Declan Burke has published four novels to date: *Eightball Boogie* (2003), *The Big O* (2007), *Absolute Zero Cool* (2011) and *Slaughter's Hound* (2012). *Absolute Zero Cool* was shortlisted in the crime fiction section for the Irish Book Awards 2011, and received the Goldsboro/Crimefest 'Last Laugh' Award for Best Humorous Crime Novel in 2012. He is the editor of *Down These Green Streets: Irish Crime Writing in the 21st Century* (2011), and the co-editor, with John Connolly, of *Books to Die For* (2012). He hosts a website dedicated to Irish crime fiction called Crime Always Pays. Declan lives in Wicklow with his wife and daughter, where he is not allowed to own a cat, or be owned by one.

First published in 2012 by
Liberties Press
7 Rathfarnham Road | Terenure | Dublin 6W
Tel: +353 (1) 405 5701
www.libertiespress.com | info@libertiespress.com

Trade enquiries to Gill & Macmillan Distribution
Hume Avenue | Park West | Dublin 12
T: +353 (1) 500 9534 | F: +353 (1) 500 9595 | E: sales@gillmacmillan.ie

Distributed in the UK by
Turnaround Publisher Services
Unit 3 | Olympia Trading Estate | Coburg Road | London N22 6TZ
T: +44 (0) 20 8829 3000 | E: orders@turnaround-uk.com

Distributed in the United States by
Dufour Editions | PO Box 7 | Chester Springs | Pennsylvania 19425

Copyright © Declan Burke, 2012
The author asserts his moral rights.

ISBN: 978-1-907593-49-9
2 4 6 8 10 9 7 5 3 1

A CIP record for this title is available from the British Library.

Cover design by Fidelma Slattery
Internal design by Liberties Press
Printed by Bell & Bain Ltd

The publishers gratefully acknowledge
financial assistance from the Arts Council.

*All characters in this book are fictitious, and any resemblance to
actual persons, living or dead, is purely coincidental.*

SLAUGHTER'S HOUND

A Harry Rigby Mystery

Declan Burke

LIB
ERT
IES

For Vincent Banville

'Crime is only a left-handed form of human endeavour.'

– W. R. Burnett, *The Asphalt Jungle*

Author's Note:
Originally bred to fight wolves and accompany their owners into battle, the Irish Wolfhound (*Cú Faoil*) is a breed old enough to feature in Irish mythology, with *cú* translating as 'hound', 'war hound' or 'Irish hound'. According to legend, the young warrior Sétanta became Cú Chulainn by killing the hound of Culann and then offering to replace it. Cú Chulainn, also known as the Hound of Ulster, owned a number of *árchú*, war hounds feared for their love of slaughter.

Thursday

1

It was a rare fine night for a stroll down by the docks, the moon plump as a new pillow in an old-fashioned hotel and the under-tow in the turning tide swushing its ripples silvery-green and a bird you've never heard before chirring its homesick tale of a place you might once have known and most likely now will never see, mid-June and almost midnight and balmy yet, the kind of evening built for a long walk with a woman who likes to take long walks and not say very much, and that little in a murmur you have to strain to catch, her laughter low and throaty, her humour dry and favouring lewd, eyes like smoky mirrors of the vast night sky and in them twinkles that might be stars reflecting or the first sparks of intentions that you'd better fan with soft words and a gentle touch in just the right place or spend the rest of your life and maybe forever wondering what might have been, all for the want of a soft word and a touch gentle and true.

It was that kind of evening, alright. That kind of place.

You ever find yourself there, say something soft, and be gentle, and true.

Me, I found myself hunched over the charred dwarf that had once been Finn Hamilton, parts of him still sizzling in a marinade of oily flesh and melting tar, and all around the rank stench of singing hair and burnt petrol, seared pork.

Midnight, and balmy yet.

I'd seen him jump. Pacing the yard below, phone clamped to my ear. 'Listen, Ben, she's under pressure at work, okay? You need to take that on— What? Yeah, I know. But look, sometimes your mum says things she—'

I heard him, first. Faint but clear from nine storeys high.

'Bell jars away . . .'

From instinct I glanced up with the next line already forming, *let's be fearless with our promises,* but by then he'd jumped, a dark blur plummeting, wings folded against the drag like some starving hawk out of the noon sun, some angel betrayed.

I guess he punched through the cab's roof so hard he sent metal shearing into the petrol tank. All it took was one spark.

Boom . . .

The blast smashed me ten feet into a heap of scrap metal, left me deafened and half blind, limbs rubbery as I scrabbled around ripping my hands on rusty steel. Stunned and flopping in the aftermath of a quake that tore my insides apart

lie down stay down

lungs pounded by hammers *O Jesus breathe, breathe* and a roaring in the ears of blood tortured to a scream

'Dad?'

coming tinny and distant

'Dad? Are you there?'

the phone two feet and a million miles away, dirt thick in my teeth

'I think you're breaking up, Dad . . .'

and the taste of roasting flesh and metal thick on my tongue.

A hot knife pierced my ribs as I reached for the phone.

'Ben?' A harsh grating. 'Ring you back, Ben.'

I lurched to my feet on spongy knees and stumbled across the yard towards the blaze. The air all a-shimmer so that his feet looked submerged, some weirdly wavering polyps. One of his moccasins came away as I pulled him free and at first I thought I'd ripped him in half. Then I thought he'd dropped a dwarf on the cab. Strange the things you think when you're trying not to think at all, dragging a man from a torched wreck and his flesh frying in lumps on the melting tar.

As I twisted my head, guts already heaving, I realised why he seemed so short.

He'd dived, come down arrow-straight, in the final instant pulling back his arms so that the impact drove his head and shoulders back up into his chest. There was still some remnant of what had once been his neck but the head had pulped like so much ripe melon.

I puked until the heaves came dry and then rang it in. Globs of grey grease spitting on the cab's skeletal frame.

2

How it began was a balmy night, twenty past ten, the caller ID flashing *Finn-Finn-Finn*. I put down the book and turned on the radio to check his mood. Tindersticks, tiny tears filling up a whole ocean.

Not promising.

Still, business is business. I picked up.

'How goes it?'

'Good, yeah. You busy?'

'Not right now.'

'How's the weather?'

'Balmy. You off on holidays?'

'Hoping to.'

'For how long?'

'Three weeks, if I can swing it.'

'You deserve it, squire. See you later.'

'Alright.'

I knocked off the cab's light and turned out of the rank,

heading west on Wine Street, across the bypass and out along the Strandhill Road. Switched off the radio. Finn played good tunes but you had to be in the mood. Some nights he went off on a jag: Santa Claus with a straight razor in his mitt, black dogs howling down the moon. Spend long enough driving a cab listening to Finn and you'd wind up with a Mohawk cruising underage whores trying to think of a politician it'd be worth the bullet to plug.

Five minutes later I was turning up Larkhill and into Herb's driveway, zapping the security gates. A stately semi-D, two bay windows to the front, five bedrooms upstairs and a cellar that wasn't on the plans. A double garage on the side. Herb'd had most of the front garden ripped out for tarmac, the better to allow the cabs come and go. Mature sycamore and horse-chestnut fringed the high red-brick walls of the perimeter.

I drove around the back, opened the garage door, eased in beside a Golf I didn't recognise, a three-year-old model that meant Herb had company. Tapped the four-digit code into the pad on the connecting door, waited for the high-pitched beep, pushed on through to the kitchen. Knocked on the kettle.

'Herb?' I called. 'I'm making a brew. What d'you want?'

'In here, Harry.'

From his tone I was expecting trouble but even at that Ross McConnell, in person, was bad news. Standing up as I crossed the hall and went in through the arch into the living room, making it look like he was being polite, waiting to be introduced, not making a fuss about being on his feet, his eyes level with mine.

Herb had a mop of curly red hair not generally seen outside of Stephen King books about killer clowns. He sat building a spliff on the coffee table, the plasma TV on with the sound muted, watching black-and-white grainy documentary footage of what might have been the Russian Front.

'Ross,' he said, 'this is Harry. I don't think you met him before.'

'Don't think I have,' he said, sounding faintly adenoidal. He took his time putting out his hand, taking in my black shoes and black pants, the white shirt and loosely knotted black cotton tie. A respectable ensemble, from a distance at least.

I guessed, from the way his lower lip twitched, that he approved more of my ambition than the actual style. 'Ross McConnell,' he said. We shook. A dry, solid handshake. Not limp and not a power-play, nothing you'd remember after except that he'd shaken your hand and met your eye doing it.

He was nothing special, Ross McConnell. A little taller than average, wearing beige chinos, brown deck shoes and a crisp pale blue shirt over a V-neck white tee. A plain gold band on his ring finger but otherwise no jewellery or gewgaws. Ross McConnell, better known as Toto, a joke name he'd been stuck with as a skinny kid because he fancied himself as a prospect, a gimlet-eyed striker in the mould of Toto Schillaci, aka the Sicilian Assassin who'd ended Ireland's hopes in the 1990 World Cup, Ross sixteen or seventeen at the time. Except Ross, aka Toto, had been nothing special. Pushing forty now and no longer skinny but not running to fat either, no sign of gym pumping or anywhere slack, the brown hair neat under a number four blade and all of it where it should and needed to be, but no more, no less. Nothing special. The eyes no harder than a bank manager's on a Monday morning and no colder, really, than that last crawling yard to the Pole. But nothing special, no.

Different, sure, because he was Ted McConnell's younger brother and de facto *consigliore*. But not so remarkable that he might get picked out of a line-up by an eye-witness to a point-blank drive-by, even on his third or fourth parade, the cops getting desperate, surrounding him with dwarfs and one-legged jugglers.

No, he was nothing special, not Ross McConnell. They never are.

'Harry . . . ?' he enquired, one eyebrow cocked. He already knew, of course. I'd have been checked out long before I slid in behind the wheel of a McConnell cab. When you're an ex-INLA blagger trying to go legit, like say for example one Ted McConnell, you need to be that bit squeakier clean than the competition.

'Rigby,' I said.

'Harry Rigby,' he said. 'Rigby, Rigby, Rigby . . .' He glanced down at Herb, who was roaching the jay, then back at me. 'You're never the Rigby who killed his brother,' he said. I nodded. 'Gonzo,' he said. 'Am I right?'

'That's right.'

'I knew him. Years ago now, but yeah. Mad fucker.'

It wasn't a question so I let it go. From the kitchen came the sound of a thin whistle. 'Kettle's boiled,' I said. 'Anyone else for a brew?'

'Ross was just leaving,' Herb said.

'I'll take a quick espresso,' Ross said. 'If it's not a bother.'

'No problem.'

He was still standing when I got back, head tilted, one whole wall given over to Herb's books, most of them hardbacks and mostly non-fiction, travel and adventure, war histories, some popular science. A Patrick Leigh Fermor biography tucked under one arm. He toasted me with the espresso, had a sip, winced at its bitterness.

'So what's it like out there?' he said. 'Busy?'

'Quiet enough so far,' I said. 'It'll pick up later on.'

'Good, good.'

So there we all were, the two of us sipping coffee, Herb on a toke in the armchair, a quarter million Germans frozen solid in Stalingrad and still hoping Von Paulus'd tell Hitler to stick his *Sieg Heil* up his Austrian hole. The silence getting brittle, Toto glancing up again at the bookshelves. I rolled a smoke and wandered over to the far wall, Herb's gallery, framed photographs from when he'd worked as a snapper, some of them standalone shots, portraits, a couple of full-length newspaper covers. The one I liked best was a *Sligo Champion* cover from a couple of election campaigns ago, Bertie Ahern touring the provinces, shocked, staring down at the egg that had just been smashed against his tie, and over it the headline, 'Bertie Scrambling for Power'.

Herb leaned forward to tap some ash, knocked a musical little tinkle out of the glass ashtray, loud enough to get Toto and I looking around. Herb cleared his throat. 'Anything cooking?' he said.

Me he was asking. I glanced at Toto. He put his hand up in mock surrender. 'I'm not even here,' he said. 'You have business to do, don't let me stop you.'

Herb nodded me on. 'Finn rang,' I told him. 'Looking three bags.'

'Oh yeah?'

'Just now.'

'He got three last month, didn't he?'

'That's right.'

'That's a lot of personal use.'

Herb didn't do half-measures. Five-ounce bags of primo bud. Sweet as Bambi going down, a kick like Thumper dreaming snares. He could've cut it with oregano, packed the bags with branch, the way some of Toto's dealers did, but Herb liked his customers happy, his trade steady and sure.

'The surfers are in next week,' I said, 'out to Enniscrone. The wild water women, something like that.'

'So he's what, dealing now?'

'I doubt it. Probably just sorting some people out.'

Toto with another book in his hand, *Schrödinger's Kittens*, one of John Gribbin's. Taking a keen interest, it looked like, in radical quantum mechanics.

'But sorting these people out,' Herb persisted, 'for money.'

'What I'm saying is, Finn doesn't need to deal.'

'Hardly giving it away free though, is he?'

'Want me to have a word?'

'Suss him out, yeah. See what's what. Last thing we want is some amateur pissing about. There's cops in Bundoran running around with boogie boards now.'

'Will do.'

Toto put his espresso down on the coffee table, held up the Gribbin. 'Herbie,' he said, 'd'you mind . . . ?'

'No worries, man. Work away.'

The Gribbin went under his arm with the Leigh Fermor. 'I'll drop them back next time,' he said. 'Harry?' He raised an eyebrow and nodded towards the hallway. 'Mind if I have a word?'

For some reason I took my coffee with me, following on as he ambled out through the kitchen, into the garage. He pressed the door-release button, said, 'How's your probation going?'

'Alright, yeah. Five more months, thereabouts.'

A wry smile. 'Thereabouts?'

'Five months, four days.'

'And you're clean, right?'

He wasn't just talking smack or coke. He meant anything that might cause him trouble if I was pulled over driving a cab in which Ted McConnell had a 40 percent stake. A daft question. I was hardly going to fess up to a sideline dealing kiddie porn from the cab's trunk. Then again, it wasn't really a question. Especially as Toto McConnell's definition of clean didn't include the bags of grass I trundled around town for Herb.

He opened the door of his three-year-old nothing-special navy Golf and got in, put the books on the passenger seat. 'This Finn guy,' he said, 'wants the three baggies. You vouch for him?'

'He's never let me down yet. Pays up front.'

'But you know him, right?'

I nodded. 'It's Finn Hamilton.'

He cocked his head. 'The property Hamiltons?'

'That's the family, yeah. Except Finn's an art dealer.'

'Bob Hamilton's boy.' Now he was nodding, filing it away. Might be useful to know somewhere down the line. 'Has a gallery down the docks,' he said, 'the old PA building. Or am I mixing him up with someone else?'

'No, that's him.'

'Nice work if you can get it,' he grinned. 'Am I right?'

'If you like art.'

He shrugged. 'I like it. What's not to like?' He turned the key in the ignition, the Golf giving a throaty roar before settling down to a purr. He closed the car door, then wound down the window. 'Meant to ask you,' he said, 'if you knew Malky Gorevan.'

Letting me know, he knew I'd done my time, or a good chunk of it, in Dundrum. And maybe letting me know he knew more, that I'd walked earlier than I should have all things considered, a six-year stretch erring on the liberal side when you go down for blowing away your brother, especially when that was enough, in the first place, to have you banged up with all the rest of the criminally insane. Tipping me off that people might be wondering why I'd skated out so soon, and if maybe some kind of deal hadn't been done, Harry Rigby agreeing to payback, a juicy morsel in the right ear once in a while, for his early release.

'Yeah, I knew Malky,' I said. 'Mad fucker.'

'Wouldn't be in Dundrum if he wasn't,' Toto said.

'True enough. How's he doing?'

Malky Gorevan had the distinction of being one of the very few ex-paramilitaries not to walk on a Good Friday pardon, partly because no one really gave a shit if the INLA ever went back to war, but mainly because Malky, who was serving multiple concurrent sentences, would have been designated Ireland's first bona fide serial killer had he not wrapped himself in the flag. If Malky ever got out of Dundrum it'd be for the short ride north to face a sheaf of outstanding warrants, Malky a hero in certain circles for being that rarest of gems, an INLA man who'd figured out the intricacies of the mercury tilt car bomb.

'Malky's Malky,' Toto shrugged. 'Last I heard he was still talking about sell-outs, Adams and McGuinness on his shit-list.' He shrugged again, Malky old news, yesterday's man. 'Listen,' he said, 'Herbie might have a bit of work for you, if you're available. No problem if you're not.'

'What's doing?'

'Herbie'll fill you in.' He stuck his hand out, and we shook again. 'Good to meet you, Harry.' The nothing-special eyes grey and cold as grave chippings. 'Catch you later.'

He reversed out, got turned and was gone. I waited until I heard the front gates close, then wiped my hand on the seat of my trousers and tossed what was left of the cold coffee into a potted bush that needed watering. Six days since it had rained.

3

'That's his fourth,' Herb groused as I came back into the living room. 'First it was a Joe Campbell, last time it was a nice hard-back on Spinoza, the feeling brain. The fuck am I, a library?'

'Maybe you need to start imposing fines.'

'Right, yeah.' A bleak grin. 'Maybe skim off the top, tell Ted it's all Toto's fault.'

Camped about six thousand miles due west, the McConnells would have been a shit-kicking rabble of inbred, rebel-yelling, crank-cooking sister lovers. They were the first to organise properly in Sligo, this something of a spin-off from the Peace Dividend up North, Ted being the kind of diehard ex-INLA who wouldn't be fully happy until everything was the way it'd been before the Ulster Plantation, when every chief had his own fief and a surfeit of spears. They'd started with dope, moved on up to coke and E, were dabbling now in H. They had hardware and were happy to use it, generally for hoot-'n'-holler drive-bys but at least once to lethal effect. Cold. Opening a van door in the

21

middle of town, three o'clock on a Saturday afternoon. One round through the forehead, two in the chest. The backsplash spattering the guy's girlfriend, the kid she held in her arms.

The dogs in the street knew Toto'd been the shooter. The problem there being, dogs don't do so well on a witness stand, tend to crumble under cross-examination.

Herb took a drag on the jay, held it down, popped a smoke-ring. Settled back in the Ezy-Chair. 'What'd he want, anyway?'

'Was asking about Finn, if I vouched for him.'

'I hope you didn't, the flaky fuck.'

Herb took a dim view of what he reckoned were Finn's unnatural proclivities for skiing, surfing and charitable innovations. Herb being of the opinion that if Finn wanted to help those less well-off than himself, which was pretty much everyone bar the Hamiltons these days, he might consider donating a chunk of Hamilton Holdings' before-tax profits instead of haranguing people to dig into their own pockets.

'I told him,' I said, 'Finn always pays up front.'

'You tell him who he was?'

'That he's Finn Hamilton, sure. The rest he knew.'

'Dundrum?'

'He knows I was in Dundrum, yeah. Asking if I knew Malky Gorevan.'

'But you didn't tell him about celling with Finn.'

'No.'

Sins of omission. What the bishops like to call mental reservations.

'Maybe that's what he was asking about,' Herb said.

'Don't sweat it. At the end there he was offering me more work, said it was there if I was available.'

'He mentioned that?'

'What's the gig?'

'A run to Galway tomorrow, there's a shipment due in. Small enough, ten grand's worth, but the good stuff. He was asking me to take it on, but, y'know.'

Herb didn't get out much, in part because he was a low-level paranoiac, but mainly because he just didn't like people. His credo was pretty simple: always assume everyone's an idiot.

He'd been a snapper once, a good one, hooked up with an agency. We'd worked as a team for a few years, freelancing local news, stringing for the nationals. I did the words, Herb took the shots, and once in a while we'd work some off-the-books research consultancy, which was a fancy name for what amounted to prowling hotel car parks for proof of some wayward husband's mid-life crisis.

Happy days.

Then Herb got his face stove in. Someone had told someone else that Herb had a photograph the someone else wanted.

I was the someone who'd done the telling. Inadvertently, as it happened.

Not that the who mattered. The bruisers were still walking around, free to stove at will. Herb stayed home, his complexion pasty, skin like old dough. The way it can get when most of both jaws and one cheekbone are underpinned by steel plate. Anyway, Herb ended up staying home a lot, huffing mucho weed. One day Toto McConnell, this back when Toto was still dealing himself, asks if Herb'll rent him some space. Herb's not interested in any sublets, but Toto's talking about turning the upstairs, the attic, into a grow-house.

A couple of years later Herb's salting away a couple of grand a month to top up his disability benefit, easy money. Two years after that, he moved out to Larkhill, went to Toto with his idea for a couple of cabs, nice cover for deals-on-wheels. A front to get him onto the Revenue's books and keep them sweet, so no one got the urge to pick up the phone and ring the Criminal Assets Bureau, wondering how no-income, disability benefit Herb could afford a four-bed on its own grounds out in the burbs.

'How come the short notice?' I said.

'His regular guy popped a kneecap last night.'

'And now he's under wraps.'

'No, I mean he popped his *own* kneecap. Five-a-side up at the Sports Complex, went in for a sliding tackle and up she blew.'

'Jesus.'

'Yeah. So what d'you think? Toto's pretty keen to get it tomorrow, has the stuff promised for Saturday night. Says he'll do twenty percent.'

'Two grand?'

'I get the impression, reading between the lines, Toto's greasing some serious wheels.'

'So we're not talking smoke.'

'Coke, yeah.'

'Shit.'

'Two grand, Harry. Five big to me for brokering, okay, but that's still tidy money for a spin to Galway.' He sat forward in the Ezy-Chair, offered across the spliff. When I declined he slotted it into the ashtray, stood up. 'Just think about it, okay? No harm at all in seeing Toto right.'

He took a little side-wobble setting off, then stabilised and headed for the hall. Right on cue my phone rang, the caller ID flashing up *Dee-Dee-Dee*.

I sat the phone on the coffee-table, rolled a smoke and let it ring out. Herb came back in with Finn's three baggies, tossing them on the table just as the message-minder buzzed, the screen lighting up to let me know I'd missed four calls from Dee.

'Reminds me,' he said. 'Dee rang earlier. Said to call her.'

'Cheers.'

'Said something about Ben's parent-teacher meeting tomorrow.'

'I got her messages, yeah.'

He plucked the jay from the ashtray, subsided into the Ezy-Chair again. 'How's Ben doing these days?' he said.

'Grand. Not a bother on him.'

'A good kid, that lad.'

Herb hadn't seen Ben in years. To be fair, though, he'd been there for Dee while I was inside, letting her know she wasn't on her own, a few quid available if she was ever badly stuck. Not that Dee took advantage, but sometimes just knowing there's somewhere out there can make all the difference.

Another favour I owed him.

'So what d'you think,' he said, 'about Toto's gig?'

'I'll do it, yeah.'

'Nice one, Harry.'

'If Dee rings again, you haven't seen me.'

'Roger and Wilco.'

I stubbed the smoke, gathered up the three baggies. Herb aimed the remote control at the TV. 'Hold up,' he said, bringing up the menu, flicking down through the options to digital radio. 'Let's see what kind of mood this fuckwit's in.'

He tuned to McCool FM in time for the last couple of verses of Townes van Zandt's 'St John the Gambler'.

'Christ,' Herb muttered.

From van Zandt to Joy Division, 'She's Lost Control'. Then straight into Big Star's 'Holocaust'.

Herb cracked first.

'There's any amount of Motown in there,' he said, pointing the spliff at his CD rack. 'I want you to bring it down to the docks, tie that part-time fucking philanthropist to his chair and tell him from me he's getting no score until I hear Smokey.'

'Will do.'

4

I took *Going to a Go-Go*, the three baggies, got in the cab. By the time I got to the bottom of Larkhill the fuel gauge was glowing orange, so I crossed town to the all-night petrol station on Pearse Road, where a taxi driver with the right contacts can get a free cup of something that smells like black coffee with every fill-up. The phone rang as I was coming up off Mailcoach Road, *Dee-Dee-Dee*.

I could have ignored it but she'd have just kept ringing.

'Dee?'

'Did you get my message?'

'What message?'

'The one I sent Herbie.'

I pulled in at the pumps, detached the hands-free and got out, phone clamped between shoulder and ear. 'I haven't seen Herb since Tuesday,' I said, ramming the nozzle into the petrol tank. 'What's up?'

'The parent-teacher meeting, Harry. I just want to be sure you remembered it.'

'You're breaking up, Dee. Can you say that again?'

'I'll fucking break *you* up. Did you hear *that*?'

'Look, Dee, you know I sleep during the—'

'We've a stock-take on tomorrow, Harry. I told you this. I can't miss it.'

'But it's okay for me to not earn. So you can do your job.'

'This once in a blue fucking moon, so you can do something with Ben? Yeah, I think that's okay.'

The old argument. I let it lie.

'I need you to do this one thing, Harry. And for Ben, not me. And maybe for yourself, too.'

Not saying it nasty. Sounding weary instead, with the little quiver she got in the back of her throat contemplating the sorry dregs of her third glass of whatever plonk was on special that week.

'Any chance we could push it back to four o'clock?' I said. 'At least that way I could—'

'Harry,' she said, no quiver now, all arrow, 'the meeting's at two. Be here at one-thirty to pick up Ben or I swear to God, I'll tell him.'

The old, old threat. Maybe she was already into glass four. The nozzle clicked, choked off the flow.

'Do you hear me?' she said.

'Why don't you just tell him, Dee?' He'd hear about it sooner or later, how the man he thought was his dad had put a bullet in the man who was but never wanted to be his father. Better it came from Dee than some schoolyard taunt.

'If I knew where he was,' she said. 'I swear, if he was home right now . . .'

'What, he doesn't have his phone with him?'

'*You* try ringing him. Go on, ring him right now, see how far it gets you.' I realised the rumble I'd thought was thunder was Dee drumming her fingers on the phone. 'One-thirty, Harry. Be here.'

She hung up. Matters weren't improved any by the news that a fifty-seven euro fill-up left me with little more than coppers in my pocket. Then I made the mistake of trying to cut through town rather than take the bypass. It was better out in the suburbs, and it was mostly suburbs, but the town was a heart-attack of concrete and chrome. Old streets, high and narrow, arteries so thick and gnarled the traffic trickled or didn't move at all. The light a frozen glare shot with greens and reds, blinking pink neon, fluorescent blues. Boom-boom blasting from rolled-down windows, deep bass pulsing out muscles of sound. On a bad night it took fifteen minutes to crawl the two hundred yards from the Abbey to Lady Erin. The mob shuffling around outside the chippers wore hoodies over baggy denims, frayed hems dragging. Night of the Living McDead. The girls in cropped tops over bulging bellies, the low-slung jeans showcasing cheese-cutter thongs. In case anyone might think they weren't wearing any underwear at all, maybe.

I skipped O'Connell Street heading west, turned north down Adelaide and then left at the new bridge onto Lynn's Dock, a grapefruit moon hanging low over the quays. Finn playing the Northern Pikes, 'Place That's Insane'. Out along Ballast Quay and the docks proper, onto Deepwater Quay, black water on my right, warehouses and depots to the left, the Connacht Gold co-op lit up like a rocket launch. Beyond the co-op loomed the unlovely Port Authority building, and behind that a jungle of weeds and a rusty marsh. Once in a while there'd be talk of turning the marsh into a nature preserve, a bird sanctuary, but no one did anything about it. The birds came and went anyway.

I turned into the PA's yard, slaloming between the potholes, tooling along in second gear, the yard lined with rusting containers, piles of scrap metal and trailers of mouldy timber. High weeds clumped in bricked-up doorways. The day had been hot and it was still warm, the acrid hum of hot tar thickening the air.

The PA building was nine stories of stark 1960s' modernism, an appropriately ugly monument to hubris, built when the docks were buzzing and Lemass had all boats on a rising tide. Polish coal, Norwegian pine, Jamaican sugar, Australian wool. Oil tankers moored offshore. Russians jumped ship and never went to sea again. The first African, a Nigerian, was a celebrity. They called him Paddy Dubh and he never had to pay when he bought a pint of stout.

Then the '70s slithered in. Crude oil went through the roof. The coal stopped coming, then the sugar. The channel silted up. Paddy had to buy his own stout. Things got so bad the Industrial Development Authority had to buy the PA building and then lease back two of the nine stories to the PA. Even that was a farce, the IDA loaning the PA the money to pay the lease.

Then the '80s, a good decade to be a weed or a rat. Everyone forgot about the docks, or tried to.

Big Bob Hamilton came in like the cavalry. By then he'd pretty much dry-lined every last square inch of Thatcher's London, and when they finally kicked out the Iron Lady, Bob took that as his cue. Came home in '91, sniffed the wind. He sold high in London and bought low all over Sligo and the northwest. Joined the Rotary Club, the Tennis Club, Golf and Lions, damn near every club in town bar the Tuesday night Chess in the Trades. Turned up on the local board of the IDA about four months before he bought up sixteen acres of dockland that included the PA building and the rusty swamp and not a hell of a lot of anything else.

Finn telling me all this from the bottom bunk in Dundrum. Sounding dull and half-muffled but telling it straight. How the word had been that Big Bob was personally responsible for the new stationery factory over in Finisklin, a staff of three working flat-out to meet the demand for brown envelopes. Serious investment on its way, a port rejuvenation, Bob all set to make a killing. The investment never did arrive, although there was a killing of sorts alright, this in '98, Finn just about to turn eighteen and right there to see his father's brand new Beamer topple off the quay and into the water, Bob still at the wheel. The official verdict was death by misadventure, even if the inquest failed to establish a satisfactory explanation as to why all the Beamer's windows might have been open down at the deepwater late one January evening.

It wasn't long after that, he reckoned, that the arson started, Finn on the fast-track to his first crack-up.

I turned into the small car park at the front of the PA and saw a sleek maroon Saab gleaming under the single bare light over the door. Which was odd. McCool FM was a one-man show, and DJs playing Leonard Cohen don't get groupies since John Peel passed on, bless his cotton socks. Which meant Finn had unexpected company or he was working middle-man, punting the baggies on.

Either way, not good.

The Saab's driver already getting out.

The baggies were under the spare wheel in the boot, so I eased up to where the driver stood, then three-pointed, reversing back into the space beside Finn's black Audi, leaving the boot tight against the PA's wall. Got out and locked the cab, strolled around towards the PA's door. The driver with a hand up, palm out, saying, 'Far enough, big man.'

His accent wasn't quite harsh enough to be Derry, the hint of a lilt suggesting north Donegal. Built like an upside-down cello, wearing a white shirt with the collar button open, a thin black tie with a loose knot. Patent leather shoes, in the reflection of which he could have flossed his even white teeth. Through the Saab's open door I could see, hung on a hangar, the top half of a dark suit silk-lined in red paisley. Italian, maybe. The eyes were eight-gauge, sawn-off.

I pulled up six inches shy of where I guessed his swing would land. 'I'm expected,' I said.

'Not by me you're not.'

'True for you.'

The trouble there was, if one guy gets to thinking he can tell you what you can do, it's only a matter of time before the rest start feeling the same. Then you're on the skids. And I was already on the skids.

'I'm going on up,' I said.

'Fine by me, big man. Just not yet.'

I craned my neck to glance up at the ninth floor, the window's dull yellow glow. 'He makes you wear a tie?' I said.

That didn't work him at all. 'You know what I like?' he said. 'Cars, threads and quim. He pays me to drive a Saab, wear good suits.'

'Two out of three ain't bad.'

'I make out.' He up-jutted his chin. 'Finn's expecting you?'

'That's right.'

He glanced over my shoulder. 'Something wrong with his Audi?'

'Other than it's not a Porsche?'

'Too fucking right.' He backed off a step, ushered me on through. 'Jimmy,' he said.

'Rigby.'

He leaned in as I went past, sniffing, his nostrils flared. I glanced up at him going by and stared straight up those sawn-off barrels, black and cold, and nary a light to guide a weary pilgrim.

'Stay useful, Rigby.'

'I'll try.'

5

Finn Hamilton was doomed from the start, named by his mother for the great hero of Irish mythology, Fionn mac Cumhaill, and left in no doubt, from a very early age, that he was expected to grow into a man apart: hunter, warrior, legend, king.

No pressure.

And then, still a kid, he sees his father drown.

I guess they were lucky it was only a few buildings he'd burned down.

He'd had his epiphany in the Central Mental Hospital in Dundrum, how to use the Hamilton name and the resources that went with it. Stopped resisting and went with the flow, folding back into the family like a fifth columnist, a saboteur bent on good deeds and charitable works. The cops turned a blind eye to McCool FM on the basis that it wasn't a commercial enterprise, its rare advertisements being on behalf of St Vincent de Paul and the Lions Club and similarly minded charities and organisations, its website offering directions and links to Aware and the

Samaritans, the Model Arts Centre and the Irish Cancer Society, as well as hosting examples of work available in the gallery on the PA's ground floor, his own included, a third of each sale going to the charity of the artist's choice.

His latest idea, still in the embryonic stage, was *Spiritus Mundi*, a loose collective of artists, musicians and writers all operating out of the PA, a kind of urban take on Annaghmakerrig, a retreat for those of a creative bent. Last I'd heard he was in talks with Blue Raincoat, offering them rehearsal space, the idea being that they'd relocate their theatre from the town centre to the docks, Finn dangling the carrot of a long-term lease on very favourable terms.

I buzzed two short and one long, waiting for the beep, the ka-chunk, before slipping inside. The tiny lobby had a single spotlight recessed in the roof, a security camera high in one corner. I glanced up at it, waited for the second beep, then pushed on through to the gallery. Finn had stripped out the ground floor, leaving nothing to distract the eye from the canvases he'd mounted on support pillars and the bare brick walls, the space echoey under a high ceiling. I left the lights off and snuck across to the window, peeked out into the yard. Jimmy was sitting half-out of the Saab, smoking and jotting down the cab's number, head at an angle, phone tucked between shoulder and ear.

The efficient type, Jimmy.

By now Bear was barking fit to shiver the foundations. I made my way through to the rear, gave the metal door the double tap, made shushing sounds, then shunted the door inwards. Bear's nails clickered on the concrete as he reared up to plant a paw on either shoulder. Full-bred Irish wolfhound. Up on his hind legs he'd have held his own in a line-out. I staggered under his weight, waltzed backwards a little, then pushed him off and tousled his ears.

'Not tonight, Bear. Sorry.'

I kicked the crutch he'd been mauling back into the pile in the corner and found the box on the top shelf, scattering a handful of bone-shaped biscuits into his metal bowl, topping up his water. Finn loved that hound, had rescued him as a terrified pup from a shelter, but he had a theory that a hungry watchdog made for an alert watchdog. Put that with Finn's prodigious appetite for psychotropic grass and a general attitude to life that if charted on a graph of ambition and endeavour would resemble a hammock, and you had a dog that was on occasion leaner and meaner than his doggie god creator intended.

While I was at it I ducked my head into his kennel to check on the bedding. It seemed fresh and clean, and by the time I backed out Bear had settled himself in a corner to gnaw at a biscuit, toying with it, three or four others still in the bowl. Which meant Finn was on the case and Bear was well fed, which was a pity of sorts. I'd been entertaining the idea of taking him out for a stroll in the yard, just to see how efficient Jimmy might be with 160 pounds of war hound bearing down at full throttle.

There was no lift in the PA building. What you got was nine stories of rusted metal stairs bolted to the inside walls. Once upon a time a set of four stairs would have taken you up to a new floor, but the insides had long ago been ripped out. Now, once you cleared the gallery space, the building was a silo all the way to the top floor. A stiff climb, but nothing a reasonably fit man couldn't manage without breaking a sweat. By the time I reached the top I could have done with an oxygen mask and a brace of Sherpas.

I rapped a tattoo on the studio door.

'Yeah, Harry?' Finn's voice came muffled. 'C'mon in.'

The studio took up most of the ninth floor, with a mixing-desk tucked into the far corner. Egg-boxes covered the ceiling and most of the walls. Finn was behind the desk, headphones around his neck. Tall and lean even sitting down, shoulders bony under the white crew-neck tee. He almost always wore the same ensemble: white T-shirt, faded Levis, brown suede moccasins, coarse blond stubble. No socks. The flaxen hair cut into the shaggy bowl favoured by post-smack Brian Jones. In behind the fringe he had a wide-awake face, an engaging grin, bright blue eyes.

Behind him were amps, processors, serried ranks of vinyl LPs. The muted rattle was The Wedding Present turned down low. It sounded like 'Brassneck', but then one Weddoes sounds a lot like the rest when it's turned down low.

The near half of the studio was dominated by a rough wooden table covered with tubes of paint, brushes in jars, palette knives. A pair of easels stood side-by-side, both covered with paint-spattered tarps. Canvases stood stacked four and five deep against the wall, some framed, some not. In the corner a Stratocaster in the classic yin-yang black-and-white stood propped on a stand, two strings missing, a third hanging by a thread.

The far wall was the reason Finn had picked the PA for his studio: a full-length window, looking out across the docks and the deepwater to the sea and Benbulben beyond. A pane had been slid aside to allow a faint breeze waft through and create a draught with the fire escape door, which was wedged open on the opposite side. On a summer evening, with the equipment humming, the day's heat rising and Finn huffing weed, the studio could get stifling, the air thick enough to chew.

The guy in the tailored suit swamping the couch under the window put me in mind of William Conrad without the moustache. Finn waved in his direction. 'You meet Gillick before?'

'I'd have remembered,' Gillick purred.

Arthur Gillick's rep was choice. Put a bullet in a cop's face at the passing out parade in Templemore, Gillick's was the number you dialled when they finally gave you your call. He'd made a name for himself starting out, this in the late '70s, all through the '80s, as the Provos' go-to silk, although it'd be pushing it to say he was politically motivated. Unless, of course, his politics stretched to some kind of convoluted anarchist theory that involved keeping every last smack-dealing lowlife, recidivist wife-beater and sticky-fingered Traveller on the streets. Last I'd heard he'd been diversifying, feeding off the economic downturn by moving into debt collecting and facilitating evictions, although his crowning glory had come a couple of years back, when he'd defended the upstanding citizen who'd strangled his daughter and dumped her body in the lake when the girl finally decided that, at the grand old age of thirteen, she was old enough to decide who took her pants down.

Now he hauled his huge frame forward, rising with the ponderous grace of a bishop who understands that without dignity a bishop is just another fat man. A large head under a flat swirl of sleek grey hair, the face full rather than fat, jowled but healthy. The tan helped. Big round eyes gave him an owlish aspect, the mouth prim and beaky under a prominent nose. He held out his hand. It was small and pudgy, not unduly encrusted with precious gems. The handshake was surprisingly dry and firm.

'Arthur Gillick,' he said.

'Harry Rigby.'

He took a beat longer to look away than he should have. Then he let go my hand. 'Harry,' he said. 'A fine, princely name.'

I slid him a leer, trying to work out if it was more odd that he was trying to needle me off the bat or that he was doing it by suggesting I was second-in-line to the English throne. Not that Arthur Gillick was in any position to start tossing rocks around the glasshouse.

'It's short for Harrison,' Finn said. 'His mother loved *My Fair Lady*, named him for Rex Harrison.'

'Really?' Gillick was amused.

'Could've been worse,' I said. 'She might have called me Pygmalion.'

'Because then,' Finn put in, 'we'd be calling him Pyggy. And that might get confusing.'

Gillick's smile didn't dim by so much as a quark but something went out in his porcine eyes.

It wasn't me he was trying to needle. It was Finn, adopted in England and raised there, given an Irish name to offset what his mother believed was a taint akin to the mark of Cain.

'I see you appreciate the classics, Mr Rigby,' Gillick said. A smooth voice, warm chocolate oozing. He gestured towards the stack of canvases. 'Are you a patron of the arts too?'

'Not since my portfolio crashed, no.'

'Ah, but Mr Rigby.' I was getting diabetic just listening to him. 'Great art is priceless, surely. Its worth resides in its power to evoke the fragility of life when juxtaposed against the, ah . . .' He glanced across at Finn.

'Against a universe almost entirely composed of dead matter,' Finn finished.

'Indeed. Particularly when art itself is generated of dead matter.'

Finn gave him a slow handclap.

'A pity,' Gillick observed, 'that this priceless wonder costs so much to hang on a wall. On those rare occasions when it sells at all.'

Finn gave him a sloppy grin and sat back in his swivel chair, hands behind his head. 'You're confusing cost and worth again, Arthur.'

A dainty bow from Gillick. 'Precisely my point to you.' A wristy little wave that finished with the forefinger pointing at Finn, thumb cocked. 'Call me,' he said. 'Let me do you this one favour.'

He took his time leaving because he'd have waddled if he hadn't. I stepped up onto the couch to where the window was open and straddled the sill, my back against the frame, foot resting on the narrow ledge outside. The rising heat carried the acrid odour of tar cut with the ocean's salty tang. I rolled a smoke and waited for the clanging to die away down the metal stairs, then reached Finn's night-sight binoculars off the hook where they lived, leaning out to train them on the cars directly below. Jimmy was still sitting half-out of the Saab.

From across the water in Cartron came the faint drone of traffic. Even fainter, from the direction of town, the tinny *whirr-whirru* of a siren, cop or ambulance I couldn't say. Someone's alarm was a waspy whine.

'He just get a call?' I said.

'Gillick? No. Why?'

'Just wondering.'

He propped his moccasined feet on the desk. 'No joy with the weed?' he said.

'I left it in the cab when I saw the bruiser outside.'

'Limerick Jimmy.'

'Jimmy, yeah, but he sounded more Derry.'

Finn made an elaborate flourish, then thrust forward. 'Tasty with a blade. Or so they say.'

'Ah.'

He clamped a headphone to one ear, eased some knobs up and down the mixing desk. The headphones slid down onto his neck again as he slumped back in the leather chair, hands folded on his midriff.

'Here,' I said, 'I never knew Gillick was a fruit.'

'Gillick a fruit?' Finn grinned. 'Try again. Man's the worst minge-hound in Christendom.'

'So why's he giving me the juju eye?'

'It's just his thing, how he remembers people. Says it's like taking a photo.' He double-tapped his temple. 'Clickety-click.'

A dull roar rumbled up from the yard. I trained the infrareds, caught the Saab pulling out through the gates. It disappeared behind the wall, then emerged onto the quay heading back towards town. I hung up the infrareds, climbed down from the couch. 'Coffee?'

'Got one here,' he said. 'You work away.'

I went through to the kitchenette and put the kettle on, stepped into the shoebox bathroom to make room for the fresh brew. Washed and flushed, then winced. The way the old cistern clanked and growled, you were only supposed to flush when Finn was playing Tom Waits, and preferably something from *Rain Dogs*.

The Stones were playing by the time I got back, 'Get Off My Cloud' cranked all the way up. Finn with a stubby jay on the go. I perched on the windowsill, sipped some coffee and nodded along. That high up, looking down the docks out over the deep-water, you could see an awful lot of nothing much at all: gaunt buildings, forty shades of shadow, the silvery-green sheen of moon on oily water.

Finn did his thing sliding knobs. Billy Bragg came on, 'A New England'. Finn lowered the volume, and I nodded towards the bathroom. 'Sorry about the flushing.'

'Just one more fucking thing, man.' He shrugged it off, had himself another toke. Which reminded me.

'Listen, these three baggies,' I said.

'Yeah?'

'Herb's wondering, it was three last month too. Says that's a lot of personal use.'

The sloppy grin. 'Depends on the person, doesn't it?'

'Yeah, but he's worried you're punting on. That it'll come back to bite him.'

'Tell him relax.'

'I'll need a bit more than that.'

'What'll he do, cut me off?'

'Don't shoot the messenger, man.'

He thought about that, then came to a decision, shrugged again. 'Fuck it,' he said, 'I'll be telling you soon enough anyway.'

'Go on.'

'The weed,' he said, 'I'm putting it away.'

'You're telling me? Three bags a month, man, that's—'

'I'm stashing it,' he said. 'Like, squirreling it away.'

'Oh?'

'We're going, Harry. Taking off in a couple of weeks, it's sup-posed to be a holiday. But that's us, gone.'

'Shit. Seriously?'

'I'll tell you what's shit, seriously,' he said. 'Raising a kid in this fucking hole any time in the next twenty years. That's shit. Seriously.'

Not the first time I'd heard that. The government kept telling us we'd dig our way out of recession with an export-led recovery. The main export, naturally, being people, and especially those still young enough to be ambitious and bright enough to read the runes.

'So where to?' I said.

'Where d'you think?'

Everyone has their get-out, the place they'll be when the plan-ets eventually align, and as long as I'd known him Finn had been angling to get away. In the beginning it hadn't really mattered where, it was all about getting out. Which made perfect sense at the time, or as much sense as anything ever made in Dundrum: when you weren't talking about getting a proper feed for once, you were plotting your escape, digging tunnels in your mind.

Except Finn never shook it off, even after he got out. And once he met Maria it was all about Cyprus, and specifically that enclave known and unbeloved by the world at large as the Turkish Republic of Northern Cyprus. A place, according to Finn, where they were building temples while Europe was wal-lowing in the filth of its caves, but was still real, still raw. Especially up in the mountains, where the light was, *pace* Durrell, God's eyeball.

He slid a record out of its sleeve, got it up on the turntable. Tim Buckley, 'Song to the Siren'.

'A big move,' I said.

'It's jump or be shoved is what it is.' He took a hefty hit off the jay, held it down. Exhaled it slow. 'It's all fucked, Harry. NAMA's on board and they're playing for keeps.'

'That bad?'

'We can hang on here,' he said, 'all huddling around a fucking candle and eating nettle salads. Or we can cash in now, cut our losses, start again. Somewhere,' he jabbed the stub of the jay in my direction, making his point, 'where family still means something.'

That was twice now. Kids, family. I felt something dislodge and shift sideways inside and it was only then I realised how much I'd miss him. His crazy schemes, the manic energy. The way he could call at any hour, or I'd call him, and we we'd shoot some pool and talk music or surfing or movies or books. Or say nothing at all. The thing unsaid, the black pool, dammed between us. Until the next time it started to seep through the cracks.

'So what's the plan? Anything lined up?'

He bob-bobbed his head, considering. 'Maria's been talking about doing something real,' he said. 'Something that matters, y'know?'

'A beauty salon that matters?'

He ignored the cheap crack. 'That'll pay its way, sure. But she wants to set up a school too, a kind of training college. Give these girls skills they can take anywhere in the world. You ever see Cypriot women? Man, they know how to look after themselves.'

'Yeah, well, if Maria's anything to go by . . .'

'Here's the kicker, though. She wants the training done through English, she reckons she read something in *Newsweek*

about how the ability to speak English is the single most important factor, world-wide, if you want to work.'

'She'd be better off teaching them Mandarin.'

'Or Russian, maybe. Anyway, the Chinese and the Russians
aren't offering education grants. The EU is, and the EU wants
Turkey, and Turkey means Turkish Cyprus. Except Maria's having huge problems converting her qualifications from here into
what's needed over there.'

'The EU's falling apart, squire. You're talking frying pan and
furnace.'

'Might be an issue,' he said, easing out from behind the mixing-desk, 'if this was about the EU and Ireland anymore, if it was-
n't about you and me and taking care of number one.' He headed
for the emergency exit. 'Excuse me,' he winked, 'while I take care
of a number one.'

He went out onto the fire escape to piss in the fresh air, as was
his wont, so that he wouldn't have to flush afterwards. Herb, I
could hear him already, would have something suitably cynical to
say about Finn Hamilton living like a prince among the Cypriot
paupers, the part-time philanthropist who'd spent a good chunk
of his extended adulescence wandering through Europe in his
customised camper van, chasing the next big breaker, the latest
fall of crisp snow, boozing, snorting, squandering money he'd
never had to earn. What I couldn't tell Herb was what a shrink
had once asked Finn during one of our group therapy sessions,
whether Finn thought he was reacting against his father's suicide,
either by blocking it out or trying it on for size.

I'd thought he was done running, that he'd learned you never
outrun it. That it's not a race but a wrestle, and the best you can
hope for is an honourable draw. I got up from the couch and

wandered over to the stacked paintings, ran a fingernail down his latest take on St Hilarion. From the other side of the room it was another of his riffs on a Gothic kind of impressionism, sheer crags and soaring peaks, barren slopes, a blowsy sunset bleeding across a wine-dark sea. But as always, up close, as the image dissolved, each stroke was a vivid scar etched into the skin of something savage that seemed almost ready to snarl, the frame doubling as the bars of its cage. Even the proverbial blind man could see, by means of braille, that the artist in Finn was not a happy man. He painted in oils, and thickly, leaving a texture so crude it was as if he worked from a palette of blood, bile and coarsely grained gunpowder, a gritty and glutinous blend that you feared to examine too closely lest a spark of light, the faintest transference of heat, cause some raw and lurking quality to spontaneously combust. He favoured for inspiration Oscar Epfs, but for me his landscapes were crude variations on early El Grecos or Caravaggios, men who had harrowed a hell of their own making, and where his canvases lacked for technique they offered a banked rage, the tensile pause in the moment before the world exploded from the frame.

Finn had found his metier inside. All the hours of the day to devote to his craft. Too fanciful to say that every artist paints out his own soul, but even my untrained eye could tell that Finn was so engaged, for better or worse. Whether it was good or bad art was almost incidental: it was startling, arresting, in and of itself. Was it worth money? Is any man's soul? Yes, with the inevitable caveat of *caveat emptor*.

I liked them, sure, but I wouldn't have wanted one on my own wall, even if I could have afforded the two or three grand they generally went for, when they went. Too unsettling, always watching it from the corner of your eye as it prowled the frame, snuffling and growling and poised to spring.

He came back in from the fire escape, got some Sonic Youth going, 'Teenage Riot'.

'Listen,' he said, 'this deal with the beauty salon.' He took one last drag of mainly roach, stubbed out the jay. 'That's kind of under wraps for now, at least until we get the red tape sorted.'

'No worries.'

'Mind you, the way things are going, it could take years.' He fiddled with the bass levels, not that there was anything wrong with the bass levels. 'No wonder the place is in the shitter. There's a million middle-men to go through, everyone's dipping their beak, except everything gets done tomorrow. Y'know?'

'Pity they couldn't be a bit more Irish, eh?'

'It's actually worse over there, if you can believe it. I wouldn't mind so much, but it's jobs I'm offering, proper investment.'

'No disrespect, but I'd say beauty salons aren't top of their list of investment priorities.'

He did the bob-bob thing with his head again, the shaggy mop falling in front of his eyes. 'The salon, sure. That's Maria's gig. Me, I have other plans.'

'Oh yeah?'

'You haven't been out there, Harry. It's like here twenty years ago, every second lot is a building site, except you have the sun, the climate. Last summer I took a wee wander, had a look at some show houses, these villa developments. One place, I got chatting with the site manager, right? Three hundred and twenty grand sterling per villa, twelve villas per development, beach-side, they're being built for a quarter of that, and even that's off the books, it's all cash-in-hand. The Turks are bunkered in, there's more Russians than flies, the border's relaxing, everyone knows the EU is on the way. That place is a gusher ready to blow.'

'You're going solo?'

'Sort of, yeah. The seed capital is coming from Hamilton Holdings but I'm the one brought it to the board, so it's my gig.'

He fleshed it out, a high-end development of two-storey apartments fronting a beach about eight miles east of Girne, one pool to each apartment block, playgrounds, a gym, putting greens, on-site restaurants and bars. Maria's salon. Hands waving as he sketched it out in the air, how the kicker was that it wasn't just a build-and-sell project, it was all about the long term. Managing the development for foreign investors, maybe tying in a car rental operation, some kind of quasi-official tour guide operation, some of the profits siphoned off for a Cypriot getaway for any of *Spiritus Mundi*'s mere anarchists who fancied a tan. Grinning all the while like the idiot second son who's just been bought a one-way ticket to Happy Valley. 'All we need now,' he said, 'is Ryanair to start flying direct to Ercan and we're minted.'

'So you're running the show for Hamilton Holdings,' I said, 'and Maria's happy as a lark working for you, managing this beauty salon.'

'The salon's a separate issue. It'll be on-site but independent. Maria's own place, like.' He grinned self-consciously, tugged at his nose. 'I mean, you couldn't give someone a wedding present with strings attached, could you?'

And there it was.

'Shit,' I said. 'Another good woman bites the dirt.'

He winced through the grin. 'If she'll have me,' he said. 'Actually, it's a pity the salon's a wedding present, I could set her on these Cypriot fuckers holding up the show. Bastards have cost me nearly three hundred grand already, and counting.'

'Christ. That's serious kickback, man.'

'No, I mean with Gillick. This time last year he was offering nine hundred grand for the PA, the sixteen acres. His latest offer, he's down to six and change.'

'Take his fucking hand off, Finn. Are you kidding?'

'Gillick's a fly fucker. Soon as I jump he'll find himself caught short, cash-flow issues, he's over-leveraged, the works. So he'll come back with, I don't know, half that, maybe less. Fifty grand up front, then I'm chasing the rest, and trying to do it from Cyprus.'

'So fuck him. Go with someone else.'

'This *is* going with someone else. Gillick's brokering the deal, he's fronting for some consortium. And the way things are now, there isn't exactly a queue for sixteen acres of Sligo dockland.'

'I wouldn't have thought so. What's he planning, a prison?'

Finn shrugged. 'Originally, this is back when everything was flying, he was talking up a self-contained village, its own shops, a restaurant or two, a pub. At the start he had a marina attached, dock-space going with every unit along the quays. He had me draw up an artist's impression, it looked good. Keeping all the old brick, the façades, he reckoned the yupniks eat that shit up with a spoon.'

'Yupniks?'

'Yuppie rednecks.' He had the grace to look embarrassed. 'Anyway, that's all scuppered for now.'

'But he still wants it.'

'Yeah, he's bunkering in, buying low. Except he's good-cop bad-cop all on his own. One minute he's all, "You need to sell

now, Finn." Next he's going, "It's a buyer's market, Finn."
Schizophrenic, the fucker is.'

'You shouldn't be dealing with him direct. Get yourself a solicitor, put some space between you. Get the solicitor to play hard-
ball.'

'Just another fucking thing, man. Gillick *is* my solicitor.'

'Right.'

'It's complicated. He's the family solicitor, always has been.
Plus there's the fact that he likes the Cyprus idea, wants in on the
ground floor.' He shrugged it off. 'Anyway, there's no panic. By the
time we get all the red tape sorted on Cyprus, he'll be throwing
money at me.'

'I wouldn't bet the farm on that one, Finn. I think we're in for
the long haul this time.'

'Yeah, well . . .' His shoulders slumped. 'Listen,' he said, 'keep
it under your hat for now.'

'I'll buy a hat special, just to have something to keep it under.'
I toasted him with my coffee mug. 'Fair fucks, man. Bon voyage.'

'Cheers.'

I drained the coffee, took the mug into the kitchen, rinsed it
out. He had The Only Ones on when I got back, 'Another Girl,
Another Planet'. 'Expecting anyone else?' I said.

'No. Why?'

'I'll bring up the score.'

He glanced at his watch. 'No need, I'm nearly finished. I'll follow you down. Oh, here.' He reached under the desk, clickety-
clicked through some CD cases, came up holding a blank.
Frisbee'd it across. He'd scrawled *Songs to Dance and Make Babies
To # VII* in flowing script on the white insert card. 'See if you can
work it out.'

'That reminds me. Herb was looking for some Motown. Some Smokey if you have it.'

'No problem. See you in ten.'

As it happened, it took him twenty. He arrived in a hurry, though. When he ploughed head-first into the cab he must have been doing damn near sixty miles an hour.

6

Sizzling flesh, burnt petrol, maybe even a whiff of sulphur. The stench of the Saturday night riots in Hell.

My guts bubbled and yawed. I stumbled across to the deepwater for a smoke, hands shaking so hard it took three goes to dig the makings out of my back pocket. Bear had stopped barking, although now and again I could hear him scraping, a low whine. I finally got a cigarette rolled, stuck my face in the smoke.

When my guts finally stopped sloshing around I rolled another smoke and went back to where he lay. Hunkered down, fingers clamped on my nose. Some words needed. It was a bit late for an Act of Contrition, and anyway Finn wasn't the religious type, so I settled for something vaguely spiritual from *Bell Jars Away*.

'I have thrown myself into your warm hold,' I whispered, 'where you bless away the shivering.'

No good reason to whisper, there being no one within half-a-mile to hear. But I didn't trust my normal voice to work.

Shuddering now, the quake taking its own sweet time to settle, aftershocks rumbling.

I kissed one knuckle and touched it to what remained of his left shoulder.

Not much, but it'd have to do.

I spent the eternity or so it took the ambulance to arrive looking for something that might do for a slim jim, this before it occurred to me to wonder if Finn might have left his Audi unlocked. He had. I was cursing him for a feckless fool, aloud, when I realised I was only doing it out loud because I knew there was no one around, never was, not that late down at the PA. I half-expected to find the keys in the ignition, but even Finn wasn't that hopeless. Two minutes, some loosened wires and a couple of sparks later and I was mobile again. The Audi was badly scorched all along its left-hand side, the windows smoke-blackened, so they looked like they'd been given a botched tint job. But it would run.

When the paramedics arrived, and looked and winced, I identified Finn and told them what I'd seen. The guy in charge seemed competent, solid, so I drifted away. He heard the Audi's door close and strolled over, knuckled the window. I rolled it down.

'You okay to drive?' he said.

'Sound, yeah.'

'Watch out for the delayed shock. If you start feeling sick, dizzy, tired, any way off, pull over straight away.' He peered a little closer, taking in the singed eyebrows, the bloody hands dried black. 'And you'll be needing a stitch or two in those.'

'I'll do for now.'

'You know you're not supposed to leave until the cops get here.'

'Someone should tell his folks.'

'The cops'll do that.'

'Yeah, but it should be somebody who knew him.'

'Fair enough, but they'll have my balls if I don't write down your reg.'

'Work away. I'll swing back this way when I'm done. If I don't find them here, I'll head in to the cop shop. Should take about an hour out and back.'

He tap-tapped the roof, straightening up. 'Better you than me,' he said, walking away.

He didn't know the half of it. I pulled out of the PA yard and headed for town. Ten minutes later I was outside Weir's Folly, the four-bed penthouse suite of which had balcony views of Yeats' Bridge to the north and Lough Gill to the east, and was officially registered as the office address of Fine Arte Investments. Two of the bedrooms had been converted into actual office space, which left two-thirds of the penthouse for the director of Fine Arte Investments, aka Finn Hamilton, to call his own, rent-free. That perk was impressive enough, given that a four-bed penthouse in the heart of town could be pulling down anything up to fifteen hundred a month, but the office address allowed Finn to claim practically every aspect of its upkeep as a tax write-off.

Money buys money.

NAMA might have been across Hamilton Holdings like some Biblical plague, but there were no eviction notices pinned to the doors of Weir's Folly. And I was pretty sure too that when I drove on out to The Grange, there'd be no For Sale signs to take the look off the place.

I buzzed on the bell again, still wondering how I'd begin. No matter how I started out it always fell apart when I got to the part where I said his name. Which was when Finn's voice cut in, talking about family and kids, his plans for Cyprus. Then the flesh spitting on hot metal, that oily, rank whiff . . .

I buzzed a fourth time, but the place was dark and it was obvious Maria wasn't home. I gave it another thirty seconds or so, then dug out my phone and dialled her number. It rang out, went to her answering machine.

'Hi, this is Maria. I'm sorry for the inconvenience, but if you leave your name, number and a short message, I'll return your call as soon as I can. Thanks, bye.'

'Maria, it's Harry. Call me back whenever you get this. It's, ah, it's important.'

I hung up, wondering if she already knew. If she was in there with all the lights turned off, sitting in the darkness with her hands cradling her belly, staring blindly into the void where her future used to be.

7

We'd been having a freakish spell, an early Irish summer, the kind that can last two months or two hours but always goes on too long. To date we'd had nearly a week of sunny days and mild nights, and the sunset earlier on had been a ruddy shepherd's delight. Which meant it'd be a bright, warm and beautiful morning when I told Herb his cab was a write-off, this courtesy of Finn, his flaky fuck du jour.

I wondered if Herb's insurance covered suicides jumping from nine floors up. Not that it mattered, any insurance hike or replacement would come out of my end. The deal we had was, anything that happened on my watch was my call.

And then there was the three baggies of Toto McConnell's finest weed, all gone up in smoke.

Just one more fucking thing . . .

I drove north out the Bundoran Road. Still shaky, thumbs drumming on the steering-wheel's leather. I felt horse-kicked and brutalised, heart pounding, mouth dry. A ripping of some fabric deep inside and I don't care if you call it the spirit or the soul or the electric charge that keeps the machine running, but it was fritzing up sparks, flashes of lightning glimpsed behind thunderheads massed along some dark horizon and only a matter of time before the storm broke and the loneliness came roaring down out of the hills, black hounds howling fit to bust a lung.

The Furies unleashed and Gonz in the vanguard, teeth bared and monstrous in a pitiless snarl.

Finn had been the only one to understand. Said his own dreams were full of kraken and creatures half-shark and half-squid, surging up from the dark depths to snatch him from the shore, drag him down. Drowning dreams, or dreams where he sat on the ocean floor trying to drink the Atlantic down, although the dreams when the slimy tentacles transformed into his father's arm were the worst, the hand grasping for Finn's, and Finn reaching, always reaching, his father's fingers slipping away beneath the waters and gone.

You didn't have to be Freud to work it out. Neither of us had needed a therapist to pick through the entrails.

How to live with it, though. Nothing in the textbooks about that. No clues to be deciphered from the clipboards they consulted, no hieroglyphics printed in invisible ink between the lines of their endless questionnaires.

I was wallowing, yeah. Anything to keep my mind off what was to come, the standing before a mother, a widow, with the worst words she would ever hear.

And then the long crawl into the deep dark hole and the pulling over of the earth to deaden every sight and every sound that might remind me I was still alive.

The Audi purred along, down the long curve into

Rathcormack, out the straight run into Drumcliffe village nestled 'neath bare Benbulben's head. The pretty little church with its lights all ablaze and somewhere in there W.B. casting his cold eye on death, and life. The Audi's tyres hissing slick on the sweat of the German tax-paper, who'd paid for every straight yard of road built in this country in the last forty years. McIlhatton ya blurt, we need ya, cry a million shaking men, and what rough beast, his hour come round, slouches towards a mother to break her heart . . .

Sweating now. The Audi veering across the white line. I sat up in the seat and flipped my smoke out the window, reached for the stereo and pumped the volume. Radiohead, 'Paranoid Android', Thom Yorke's wailing about raining down from a great height. Nice timing, Thom. The kicker being that Finn had the Audi's stereo tuned to McCool FM, the personalised Spotify pre-records he'd broadcast to the world all night, or that part of the world within a fifteen-mile radius of the PA building at least.

Too much.

I dug out his CD, *Music to Make Babies To*, slipped it into the deck. Hoping for a little distraction. Finn's compilations were musical crossword puzzles, each song a clue. Except Rollerskate Skinny were first out of the traps, 'Swingboat Yawning', and that was way too close to the bone, *heaven to be overcome, what are you going through the only thing I can ask you*, even before they hit the whimsical hook, *Now my future is all behind me . . .*

I knocked the stereo off and drove on. Shuddering from a bad case of the grace of Gods and but fors. My brain popping sparks as it tried to weld two irreconcilable truths, one Finn over this side, the easy-going guy with the big plans and a sloppy shit-don't-matter grin, the other a flattened lump of burnt flesh and shattered bone. No sense to it, no logic.

Except that was Finn. Always had been. A two-piece jigsaw, no way of making it fit.

Now my future is all behind me . . .

Maybe Herb was right. The part-time philanthropist, he called Finn, the rich kid dabbling in poverty for the photo ops and tax-breaks. 'Pro fucking Bono,' he'd sneer whenever Finn's picture appeared in the *Champion* or the *Weekender*. It was perfect for Herb that Finn was into skiing, snowboards. 'Because it's all fucking downhill.'

Yeah, maybe. It doesn't get much more downhill than nine stories high and gravity singing its siren song.

8

The first Hamiltons came over with Cromwell and slaughtered enough Papists to earn themselves a plot in hell. Or Connaught, as the locals called it. The townland is still there, the pretty little village of Manorhamilton in the county of Leitrim, although these days the rack-rents are called austerity measures and we scarf McBurgers rather than scabby black spuds.

The point being, the Hamiltons and their carpet-bagging Anglo-Irish ilk had only been in Ireland for five hundred years.

Around here, that just about qualifies you as a blow-in.

I'd been out to The Grange once before, for a wedding reception, but even so it took some finding in the high-ditched labyrinth on the peninsula southwest of the village of Grange itself. A faux-Georgian pile, of course, although to be fair to the Hamiltons, it was only faux because the original Georgian structure had been torched back in 1921 during the IRA campaign to ethnically cleanse Ireland of Protestants, and specifically those of the land-owning class. But the Hamiltons were a hardy breed, perennials. The kind to thrive on slash-and-burn. It helped that one of Donald Hamilton's brothers, one of the minor artists of the Celtic Twilight now long eclipsed by Jack Yeats, had been bounced into the Senate in 1924 as one of the Free State's token representative Protestants.

The Audi purred up out of the small wood of oak and sycamore into a sunken dell, smooth lawns running from the forest fringe to either side of the house and curving up and behind to form a steep-sided bowl. A round loop of gravel had fallen short of lassoing the house and had had to content itself with an oblong fountain instead, a trio of arrow-pinging cherubs perched on its rim, a Mexican stand-off in marble. The obligatory Merc was parked out front, a shiny black Lexus tucked in behind, and one of those ridiculous urban jeeps, a Rav4. Spotlights popped on as I cleared the trees, bathing the house with a bluey glow. Squared-off and stolid, exuding a hunched defiance despite its three storeys. Red ivy put a blush on the functional grey stone but had the perverse effect of emphasising the austere lines and harsh angles. Wide steps narrowed to a front porch under a portico that had been swiped along with the Elgin marbles. The flowerbeds were neater than a double gin.

I hauled up the wide steps. Shivering now, a salty Atlantic breeze gusting around the corner of the house. Apart from the ivy, the door's fire-engine red was the building's only splash of colour. A brass door knocker in the shape of an elephant's head was inviting but a lusty swing on its trunk revealed it as ornamental. I pushed the button set into a steel plate to the right of the door. Almost immediately the speaker above the button crackled.

'Yes?'

'Harry Rigby. I'm a friend of Finn's.'

'Yes?'

'There's been an accident.'

An intake of breath suggested he was about to try another affirmative query, but then a bolt slid back. The hallway, when the door had finally swung open far enough to allow me slip inside, looked like it had been designed with fat giraffes in mind. He made to speak but then stood back and let me through. 'I'm Simon,' he said, ushering me across the tiled hallway into a study with French windows set into the opposite wall. The other walls were taken up with shelves of leather-bound volumes, although here and there the grotesque exaggerations of modern portraiture leered from the gloom.

He gestured towards an armchair of dimpled green leather, waiting until I'd sat down before perching on the edge of its facing twin. On a squat table beside his chair sat a cut-crystal decanter, a green-shaded lamp and an empty balloon glass. A leather-bound book lay open and facedown on the chair's arm but I couldn't make out the title. I couldn't work him out, either. Forty-something, quietly spoken, with a receding hairline and grey at his temples. His eyes, keenly alert, were also grey. Which made him old and smart enough to know better than to be seen in public wearing black trousers with a charcoal satin stripe running down the seam.

'It's bad,' he said. 'You'd have phoned if it wasn't bad.'

'It's the worst. I'm sorry.'

The eyes seemed to blossom, then narrow. 'He's dead?'

I nodded. He swallowed dry. His eyes glazed over. 'How did it happen?'

Even as I told him he was frowning, shaking his head. 'Suicide?' he said when I'd finished. 'Finn?'

'That's why I thought Mrs Hamilton should know. Before the cops get here.'

'Of course. She'll appreciate that. Thank you.' He didn't seem to be aware that he was shaking his head all the while. 'You're sure?' he said then. I nodded. 'But why would he . . . ?'

'No idea. I'm sorry.'

He licked at dry lips. 'She's asleep, of course. I should wake her, but . . .'

He didn't move.

'The news won't be any worse in the morning,' I said.

'No, I don't suppose it will.' He was humouring me, buying time. Right then he was miles away, or maybe just upstairs telling a woman the worst news she would ever hear. 'Do you have children, Mr Rigby?'

'A son.'

'If it was you,' he said, stalling, 'would you rather find out straight away?'

'I would, yeah.'

'I think I would too.' He thought it over, then noticed my fidgeting fingers and prescribed a brandy for the shock, poured us both a couple of inches. He sluiced his down without waiting for a toast. I wanted that brandy so bad I almost inhaled it having a sniff, but I was a taxi-driver on my way back in to meet with the cops, so I let it run up against my lips and slip away again. Just enough for a taste, to observe the ceremony.

'I'll wake her,' he said. Dutch courage. 'She should know.'

I stood and fished a card out of the back pocket of my jeans. 'If you need me for anything, you can get me at that number.'

He glanced at it, distracted, then showed me to the door, thanked me again. He was still standing at the top of the wide steps when I pulled away down the drive, his stance loose, the shoulders slack, and I'd have bet everything I owned he'd have stood there through winter if it meant he didn't have to climb those stairs and wake the woman who slept so blissfully unaware.

9

'What I don't like about it,' Tohill said, 'is you were there when it happened.'

'When it happened, yeah. Not where it happened.'

'Don't be cute.'

'I was down in the yard. The big decision was made nine storeys up. It was all over by the time he got down as far as me.'

'Says you.'

'It's me you're asking.'

'Let's not try to be too smart, hey?'

'What's that, policy here?'

The interview room was tricked out like a little girl's bedroom, pastel pinks and blues. Some new EU directive, no doubt, designed to minimise the invasiveness of the interrogation process for those thugs and scumbags who suffered from a sensitive disposition. The lighting subdued, not so much as a cigarette burn or graffiti scar on the formica-topped table. The smell of paint was fresh enough to give me a faint headache.

Tohill stalked the room with his hands in his pockets, fair-haired, late thirties, his face a scuffed steel-toe boot. He liked me as well as he'd like any other ex-con who'd left the scene of a crime.

We'd chewed that one over. Last I'd heard, suicide wasn't a crime. Tohill was of the opinion it wasn't suicide until he said so. Now he leaned on the back of the chair across the table and ducked his head so his pale blue eyes were level with mine. 'Let's just go over it one more time.'

'Sound, yeah. Can we get someone in, make this the official statement?'

'You in a hurry?'

I was exhausted. There'd been a single uniform standing guard at the PA when I'd dropped back the Audi, who'd just stared, waiting for the punch line, when I'd asked if he could ring for a squad car to take me in to the station. So I'd hoofed it, in along the docks and all the way across town, a long and solitary hike, begrudging every last plodding step. Not exactly the Bataan Death March, okay. But I'd been badly shook for about two hours by then, and it felt like every cell in my body was screaming to shut down, just blank it all out.

And now Tohill looked to be in the mood to break out his Bud White impression.

'I get the impression you're the thorough type,' I said. 'So I'd say you went up there, had a good look around. And if you'd found anything, what they call signs of a struggle, I'd be having this conversation with my brief.'

'I found your hands ripped to shit,' he said. 'That looks like signs of a struggle to me.'

'Maybe it does, if you're willing to get up in court and say I tried to batter Finn off the roof with a pile of scrap metal. And I'm talking about the studio. They find anything up there?'

'Should they have?'

'How would I know? I didn't go up there.'

'You did go up there.'

'I mean after. I didn't go up there after.'

'You weren't curious?'

'That's a sick question.'

The wide grin suggested that he genuinely enjoyed that one. 'You're telling me *I'm* sick?'

He had all night, a charred corpse and an eyewitness who'd done seven years in the home for the criminally bewildered for shooting his brother in cold blood. Promotions have been grubbed from a lot less.

A Catch-22 bind, no matter how it fell out. If I copped to insanity when I blew Gonzo away, then I was a loose cannon, liable to blow any time, maybe heave a friend through a window nine storeys up.

The flip side being, if I claimed I'd been stone cold sane when I punched a hole in my only brother's chest, same deal, I was capable of anything.

So I picked a spot on the wall over his head and stared.

'See, what I'm not getting,' Tohill said, flicking some pages in the folder on the desk, 'is why this guy might want to jump. If it was you, grand, you're off your bap, we'd all be home tucked up right now wondering why you couldn't have jumped in the water, saved us the hassle of cleaning up the mess. Only this guy looks like he had it all.'

It was a fair question, the one that had been bugging me all night. How Finn had been so upbeat back at the PA before he jumped. If he'd been down, sure, it'd make sense, the black dog snarling and chasing him out onto the ledge. Except Finn, when he was down, could hardly walk. It was when he was up that he wanted to jump, burn off the evil buzz.

Bell jars away . . .

'I mean,' Tohill said, 'if you'd been smart about it, torched the building and *then* said he'd jumped from the blaze, we'd all be thinking it was Finn the firebug, he just couldn't help himself. Am I right?'

The spot on the wall was maybe a damp patch they hadn't treated, just painted over.

'Hey!' Tohill pounded the table with a clenched fist. I started in the seat, a jagged pain darting down my left ribs.

'Look,' I said, breathing out slow, 'I came in here to do you a favour. I don't need to—'

'Bullfucking*shit*. You're about this close,' his thumb and forefinger pressed together, 'from an obstruction of justice charge. Yeah? Because right now I'm wondering what the big fucking deal is, what it is you're trying to hide.' He poked a stubby forefinger into the pristine formica. 'So my advice to you is to open your fucking mouth and have something half-intelligent come out. Otherwise we're in for a long fucking night.'

The pain ebbed, subsided. A cold sweat prickling my back. 'Are we making movies?' I said. I glanced up at the camera high in the corner, its green light blinking. 'Tell them be sure to get my good side.'

'You want me to tell them to turn it off?' he said. 'So we can have a proper chat, like?'

Dee once told me I had eyes like a jilted shark. I met his stare and then shut down the lights, let him see what sick really looked like. 'Just you and me,' I said. 'A proper chat.'

A twitch under his right eye, a faint narrowing. Then he rolled his shoulders and grinned. He fancied his chances. 'Maybe we'll do that,' he said. 'Just not here, yeah?'

'You'll know where to find me.'

'Fucking right I'll know where to find you. Because right now you're headed for a padded cell again.' He straightened up, jammed his hands into this pockets, took a little stroll around the room. 'Go back to the start,' he said. A faint smirk. 'Tell me how you and Finn were bunk buddies.'

'We shared a room, yeah.'

'A *room*?' He chuckled. Easily amused, Tohill. 'Where was this, the Radisson?'

'They called them rooms. Part of the rehab process.'

'Normalisation,' he nodded, 'am I right? So you don't feel a freak for blowing a hole in your brother. I get it. So there you are,' he said, rolling his shoulders again, 'all cosy in your room, and Finn Hamilton wanders in stinking like the pit lane at Le Mans. Did you jump his bones straight away or give him time to settle in?'

He was old school, Tohill. He'd be checking to see if I wore white socks next, asking if I liked to jazzercise to Liza Minelli show tunes.

'What I don't get,' Tohill said, flipping idly through the pages of the folder, 'is how you got such soft time. Like, here it says fit to be tried, and you were up on murder, there was just you and him in a room, you shot him. Right? Black and white. Except then you're allowed plead self-defence *and* temporary insanity?' He waited. I stared. 'Next thing we know,' he flipped a couple of pages, 'you're remanded to Dundrum for observation, assessment. Which is supposed to last two weeks, max, except you're in there four years.' Again he paused. 'Maybe you're more complicated than most,' he said, 'but four years' worth?' He pursed his lips, made a sucking sound. 'And then you get transferred to the mental hospital here, nice and easy, not a single objection. Even though,' he flipped back a page or two, 'I'm not seeing any gold stars, no one raving about how you're a model prisoner. What, you think this is funny? I'm some kind of comedian?'

'No, it's not that.'

'Then what's so fucking funny?'

I shouldn't have rolled him the shark eyes. Bad things happen. Cogs and gears slipping their mesh, something flapping free in the back of my head.

'Sitting on the sidelines,' I said, 'cribbing and moaning, is a lost opportunity.' I knew it by heart. 'I don't know how people who engage in that don't commit suicide because frankly the only thing that motivates me is being able to actively change something.'

'The fuck has that to do with—'

'It's a quote, Tohill. From our former Lord and Master, Bartholomew Ahern, you might know him better as Bertie, not necessarily of the Wooster variety. That was his measured response when asked about those critiquing an economic policy driven by an accountant and former Minister for Finance who never learned how to open a bank account. A persuasive guy, though. They've been topping themselves in fucking droves ever since.'

'You're saying this is why Finn Hamilton jumped.'

'I'm saying, I'm with Bertie. About not sitting on the sidelines, whinging about how shit everything is.' I leaned forward, tapped the folder. 'Being what they call proactive about changing stuff.'

'Go on.'

'Gonz was the crazy, Tohill. Mad fucker. He'd killed once already, once I knew of. Was already diving for a gun when I pulled the trigger. Sanest thing I ever did was cut that fucker down. Him or me, yeah? Doesn't get more logical than that. Except then they said I was the crazy, because I was waiting and ready. What they call malice aforethought. That judge, if he'd ever been in the Scouts, I'd have walked away a free man. Dib-dib-dib, be prepared, you know the drill. But here's the kicker, Tohill – that mental hospital, man, if you're not mad going in you're hinky as fuck coming out.'

'What's that, a threat?'

'Why would I threaten you? You're not even in the game.'

'Game?'

'The *game.*'

'I don't get it. What fucking game are you—'

'I'll take a bet with you now, Tohill.' I leaned in. 'I'm betting you've never slotted anyone. I'm betting you don't even *know* anyone who's ever put a man away. Tell me I'm wrong.'

It was in his eyes.

'I took Gonzo off the map,' I said. 'And yeah, it was me or him, but I did it. You think the world isn't a better place without him in it? That was me.' I touched a thumb to my chest. 'Me. Not you, not any one of you. Me. So if you need to know why I did four years of what they call soft fucking time, go find yourself a guy called Brady, last I heard he was calling the shots in Harcourt Street. A cop, yeah, but a cop who knows how the game works. Tell him I sent you, he'll give you anything you need to know. As for this bullshit, I've had a long fucking night and I'm legally entitled to make a statement,' I glanced up at the lens, 'which I'm now officially requesting. So either take my statement and let me go, or arrest me and let me get some sleep.'

He stared awhile, lower jaw moving like he was grinding corn. Then he left the room. He came back with a uniform who wasn't old enough to shave. The clock on the wall read 5.23 AM.

I stuck to the story. How Finn'd rang to say his Audi was giving him trouble, which was why he'd needed a cab. He'd been smoking a little dope, sure, but he'd been upbeat, making plans to get married and move to Cyprus. The last thing I'd expected was for him to jump, but he did. *Sic transit gloria mundi.*

The uniform went away to type up the statement.

'This dope he was smoking,' Tohill said. 'I don't suppose you know where he got it?'

'No idea.'

'Smoke a little with him, hey?'

'That'd violate the terms of my release.'

'Still, maybe we should have you take a piss test.'

I allowed that one fall pat, let him feel exactly how small was something so big. He tugged on his nose. 'Just so you know,' he said. 'It wouldn't cost me a second thought to put you back in the bin.'

'What it'd cost is about quarter of a million a year to keep me there,' I said.

'Scum like you, it's worth it.'

He looked worn down, shapeless and shabby. He'd have been better off investing his tax dollar in a decent suit.

The uniform brought the statement back in to be signed. Tohill leaned against the door-jamb rolling his neck in clockwise circles while I gave it the once-over.

'For Christ's sake,' he sighed, 'just sign the fucking thing.'

'No problem. Once I'm sure it's all my own work.'

There was a knock at the door. Tohill stepped out. I rolled a cigarette, tucked it behind my ear. Tohill came back in, rolling his shoulders.

I glanced up in the corner. The green light had stopped blinking.

Shit.

He picked the statement off the table, nodding as he read through. 'Remind me,' he said, 'how there was no one else at the PA when you arrived. Although first,' he crumpled the statement and tossed it in my face, 'let me tell you how we just had a call. From someone you might know. The name Gillick ring any bells?'

'Gillick?'

'He's what you might call a concerned citizen. Public-spirited. Heard on the radio about a suicide down at the PA building, thought he could help with our enquiries. Clarify a thing or two.'

'Sounds like a real gent.'

'Says he was down at the PA earlier on, consulting with his client, Finn Hamilton. Strange place and time for a consultation, I'd have said, but anyway, Gillick noticed this guy who came in, Rigby he called him. About five-eleven, dark hair, medium build running to skinny. Early forties. White shirt, black tie, had the look of the loser in a Travellers' bare-knuckle brawl.'

'Be some coincidence if it wasn't me.'

I wondered if he knew his right hand was balled, the knuckles gone creamy. 'You just made a statement that could put you away for two years. And that's before they open your old file, wondering if you're not starting to get squirrelly again.'

'I didn't mention Gillick because you were asking if I'd seen anyone who'd push Finn out of a window. Gillick was long gone by then. And anyway, he's Finn's solicitor, or was. Why would he push Finn anywhere?'

'Smart,' he said. He was fast. Grabbed my tie while I was mid-blink, rammed the knot up under my Adam's apple. Enough squeeze to cut off my air, not so hard he'd do permanent damage. 'But you'll need to smarten up, Rigby. Otherwise you're looking at—'

Another knock on the door. The uniform popped his head in. 'Sir, that solicitor's – shit. *Sir?*' Tohill turned his head. 'That solicitor's arrived, sir. Wants to see his client.'

The door closed. Tohill let go, shoving my head back, then leaned in so close I could tell he'd had Bolognese for dinner, heavy on the garlic. 'I'll fucking nail you both,' he said.

I loosened the knot, working it free with a forefinger. 'You should floss,' I croaked.

He slammed the table with the flat of his hand but I didn't jump any higher than a Mexican flea. A sour chuckle, then he hawked and spat.

'Thanks,' he said.

'No problem,' I said, wiping gluey spittle from my cheek with the tail of my shirt.

'Sometimes you forget why you do the job. Scum like you, you're a refresher course.'

'They also serve who stand and wait.'

He made a point of straightening his tie and then he was gone. I mopped up the last of the phlegm. The stench of garlic hung in the air but at least I wasn't smelling burnt pork anymore.

10

While I waited for Gillick to pay for the coffees I thought about how I didn't have a solicitor, couldn't afford one, hadn't asked for one and hadn't needed one, not until a solicitor rang the cops.

He'd walked me out of the cop shop, asked me to join him for an early breakfast. I told him sure, so long as it featured grilled kidneys, at least one of them his, then walked on. Thirty seconds later the maroon Saab cruised by, Jimmy rolling down the window. He pulled in, double-parked. 'I'm the one has to pick up the toys,' he said, 'when he throws them out of the pram.'

'It's been a long night, Jimmy. Last thing I need now is coffee and bullshit.'

'Let the man buy you breakfast. He's happy, I'm happy, you're fed.'

'I'm too tired to eat, man.'

'I'd take it as a favour. Never any harm in having a favour out there, is there?'

A fair point, especially when knocking it back meant Jimmy

believing he owed me something different. I shrugged.

'So eat breakfast,' he said, 'smile and nod. Then we all go home.'

I thought about breakfast, felt my guts constrict. I thought about home. Same result. I went around to the Saab, got in.

Jimmy drove us to the all-night truck stop north of town. Took our orders and went inside while Gillick and I strolled around the back to the enclosed smoking area. Wooden picnic tables, overhead heating.

Gillick looked sharp for six in the morning. An open-necked shirt in pale blue, tan Chinos with a sharp crease. Tasselled loafers, a sports jacket with corduroy elbow-patches, a faint whiff of cigarette and jasmine. Or maybe, given the hour and Finn's verdict on his reputation, Jasmine. He eased his bulk onto the picnic table seat and placed a slim crocodile-skin briefcase on the table. Got his elbows set on the briefcase so he wouldn't soil the elbow-patches, then lowered his middle chin onto the point of his steepled fingers.

'What exactly did you tell them?' he purred.

'It's all in the statement.'

'Surely you didn't sign anything.'

'What's it to you?'

He dipped into his hip pocket and put down a card. 'I'm the Hamiltons' family solicitor.'

'So?'

'The bulletin said someone was helping the Gardaí with their enquiries. That had to be you.'

'So?'

'I wanted to be sure you weren't unnecessarily detained.'

'I was doing just fine until you showed up.'

'Possibly.' Jimmy arrived with a tray, black coffee for Gillick, a sausage sandwich for me, some orange juice. Gillick waited until Jimmy had ambled off before continuing. 'But it's unlikely you'd have gone to see Mrs Hamilton after you left, would you?'

'I was already out there,' I said through a mouthful of sausage and bread. Crumbs rained down.

'So I understand.' He pulled his beaker of coffee back out of mortar range. 'I'm also given to understand you didn't speak with Mrs Hamilton.'

'She was asleep.'

'She's awake now.' He heaved a sigh that set his lowest chin a-wobble. 'Her only son has just died. You were the last person to see him alive.'

'I can't tell her any more than I told the butler.'

He coughed delicately, the hand not quite covering a wry smile. 'I believe Simon's official title is Household Manager.'

'That doesn't change what I told him.' I put aside the sandwich, which had been made from genetically modified plastic pork, drank off the orange juice and dug out the makings. 'Although, thinking back, I left out the bit about you being there. Maybe the lady needs to talk to you.'

'Mrs Hamilton is fully aware that I was speaking with Finn this evening. And why.'

'So you're saying she wants to ask me if you pressured him into jumping.'

He flushed. 'I don't anticipate my clients' needs, Mr Rigby. I simply act as directed, when directed.'

'The organ-grinder's monkey.'

The prim little beak took on a wet-lipped pout. 'As I understand it,' he said, 'you were very close to spending a night in the cells for obstruction, failure to cooperate and wasting police time. That wouldn't go down very well with your probation officer, would it?'

'What goes down well with my probation officer is a naggin of Scotch between high tea and cocktails. You think she gives a fuck where I spend the night?'

'Maybe she could be persuaded to take an interest.'

I was exhausted, sure, the adrenaline buzz long gone, the shock of Finn's death a sponge sucking me dry. But some days, Jesus, it's like everyone, everywhere, its putting the squeeze on.

'What exactly is it Mrs Hamilton is hoping I'll say?' I said.

'As I said, I never try to second-guess my—'

'Hold on,' I said, putting the roll-up between my lips, patting my pockets for the Zippo. He reached into his breast pocket and held out a gold Ronson. I dipped my head towards the flame and came back with an arm around the crocodile-skin briefcase. He grabbed for it, but his reflexes were those of a man who spent half his life drinking lunch and the other half filling out expense claims. I set the briefcase on my lap, flicked the clasps. The dictaphone was a neat affair, digital, matt silver, not much bigger than the Ronson, and had been recording for almost twenty minutes. I turned it off, put it in my breast pocket, slid the briefcase back across the table.

'Give me a clue,' I said. 'What were *you* hoping I'd say?'

'That's purely for my own protection. In case a dissatisfied client tries to misrepresent my advice at a later stage. It's standard procedure.'

'For one, I'm not your client. Even if I was, it's illegal unless you tell me you're taping the conversation.'

An oily grin slid away to disappear between the first and second chins. 'Few things in life are entirely legal, Mr Rigby.'

'Like you playing both sides with Finn, say.'

Maybe the click-click of the briefcase clasps drowned me out. 'Despite his popularity,' he said, opening the case and extracting a cheque book, 'Finn didn't have many close friends.' He closed the case again, laid the cheque book on top, located the fountain pen in his breast pocket. 'I believe Mrs Hamilton is now reaching out to one of those friends in an attempt to distract her from her grief. Is it too much to ask that you would play that role on what is probably the worst night of her life?'

'Yes.'

He uncapped the pen. 'You'll be paid for your time, of course. I'd imagine it'll take two hours, including the journey out and back. Would three hundred euro be acceptable?'

I thought about Finn's broken, torched body. I thought about a grieving mother's agony. I thought about the three baggies Finn had ordered before he jumped, Toto McConnell's weed gone up in smoke.

'Make it five,' I said, 'cash.'

11

It might have been Marx. Or Engels, maybe. Anyway, someone once said man would never be free until the last priest was hanging from the entrails of the last banker. Or words to that effect.

Funny he didn't mention lawyers. Maybe he thought they'd be impossible to exterminate, like roaches and hope. I wasn't so sure. A garlic-tipped silver bullet, a stake through the heart – it's worth a try, at least.

I was spared Jimmy. Gillick drove, the Saab sounding like a horny angel, smooth and silent but for a smug little hum. Up front the interior was polished leather and walnut. The dash panel, luminous with blues and reds, had been lifted from a Lear's cockpit. We were passing Drumcliffe Church when he finally spoke. Working for casual, coming off strained. 'So what did Finn have to say?'

'About what?'

'Please, Mr Rigby. I thought we were beyond games.'

'No, you thought you'd bought me.'

'That's not—'

'And what you really want to know is what he said about you.'

'I'm afraid I don't follow.'

'Like fuck you don't. It's why you're whizzing around town at five in the morning, springing desperadoes from the cells. So Mrs Hamilton talks to me, not you, and forgets to ask why you were at the PA hassling Finn.'

'I was there,' he said, 'at Mrs Hamilton's request. And I object to the—'

'You're up this early for the good of your health? What's next, a sitz bath?'

A sigh. 'Mrs Hamilton,' he said, 'is not just a client of long and good standing. She is a friend, as was her husband. If she calls on me at an inconvenient time, that simply confirms how badly she needs me.'

'Thou good and faithful servant.'

We were coming up on Monaneen Cross. He indicated left, shifted down and turned off towards the sea. The horizon turning grey, the Donegal mountains a faint purple haze on the horizon. 'A touch of inferiority complex can be a healthy thing, Rigby. Just don't let it cripple you.'

'What happened to the "Mister" bit?'

He liked that. 'You'd rather I called you Mr Rigby?'

'You're getting well paid to do it. And I'd say you're on triple time for anti-social hours.'

He slowed into a crossroads, eased across. 'May ask as to why you didn't tell our friend Tohill I was at the PA tonight?'

'He never asked.'

A soft chuckle. 'Jimmy will appreciate the sentiment.' He waited. 'And is that, definitively, all it was?'

He should have brought Jimmy. The more he talked, the more I was wondering why he was worried I had something on him.

He indicated left, turned up through the iron-wrought gates, crunching gravel as we rolled on into the small forest of oak and sycamore. Up ahead I saw a badger waddle off the road into the ditch, its eyes gleaming greenly in the halogen glare. 'I understand you used to be a private detective,' he said.

'Research consultant.'

'Of course.' Another chuckle. 'You know, I might require the services of a research consultant one day.'

'I'd say your kind of operation needs that kind of service every day. What's wrong with the ones you use now?'

'Nothing, they're all perfectly fine. But I am blessed in having a large number of clients. Sometimes I need to outsource.'

'Squeamish about the debt collecting, are they?'

'In the current climate, Mr Rigby, you diversify or die.' The faintest of sneers. 'I'd imagine you appreciate that better than most.'

'And you think I'm onside because I don't squeak to the shades.'

'If by that you're asking if confidentiality is important to my clients, then yes.'

'I'm retired.'

'I heard.' He cleared his throat. 'Harry J. Rigby, former research consultant and freelance journalist. Tried in 2004 for the murder of one Edward aka Gonzo Rigby, but not convicted, this on the basis that you claimed temporary insanity and were subsequently referred to the Central Mental Hospital for assessment, which for one reason or another took the best part of four years.' He glanced across. 'I'm no expert, but I'd imagine killing your own brother is as good a way as any to become the least private eye in town.' He waited. I let it hang. 'So why come back?' he mused. 'It's either the boy or a lack of imagination.' Again he waited. 'I'm betting it's the boy.'

'Mention my son again and I'll put you through that window.'

'How dramatic.' He tugged on his nose to disguise a wry smile, his Blofeld impression beginning to grate. 'I am impressed.'

'Stay that way, you'll save on windows.'

He sniffed at that. 'Look, Rigby, this isn't a moral issue. You did what you did, and your actions couldn't be condoned by any civilised standards. But as far as I'm concerned, you've served your time, paid your debt to society.'

'Society charges interest.'

'Undoubtedly. Otherwise you wouldn't be driving a taxi.' I let that one bowl on through. 'Understand that I'm not offering you a permanent position. But your reputation precedes you, and your actions tonight confirm that you're a man who can be trusted to negotiate, shall we say, potentially treacherous situations without succumbing to the urge to unburden yourself unnecessarily.'

'You want muscle. A reducer with a killer's rep, who'll keep his mouth shut if the cops start to squeeze. Someone like your friend Limerick Jim, say.'

'Not quite,' he said. 'For one thing, you lack his physique.'

'And his way with a blade.'

'Ancient history, Mr Rigby. And you of all people, surely, wouldn't deny Jimmy his right to rehabilitation and reintegration.'

We circled the fountain, passing the Merc and the Lexus, the Rav4 jeep. A red Mini Cooper tucked in behind that I hadn't noticed earlier. Gillick parked beside the wide steps, turned off the engine. He was too bulky to turn all the way around, so he peered at me over a well-padded shoulder. 'Can you honestly say you enjoy driving a taxi?'

'More than life itself.'

'There are more profitable ways of making a living.'

'I'm my own boss. I work when I want to. The bills get paid.'

'And that's the sum total of your ambition in life?'

'My lack of ambition breaks my heart. Every day I wake up weeping for the want of an urge to take a sledgehammer to some poor fucker's front door. What's so funny?'

'This posturing,' he said. 'Your contrived antipathy towards money. And yet all it took was five hundred euro in cash to lure you here tonight.'

I didn't like the sound of that 'lure'.

'Money's not the issue,' I said. 'Money's fine. If the sun ever goes out, we'll have something else to help the world go round.'

'So it's not the money per se, it's who offers it.'

'And the why.'

'Undoubtedly. But money is a wonderfully democratic concept, Mr Rigby. It cares not a whit for the history or social position of the person who spends it.'

'Money's a gun. Harmless until it winds up loaded in the wrong hands.'

'Loaded?'

'With influence, access, self-interest. For such a democratic concept, money seems awfully dependent on wearing the right tie in the right place.'

'You need to attend a polling booth to vote,' he purred. 'And they'd hardly be inclined to let you in if you arrived naked, would they?'

'I don't know. Depends on how badly the Germans need the latest referendum passed.'

He nodded, smiling indulgently. 'I'm not asking you to come to work for me, Mr Rigby. I'm simply suggesting that, should the opportunity arise, you might—'

'I'm allergic to evictions, Gillick. Crying kids bring me out in a rash.'

He inclined his head, slid me another oily smile. 'Think it over. Talk to Jimmy if you want. If you change your mind, my door is always open.'

'With all due respect to Jimmy, my probation depends on me not knowingly associating with known criminals.'

'Everyone who comes to me is innocent until proven otherwise. That's the law.'

'The law is what the law says it is.'

'Your loss.'

'I'll live.'

'Yes,' he said with an apologetic wince. 'But how well?'

12

A stone staircase swept up and around to a first-floor balcony but we didn't go up there. Simon and Gillick went away into the shadows at the far end of the hall, leaving me dawdling outside the study without so much as a fat giraffe for company. I heard Simon knock on the mahogany doors at the end of the hallway. They waited for a summons and then merged with the gloom.

I rolled a smoke and set sail down the plush Tigris of Persian carpet. Outfitting that hall cost more than I had earned in my entire life and even at that they hadn't included a single necessary object. The chandelier was a Milky Way in crystal, the walls covered with the therapeutic dribbles of blind amputees which constitute modern art, a couple of facing Knuttels giving one another a slit-eyed dare, a few blobs that could well have been sunrises or sunsets or psychedelic cow-pats on a low simmer. There were potted palms at regular intervals, the pots burnished copper and the foliage clipped tight, the leaves dusted, gleaming. The pots, at least, were useful for tipping ash into. The spindly legs on the facing set of antique velvet-covered couches suggested they'd been designed to accommodate Tinker Bell and her little friends, even if the little friends would have to take turns sitting down.

It struck me as odd that no room had been found for even one of Finn's landscapes, but then the décor was exquisitely refined, a statement of intent that let you know, in discreet whispers, that you were entering a home in which elegance was prized above passion, taste rather than feel. It was the interior design equivalent of a dinner party conversation, archly polite and excessively mannered, the ultimate goal being a consensus of no consequence lest any guest take offence. In that hallway a Finn Hamilton would have stood out like a turd on a communion wafer.

Yeah, and maybe it was just that Saoirse Hamilton didn't want any reminding that her son had learned to paint in a loony bin.

He'd spent months sleepwalking up and down the drab olive corridors, the doctors fiddling with his dosage. You'd come upon him standing stiffly in some alcove, vacant and dull, a thousand-year stare in the dead blue eyes. Like some waxwork crafted in praise of futility. A terracotta soldier escaped from the Forbidden City, fully biddable but useless for the want of orders, some final doomed assault on an impregnable hold. Even the perverts steered clear.

But if he was a basket case when he was down, the up days were just as bad. This cruelly manic energy that had him bouncing off walls, on his knees in the shower punching tiles. A black crackling in the veins that burned off caution and fear, made him a prodigy as a kid, a skateboard *wunderkind*, a BMX champ. Telling me all this from the bottom bunk, never able to meet my eyes. All the while racking up an A&E rap sheet of broken bones and concussions, a twice-fractured skull, a detached retina. Sacrifices on the altar of Finn, tokens offered up as he pushed beyond his limits against the ungiving world, graduating to fast cars and skis and snowboards, from riding waves to piercing them from cliffs that were never quite high or sheer enough.

The shrink's theory was that it was this urge that manifested itself in the torched buildings. That they were straw men, projections of himself. It sounded simplistic to me, but Finn allowed she might be right, this on the principle that nothing good ever came of disagreeing with a woman with cell keys jangling at her hip, metaphorically or otherwise.

Mainly he agreed because she encouraged him to paint, to express himself, to purge as benignly as polite society requires. In the end he learned to harness if not quite tame it, to suspend himself between high and low, a canvas primed and stretched and pinned so tight to the wood you could hear the hum.

'You've come to the wrong place.'

When I glanced up the staircase she was already halfway down, gliding, one hand on the banister, wearing paint-spattered dungarees and not a lot of anything else. Barefoot and on the verge of giggling, although maybe that was the way genetics had the baby-pink lips primed. I watched her all the way down the stairs and she wasn't the slightest bit surprised.

'The body's in the morgue,' she said. 'What's left of it, anyway.'

Six feet away and gaining fast. Shy as Gilda. She wore no make-up but the skin was a flawless latte tan, the eyes almond-shaped and the kind of elusive blue you find buried deep in a diamond. Late teens, if memory served, maybe a little older.

'I'm not the undertaker.'

'You're not?' Close enough now to see the pants, white shirt and black tie for what they really were. A faint blush spreading under the latte tan, embarrassed at mistaking me for one of the menials. 'You knew Finn?'

'That's right. I'm Harry.'

'I don't remember him mentioning you.' She held out a delicate hand. 'I'm Grainne.'

'I know.' I gave the cool flesh a faint squeeze. 'We've met before,' I said, 'at Paul and Andrea's wedding. I'm sorry for your loss.'

'Why?' A blaze of cobalt. 'Was it your fault?'

'I was there.'

'You mean you could have stopped him.'

'If I'd known,' I said, 'yeah.'

'Against his will?'

'If I had to.'

'Some friend.'

'A better one than I feel right now.'

The blaze flickered, snuffed out. 'It's traditional to feel personally responsible. You'll get over it.'

'Glad to hear it.'

'Do you think I'm cold?'

I thought she was vacant. Still in shock, and sedated. Once you got past the cobalt haze the eyes were a little too rounded for their sockets, the gaze dislocating when she tried for a piercing stare. They were diamond eyes, alright, cold and glittering and ageless.

'I think you might *get* cold,' I said, 'running around like that. Do you paint anything other than dungarees?'

She giggled, but it wasn't at my crack. 'I remember you now,' she said. 'You were at the wedding.' She frowned. 'Who was it got married?'

'Paul and Andrea.'

'That's it, yeah. She wore that retro dress.'

'She did.' I wondered what was taking Simon and Gillick.

Grainne giggled again. 'Are you okay?' I said.

She shook her head, blinked heavily. 'I am trying,' she announced, picking her words like some drunk negotiating a flash of clarity, 'to remember if there is such a thing as a fear of not falling. Wouldn't it be funny if Finn suffered from some kind of reverse vertigo?'

I thought about the crisping blob of broken jelly that had once been her brother. 'From here, maybe.'

'Although technically speaking, vertigo's not so much a fear of heights as falling off them. I really do hope he enjoyed it.'

Everyone copes with death their own way. Some weep and wail, don sackcloth. Others play it cool, make with the cheap jokes and hope they'll get slapped so hard it'll make them cry.

We were still holding hands. I let go.

'You're a sentimentalist,' she said. It was an accusation. 'You're just like all the rest, you don't want to hear the truth.'

'Maybe it's just you they don't want to hear.'

The elusive blue blazed again. She made a sound like a curious cat. 'Oh, you're different. You and I, we should talk.'

'Any time. Just ring the Samaritans, I'm always on call.'

I shouldn't have dropped her hand, but it was late, I was exhausted, and that's when mistakes get made. She raked me down the left cheek. No back-lift. She just reached and clawed.

It was too smooth. I wasn't the first.

I backed away with a hand to my cheek, checked the damage. She'd drawn blood. The sight, or maybe the scent, seemed to enrage her. This time she lunged, swinging wild. I planted a palm on her forehead. She made a couple of swipes that grazed my chest and then tried to kick in my shins with her bare feet, grunting all the while through bared teeth, a bubble of saliva in the corner of the baby-pink lips.

I heard a door open.

'If you would be so kind, Mr Rig—*Grainne!*'

She came out of it like overstretched elastic, snapped and sagged and pee-yonged away up the staircase. A door slammed.

I found an Abrakebabra napkin in my pocket and dabbed at my cheek while Simon apologised on Grainne's behalf.

'She's distraught, as you might expect. The doctor gave her some sedatives but . . .' He tailed off, shrugged. 'She's a law unto herself at the best of times.'

Scupper that. Simon made excuses, not apologies.

'Any chance we could get this done?' I said. 'I've had a long night.'

'Of course. Come this way, please.'

I went that way holding the napkin against my cheek, hoping the bereft Mrs Hamilton wouldn't suck out my eye in a paroxysm of grief.

13

I was expecting a couple of priests, maybe even a monsignor, but I had to make do with the bishop-sized Gillick. He stood to one side of the marble fireplace, his body language, consciously or otherwise, mimicking the chest-puffed profile of the patrician figure in the portrait on the chimney breast.

Bob Hamilton, I presumed, larger than life, although he'd been plenty large in life. A swarthy cove to begin with, the artist had given him a piratical mien, placing Big Bob on the deck of a yacht where the breeze could amuse itself for all eternity in ruffling his dark curls, or at least until someone decided a Knuttel molls-and-gangsters pastiche was more in keeping with the ambience. Gillick's presence suggested that that day wouldn't be long coming. The brandy balloon in his chubby fingers gave the gathering an incongruous air of celebration.

That room could have fit a small helicopter, although the pilot would need to be the barnstorming type to avoid mangling the by now obligatory squiggles and scrawls that defaced three walls.

The fourth, the rear wall, was composed entirely of glass. The crushed-velvet drapes were drawn back, affording a view of a dawn-drained North Atlantic that stretched most of the way to Iceland and a sky like Carrera marble, hard and cold behind the faint pink blush.

Gillick looked pretty comfortable standing beside the fireplace. The nonchalant stance made me wonder if his relationship with Mrs Hamilton was one that required him to stand by that fire on a regular basis, lapping brandy out of a balloon big enough to breed guppies.

I couldn't fault his taste. In among the high-backed Victorian armchairs, French-polished mahogany and a foot-high brass Cupid pinging his arrow from the distressed-oak coffee table, Mrs Saoirse Hamilton was by some distance the best preserved antique in the room. She reclined on a couch angled towards the log fire, the flames taking their cue from her auburn mane. The ripe side of fifty, luscious as fresh mango, she wore a knee-length nightgown in lavender silk that most women would have happily worn to a wedding, this providing they had a grudge against the bride. A peignoir trimmed with lacy frills would have completed the look, but she'd accessorised, using the word loosely, with a fluffy pink bathrobe, Dennis the Menace-striped leggings and knee-length riding boots. None of which disguised the fact that she had more curves than the Monaco Grand Prix. The drawl suggested she gargled Sweet Afton.

'Mr Rigby. So good of you to come.'

'I'm sorry for your troubles, Mrs Hamilton.'

'You are too kind.' She inclined her head towards the facing armchair. 'Please, won't you sit?'

I sat. She held up her glass. 'Will you join us in a toast?'

It wouldn't be her first and they'd have drank on without me, so Simon built me a Jack and ice. We toasted Finn in silence. 'Gentlemen,' she said, 'could you leave us for a moment?'

Being no gentleman, I was expected to stay. She watched Simon and Gillick leave, then turned dreamy eyes on mine. Grainne had been sold short with the cobalt blue. Her mother's eyes were the Aegean on a hazy June dawn. 'What can you tell me, Mr Rigby?'

'Not much more than I told Simon, I'm afraid. Sorry.'

'Yes. Simon told me you were here earlier. Very thoughtful of you, Mr Rigby.'

'Anyone else would've done the same.'

'I wish that were true. But I am inclined to believe that most people would have washed their hands of the whole sorry mess.'

'I knew Finn, Mrs Hamilton. I thought it'd be better coming from me than the cops.'

'So I understand. Unfortunately, Simon was rather vague on the details. Apparently Finn jumped off the PA building shortly after speaking with you.'

'That's right.'

She flicked some wayward silk back up onto her ankle. 'And how was Finn when you spoke with him?'

'Good form, yeah. He was, y'know, Finn.'

'And you noticed nothing that might . . .' She hesitated, then steeled herself. 'That might explain why Finn would want to take his life?'

'Nothing. Really.'

'May I enquire as to what it was you spoke about?'

'It was Finn who did most of the talking. He was pretty excited about this new development.'

Her forehead shimmered, which I took to be a Botox frown. 'Development?'

Gillick, already under some strain hoisting the brandy balloon, had obviously left the heavy lifting to me.

'It was supposed to be a surprise,' I said, 'a wedding present. Luxury apartments, with a salon for Maria.'

'And where exactly,' she drawled, glancing away to rearrange some more silk, 'did he propose to establish this development?'

'Cyprus.'

'*Cyp*rus?'

'That's right. Northern Cyprus.'

'They were going to live there?'

'So he said, yeah.'

'For how long?'

'All going well, for good.'

She considered that. 'And did he say when this was likely to happen?'

'He wasn't sure. Red tape was holding them up at the Cyprus end. And he was funding it from the sale of the PA building, so . . .'

Her forehead glistened. 'The PA?'

'The Port Authority building.'

'I know what it *is*, Mr Rigby.' She sat up straight, sloshing some martini onto the cuff of the fluffy bathrobe. 'What is it exactly,' she said, a cold storm brewing in the Aegean dawn, 'you are trying to achieve?'

'Sorry?'

'The question is straightforward. What is it you hope to achieve by telling me lies?'

'What lies? I don't—'

'That property wasn't Finn's to sell, Mr Rigby. It belongs to Hamilton Holdings. And no one knew that better than Finn.' A mocking smile. This much, at least, she was sure of. 'So how could he have been planning to sell it?'

'I haven't the faintest idea. You wanted to know what Finn was talking about tonight, and I'm telling you.'

'I don't believe you.'

'That's your choice, but Finn told me he was selling the PA. If you're saying he couldn't, then I don't know, maybe you should be having this conversation with Gillick. Maybe there's some loophole in the setup that allowed Finn to sell.'

She stared imperiously, and I guessed I was supposed to find a hole to crawl into, or just whimper a little. I sipped some Jack.

'You do appreciate,' she said, 'that what you've just told me is entirely ridiculous.'

I wondered how ridiculous she'd find it if I mentioned Finn's sudden desire to settle in a place where family still meant something. I set the Jack on the coffee table, being careful to avoid the glazed tile coasters. 'Here's what I don't appreciate, Mrs Hamilton. Getting called a liar. Spending half the night in the cop shop for trying to do the right thing. Having my taxi wrecked.' I fingered my grazed cheek. 'Let me know when you've heard enough. There's more.'

'If it's compensation you're—'

'I've been paid, Mrs Hamilton, not bought. The Queen's shilling doesn't go as far as it used to these days.'

If looks could kill I'd have been cremated on the spot. 'How dare—'

I stood up. 'You want my advice, buy mittens for your daughter. Some day she'll attack someone who matters.' I made for the door.

'Mr Rigby.'

I kept going.

'Please?'

I faltered, then stopped and turned. 'Allow me to apologise,' she said huskily. 'As you can imagine, this is a fraught time.' She gestured towards the armchair. 'Please?'

I figured Gillick had had his five hundred euro worth, but there was a catch in her throat when she said the word 'please' that suggested she'd licked it off a leper's tongue. I sat down again, retrieved the Jack. She settled back into the couch and composed herself. 'I presume you know that Finn and I have been estranged for some time?'

'Mrs Hamilton,' I said, 'what exactly do you want?'

She compressed her lips, then drained the martini and sat up rearranging more silk. From under a cushion she drew a beige manila envelope and from that she slid an A4 sheet of paper. 'I'd like you to read his suicide note, Mr Rigby.'

My guts flipped over. I felt trapped, the room shrinking, a clammy claustrophobia sucking on my lungs. 'If it's all the same to you . . .'

'It's not.' She softened her tone. 'You knew him, Mr Rigby. Perhaps you can help me make sense of it all.'

'You should probably talk to Maria.'

She fixed me with the pair of cobalt skewers. 'You weren't to know, Mr Rigby. But my orders are that that whore's name is not to be spoken in this house.'

'With all due respect, orders aren't really my thing.'

97

I waited, tensed up, while the sedatives and martinis waged war in her eyes. I was guessing she'd be a lot more brutal than her daughter when she finally let—

Shit.

Like father, like son.

I cursed myself for not seeing it before. For not trying to understand how it might feel to be Saoirse Hamilton, so used to having her every whim indulged and command obeyed, now rocked to her core by the suicide of both husband and son. A bereft queen skulking behind her throne, terrified and uncomprehending as she ducked the chunks of masonry shaken loose by some blind and barbarous emissary of Fate.

I could sympathise, sure. If it was Ben who'd just topped himself, I'd be lashing out myself. But Maria deserved better than crude abuse, even from a woman who was for now little more than agony made flesh, an old wound ripped open to be salted all over again.

'Does Maria know?' I said. 'Has she even been told?'

'I'll remind you,' she said, 'that you are under my roof.'

'And I'll remind you I'm here as a favour to Finn, not you.'

His name seemed to clarify something. She still glared, but her eyes were fully clear now, focused. She tapped the sheet of paper in a way that made me feel like a whole row of violins. 'Hey Joe,' she said, 'where are you going with that gun in your hand?'

It was obscene. She read all the way through to the end in a husky monotone. When she was finished she raised her eyes to mine. 'Can I ask you, Mr Rigby, what you make of that?'

'It's a song. They're lyrics.'

'That much I already know. What I am asking is, why do you think Finn would have left those lyrics in particular?'

'He liked the song. It was one of his favourites.'

'I understand. But you will appreciate what I mean when I say that they do not appear to be entirely relevant. This,' she continued, glancing down contemptuously, 'seems to be about shooting an unfaithful lover. Whereas most suicide notes, if I am not mistaken, will at least attempt to explain why its writer killed himself.'

'Maybe it does.'

'So you believe,' a triumphant trembling, 'he was distraught about her infidelity.'

'Maria's?'

Her mouth tightened in the corners. 'Who else?'

'That's a hell of a leap. What I'm saying is, you'd need to have been inside Finn's head to know what he meant.'

'Can I ask you to try?'

'He was suicidal,' I said. 'No one can—'

'Mr Gillick tells me that you shared,' and here the corner of her mouth turned down, 'a room with Finn. For almost a year.'

'A cell, yeah. That was a long time ago.'

'Mr Gillick also tells me you were a private investigator.'

'That was a different life. And anyway, I—'

'Would you mind?' She held out the note. 'Perhaps, given your experience, you might spot a clue.'

A clue, of course. One brief scan of the note would reveal to master sleuth Rigby that Colonel Mustard had used the lead pipe to batter Finn off the roof of the library.

'Please?' she said, proffering the sheet of paper. 'I would consider it a very great favour.'

First Jimmy, now Saoirse Hamilton. People I wanted nothing from kept offering me favours.

'All I crave,' she said, 'is a tiny corner of my mind where I might find some measure of peace. If you refuse,' she chuckled the coldest sound I'd ever heard, 'I may be forced to request a priest.'

I took the note. A copy, obviously. The cops wouldn't have released the genuine article yet. It was written in his familiar flowing script, and while it would take a handwriting expert to say for sure, the writing looked like his, normal and unstressed. Apart from the notations between the lines, which were basic chord progressions, there were no additions. It wasn't even signed.

'Well?' she prompted.

'Like I say, the song is one of Finn's favourites. This is the Hendrix cover, Jimi Hendrix, which most people consider definitive. Finn preferred Love's version, it has more of an energy, sounds more desperate.'

'Go on.'

'Finn knows the song by heart. There'd be no reason for him to scribble out the lyrics for himself, it'd be like the Pope doodling a Hail Mary.'

'Your point, Mr Rigby?'

'I'm not being flip. I'm just trying to eliminate possibilities. You told me that this is a suicide note, and I'm suggesting there are other options.'

'Such as?'

'The most probable, going by the notations, is that he was writing out the lyrics for someone who wanted to learn the song. A talented beginner, maybe. It's not the easiest song in the world to play but the chords here are fairly straightforward.'

'You don't believe it's his note?'

'It's his writing, sure, but Finn was his own man. If he had something to say, he'd have said it in his own words.'

She pressed a forefinger to her lips, then used a knuckle to snick a tear from the corner of her eye. She beckoned for the note. 'Thank you,' she said.

'For what?'

'Confirming my sanity.'

'What I believe and what's true aren't necessarily the same thing, Mrs Hamilton. And—'

'Saoirse, please.'

'Okay.' She was fairly pouring it on now. First the tears, now the brazen familiarity with the lumpen prole. 'What I'm saying is, just because – whoa.'

She'd balled the note and tossed it on top of the log fire. While she crossed to the bar I watched it shrivel into a petrol-blue flame. She came back with a fresh martini, a Jack. She handed me the glass and perched on the edge of the couch, hunched forward, one knee crossed on the other. Her tone was brisk.

'Estranged or not, Mr Rigby, I know my son. He would have left a note. And if he did write a note, it shouldn't be too hard to find, even for,' she cleared her throat, 'a retired investigator. It's not the kind of thing you hide.'

I thought she was right, but then suicide is by definition out of character. And once a man finds himself out in the badlands, out beyond rule and law and custom, who knows what anyone might do?

'Sorry, Mrs Hamilton, but I'm not the man for—'

'I would like to retain your services, Mr Rigby. I want you to find for me, if it exists, Finn's suicide note.'

'With all due respect, Mrs Hamilton—'

'Saoirse.'

'—I'd be wasting your time. I've been away from the game too long and I've no intention of ever going back. On top of that, the cops have already been over the studio. Like you say, if Finn did write a note, he wouldn't have hidden it. He'd have left it to be found.'

'Perhaps he didn't leave it at the studio.'

'So you go to his apartment. If he wrote one – and not all suicides leave a note – it'll probably be there.'

'That would be impossible.'

'I'm sure, under the circumstances, Maria would—'

'Mr Rigby, I have warned you once. I will not warn you again.'

I put the Jack on the low table, stood up. 'You have my sympathies, Mrs Hamilton. Really. But looking for a suicide note that probably doesn't—'

'I'm begging you.'

You can tell when people use a phrase for the first time. The virgin words sound awkward, the tongue fumbling its way around syllables rough as broken teeth. Her face was turned up to mine, imploring. The fluffy robe had fallen away to reveal an expanse of décolletage, but it was the naked want in her eyes that made me avert my eyes. A raw and secret savagery.

'Simon has my card,' I said. 'If you still feel this way tomorrow morning, then call me and we'll talk about it again.'

I said it as gently as I knew how, but a dismissal is a dismissal and Saoirse Hamilton wasn't practised at being gracious when denied.

'Do you think it might be possible for a mother to *ever* stop wondering why her son would do such a thing, Mr Rigby?' Each word was a scourge. 'Can you honestly believe that one day will make any difference to how I feel?'

I considered that. 'Gillick told you I did time,' I said.

'Yes, he did.' A faint sneer. 'And why?'

'Then you'll appreciate why I don't want to be the one to raise false hopes. Goodnight, Mrs Hamilton.'

I felt like a toe-rag walking away. Still, a glass shattered against the frame as I opened the door, spraying me with Jack.

That helped.

14

You know you've arrived when a solicitor says you lack even a shred of human decency, by the shred being how lawyer types measure decency.

I was living that year on Castle Street, three floors up from a coffee shop, Early 'Til Latte, which was already open when Gillick finally dropped me off, the sky gunmetal grey, dawn cocking the hammer. On the second floor was the tiny landing where I'd once had an office. Back then I'd called myself a research consultant, but I was generally the only one who called. Now I lived on the floor above, under the eaves. One of Hamilton Holdings' minions would have described it as a penthouse with potential, although less Joycean fabulists would call it disused attic storage. A single room of sloping ceilings with low wide windows facing east and west, the stairwell of the bare wooden stairs taking up most of the south wall. A one-ring gas stove in a corner, some books and CDs on the windowsills, a squat hurricane lamp on the floor beside the fold-down couch. No electricity, but I mostly worked nights, so that was okay too. The bathroom was in a closet off the landing below. The décor boasted flaking paint and patches of damp, the colour scheme canary yellow trimmed in blue. A family of mice nested in one corner and I did what I could to respect their privacy.

I was so tired unlocking the door that it took me three keys to realise it was already unlocked. I pushed on through.

'Dutch?'

'Out on the roof.'

Dutch ran The Cellars, the pub across the street. Sometimes after work he dropped by for a smoke to wind down before going home, a game of chess on my nights off. If I wasn't there he'd let himself in, do the needful, head off again.

Unusual for him to stick around, though. He must have heard.

I ducked out through the east window onto the flat tar roof, where Dutch had unfolded the deckchair, got himself comfortable. From there the view was rooftops down as far as the river, then the bay opening up beyond Yeats' Bridge. Benbulben a purple haze ten miles out. Dutch peered up at me, bleary-eyed.

'Christ,' he said, 'what the fuck happened you?'

'Finn Hamilton jumped off the PA.'

'So I hear. Didn't know he landed on you.'

'Damn near did.'

I took a hit off the spliff he offered, ignoring the stale whiff of blood caking black under my nails. He nodded along while I filled him in, gloomy but unsurprised. He'd known Finn, had hosted his band once in The Cellars, the usual deal, the boys drinking free for as long as they played. Which didn't exactly put a hole in Dutch's pocket. Finn's boys were a Rollerskate Skinny tribute band, or more accurately a tribute band playing the

Horsedrawn Wishes album, a loose setup with his mate Paul on drums, a couple of the lads who jammed up in Dude McLynn's on bass and rhythm, Johnny Burrows picking away, Finn taking the lead and vocals. That night they'd been bottled off after two songs, Dutch lobbing lemons from behind the bar. Spanners trapped in a spin-cycle, he reckoned, until I gave him the CD and he realised that was how they were supposed to sound, the Pistols trying on Beethoven's Ninth. Dutch didn't buy it. 'So he's put together this tribute band to play what you're telling me is the greatest album of all time, except the real band went bust because they couldn't play it live, couldn't tour. Is that it?'

In a nutshell, pretty much.

That was Finn, though. Watching him up there that night on the non-existent stage, ducking bottles, putting all that effort into playing songs nobody knew or cared about, not giving a shit what the audience liked or thought it wanted – yeah, sure, he was a dilettante, self-indulgent. But you'd want to have a dead soul not to applaud the nobility of the gesture, the quixotic purity of it all.

And maybe that was the problem right there. That Finn had surrounded himself with people who'd encouraged his every extravagance, who'd clapped him up onto the stage knowing the whimsy could only end badly, or out onto those cliffs to watch him dive, cheering him all the way out onto that ledge nine storeys up.

'And you're feeling guilty enough to try,' Dutch said when I told him Saoirse Hamilton wanted me to find Finn's suicide note.

'His sister says it's traditional.'

'Bullshit.' He yawned and scratched at his skull stubble. 'Say you were even psychic, you twigged to what he was planning. Okay, you could've stopped him. This one time.'

'Once might have been enough.'

'Don't beat yourself up, Harry. There's an epidemic out there, blokes jumping every day. And you know blokes, the first you'll hear is the splat.'

'They're not fucking lemmings, Dutch. Every one of them has a good fucking reason to go.'

'Reasons plural. It's never just one thing.'

'Sure, yeah. But I'd say if you went through every last one, money'd be an issue somewhere along the line. And whatever else Finn had going on, money wasn't a problem.'

'Harry,' he said quietly, 'the guy was a diagnosed schizo. I mean, that's how you met him, right? All fucked up over his father, traumatised, he's burning down everything that can't run away.'

'I told you that in confidence, Dutch.'

He looked pointedly over both shoulders. 'Who else is here?'

'Anyway, that was all a long time ago.'

'So was the Big Bang, and we're still dealing with that shit too. And the guy was smoking his head off, Harry. Not exactly what the doctor ordered, eh?'

'You're saying I enabled him.'

'Fuck *that*. You didn't sort him out, he'd have gone somewhere else.'

'He didn't, though, did he?'

'Don't *do* that, Harry. Seriously, can you hear yourself? You're like a teenage girl.' A mincing tone. '"Should I have known? Was *I* the reason he jumped?" You'll be starting a fucking Facebook page for him next.'

'Yeah, well, something sent him out that window.'

He exhaled a long draw and held out the spliff. 'And you're

sure,' he said, serious now, 'it was something and not someone.'

'I was the only one around.'

'Far as you know. How long were you up there?'

'In the studio? Twenty minutes. Maybe more.'

'Plenty of time for Gillick, this Jimmy guy, to get around the back. Up the fire escape. Or anyone else, for that matter.'

'Possible, yeah, except the cops didn't find any sign of a struggle. Jimmy's a big man but Finn's tall, he wouldn't have gone out that window easy. And anyway, why would Gillick want him gone? He's the family solicitor, he's horse-trading with Finn for the PA.'

'Except you're saying, the mother reckons that couldn't happen.'

'That's what she told me.'

'Maybe Gillick found a way around it.'

'That's what I said. But Gillick's in tight there, covers all the legal shit for Hamilton Holdings. Always has. I doubt he'd blow a sweet deal like that for a one-off on the PA, a piece of shit no one wants.'

'So maybe it's someone else.'

'Who? Finn's a good guy, Dutch, he's in the *Champion* every second week with some charity or other. Runs the artist's co-op, Christ, he's out on a limb for—'

'Sure, yeah. But a good-looking guy like that, plenty of cash to flash, he liked to put it about . . .'

'Not since Maria. Not that I heard, anyway.'

'He'd hardly go broadcasting it on the radio, would he?'

'No, but he was making plans, getting married. Moving to Cyprus.'

'Sure,' Dutch said, 'one step ahead of the posse, some father waving a shotgun. I mean, this Cyprus move, it's all a bit sudden, right?'

'Last night was the first I heard of it, yeah. But who knows how long he was planning it? And anyway, it was nothing he actually said, but . . .'

'What?'

'He mentioned kids, Dutch. How Cyprus was this great place for raising a family.' I shrugged. 'I got the feeling, just the way he was saying it, that Maria is pregnant.'

He winced. 'Fuck.'

'Yeah.'

'How is she?'

'I don't know. I went around there but she wasn't home, and I couldn't raise her on the phone.'

'Does she even know?'

'No idea.'

'Christ.'

'I should ring her again,' I said, and suddenly the tiredness was an ache in my bones.

Dutch hauled himself out of the deckchair, laid a hand on my shoulder. 'A few more hours won't hurt. Get some sleep, get your head straight.'

'Yeah, maybe.'

'And Harry, this suicide note bit.' He shook his head. 'Don't get sucked in. Family shit like that, you don't want to get involved. The mother wants it found, let her find it herself.'

He left. I tumbled into the deckchair, had one last suck on the spliff and waited for what Mailer once called the biles and jamborees of the heart.

Nothing stirred.

Too soon, maybe. Still in shock. Too numb to feel and too exhausted to start building bridges between what had been and what would have to be. And maybe it was just that he wasn't dead, not tonight. Not until I closed my eyes and rolled across the stones and woke up tomorrow with Finn sealed in yesterday's tomb.

Just one more fucking thing, man . . .

Yeah, I could nearly hear him now, that hollow chuckle, how being dead was just one more fucking thing. It had been our mantra inside, our koan. No matter how bad it got, it was just one more fucking thing, no worse there is none . . .

*

The night I met Finn he was walked into the cell, eyes glazed, a screw to each arm. And yeah, he stank like the pit lane at Le Mans. He crawled onto the bottom bunk and lay on his back all night, hardly able to breathe, unblinking and endlessly fascinated with whatever it was he saw in the pattern of rusty springs and bare mattress above his head. Next morning I tried to rouse him and if he hadn't been warm I'd have said he was dead. I left him to it. A good-looking guy with a shaggy mop of blonde hair and wide blue eyes. Bad enough, but he was limp and vacant, passive and beyond caring. A walking invitation to the kind of man who doesn't need an invitation, prefers not to be invited.

The days spun out. Finn slouched through them dull and unaware. He moved when they told him to, popped every pill they put on his tongue. A tiny jerk of the head when spoken to, as if called to from the top of a very deep well. His face hardly changed. Asleep or awake, it was a hard-cornered mask. About the only muscles that moved were those hinging his jaws. He chewed with a mechanical indifference, staring into the space between the shoulders across the table. None of which was unusual in Dundrum.

He'd been there six weeks or so when we finally clicked. A group session, shooting the shit with the shrink and lying through our collective teeth, when Finn, at my shoulder, started in with this sing-song murmur. *'Trying to get well, no lies here lies . . .'*

I glanced across and caught an anarchic flicker in the pale blue eyes. The line triggering the next, so that we half-hummed it together, *'Swab the temples of the untapped dreamboy, a jagged day in life . . .'*

He nodded. 'So how's that temple swabbing coming on?'

I shrugged. 'Just trying to get well.'

And just like that, it was on.

Sometimes that's all you need. One line, the faintest of connections. Both of us convinced of Rollerskate Skinny's greatness. *Pet Sounds*, according to Finn, being the tinkling of nursery rhymes on a xylophone by comparison.

But yeah, it all flowed from that one line. By the end of the week he'd told me about his father drowning, Cap'n Bob going down with the HMS BMW. How the big fat joke was that it'd been his mother, Saoirse, who'd filed the papers and had him locked up. Saoirse, meaning freedom. This after Finn had moved on, moved up, from torching sheds and half-built houses on derelict estates, had been caught gas-handed outside The Grange itself.

I'd told him about Ben, how he'd been born five days overdue, which made him, as close as science could guess, nine months, three weeks, five days and forty-two minutes old when I held him for the first time. Not much bigger than a volleyball, even swaddled, a tiny and badly peeled turnip wobbling on the skinny neck. How I'd cradled him in my arms and made no extravagant promises: no harm would come, I'd whispered, so long as I had any part to play. How that was promise enough to put a bullet in his father.

I'd told him that Ben wasn't mine, okay, but that blood doesn't think, doesn't feel and doesn't hurt. Blood pumps and blood bleeds and that's as far as blood goes.

We laid it all out, every card on the table. A weird kind of poker with no bluffs or blinds, where everyone walked away a winner. I even told him my real name, what Harry was short for. I'd never told anyone that, not even Dee, not even when we were good.

He'd done eleven months. The night before he checked out, he popped his three pills and said, 'Listen, just tell them what they want to hear. They think you're a looper anyway, always will. What they need to believe is you've convinced yourself, not them.'

He'd walked out of Dundrum with a stack of canvases and an idea. Took a couple of months to work up the outline of a project, then went to the financial controller of Hamilton Holdings to sound her out with an informal proposal. Three days later he was standing before the board making a proper balls of a PowerPoint presentation. Didn't matter. The idea was sound, and by then Hamilton Holdings had one foot in NAMA and hurting bad, looking for ways to diversify. And so Finn was appointed to the official position of art consultant with Fine Arte Investments, a division of Hamilton Holdings dedicated, according to the literature, to the creation and management of art portfolios for the discerning investor.

It didn't exactly work out like that. Very few of the clients even wanted to see the art. 'The fucking price tag, yeah, that they'll frame.' Finn's role was to match a client to a particular work, so that it looked to the casual observer that there was some kind of coherence to the portfolio, and then get busy donating the pieces to any place that'd make space on its walls – hospitals, town halls, municipal buildings, libraries. The idea being that charitable donations could be written off against tax. 'Leave a painting long enough on someone else's wall,' he reckoned, 'it pays for itself. Then sell the fucker on.'

Telling me all this when he came to visit me in Sligo Mental Hospital, where I'd been transferred for good behaviour after three years in Dundrum. Not exactly a halfway house, but a sign they believed you'd convinced yourself that life didn't have to be one long sadomasochist piñata party.

In theory, the transfer was supposed to aid my reintegration into society, especially when it came to Ben, giving him access, making it easier for Dee to bring him for visits.

It never happened. My fault. Couldn't face him.

Dutch dropped in every now and again, kept me posted about Dee and Ben. They seemed to be doing just fine without me.

Finn came by more regularly, maybe once a month, each time with a new Big Idea. The biggest, I guess, being the day he arrived after three months' radio silence, tanned like good leather and a gleam in his eye. He'd gone to Cyprus to see if he couldn't see what Oscar Epfs had seen, that famous light, wondering what it might do for his landscapes. He'd even tracked down Deirdre Guthrie, herself a flamenco dancer under the *nom de plume* Candela Flores and scion to the Guthrie family of artists, who as a young girl had been more or less adopted by Epfs, aka Lawrence

Durrell, during his stay in Bellapais, that quasi-mythical village eyrie high above the flat plain of the northern coast.

Finn had never said so, not outright, but I'd always presumed the Spiritus Mundi gallery, which was organised according to a loose co-op structure, was both inspired by Deirdre Guthrie's gallery in Bellapais and some kind of self-flagellating bohemian reaction against his official position as consultant with Hamilton Holdings. Or Ha-Ho Con, as Finn referred to his tie-wearing alter-ego.

He'd taken a room at Guthrie's Garden of Irini, rented a moped, rang home to say he was taking a sabbatical. Spent the next few weeks roaming the hills, drunk on the light and what was appearing, by some kind of alchemy, on his sketchpad. One evening, eating alone near the village of Ozanköy, he'd met Maria Malpas, recently graduated from the exclusive Gilligan Beauty Group on Grafton Street, Dublin, and CIBTAC-certified in the fundamentals of beauty enhancement, including hot stone therapy and Hopi ear candling, who was then working as a waitress at her family's restaurant, which required three generations of hands at the pump, even those with perfectly manicured nails, during the crucial summer season. He was thirty, feckless, with money to burn; she was twenty-one, the eldest daughter of a farmer who scratched a living from the barren slopes of Bespamark, the five-fingered fist punching the impossibly blue sky, according to Finn, like the Turkish Cypriot equivalent of a Black Power salute.

It can be easy to be sceptical about such things, but the way Finn told it he was on a Durrell binge and the first time he saw Maria he understood, no, *felt*, Durrell's description of Aphrodite, the goddess who seemed to hover somewhere between the impossible and the inevitable. She reminded me of Diane Lane in *Streets of Fire*, which some would say is pretty much the same thing.

That night he told her he was an artist, a landscape man, and that she was the first portrait he'd ever wanted to paint. She'd shook her head. If he'd been a sculptor, she said as she placed the little wooden treasure chest containing the bill on his table, he might have stood a chance. But a painter? A necrophile, dabbling in dead materials. True artists, she said, skimming immaculate nails along the fine line of her jaw and tilting her chin, worked only with living flesh.

Cypriot father, Irish mother: the combination, and the subsequent sundering of the marriage, had left her garrulous, fiercely independent and disinclined to suffer fools, gladly or otherwise. She told a good story about a sunny Mediterranean paradise, of hot days and balmy nights, glorious beaches and razor-backed mountains, verdant plains dotted with olive trees, lavender, bougainvillea. A plucky island enclave populated by a disarmingly hospitable people, a trait that was all the more remarkable given that they'd been disowned by the world and were making their way through hard work and the bloody-minded survival instinct of a people who escaped a genocide barely a generation before.

Finn told a different story. The place thrived on graft, alright, most of it Russian. A warm, dry climate perfect for laundering dirty cash, especially once the border controls with the South were relaxed in the build-up to the inevitable EU accession. The place fairly glittered with new nightclubs, shiny casinos, exclusive villa developments and roughly one currency conversion outlet per every tourist. The official economy was hooked to a drip of inward investment from Turkey, just as the country's very existence depended on the Turkish army bases, from which the soldiers emerged to do their dancing, in horizontal fashion, upstairs in the shiny nightclubs. 'Throw in the bad drivers,' he said, 'it's like Norn Iron used to be, with a better class of mosquito.'

Not that he'd say so in Maria's presence. She was happy enough, being a pragmatist, to acknowledge that growing up in Ireland had given her opportunities she could never have expected in Cyprus, but she'd never made any secret of the fact that she planned to return home to live, to settle down. Finn had always seemed easy about the prospect, so long as it remained a prospect, and for the past three summers they'd loaded up Finn's camper van with clothes, blankets, toys, crutches and whatever else they could get their hands on, driving across Europe and down through the Balkans, south along the Turkish coast to Taşucu and the five-hour ferry ride across to Girne, liaising from there with the SOS Children's Programme to distribute the swag wherever it might do some good. Spending the summer on her father's farm, Maria working as a waitress, Finn tramping the hills with a sketchpad in his satchel, drinking in the light.

The big revelation, apparently, wasn't that she made Finn happy, or even that she allowed him to believe he was entitled to be happy. It was that he wanted to make her happy.

Bell Jars awaaaaaaay . . .

The sun was crawling up from behind Cairn's Hill to give the Ulster Bank's sandstone a pinkish glow. It was already warm, the air shimmering, as peachy fresh as a schoolgirl on her first night on the game. I felt myself drift, allowing that Dutch's advice was sound. Saoirse Hamilton had had a hell of a shock, and the scrambling effect of a martini-sedative cocktail wouldn't have helped any, but even at that, just a passing mention of Maria had primed her ready to blow. If it turned out that her prospective daughter-in-law was pregnant, the collateral damage could take out anyone who'd got a little too close.

And maybe that was reason enough to jump, if you were Finn and fragile, the kind who'd always had it easy and maybe too good, the world your oyster with Guinness chasers. No brakes, no drag. Life as a downhill freewheel with a warm breeze on your face, a fiancée who believed you were some kind of snowboarding Carnegie, hiding out in your studio to paint and play your tunes, no rent to worry about, no pressure to bend.

I'd been jealous of how easy Finn had it, sure. Who wouldn't be? But I'd never envied him, never wanted his life.

And maybe Finn didn't either. Maybe his father's suicide had left him frailer than anyone thought, brittle inside and squeezed by all those big small words: love, duty, trust, hope. And maybe, just maybe, trapped between Saoirse Hamilton's immovable object and Maria's irresistible force, Finn had finally snapped.

Just one more fucking thing . . .

No thanks, please.

Friday

15

The sun was a diamond, hard and bright and more trouble than it was worth.

Herb looked nowhere as hard or bright but he looked like a whole lot of trouble. Somehow he managed to loom over the deckchair without blocking out any of the glare. I shaded my eyes and rolled my neck anti-clockwise to ease the stiffness, head no heavier than a baby grand.

'What?' I said, tasting the stale Jack wafting up off my shirt.

'This shit with Finn. Where do we stand?'

Dutch, the dopey prick, had left the door unlocked going out. I made to haul myself off the canvas and realised some perverse vampire had been around during the night, swapping the blood in my veins for a sticky warm sweat. So I closed my eyes again and gave him the spiel.

'Fuck *that* fucking idiot,' he said about ten seconds in, which was good, because each word was taking a minute off my life. 'What'd you do with the grass?'

'It's looked after.'

'You don't have it here?'

'No.'

'So where is it?'

I half-cranked an eyelid. 'Why, what're you going to do? Go get it?'

He stared. Then he said, 'Are you drinking this shit or what?'

A beaker of hot black nectar from three floors below. I chugged the first half in two long swallows, going for the burn as much as the jolt, then subsided back into the deckchair again and studied the minor miracle that was Herb out and about in broad daylight.

'You get my message?' he said.

I patted my pockets, came up with the phone. Switching it on I tried to remember when I'd turned if off. For Tohill's interview, probably. 'Remind me,' I said.

'Christ.' He toed the black Adidas hold-all at his feet. 'You're still on for Galway, right?'

Some chirps and beeps from the phone. Five missed calls. One from Herb, one from Dee, a punter looking to score, two I didn't recognise.

Nothing from Maria.

'You're kidding, right? A run to Galway now? After all the shit last night?'

'Last night,' he said, 'you said you'd do it. Which is what I told Toto.'

'Yeah, well, you can tell him different now.'

'Alright, I will. Just cough up the weed and I'll square it away.'

'The weed,' I said, 'is stashed in the PA. I can't get to it while the place is a crime scene.'

Herb nodding along. 'This is what Toto's saying, yeah. So you're on the hook for it until such time as he gets it back. Which means, Galway.'

'Fuck that, Herb. Last night I was doing a dope run for *you.*'

'Sure, yeah.' Defensive now, fighting a losing battle on two fronts. 'A dope run for someone you vouched for to Toto.'

'I was vouching for Finn paying for the weed, not jumping off any buildings.'

'Except he jumped, didn't he? And I'm guessing he handed over no cash before he went all triple-back fucking flip into the cab.'

'Fuck's sakes, Herb.'

'It's not my call, Harry.'

'Alright. Fuck.' I realised why Herb was out and about, driving a spare cab into town to save me traipsing all the way out to Larkhill. Which was nice. I took a stab at escaping the deckchair's tractor-beam, fell back. 'Want me to run you back out home before I go?'

'No go, Harry.'

'No go what?'

'Toto reckons you're getting no more cabs until you've cleared the debt.'

I squinted up at him. 'So what, I'm taking the bus to Galway?'

He shrugged, glanced away across the rooftops. 'You can't borrow Dee's car?'

He wasn't glancing away to admire the sooty chimneypots. Toto had told Herb to tell me to borrow Dee's car. This to let me know, he knew who she was, what she drove. Where she lived, and who with.

A cold sweat starting to ice in the small of my back.

'This'll be a car I'm not insured to drive,' I said slowly, 'to go to Galway and pick up a score. What're you on, PCP?'

'She won't loan you the car?'

'If I swear I'll drive straight into the first cement truck I meet, maybe.'

'Tell her you've a regular fare, he's flying out of Knock. You can't let him down.'

'That's a two-hour round trip, max. I'll be gone, what, five or six hours?'

'So you get a flat tyre or some shit. Listen, Harry, it's a ten grand score. There and back, you pay off on the weed. Simple.'

The torque started to bite, the inevitability of it all winding tight like some metal band slowly crushing my skull. Sparks flaring behind my eyes. Herb waited while I rolled a smoke and sparked it up, coughed out some lung I wasn't using right then. 'I'll need a couple of hundred up front,' I said. 'I'm behind on Ben's maintenance. And Dee'll need some kind of sweetener if she's to lend me the car.'

He thought about that. 'Done,' he said.

'I'm making no promises. It'll all depend on what kind of mood she's in.'

'Horseshit. She'll be in a bad mood, she'll be looking at you. Your job is work around that. A grand is a grand.'

If there was a flaw in his logic, I couldn't see it.

16

When Herb left I had myself a Mexican shower in the tiny bathroom downstairs. The mirror could have hung in Saoirse
Hamilton's drawing room, titled 'Something the Cat Coughed
Up'. A mad and possibly evil taxidermist had fitted me with the
eyes of a dipsomaniac racoon. The blackened blood under my
nails washed out easily enough, but the shave proved rather more
Herculean. The tremors in my hands could have had Richter
shuddering in his grave, and the shredded hands and gash above
my eye had already filled my laceration quota for the week.

I brushed most of the fuzz off my front teeth and went back
upstairs to change my Jack-soaked shirt for its greyer but slightly less damp and sticky twin. The tie and pants were of yesterday's
vintage, but I figured Ben would need every scrap of help he
could get at the PTA meeting, and a scruffy shirt-tie combo was
better than turning up a tattered coat upon a stick.

Then, primed for another day, powder dry-ish, my trust in
God no shakier than usual, I shouldered the Adidas hold-all

containing ten grand and stumbled down the three flights of stairs and into Early 'Til Latte, where I had Inez put a small bucket of triple-shot latte on my tab. While the elixir brewed I sat in at the computer terminal at the rear of the shop and typed 'Tohill Garda Síochána detective' into Google.

He was a new one on me, Tohill. I don't spend a lot of time hanging around the cop shop logging the new arrivals, but generally speaking, when you drive a cab in a place of Sligo's size, it's not long before you know all the cops, by sight at least. Which meant he was probably a recent transfer. What I wanted to know was why, and if he had form.

Nought-point-two-eight seconds later I had 2,311 results. Only the first seven related to Detective-Sergeant Daniel Tohill of An Garda Síochána, but there was more than enough in that little lot to suggest that Saoirse Hamilton's desire to find Finn's suicide note, if such existed, was prompted by rather more than a grieving mother's need for closure.

I sipped on the bucket of latte and ran another search, this time on Hamilton Holdings, which almost caused the modem to melt down. Most of the results, when I refined the search to include only the last year's offerings, confirmed that Finn hadn't been exaggerating. The Hamilton Holdings website still claimed that the company could provide the only property investment portfolio I'd ever need, with blue-chip returns available in Spain and Portugal, the Balkans and Florida, but the main thrust of a quick sample of clicks was that Hamilton Holdings was effectively owned by NAMA, which was hell bent on offering everything on the Hamilton books at fire-sale rates. Or would, once it had negotiated the barbed-wire legal hoops erected by one Arthur Gillick.

Let me do you this one favour, he'd said. Half an hour later, Finn was a scorched lump of frying flesh.

Which was possibly why Detective-Sergeant Tohill, an upstanding and well-regarded member of An Garda Síochána, but currently seconded to the Criminal Assets Bureau, was reserving his opinion as to whether Finn had jumped or been pushed.

All of which left this tattered coat fluttering in No Man's Land, bogged down in the mud and likely to be crushed between the inexorable creeping advance of opposing forces.

Unless, of course, one of Toto McConnell's snipers took me out from the flank first.

I sipped some more latte and logged off, wiped my searches. Wondering how much Saoirse Hamilton might be prepared to pay me to go looking for Finn's suicide note, and what Tohill might be persuaded to do if I found it.

I strolled along Castle Street and turned right up Teeling Street towards the cop shop. Paused at the corner for a quick sketch around to make sure no one was watching before sidling across the road into the station, a squat block of Stalinist functionality rendered even greyer by the retro-Gothic glory of the Courthouse across the way. It wasn't even noon but the shade on the desk was in dire need of a second shave. Bull-shouldered, a blocky head, small eyes set wide apart. His greeting registered somewhere between a snort and a bellow, and if it wasn't for all the budget cuts I'd have assumed he was an actor employed to remind visitors they were about to enter the labyrinth.

'I need to see Detective-Sergeant Tohill,' I said.

'In connection with . . . ?'

'It's in connection with Detective-Sergeant Tohill.'

'Sorry.' He had yet to look up from the sports pages. 'Never heard of him.'

'Maybe he's top secret. He's a big shot, I know that, gets to spit in people's faces.'

The head slowly came up. His eyes were stale mercury. 'You want to make a complaint?'

A comedian, this guy. 'I just want to talk to him. Sign that statement I made last night.'

The mercury glistened. 'Hold on there,' he said, reaching for the phone. He turned away hunching a shoulder, so all I heard were some grunts and a snort, possibly a fart. 'Says he'll see you outside,' he said, crunching the phone down. 'Five minutes.'

A man can get a bad name for himself loitering outside a cop shop, so I strolled across the road and rolled a smoke while pretending to read the plaque on the wall of the building facing the Courthouse that bore the legend, *Argue and Phibbs, Solicitors.*

A horn parped behind me. Tohill was double-parked and waving me across. I did a little shoulder-rolling and pfffing, then slouched over to his Passat and slid in, tucked the hold-all between my feet. 'A rum pair, Argue and Phibbs,' Tohill grinned as we edged forward, heading south up the Pearse Road. 'Apparently, during the 1920s, they were planning to take another partner on board, an English lawyer called Cheetham.'

'Hilarious, yeah. The law, it's just a sick joke, right?'

'Can't fault the lads for a sense of humour.'

'It's like William Gaddis said, you get justice in the next world—'

'And the law in this. So I hear. Funny,' he said, 'but I wouldn't have had you down as the religious type.' He took my silence for assent. 'So I guess we're all stuck with the law. Tell me more about wanting to sign your statement, go back inside for wilful obstruction.'

'A couple of things first.'

'Go on.'

'Gillick I know nothing about. Last night was the first time I met him.'

'Okay.'

'Second thing is, I know nothing about Finn that might interest the Criminal Assets Bureau. Far as I know, he was clean.'

'Duly noted.'

'Same goes for the Hamiltons. About all I know there is what Finn told me last night, they're up to their oxters in NAMA.'

'Great. Is there anything you *do* know?'

'A few bits and pieces, yeah. First I need to find out what they'll buy me.'

'That'd depend on what they were worth, wouldn't it?'

'Sure.'

There was silence then, until we rolled to a stop at a red light opposite Markievicz Park. 'I won't know what they're worth until you tell me what they are,' he said.

'I get that,' I said. 'But first I need to know what the market's like.'

'I don't follow.'

'What I'm wondering, why I'm here, is why CAB is interested in Finn. I'm also wondering if CAB taking an interest wasn't what pushed him off the PA.'

A grin wrinkled in the cracked leather of his tough boot face.

'You think it's funny?' I said. 'That Finn jumped?'

'Not at all. Where are we going, by the way?'

'Rasharkin.'

'Where's that?'

We were passing the Sligo Park Hotel by then, driving south towards Carraroe, so I told him to head for Maugheraboy, skirt the town, come in through the industrial estate at Finisklin. He turned west off the Carraroe roundabout across the new road, an arrow-straight model of everything the modern bypass aspires to be, apart from the fact that it cuts straight through the town and splits it in two. Took the Oakfield Road, the ditches a-bloom with dusty blue blossoms and silky-peach leaves.

'Last night,' he said. 'I was out of order.'

'The intimidation or the spitting?'

'The spitting. That's not me.'

'Then you'd want to watch out for that evil twin of yours. A fucking pest, he is.'

'See it my way. You're telling barefaced lies, signing off on a statement.'

'Keep it up. They'll have Tom Hanks play you in the movie.'

In theory, a cop car is a place of work, which meant no smoking. That didn't stop Tohill finding a cigarillo in his breast pocket, sparking it up. I went for the makings and followed suit.

'Okay,' he said, exhaling heavily. 'So now we've established that you're a radical free-thinker, you're out there on your own believing all cops are fascist pigs. I'm some kind of Nazi, right?'

'Try Black and Tan.'

'Nice. Historical. I like it.' He tapped ash from the cigarillo. 'Except here you are, chasing me up for quid pro quo. What's that make you, some kind of collaborator?' He winked, but there was no humour in it. 'And you weren't so proud the last time either, were you? Happy enough to let Brady pull some strings when you killed your brother, buy you easy time in Dundrum.'

'Buy *me*?'

'That's what the man said.'

'Funny, that. Because the way it was *sold* to me was, I'd be doing them a favour keeping quiet about this dirty cop who was in bed with ex-paramilitaries, the guy looking to establish a nice little coke empire for himself. And then I go and take Gonzo out, save them the bother, all those pesky reports and public inquiries and therapy sessions. The least they could do, they reckoned, was make sure my pillows were nice and soft in Dundrum.'

He drove on. A glorious summer day, a warm sun high above Queen Maeve's grave on Knocknerea. Midges swarming the hedgerows in search of a pharaoh to plague. 'I spoke with Brady this morning,' he said. 'Not very talkative, is he?'

'Can't say I know him that well.'

'He's not particularly fond of you, either. Said I should carry one of those forked sticks snake-handlers use, and wear Kevlar. Maybe grow an eye in the back of my head.'

'He said a lot for someone who doesn't like to talk.'

'I'm good at deciphering meaningful silence.' He took a long drag on the cigarillo and exhaled slow, came to a decision. 'He said you were a stone-cold killer, no doubt about it. Ice all the way down. But he reckons you know how to keep your part of a deal. So quid-pro, yeah? I tell you about Finn and CAB, you give me what you have on Gillick, anything he said last night, at the PA or after he picked you up. How's that?'

'Sounds good.'

He inclined his head towards the back seat. 'There's an *Irish Times* back there. See page seven, three paragraphs down the right-hand side.'

It was a report on a court case, in which a named Italian art dealer was suing an unnamed purveyor for breach of contract and damage to reputation. The gist was that the Italian had been peddled a fake Paul Henry landscape, although things were complicated by the fact that the Italian wasn't trying to sue the purveyor, who swore he bought the Paul Henry in good faith, but instead a third party who had sold the purveyor the fake. The third party was also unnamed, and was currently lobbing in all kinds of injunctions to slow proceedings down, soak up the Italian's war chest. The judge was to make a decision today as to whether the third party could be named and dragged into the mire.

By the time I'd finished reading we were cruising around by Finisklin, on the docks aiming for Hughes' Bridge.

'I take it the third party is Fine Arte Investments,' I said.

'I'd be in contempt of court if I confirmed that,' he said, nodding.

'Shit.'

'Actually it's pretty clean,' Tohill said. 'Iceberg tips generally are.' He tapped some ash. 'A nice scam, if you've the money to get in on the ground floor. Buy a painting for some investor who wouldn't know a Pollock from a boot in the hole, knock off a copy, put the fake into circulation under the investor's name. The original goes to someone who can keep his trap shut.' He shrugged. 'What's daft about it is, the fake retains all the value and the original gets sold at a discount because it can't go on the open market. Fucking art, eh?'

'They know what they like.'

Irish gangsters had been targeting art long before the Criminal Assets Bureau was set up, the idea behind CAB being to target the gangs and their untouchable wealth, which was generally salted away in offshore accounts and real estate. A noble endeavour, given that the Bureau was a kind of monument to the murdered investigative reporter Veronica Guerin, and largely effective, although the gangs had adapted quickly, found other ways of laundering their cash.

Back in the day, the IRA, or the General, would just wander up to Russborough House of a dark and stormy night and filch an occasional Goya or Vermeer from the Beit's private gallery. This latest scam was a bit more sophisticated. Buying the originals low, stashing them away. In ten years' time, maybe more, there'd be a hoo-hah about a painting hanging in some gallery, an expert taking a close look during an exhibition and querying its provenance, maybe declaring that the certificate of authenticity was real enough, a pity about the actual painting. And hey presto, the original is discovered lying in some cellar or up in somebody's attic, worth at least what the market had been prepared to pay when it first disappeared, and very probably more.

No wonder Finn'd been planning to bolt for Cyprus, and Northern Cyprus at that. The TNRC not being renowned, exactly, for its alacrity in responding to extradition requests.

'So who tipped you off?' I said.

'I'd be in contempt of court,' he said, staring straight ahead, 'if I named our source as Finn Hamilton.'

'*Finn?*'

'The very man.'

'The flaky fuck.'

Tohill nodded agreeably. 'So you can see why we might be interested in why Gillick swung round to see Finn so late last night. Specifically, if Finn mentioned anything about what Gillick might have said about how Hamilton Holdings propose to deal with the judge's decision today, which is very likely to rule on behalf of our Italian friend.'

'It never even came up.'

'No?'

'Gillick was taking the piss out of Finn alright, about how much his own paintings were worth, or weren't. But that was about it.'

'What exactly did he say?'

'I dunno. Something about how art is priceless because dead materials, paint and canvas, make something come alive.'

'And that's it?'

'Pretty much.'

'What about after, when Gillick took you for a spin?'

'Nothing, no. He wanted me to go see Saoirse Hamilton, I was the last person to see her son alive.'

'What'd she say?'

'What you'd expect. She wanted to know what kind of form he was in, why he might've wanted to jump. I didn't tell her anything I hadn't already told you.'

'And that's all you have?'

'Far as they're concerned, I'm the hired help. Not the type that gets confided in. All I can tell you is that they were both asking me pretty much the same questions you are, wondering if Finn said something. But separately, yeah? Gillick quizzing me on the way out there, Saoirse Hamilton waiting until Gillick was out of the room before she started in on me. Like they were worried Finn was saying something he shouldn't.'

We were stuck in traffic, Hughes Bridge a bottle-neck.

'Now I know he was talking to CAB,' I said, 'it makes more sense. What I don't get is what was in it for Finn.'

Tohill nodded. 'You're right, you don't get that. How are you fixed now with Gillick?'

'Great, yeah. Last night he offered me a job. Promised to take me away from all this.'

'What kind of job?'

'Oh, y'know. Evictions, debt collections, that class of a lark. Generalised thuggery. I'm guessing he's concerned his boy Jimmy might keel over from 'roid rage one of these days.'

'His boy Jimmy being James Callaghan, aka Limerick Jim.'

'The very man.'

'I doubt you'd be replacing him, Rigby. Not unless you're hiding some serious lights under your bushel.'

'I could learn to use a knife. How hard could it be?'

'Harder than pulling a trigger, I'd say.' A grating now in his tone. 'For one, you need to get up close, make it personal.' He looked across, a bleak quality in his eyes suggesting he'd like nothing more than to put the hard old boot of his face right through mine. 'Besides, you wouldn't have our friend Limerick Jim's range. His depth, maybe, but until you've blown a car bomb outside a hospital's ER department you're only in the ha'penny place.' The cigarillo switched sides. 'Say you were to take Gillick up on his offer, though. Sit down with him, have a chat about this job.'

'Work some freelance, sure. All wired for sound, no doubt.'

He shrugged. 'You want to volunteer, great. It'd set my mind at ease, I wouldn't have to worry about how maybe you're onside with Gillick. Leaving my mind so placid, maybe, that it'd let that obstruction of justice charge sink all the way down to the murky depths.'

'You want me to tout?'

He winced, inhaling in a little hiss. 'Tout's an ugly word, Rigby.'

'It's an ugly business.'

'It is that,' he conceded. 'Was it any more handsome when you were calling yourself a private eye, got paid to blow the whistle?' He flicked some ash. 'Didn't think so. And anyway, it's no uglier than a bullet in the back of the head.'

'And there's the threat.'

'Absolutely. Only it's not coming from me.'

'So who?'

He jammed the cigarillo in the corner of his mouth, talked around it. 'Gillick's lodged a proposal at the Town Hall, wants to build a village down at the docks.'

'I heard.'

'From Finn.'

'Yeah, but he reckoned it was a bust. Five years ago, okay. But now? Who's going to fund that kind of development? Who'd buy into it?'

'Finn mention anyone else involved?'

'Nope.'

'Any ideas?'

'I don't move in those kind of circles, Tohill.'

'Me and you both.' A rueful grin as he worked the solidarity angle. I rubbed at my cheek where his snotter had landed. The grin died fast. 'Look, all I'm asking is if Finn mentioned any names,' he said. 'Or anything at all that might help us pull a thread.'

'What kind of thread?'

'Gillick's name is all over the planning applications, but we know he doesn't have the capital to carry it off on his own. Like you say, he's into debt collection now, scraping what he can out of the Hamiltons to keep NAMA at bay.'

'You're saying, I should nail down the contract on this job he's offering.'

He scratched his jaw, the fingernails blunt and faintly yellow. 'Gillick's pulling strings behind a research-development company set up to pursue the proposal. Said company being the kind, you'll get a tan if you want to sign the AGM's minutes. There isn't a single connection to Hamilton Holdings.'

'The rat deserts the sinking ship. So what?'

'Except Gillick's the solicitor for Hamilton Holdings, covers their whole portfolio. Including the PA building.'

'Liquidating assets on the sly. Doing NAMA's job for them.'

'Sure. But who's buying?'

'No one, according to Finn.'

'No one official, anyway. And Gillick's a big man, Rigby. Throws a lot of shade. So you tell me why he'd want to keep his backers' money out of sight.'

'I'd imagine it's dirty.'

He grunted. 'Okay, progress at last. Next question: why's Finn Hamilton a midget in the morgue?'

I flipped my smoke out the window. 'Maybe he couldn't take the pressure of touting.'

'Finn was remarkably cool about helping us with our inquiries. A model fucking citizen, that lad.'

'Finn's the kind, he'd be too lazy to let it show.'

'You think?' A careless shrug. 'Me, I got the impression he liked it. Got off on the kick. You see it a lot, people think they're playing God. A little power goes a long way.'

Sounded like Finn, alright. Something slimy squirming in my

guts as we turned right at Feehily's Funeral Home, towards the hospital. Tohill cut left for Rasharkin and then we were crawling along in second gear, a funeral at St Joseph's Church spilling out, more traffic backed up. We inched by, rolled on down the hill to Rasharkin. Tohill pulled up opposite Abbott's beside the alleyway that cut into the estate. I released the safety belt. 'One thing,' he said, his jaw set hard.

'What's that?'

'When you were up there last night, talking about nothing with Finn. You see any binoculars?'

'The infrareds? Sure. I used them myself after Gillick left. So don't go trying to nail me for—'

'They were gone by the time we got up there.'

'Maybe he'd put them away.'

'We tossed the place, looking for infrared binoculars specifically. No go.'

'Why the binoculars?'

'Because Finn saw something one night through them. The landing, we assume, of what's known as undisclosed imports. Very probably coke or smack. This being the added bonus,' he said, 'to Gillick's proposal to rejuvenate the docks. They'll have privately owned facilities, harbour masters recruited for their ability to look the other way. Warehouses guarded by their own security firm. Point being, if there's no infrareds, how'll we prove Finn saw what he saw?'

'How could you prove it anyway? Put a corpse on the stand?'

'If someone took the infrareds, there's a reason they took them. If we find out who, it's a thread. Pull that, things might start to fall apart.' He closed his eyes, pinched the corners. 'So that's where we are. Or were, until Finn went out that fucking window.'

'I'm still not seeing what it has to do with me.'

'You were there.'

'Okay. But Finn told me nothing about any of that shit. All I saw was a guy planning for a big future, then taking a dive.'

'Maybe, before he went, he told you what he'd seen.'

'He told me nothing.'

'Sure. But if you say he did, how can they prove otherwise?'

'First I'm touting, now I'm perjuring myself. Is that it?'

'They'd be Finn's words, your name on them. Confirming his statement.'

'Fuck *that*.'

'Worst case scenario, we get an injunction against Gillick, tie him up.'

'Stymie the development.'

'Indefinitely, yeah. We have precedent, so we're solid there.'

'Nice job.'

'Could be, yeah. All we need is—'

'I mean, your job. It's a nice job.'

He frowned. 'Don't get all fucking moral on me now, Rigby. You burnt that fucking bridge a long time ago.'

'I'm just saying, you've a job. Which is nice.' I pointed across the road at the Abbott building. 'Don't know if you heard, but a couple of months ago those guys announced 175 new jobs in there.'

'So?'

'So the last time anyone announced new jobs in Sligo was Queen Maeve, she was short a few spears for her little jaunt to the Cooley Mountains.'

Tohill wearing a poker face now, jaw and lips hard and straight as pokers. 'This is *dirty* money we're talking about here, Rigby.'

'Tohill, man – do you seriously think anyone in Sligo gives a fuck about who's investing? Someone wants to create jobs with laundered cash, so what? No Dublin bastard'll do it. If Sligo drifted off to fucking Iceland next week, it'd only make the news because the deer got frostbite.'

He was chewing the butt of the cigarillo into a soggy mess. 'Let me clarify where this dirty money comes from, Rigby.'

'I know where—'

'In this case, specifically, we're talking about the boys still fighting the good fight. Y'know, the Socialist Republic lads who knock off a bank here and there to grease the wheels.'

'Fuck the fucking *banks.*'

'Yeah, well, these raggy-arsed philanthropists, they're socialist enough to want to share the wealth, only they do it in kind, pumping heroin into their own back yards. Or they'll splash the cash by trafficking in women, spread a little happiness there if you've a few quid to spare and don't mind screwing a zombie. You have a problem with that? No worries, here's a double-tap in the knees, no charge. Or maybe they'll bugger you to death with sewer rods and then rape your grieving wife, on the off chance she might get some daft notion about justice.'

'You're forgetting the bullet to the back of the head.'

'You can live with that?'

'You'd be surprised by what I can live with.'

'Surprised, no. Disappointed, yes.'

'That's cute. A disappointed cop.'

He thought that over. 'Tell me this,' he said. 'How long d'you think it'd take me to have your taxi licence revoked?'

'Dunno. Ten minutes?'

'Don't be daft. It'd take at least a day.'

'You're giving me a whole twenty-four hours?'

He shrugged. 'Don't thank me. I blush easy.'

I thought about that. Not for long, or I'd have laughed out loud at Tohill's big play, taking away a licence to drive a cab that'd gone up in flames. Instead I thought about how perjuring myself would go on the record, there in black and white should Tohill ever decide he needed another favour from an ex-con.

'I'm signing nothing,' I said. 'And I'll be wearing no wires.'

'Your call. But if we do it the hard way, have you up on the stand to testify you saw infrareds in Finn's studio, actually used them, this to corroborate Finn's statement about what he saw, then you'll be stepping down without a friend in the world. So think on about your new friend Gillick, how you might like to have a chat with him in the very near future, reminisce about Finn.'

I opened the door and made to get out, then hesitated. 'There was one thing,' I said.

'Oh yeah?'

'This goes under the radar. Call it an anonymous tip.'

He leaned towards me, turning his head away as he put a fore-finger behind his ear. 'It'll go no further than these four doors,' he said.

'Wouldn't be much point in me saying it then, would there?'

'No, I mean—'

I hawked up a goober, spat in his ear. By the time he struggled out of the safety-belt, got his door open, I was halfway down the alleyway and gone.

17

Sligo gets to call itself a city because it has a cathedral and smack. The sprawling suburbs are just the lily's flaking gilt. Rasharkin lies to the north-east, a mile from O'Connell Street and just inside the borough boundary, seventy or so three-bed semis loosely arranged around a central green, an estate twenty years old and aging fast. Damp patches discolouring the red-brick facades.

Dee's tiny lawn needed a trim and a sprinkle, its border beds a riot of dandelions and bindweed, the grass crunchy with tinder-dry moss. Three doors up from where I stood behind her living room window, twitching the curtain, a burnt-out Ford Focus sat skew-ways across the mouth of the alleyway.

No Tohill appeared.

A stupid thing to do, gob in a cop's ear. But if you sit still for menace, just once, it never ends.

Ben was sitting Buddha-like before the TV, thumbing furious-ly at the Playstation gamepad, his face a ghastly kaleidoscope of greens, reds and yellows. FIFA 2012, the curtains pulled tight to eliminate sun-dazzle on the screen and the possibility that he might accidentally glimpse real people outside kicking an actual football around. He wore Puma trainers, beige tracksuit bottoms with white piping and an orange football shirt bearing the legend 'V. Persie' above the number nine.

I hunkered down behind, tousled his shock of dirty-blond hair. 'Hey,' I said.

He wriggled out from under without glancing away from the screen. 'Hey.'

'How's tricks?'

'Fine.'

'Yeah? Who's winning?'

'Me.'

'Where's your mother?'

'Upstairs.'

Two syllables was progress of sorts and akin to an entire conversation from a twelve-year-old lad. Or my twelve-year-old lad, anyway. 'Want a coffee?'

'No.'

'No what?'

He pfffed his cheeks. 'No *thanks.*'

I went through to the kitchen and put the kettle on, slid open the patio doors and stepped out to roll a smoke. Dee was death on smoking in the house. She said a smoker's house was harder to sell and Dee was always hoping to sell. There were all kinds of reasons, but mainly it was that she didn't feel right still living in the house we'd bought when she got pregnant with Ben. Said she looked around some nights and felt baby snakes slithering in her pants. Hard to say if she was casting aspersions on my six pounds of dangling dynamite or just being sentimental. Dee can be tough to second-guess.

The garden was small, enclosed on three sides by a high pitch-pine fence that blocked out most of the sunshine and all the neighbours. A wooden shed sagged in the right-hand bottom corner, one of its window panes cracked and lined inside with a Cornflakes box. Flagstones led from the tiny patio to a rotary washing line that *skreeed* whenever the breeze changed its mind. The grass was lush, ankle-deep and clumping where the dog shit had been left to rot.

Dee came through onto the patio humping a half-full basket of laundry on one hip.

'Boo,' I said.

She whirled, clamping the free hand to her chest. '*Jee*sus!'

'Dee.'

She glared daggers as the fight-or-flight blush spread like bushfire across her face and throat. 'Will you for Chrissakes *knock* the next time? No, first ring ahead, *then* knock when you get here.'

'Can do, will do.'

She was a good-looking woman, Dee, angry, alarmed or otherwise, although my experience of her was that she was generally angry or alarmed. A sun-rinsed blonde with wide-set eyes, chipmunk cheekbones and Pirelli lips. The white blouse had wide sharp collars and the rest clung to her all the way from the neck to the flared hips, where a hint of flat belly peeked out from above the bottom half of a trouser suit in dark charcoal with a faint grey pin. The ox-blood boots had a two-inch kitten heel and looked like they could kick holes in a bishop's dreadnought hull. If they didn't, the eyes could always laser through instead. I balanced the cigarette on the windowsill and took the laundry basket from her, shuffled down the flagstones to the rotary line, began pinning up the damp clothes.

She leaned back to glance into the kitchen, then picked up the cigarette. 'This is a straight, right?'

I nodded and she had herself a drag, closing her eyes as she exhaled. 'You got my message,' she said without opening them.

'The parent-teacher meeting, sure.'

'You didn't listen to it, did you?'

'Nope.'

Now her eyes opened, found me and bore down. A sizzle in my groin, and not just because I was pinning up a pair of sheer grey lacy panties. 'How come?' she said.

'Because I don't listen to messages, Dee. Everyone knows this. You listen to a message and you ring whoever left it, and then they tell you the whole story all over again. So neither ear feels left out, maybe.'

'Or maybe,' she said, doing something pouty as she tried to pop a smoke ring, 'it's just too much hassle, you being permanently stoned or asleep.' A twitch in the corner of her mouth, something smiley but sad. 'I swear, one day you'll ring me to remind you where Ben lives.'

No pain like an old pain.

'Hey, Dee? You're the one forgot which brother she was supposed to be sleeping with. So let's cut the—'

'Is that all you've got?' She flipped away the cigarette, slid the patio door closed, then advanced down the flagstones with her arms crossed. 'The only reason I ask is, every time there's any kind of dispute you bring it up.'

'You're the one who brought Ben into it.'

'Don't you fucking start on—' She pulled up short, tilting her head as she peered at me. 'Oh for Chrissakes,' she said, 'do *not* tell me you were fighting again.'

I couldn't decide which was more disappointing, that it'd taken her that long to notice the gash in my forehead or that she thought I ever stopped fighting.

Ben's Sligo Rovers shirt was the last item to get pegged up. 'It was Finn,' I said.

'You were scrapping with Finn?'

She hadn't heard. 'Not exactly.' I rolled a fresh smoke while I told her the story, Finn's swan dive, keeping it brief, already tired of how pathetic it all sounded, how sordid and final.

Death can be heroic or shocking or at the very least inevitable, but generally there's a vital one remove, the instinctive disassociation. Nobody ever thinks they'll get cancer or be hit by a bus, or get so old their brains will melt into mush.

Suicide is different. It lives under the skin, too close to the bone. There's no comfort in it, no perverse schadenfreude to be mined. It's in all our gift.

Her eyes gleamed. The words were salt on ice, her rigid stance softening, the arms uncrossing to open into what might have become a hug before she caught herself, remembering. The hand that had launched itself towards my left shoulder, perhaps to pat it, or maybe to cup my cheek, wound up covering the O of her mouth.

'Crap,' she said. 'Harry, I'm sorry.'

But it was there in her eyes. First Gonzo, now Finn.

I was some kind of jinx.

God help me, but for a split-second I couldn't help but wonder if she'd been sleeping with Finn too.

'Listen,' I said, 'I need to borrow the car.'

The damp eyes froze. '*The* car? You mean *my* car.'

'That'll be the one, yeah.'

'Not a chance in hell.'

I could tell she was gauging how likely it was I'd invented Finn's suicide just to soften her up.

'The cab's off the road,' I said, 'and I've a regular looking to be brought to Knock. I can't afford to turn him down.'

'You're not even insured on my car. And anyway, I need it to get to work.'

'You could always ring a cab.'

A snort. 'You want *me* to ring a taxi so you can bring a fare to Knock?'

Dee confused sarcasm with irony. Not a fatal flaw, but still. 'I'll pay you back this evening,' I said. 'And don't sweat me not being insured. Nothing'll happen.'

'A nothing like whatever it is has your cab off the road, say.'

'That was Finn. He landed on the taxi, blew it to shit.'

You'd have thought, her eyes being so expressive, that Dee would have made for easy prey at poker. Except she went the other way, piled on the tells, so I couldn't work out if she was wishing I'd been the one who landed on the taxi or been in it when Finn hit.

Probably, the laws of physics allowing, both.

'It'll only take a couple of hours,' I said. 'And I need to get the cab back on the road. If I can pick up a fare in Knock for the trip home, I'm halfway there.'

The lies always came easy for Dee. The trouble there was, Dee started out from a point where she simply presumed I was lying.

'That's your problem, Harry. You're always halfway there.'

'Jesus, Dee, give me a break. I could really do with one around now.'

That bought me an arched eyebrow, but at least she didn't say that I always needed a break around now, 'now' being roughly any time the maintenance payments fell due.

Credit where it's due, though. Dee had never held out her hand. Not once. Then again, Ben being Gonzo's boy, genetically speaking, mine was a voluntary offering with no legal obligations enforceable.

She'd managed just fine while I was inside. A consultant's PA when I went in, she'd moved sideways into the hospital's IT department, started off uploading data, the drudge work. I don't know, maybe it was a kind of penance. Gonz had been a psycho and I'd known I'd pull the trigger long before he dived for that gun, but women always blame themselves. Guilt puts you centre-stage in all the best dramas. Anyway, Dee had put in the hours. Plugged into the system and got herself on the inside track, multi-tasking like an octopus in a pool-hall brawl. Now she ran the IT department, and if she occasionally complained of a mild concussion from bumping her head off the glass ceiling, at least she was trapped in the bubble, a recession-proof public servant peering out at the rubble of an economy laid waste.

Which meant Dee didn't actually need my money. Just as well, because it'd have broken her heart to have to depend on me ever again. The payments I made went straight into a special credit union account she'd opened for Ben's college education.

'What time's the fare?' she said.

'He's flying out at six. Wants picking up at three.'

'Okay,' she said. 'You'll still be back.'

'Back for what?'

'This is why you need to listen to your messages, Harry. So you can stay in touch with the human race.'

'Back for what, Dee?'

'I'm going out tonight. I need you to sit with Ben.'

'Babysit?'

'Nope. You'll find out why at the PTA meeting.' She glanced over her shoulder, lowered her voice. 'His grades are on the slide and I mean badly. And he's a bright boy, it's not like he's . . . y'know.'

'Dense, yeah. Like his father.'

'We need to show solidarity on this one, Harry. Ben has to realise that this is a serious issue. He starts secondary school next year, and if he goes in with the wrong attitude, with shit grades, then he's fucked from the start. They'll stream him wrong, he'll be way down the line, doing fucking woodwork with rubber fucking saws.'

'Alright, yeah.' I held up a hand. 'I get it. It's all my fault.'

'Jesus fucking Christ,' she hissed, 'grow *up*. This isn't about *you*.' She was pale now, cheekbones burning. 'It's about you doing the right thing, telling Ben what's what.'

'That if he doesn't shape up, he'll turn out like his father.'

'Something along those lines, yeah.'

'Which one? The psycho killer or the jailbird?'

The full lips thinned. 'Flip a coin.'

18

There was every chance Tohill was still lurking somewhere around the estate, but if he was he'd be looking for an expectorating desperado peeling rubber in something high-powered and very probably stolen.

I was banking on Dee's car trundling by under his radar, the perfect nuclear family aboard, its driver so devotedly and patently harmless a husband and father that he could wear his son's baseball cap and wife's Gucci shades whilst piloting a pea-green Mini Cooper without spontaneously combusting from shame.

'You break them, you buy them,' Dee said when I wrapped on the shades. Ben snickered from the rear. I drove along through a Gucci-tinged world, honing my justification should Tohill pull us over. The problem being, as I saw it, that the *homo sapiens* is trapped roughly halfway between micros and cosmos, derived from quantum chaos yet peering at the stars, smart enough to appreciate the elegance in every part of the universe that is not human and yet so unevolved we confuse harmony with order;

and being human, crave that which is beyond our reach, and wish to tame that which we do not understand, never realising, or at least not admitting to ourselves, that we are the elements out of kilter with all else, an army of intestinal parasites declaring war on their host, eternity, until it hands over the one quality it does not possess: justice.

Hence the loogie in Tohill's shell-like.

I dropped Dee off at the hospital, crossed town to Ben's school, the lunchtime traffic heavy but moving. Ben stayed in the back, a Gameboy plink-bleeping in his hands.

'Good news and bad,' I said.

'Uh-huh?'

'This meeting. I won't have time to see all your teachers.'

'Cool.'

'So we'll have to focus on the ones giving you bad reports.'

'Crap.'

'So who do I need to see?'

'Dunno. All of them?'

He was exaggerating, sure, but not by much. The school had a system whereby you were handed an A4 sheet as you went into the gym where the teachers sat at desks attending crocodile lines of parents. An hour later, we were back outside staring at the graph of Ben's progress report, which strongly resembled the Black Run at Klosters. He was good at art, computer studies and religious instruction.

'Looking on the bright side,' I said, 'you'll make a marvellous cyber-pope. Your grandmother would've been so proud.'

He squirmed, shoulders hunched as he scuffed at the Mini's tyres.

'Listen, Ben, we need to talk about this. I'm serious, now. We'll sit down later on when I get back from Knock, but in the mean-time,' I rattled the A4 sheet, 'I need you to really think about this.'

'Where am I going now?'

'To class. Where else?'

'But there's no class today.'

'You're kidding me.'

'It's parent-teacher day, dad. All the teachers are busy.'

'So your grades are failing, and the best thing they can think of is to give you the day off?'

He hoisted a shoulder, let it slump. 'Ben,' I said, 'I need to work. I've a run to Knock to do.'

'Sorry,' he said.

His quiet tone was a blade in the heart. 'It's not your fault, son. Look, who usually keeps an eye on you when your mother's out?'

He frowned at the idea of being babysat. 'Katie,' he said. 'But she'll be at school.'

'Of course she will. Okay, get in.'

I rang Dee. The conversation was brief and terse. No, she had-n't known Ben would be free for the afternoon. Yes, Katie was out of the loop. Yes, leaving a twelve-year-old at a loose end for the afternoon was insane. No, the problem was mine, deal with it.

Exeunt Dee, pursued by bears.

'Right,' I said, climbing into the Mini Cooper. 'Looks like it's you and me.'

Another shoulder slump, the Gameboy plinking away. But I could've sworn I caught the glimpse of a grin behind the unruly fringe.

I cut back through town, across the bridge and out along the docks, turned into the PA's yard. The scorched hull of the cab was still in place, and I wondered who'd be paying for it to be towed away.

'What're we doing here?' Ben said.

'Seeing a dog about a dog.'

He rolled his eyes, then noticed the burned-out cab, the scorch marks on the wall of the PA, the X of yellow tape fluttering at the door. A uniformed cop shading her eyes as I pulled in beside Finn's Audi. 'Hey,' he said, 'is this, like, a crime scene?'

'You'll be seeing a crime scene soon enough, son. Your mother's lining up a firing squad.'

He crossed his eyes this time, went back to the Gameboy. I got out and waved at the cop to acknowledge her presence, taking care to step across the black rubbery smears. She put away the mobile she'd been texting on and raised a firm hand, palm facing.

'This area,' she announced, 'is off-limits to unauthorized personnel.'

I kept going, wondering if that was the standard spiel or if she was auditioning for *CSI*. She had the looks for it, quirky and fey, striking grey eyes, a button-cute chin.

'I appreciate that,' I said, nodding agreeably. 'But I'm here to feed the dog. You've heard him, right?' I edged by her, kicked the metal door. My reward was a fusillade of deep-throated barks. She flinched, but she was adamant. No dice.

There followed a quick chat about her orders and my responsibilities to my dead friend Finn and Bear's voracious appetite. The ISPCC got a mention. Then I told her about how Bear had broken out the last time he'd been let go hungry for two days. 'Go ahead and ring it in,' I said, nodding at her crackling radio. 'Maybe the dog-handler guy will come down and take care of it.'

Budgets being what they are these days, that was about as

likely as some doggy Jesus wandering by with a basket of loaves and fishes.

'Listen,' I said, 'I was in there last night, they already know that. So it's not like I'd be polluting the crime scene or anything. But look,' I shrugged, 'I don't want to get anyone in trouble.' I kicked the door again. Bear hurled himself at the other side of it, howling up a storm. 'I mean, it doesn't have to be me who feeds him, just so long as he's fed.'

'I don't have a key,' she said.

Thirty seconds later I was around the back and hauling myself up onto the rusted fire escape. It didn't yaw any more than an oak in a storm, but then I'd have been leery of climbing an oak in a storm too. The stench of drying kelp was thick as a shroud.

The emergency exit door had a deadbolt on the inside but I was guessing that Finn hadn't bothered to lock up before he took his last dive. For once I was right. I slipped my fingers into the gap between the reinforced metal and the frame and gave a hefty tug, and it came away so easy that it nearly toppled me backwards over the waist-high barrier.

Inside was a dead stillness and the whiff of stale smoke and tortured howls echoing up from downstairs. I opened the studio door and called down to him. A pause, and then came a metallic pounding, the clickering of his toenails an ominous tattoo.

He was all business now, no howling.

'Bear! *Good* boy. Good *boy*, Bear!'

The acoustics confused him and he skittered to a halt three landings below. A querulous whine. I advanced down the steps slowly, calling his name, and soon we were reunited in a slobbery blizzard. I pushed him off and led him down to the ground floor, scooped three cans of ground meat into his bowl. He wolfed it down, one quizzical brown eye watching me as I poured fresh water. I knew this because I was keeping a quizzical eye on him. All dogs, when you go back far enough, were wolves once, but the wolfhound, to the best of my knowledge, was the only breed specifically bred to hunt its own ancestor.

Hard to trust any dog that disloyal or stupid, or both.

Once he was finished eating I opened some more cans of meat and dumped them out, left him to it. Back up in the studio, blowing hard now, I took a quick rummage through the drawers beneath the mixing desk, one eye cocked for Finn's note, the other for his binoculars. Not that I had a lot of hope of finding either. He wouldn't have written a note and then hidden it away, and I only had Tohill's word for the infrareds being missing.

The place had already been dusted, and my prints were all over it anyway, so I tossed the kitchen too: cupboards, fridge, freezer, bin. No joy. Back into the studio, a sooty residue thick on my fingers. I was running out of time, and the cop'd be wondering if I hadn't fed myself to Bear. I crossed to the window, which had been left open, poked my head out to make sure she was still there. She was strolling in a wide circle, texting on her mobile again, once in a while glancing at the PA building. But all seemed calm. Ben hadn't even begun to spin doughnuts in his mother's car, being more intrigued by Finn's Audi, walking around it, admiring its lines. The water beyond was flat and still, petrol-blue opposite the PA, darkening to magenta as it neared the deepwater. Sounds wafted across from Cartron on the faint breeze, the low thrum of traffic, a gull's screech, children's laughter from the schoolyard on the point.

I checked the window frame to see if I could spot any scratch marks, any pattern in the peeling paint that might suggest he hadn't actually jumped. That he'd toppled out, made one last despairing grab. There was nothing, but that didn't mean a lot. Life isn't like the movies. Things don't happen in slow-mo, and the reason accidents happen is that by the time they start happening, it's already too late. Lean a little too far when you're nine stories up . . .

It hit hard. A low blow that convulsed my gut. Nine stories mightn't sound like much, not until you're up there looking down. My head spun, and I closed my eyes against the dizzying drop. That and the possibility of glimpsing the ghostly outline of a body in freefall, arms and legs flailing in a tangled whirl as they sought purchase from the pitiless air.

Except I hadn't seen Finn fall. He'd dived. Streamlined and arrow-straight.

But it wasn't his jumping, or diving. It didn't matter a damn how he'd gone. What sickened me was his going, stepping off knowing what he knew was nestled in Maria's belly and growing.

I eased back in, slow, no sudden moves. Slid down on the couch, a hot sweat prickling my hair.

Sure, you could say, if you really wanted to exonerate him, that Finn jumped not knowing what he'd be missing. That he was to be pitied for that.

Not me.

Finn Hamilton was dead because he was a selfish prick, period.

I sat there staring blindly and tried to put myself in his place, perched out on that ledge, but it wouldn't come. Not with children's laughter on the breeze and Ben down below. Not with—

It was tucked away in the corner, partly wedged behind a stack of landscapes. His first ever portrait, maybe. Even from across the room I could tell it was a pretty good likeness. Up close, when

I'd tugged it free, and even splashed as it was with red paint, the canvas ragged where it had been slashed with a blade, you could see he'd caught Maria's wicked smile, the mischief in her eyes.

So you believe he was distraught about her infidelity . . .

The sweat dried cold so fast I almost heard it tinkle. It wasn't exactly a suicide note, but it'd confirm Saoirse Hamilton's suspicions, and her prejudice to boot. Guts bubbling, I took the palette knife and dug in under the frame, sliced the canvas out. There was a moment's relief when I rolled up the canvas, blotting out the sight of those mischievous eyes, but then the disgust roiled up in a wave, setting my guts a-chunder. I barged through the bathroom door with seconds to spare, puke spattering the toilet seat and the cistern, each successive heave yielding less and less, and there wasn't a lot down there to begin with, just bile and black coffee. Finally I was empty and retching dry.

I knelt there with my elbows on the rim, too weak to rise, heart pounding.

Da-*dum*, da-*dum*, da-*dum*.

That most simple and profound of symphonies, soundtrack to the seven billion or so miracles wandering the only lump of rock and water capable of hosting them for about six trillion miles in any direction.

What a waste.

I washed my face, gargled away the taste of bile, then wadded some handfuls of toilet-paper and wiped down the cistern, the spatters on its seat. Flushed the toilet and went back out into the studio, closed the window, hurrying to leave now, the big room suddenly claustrophobic and closing in, its silence so complete I could hear the crackle of static electricity as the carpet fibres crushed beneath my—

No clanking. No Tom Waits growl.

The toilet hadn't flushed.

I went back into the bathroom, thinking I'd jammed up the toilet with the wadded papers, but no. Which meant something was interfering with the mechanism inside the cistern.

I was betting on a pair of infrared binoculars.

I lost.

The cistern was empty, unless you counted cistern-like stuff such as water and an overflow tube and the filler valve and a red plastic float. Definitely no binoculars.

Slowly, I depressed the handle, flushing again. Everything worked as it should, the red float descending, the flush valve rising.

The water didn't stir.

I tried again. This time a single bubble rose to the surface.

I rolled up a sleeve, slipped my hand under the mechanism, finger-tipping my way around the base of the cistern. It felt pretty rough, for porcelain. Dimpled and slightly spongy.

Aeroboard, yeah. A false bottom.

Underneath, waterproofed in cling-film, a narrow padded envelope.

The chances of it being what I was looking for were slim. Who writes a suicide note and hides it away under a false bottom in a toilet cistern?

The *screak* was the fire-escape door opening. I stuck the package into the waist of my pants, leaving my shirt untucked to cover the damp stain, and braced myself for some of Tohill's TLC.

But when I popped my head out of the bathroom, it was only the cop.

'What're you doing up here?' she said. 'The dog's downstairs.'

'Sure, yeah. But I got caught short, y'know,' I jerked a thumb over my shoulder, 'and the bog downstairs doesn't work.'

'So you came all the way up here.'

'Wouldn't you?'

The faint flush at her cheekbones told me no, that she'd been sneaking off into the weeds behind the PA.

'Out,' she said.

'I should flush first,' I said, and ducked back into the bathroom, fitting the cistern lid back in place under cover of the clanking and growling. Then I hustled out into the studio, patting my stomach to disguise the bulge beneath my shirt. 'Shouldn't have had that curry last night,' I winced. 'It'll be a danger to shipping, that.'

Her mouth twisted in disgust, and I slipped by her out onto the fire escape. 'Listen,' I said as she pulled the door to behind us, 'I wouldn't fancy both our chances on this.' I gave the guardrail a hefty tug, let her see it wobble. 'Ladies first, though.'

'I'd say we'll be okay together,' she said. 'You go on ahead.'

She was saying the right things but sounding tight about it, tense. It could've been the prospect of descending the fire escape, sure, and it might have been that she'd rang it in, been told to keep me close until back-up arrived.

Both, probably.

'Fair enough,' I said, and took off. Two steps at a time, then three.

'Hey,' she called, but by then I was two flights below her and moving a lot faster than she was willing to risk. She was still halfway down when I hit the ground at a sprint. I slid into the driver's seat of the Mini-Cooper, blowing like a surfacing whale.

Reversed back, slammed the Mini into first, put the boot down in a tight curve. Glanced in the rear-view.

No Ben.

I jammed on, gravel crunching. Leaned back to see if he'd lain down, was taking a nap.

Heard a horn parp.

Finn's Audi. Ben frowning. Wondering why I was leaving in such a hurry.

A smart kid, though. I wished his teachers had been there to see him clock it all at once.

Me, barrelling out of the Mini Cooper and brandishing the Adidas hold-all, waving him across to the passenger seat. The cop red-faced as she hurried around the corner of the PA, radio clamped to her ear.

Ben had already scrambled across into the passenger seat when I yanked the Audi's door open, tossed the hold-all into the back seat.

'What is it, dad?'

'Police harassment, son,' I said, locking the doors and reaching under the steering column.

It took about five seconds to get the Audi sparked. By the time I straightened up, the cop was advancing with her arms outstretched.

I revved the engine, which stopped her dead, then rolled the Audi back, punched it up into first.

She had her eyes closed, shoulders sagging and the very picture of relief, as we roared past her heading for the gate. Ben flipping her the bird, screaming, 'Grand fucking theft *auto*, motherfuckers!'

It was on the tip of my tongue to chastise him for his language, his lack of respect, but then I was driving a stolen car with ten grand of dirty cash on board, this for a coke buy, my twelve-year-old boy along for the ride. And that was without getting into the whole deal about me being an ex-con for blowing a hole in his father.

I glanced in the rear-view to check if the cop had followed us out and for a split-second caught a glimpse of Gonzo's shade in the back of the car, the skull-like leer an unspoken question asking how much worse off Ben could have been, really, if Gonz had made it all the way down to that gun he'd been diving for and put me away for keeps.

19

It's the heartbreak of many a retired and visiting New York cop that the sun does not, in fact, go down on Galway Bay. What actually happens is that the sun declines to a point roughly west of the Cliffs of Moher before disappearing behind the bank of ominous cloud permanently massed above the Aran Islands. You could've fried an egg on the stones when we were leaving Sligo, if you'd had an egg. Galway, on the other hand, and as always, was shrouded in a pea-soup drizzle.

We hit Supermacs on Eyre Square. Ben was ravenous, but the aroma of frying meat put me in mind of burnt pork.

'Gift,' he said, swooping down on my plate.

It was the first time he'd looked lively since leaving Sligo. He'd slumped in the front seat the whole way, the Gameboy silent in his lap, answering any question with grunts and mumbles. Nodded off not long after passing Knock, when I'd asked if he wanted to divert and see if we couldn't rustle him up a miracle, only waking when I shook his shoulder in the underground car park off Eyre Square.

Shock, I guessed. It's one thing, when you're a kid, to throw snowballs at cop cars, hope they'll give you a chase. Another thing entirely to be party to a getaway, especially when your old man is the wheelman.

Now he was throwing what he thought were surreptitious glances at a trio of young girls two booths away. 'Forget about it,' I said. 'They only talk Irish in Galway.'

A quick grin. 'Monty was at the Gaeltacht last summer,' he said. 'Said they were all gael-goers.'

'Oh yeah? What's a gael-goer?'

'Y'know.'

'I've heard.'

The familiar pang squeezed my heart as I realised how quickly he was growing, how much I'd missed while I was inside. Even now I was still getting it wrong, buying him gifts more appropriate for an eight-year-old, starting conversations he'd outgrown by years. He was tall for his age and yet to fill out, the shoulders and chest thin and unformed. His complexion was pale and riddled with acne, the face gaunt and shadowed from sitting too close to flickering screens. He had long lashes over round brown eyes, his mother's eyes, and he might even have looked effeminate if it weren't for the strong chin, the abrupt nose.

'So what about this girlfriend I'm hearing about?' I said. 'She a gael-goer too?'

A faint reddening joined up the acne dots one by one. 'What girlfriend?'

'There's more than one?'

He shook his head. 'There's no girlfriend, dad.'

A doleful note in among all the defiance that made me ache for him. 'Okay,' I said, 'kidding aside, we need to talk.'

He made a point of sucking hard on the dregs of his Pepsi. ''Bout what?'

'About school, what d'you think? Your mother and I—'

He rolled his eyes. I paused. We stared.

'Okay,' I said, 'no bullshit. So here's the question. You want to turn out like me, some fuckwit drives a cab?'

He was genuinely flummoxed, albeit intrigued by the foul language. 'What's wrong with driving a taxi?'

'There's nothing *wrong* with it. But you work long hours for fuck-all money. Sometimes you have to deal with drunken assholes. And some of them can be dangerous.'

'Mum says they should be more worried about you.'

'Is that a fact? What else does she say?'

'About you? Not much.'

'Believe it or not, that's actually a good sign. You'll learn all this yourself the hard way.'

Ben scratched at a stain on the knee of his tracksuit. 'Dad?'

'What?'

'Are you ever coming back to live with us again?'

'That mostly depends on your mother. Although,' I said, wincing as I heard it out loud, 'if I don't it'll be my fault, not hers.'

'Who cares whose fault it is?'

'It's complicated, Ben.'

'It's *complicated*,' he mimicked. 'Everything's complicated when you're old,' he groused.

'Older.'

'Old.'

I grinned. 'Look, we need to have this talk.' He crossed his eyes. 'So what do you want to do with your life?'

He shrugged. 'I dunno.'

'I mean, what do you want to be when you grow up?'

'Oh.' His chin came up. 'Play football.'

'You mean professionally.'

He nodded.

'Nice one. But on the remote off-chance you don't become a footballer, what would you like to be?'

'Dunno.'

'You're good at art, right?' He nodded. 'I mean, you like it.' He nodded again. 'And computers, you're good at them too. And you're always on the Playstation or Gameboy.'

'So?' he said defensively.

'So how would you like to design computer games when you grow up?'

His eyebrows met in a downy tangle. 'Design games?'

'Someone has to. They don't just appear by magic. And people get paid good money to come up with new games. If you want, I can introduce you to this guy I know, he's a whizz at computers. He'll show you how to get started.'

He glanced up warily. 'Yeah, okay.'

'I'll clear it with your mother first, but I don't think she'll have any objections.'

'You think?'

'Hey – if your mother has a problem with anything you do, it's for your own good. Hear me?'

'Yeah, right.'

'Okay.'

I rang Herb.

'You get it?'

'Not yet. Just heading over there now.'

'How come?'

'Mice and men, Herb. Listen, quick question.'

'Shoot.'

'Say you wanted to set someone up with a suite for designing computer games.' The twitch to my left was Ben cocking an ear. 'What're we talking?'

'All depends on what you need.'

'Top of the range. No expense spared.'

'What're you building?'

'Shoot-'em-ups. Football. The usual.'

'Couple of grand'll get you the beginner's basics.'

'Two grand, okay. Cheers.'

Ben looked up, the brown eyes wide and probing. 'Is that two thousand euro?'

I nodded.

'Fucking hell,' he breathed.

'Watch your language.'

'You watch yours.'

'Okay,' I said. 'I'll make you a deal. We can swear all we want, so long as we do it in Irish.'

He groaned and threw me an up-from-under eye that would have put the Gorgon off her feed for a week. 'You're funny when you try to be funny, dad. Not funny ha-ha . . .'

'Funny peculiar,' we chimed. It was Dee's line, but the pronunciation of dad was all his own. Slightly drawn out, as if he was being sardonic. Or maybe he just didn't get to use the word enough to be entirely comfortable with it.

'Start thinking,' I said.

''Bout what?'

'Some game you'd like to play that hasn't been invented yet.'

He frowned, lips pursing. Then it hit him. His jaw dropped, and the round eyes grew rounder. I laughed and reached and ruffled his hair and he was so shocked he didn't even flinch.

*

I gave Ben five euro and pointed him at the amusement arcade beside Supermacs, told him I'd be back in half an hour. Then I cut down Shop Street, into Quay Street, making for the Crescent.

The phone rang when I was crossing the bridge. No caller ID.

'Hello?'

'Mr Rigby?'

'Who's this?'

'Saoirse Hamilton, Mr Rigby.'

I gave the hold-all a little swing. Tucked inside, along with the ten grand in cash, was a cling-filmed envelope. 'Yes?' I said.

'I have not changed my mind. I am hoping that you have changed yours.'

'About finding Finn's suicide note.'

'Correct. I wish to retain your services.'

'I'm sorry, Mrs Hamilton, but I really can't afford to take time off work to go chasing something that probably doesn't exist.'

'You will be well rewarded for your time.'

'I appreciate that. But it isn't just a matter of time, is it?'

'No,' she said, 'I don't suppose it is.'

'If I get in the cops' way on this,' I said, 'they won't be happy. I've already had one guy threaten to revoke my cab driver's licence. And if things get really skewy I could be considered in breach of release conditions.'

'I understand,' she said. 'How much?'

'Well,' I said, 'it's not really a case of—'

'How much, Mr Rigby?'

'Ten grand. Cash. Non-sequential notes.'

'Ten thousand euro?'

'It's what they call danger money, Mrs Hamilton. I didn't ask to get involved in this, but now I am, and you're asking me to dig myself deeper. I think I'm entitled to get paid for my trouble.'

It was hard to tell with the breeze swirling around the river, but I got the impression she'd covered the receiver to confer.

'Ten thousand euro is a substantial amount of money,' she said.

'Yeah, well, the cops'll do it for free if you ask nice. But then, you get what you pay for these days. So maybe you'll want to shop around, get the best price out there.'

'I fail to see the—'

'And listen, just to show there's no hard feelings if you do decide to run with someone else, I'll tell you now that if it was me I'd try the PA first. Pretend like you're there to feed the dog, then run upstairs to Finn's office, check the cistern in the bathroom. There's a false bottom in there, perfect for hiding things under.'

Silence now. Nothing but the breeze and the phone's hiss.

'What did you find, Mr Rigby?'

'I'll put it this way. If the cops find out I have it and didn't turn it over, it'll cost me a hell of a lot more than ten grand.'

'I understand. Be so good as to come and see me, Mr Rigby. I may have more work for you.'

'I'll do that.'

'When shall I expect you?'

'I'm in Galway right now, so it'll be a few hours. Why don't I call you when I get back to town?'

'Very well. My number is—'

'That's okay, it's in my phone now.'

She hung up. Not a woman to waste words, Saoirse Hamilton.

Not a woman to waste money either, I'd have thought. Ten grand mightn't sound a lot in the grand scheme of things, but it'd have made a pretty good price for one of Finn's canvases, say, and Saoirse Hamilton was forking it over sight unseen, unframed.

Maybe I should have asked for fifteen. Hell, it was all NAMA money anyway, courtesy of the endlessly generous Irish taxpayer.

The Crescent is a short curving street of three-storey Georgian relics halfway to Salthill. Quiet, respectable, affluent. Galway's Harley Street, doctors and nothing but. Franny Moore, aka Dr Robert, had a place that backed onto the narrow alley behind the Crescent and running parallel. He also rented the lock-up directly across from his back yard. With the garden's high walls and the alleyway's curve, you'd need to be hovering overhead in chopper to see what was happening. X-ray vision might have helped. I laid out the ten grand and Franny placed its equivalent in primo coke in the hold-all. Up at the top end, ten grand doesn't buy you much by way of quantity.

It all took about ten minutes. By the time I made it back to Eyre Square, Ben was waiting, damp and huddled under an awning, his eyes dark hollows.

'What happened?' I said.

'Mum rang.'

'Shit. What'd you say?'

'What you told me to say.'

'So we're in Knock, right? Waiting for a delayed flight to get in.'

He nodded. Sullen, withdrawn.

'Good lad,' I said, feeling a lot like something he'd scraped off his shoe.

'She said to say she's owed twenty euro for her taxi home.'

'Christ, what'd she get, a stretch limo?'

No reaction bar a sudden shivering. I hustled him back to the car, got back on the road, the heater on full blast. Ticking things off my mental to-do list once we were back in Sligo: drop Ben off, swing by Herb's, take a squint inside the cling-filmed envelope before heading out to The Grange, just to be sure I wasn't selling myself short with the ten large.

We were halfway home, the sun a golden glare in the rear-view mirrors, when Ben finally roused himself, jolted from his torpor when we crossed the disused railway tracks outside Ballindine. He blinked, rubbed his eyes, and said, 'I'm starving.'

'How could you be starving? You just ate two cheeseburgers.'

'That was three hours ago.'

'Seriously?'

I pulled in at the petrol station. Sent Ben on ahead with a fifty to pay for the petrol and rustle up some munchies from the change, watching him while I filled up, insouciant among the milling adults. It was hard to resist the sudden rush of ridiculous pride.

Okay, so Ben was Gonzo's kid, and I favour Darwin, and what genes know about second chances you could stick in Gregor Mendel's ear and still have room for a ball of wax. And Gonz died diving for that gun.

But if Ben's resentment of his mother was any kind of guide,

Dee was doing a fair job of raising a young boy on her own. Ben was smart and creatively inclined, sensitive to a fault. Sociable too, if his welcome at the school was anything to go by. His apathy towards his grades didn't fit the pattern, but I was guessing the clipboard crew would find a parallel or two between his slipping grades and the sudden appearance of a father figure who'd been away for a long time, and who was still missing a lot more than he was around.

Whose big idea of a father-son day out was a coke-run to Galway in a stolen car.

Ben came back across the forecourt clutching a brown paper sack and stifling a smile. Slid into the passenger seat.

'Change,' I said, knowing what was coming.

He handed me seven cents, snickering, then opened the sack. Flakes, Mars Bars, Twix, Choc-Ices, Jammy Dodgers, cans of Pringles and Sprite. My throat was parched, so I guzzled half a can of Sprite and lucky-dipped a Mars Bar.

Got back on the road again, the low sun dazzling in the rearview. I adjusted the mirror so it angled out over my left shoulder, dipped the driver's side mirror, had Ben do the same. In a hurry now to get back home, run the necessary errands, draw a line under the day. Ben munching steadily through the can of Pringles.

'How about some tunes?' I said.

'Uh-oh.'

'Uh-oh what?'

'Your music is rubbish, dad.'

I pointed at the stereo, a five-disc CD player. 'This car,' I said, 'belongs to a guy who runs a pirate radio station.' I didn't want to get into the past tense, spoil the buzz. 'I guarantee you you'll find some good stuff in there. Press any button you like.'

He left a chocolatey smear pressing the third button. A hum and a whirring, then a hiss. 'Swingboat Yawning' kicked in, the scratchy guitars, the sing-song vocals, *digging trenches in the stars again*. My guts constricted, but at least it hadn't come in on 'Bell Jars Away'. Ben wobbled his head a little, considering.

'That CD's broken,' he said.

'No, it's Rollerskate Skinny.'

He gave it about ten seconds. 'That's pants,' he declared.

'Give it a chance. Any Sprite left?'

'It's gone.'

'Greedy shite. What's left to eat?'

He snorted back a giggle. 'Nothing.'

'It's *all* gone? The whole *sack*?'

He nodded, on the verge of more giggles.

'Christ,' I said, 'you must have hollow legs.'

Which was when it all finally clicked into place. Haunted by Finn, maybe, a flashback to bombing along in his Audi, *Horsedrawn Wishes* up full blast. Finn with his window down and a fat spliff drifting sparks in the breeze.

I glanced across at Ben and saw Finn grinning up at me, a fun-loving kid with gaunted eyes and a life sucked dryer every time he drew on a jay. Saw greyish globs spitting, frying, on the cab's skeletal frame.

Saw what I should already have seen. Or might have seen, had I been around to see.

Maybe. I'm not really the noticing type.

Right there I decided it was time to swing in behind Dee. Until now I'd been feeding her the line that it was best for Ben if I stayed at arm's length, so he wouldn't get teased and maybe bullied and one day tainted for being the son of an ex-con. But that was horseshit. The truth being that I was really trying to achieve some kind of retrospective exoneration if Ben lucked out and became a fuck-up too.

Besides, Ben already knew I'd been away doing time. Some day, it was inevitable, he'd find out why, and for who. When he did he'd make his own decisions about what and who was right and wrong, and maybe then he'd come to the same conclusion I had. That dad by default was better than no dad at all, for both of us.

If he didn't, he didn't. But until then I'd do whatever it took.

I switched off the stereo. 'Ben?'

'Uh-huh?'

'How long have you been smoking dope?'

He denied it, naturally. I'd have been disappointed if he hadn't. But he blushed to the bone and wouldn't meet my eye. We shouted for a bit, Ben shrill and defensive, but as a mismatch we were up there with Kong and Fay Wray.

'You're half the time zonked,' I said. 'Grades sliding off the map. Eating your own weight in munchies and giggling like a girl on a wonky swing.'

A sullen snort.

'Ben, man – you're *twelve.*'

'So?'

'So get that fucking look off your face or I'll smack it off.'

He rearranged his features into something pale and hollowed, stared straight ahead.

'How long?' I said.

'How long what?'

'How long have you been smoking?'

He shrugged. 'Couple of months.'

'How much?'

'Dunno.'

'One a day? Five? How much?'

'Depends.'

'No. It *used* to depend. Now it doesn't *depend* so much because you've smoked your last joint.'

No answer. 'I know what you're thinking,' I said. 'How am I going to stop you?' He shifted in his seat, hunching a shoulder to hide the sly grin twitching in the corner of his mouth. 'Easy,' I said. 'I go to the cops, tell them some fucker's selling my kid drugs at school.'

'Dad—'

'That way, everyone'll know it was you who squealed. Yeah? Who'll sell you dope after that? And unless things've changed since I was in school, you'll be due a kicking or three as well. Am I right?'

His shoulders quivered. 'It's not like I'm smoking it every day,' he said. A quavering note in his voice.

'I don't give a shit about what it's not like. From now on, it's out. Jesus, Ben, it's a gateway drug.'

'Chill, Dad. I know what—'

'You haven't a fucking clue, Ben. And tell me to chill again, and I'll chill *you*. You hear me?'

'Jesus,' he muttered, 'it's only a few smokes. It's not like I killed anyone.'

For a split-second I froze. 'What'd you say?'

'Nothing.'

'You said something,' I said, 'about not killing anyone.'

He shrugged, edged away from me. His Adam's apple bobbing

hard. 'It's only dope, dad.'

A throwaway remark? Or did he know?

Either way, he was right. I softened my tone. 'I know what I'm talking about, Ben. You think you're the first kid who ever smoked some weed?'

An up-and-under glance from behind the fringe, quizzical. Honesty being the most shocking policy, I went the whole hog. 'Yeah, I smoked it too.' This time I ladled on the past tense. 'And I'm telling you it's a gateway drug. I started off smoking hash and wound up smoking sixty cigarettes a day.' I left out the speed, E, acid, poppers, coke, shrooms and PCP. I had a feeling I'd need another shock or two up my sleeve in the years to come.

'Cigarettes aren't real drugs,' he said.

'They'll kill you all the same.'

'Yeah, but I mean—'

'They're not illegal, sure. But just in case there's any confusion, here's the way it is. If I catch you smoking hash again, I'll break your fucking fingers to stop you rolling up. Are we clear?'

Over the top, maybe, but it had the desired effect. He slumped back in his seat, shocked at the ferocity of the threat. His skin so pale it seemed to glow in the gathering dusk. Once in a while he'd sniffle, then wipe his nose with a defiant slash, sleeve tugged down across his wrist. After a while, in a small voice, he said, 'Are you going to tell mum?'

'*Tell* her? I'm going to have to move back *in* with her.'

A half-choked giggle. He looked across at me, eyes huge and watering, hopeful.

'Tell you what I'm going to do,' I said. 'This once, this one time only, I'm giving you an amnesty. You know what an amnesty is?' He nodded, which was something of a thunder-stealer. 'Okay, so the amnesty is that I don't tell your mother, I don't go to your school, I don't blow the whistle to the cops. Now you tell me, what're *you* going to do?'

He gulped it out. 'Not smoke hash.'

'Correct. I mean, Ben, if you keep smoking that crap, football's out. Forget about it. Your lungs haven't even formed properly yet. Sucking that shit down, you'll cripple yourself. You know hash is ten times more cancerous than cigarettes, right?'

He shook his head. 'No,' I said, 'they never tell you the downside. Then there's the mental problems.'

'I never even had a bad dream,' he said.

'Not yet, maybe. But they've done studies into the long-term effects of smoking dope. Know what they found?'

'No.'

'Neither do they. And I don't know about you, but that scares the shit out of me.'

'Maybe it doesn't *have* any effect.'

I admired his guts, the way he wasn't taking it lying down. But he had to learn. 'I knew this guy,' I said, 'he was chilled, like you'd say. Nice guy, friendly. Liked a smoke. Guy was rich, had a good-looking girlfriend, no problems.'

'So?'

'He jumped off nine stories for no reason anyone can see. Last night. You're sitting in his car right now.'

That got him. 'Remember the crime scene earlier?' I said. 'I was there when it happened. The guy hit so hard he looked like a dwarf after. Smashed every bone in his body. It'll be in the paper tomorrow, look out for it. His name was Finn Hamilton.'

'He jumped because he was on hash?'

'This is what I'm saying. No one knows *why* he jumped. But

yeah, he smoked a lot of grass, for years. And I don't care what it is you're taking, acid or fucking bran flakes, you do something for years, it's going to have an effect. You want to turn out a mentaller?'

'No.'

'Well then.'

He didn't speak for half an hour. I let him stew, cranked up the stereo, let Rollerskate Skinny take us home. We came off the Tubbercurry bypass and I'd just dug out the makings to roll a smoke when my phone rang, caller ID flashing *Dee-Dee-Dee*.

I handed the half-rolled cigarette to Ben, picked up.

'Dee?'

'Where are you, Harry?'

'Right now I'm on a bad stretch for talking on the phone. I'll buzz you back in ten.'

'Are you far away?'

'Twenty minutes, depending on traffic.'

I hung up. Ben, sucking in his cheeks to suppress the smile, handed me the cigarette already rolled and roached. I shook my head, then grinned and sparked it up. Rollerskate Skinny adding a touch of melancholy with 'Bell Jars Away', Ken Griffin plaintive, *this motionless ease, measure me by . . .*

'Okay,' I said. 'How this amnesty works is this. You'll know by the time you're eighteen if you have what it takes to make it. I mean as a footballer. If you haven't been scouted by then, you never will. Plus, with your grades back up, you'll probably be heading off to college, where it's practically the law you have to smoke dope.'

'Really?'

'No. Look, Ben – what I'm saying is that from now on, and

until you're old enough to get your shit together, I'm on your case. Hear me? I'll be dropping by regular, checking you out. And you can't kid a kidder. I'll know. Trust me. I'll be checking for hot-spots, smelling your clothes, making it so fucking hard it won't be worth your while smoking. And if I get the faintest whiff that you might even be thinking about having a toke, I'll be off to the cops, dobbing your mates in. How's that?'

He wasn't happy, but if he hit eighteen still hating me I'd figure I'd done a half-decent job.

'Mum doesn't have to find out?'

'It's a clean slate, Ben, but it's a one-time offer. Screw up again and you're fucked. She'll send you away to military school. In Gdańsk. Christ!'

The phone ringing again. *Dee-Dee-Dee.* The road had straightened up, the long run down towards the Collooney roundabout that was there but already invisible in the gloom. I picked up.

'I'll be there in ten fucking minutes, okay? Chill.'

Ben sniggered. I cocked an eyebrow at him, and that was all it took.

Hard to say looking back, but if I hadn't been juggling Dee, the phone, steering wheel and a cigarette, then maybe I'd have seen it coming. Maybe if I had readjusted the rear-view mirror when the sun finally went down I'd have caught more than a blur in my peripheral vision. Maybe if I hadn't let myself be distracted by Ben's snigger.

Maybe, maybe, maybe . . .

The world shunted ten feet to the right, the Audi shivering like a harpooned whale as it veered onto the hard shoulder. I dropped phone and cigarette, yanked hard on the wheel. Swerved back on line, clipping the white reflector poles marking the grass verge. Then a pole flickered up over the bonnet to smash the windscreen, glaze it milky.

The wheels on the left skidding out, sliding away on the grass verge. A steep slope beyond, a narrow gully.

I think Ben might have been screaming. My last lucid thought was, *O Christ, it's going to kill him too.*

Then someone buried an axe in the equator. The car flipped over, seemed to hang upside down, poised in mid-air.

We hit with a crunch, the screech of metal rending, the harsh splintering of glass. The someone buried the axe in my skull. The world split in two.

20

Most Irish cops, freshly minted, are sent to Dublin once they leave Templemore. The idea being, if you can handle the Dublin streets anywhere else will be a doddle. If you grew up in Dublin, they'll probably send you to Limerick. Same idea, more knives.

The last place they'll send you is home, the theory being that you're far less likely to be bribed, corrupted, threatened or inclined to turn a blind eye if you're parachuted into a place where you know no one and no one knows you, or your family.

This also applies to the judiciary.

Why it doesn't apply to the politicians is anyone's guess. Maybe they're born of nobler stuff than cops and judges.

Anyway, the theory is sound, but in practice it has its drawbacks. For one, it promotes a them-and-us mentality, which means most young cops pick up their local knowledge from other cops, which in turn means that one cop's personal experience can filter down through the years into a prejudice against a particular individual or family, and become a self-perpetuating myth.

The fact that such prejudice is generally hard-earned and well-deserved is neither here nor there.

The cop stationed outside the door of my room, Pamela reckoned, was nervous. Not because he knew me, but because the only things he did know about me were that I'd done time for killing my brother and was liable to embark on a homicidal frenzy when I woke to discover that the hospital corners on my sheets weren't sharp enough to shave with.

So Pamela said. I didn't have the strength to check the colour of the sheets, let alone the quality of the corners.

I'd woken drenched in sweat to a world that was shorter and narrower than when I went away. The ceiling lower, pressing down. For a second I'd thought I was back in my cell, that it'd all been another dream. But the sheets felt crisp.

Then came a muted beep.

I sensed rather than smelled the cloying blanket of antiseptic warmth. A tube in my arm, the bag of clear fluid suspended high above my head. Beneath that a bedside locker, and on top of that a jug of water, a plastic beaker standing sentry, half-full.

My throat felt like it was growing cacti for fun. I reached for the beaker and—

Bad mistake.

I'd been booby-trapped, some sadistic fiend laying in tiny coils of molten razor-wire just below the skin. Ripped free, they sent an agonising jolt whiplashing out from under my left eye, all the way down through my shoulder and into my left elbow.

I lay there panting hot and raw. Sweat or tears or something acid burning my right eye.

I must have grunted.

'You're awake.' She swam into view with a swish of starch, her shoes all a-squeak on a floor carpeted with orgasmic mice. She tried for severe but she was too surprised to make it work. 'How are you feeling?'

'Shit.' A croak. 'How's Ben?'

'He's fine. Do you want a drink?'

I nodded. Another bad mistake. My head felt like a balloon going over an underwater falls. The wooziness spiralled away down my spine, became a whirlpool. She held the beaker to my lips. 'Sip at it,' she said.

It took a combination of Napoleonic ambition and Puritan masochism, but I managed three sips. It was warm and tasted faintly of dust and something antiseptic but as it trickled down my throat the cacti blossomed into a field of damp buttercups, gleaming. She took the beaker away. 'Are you in pain?' she said.

'Ben.'

'You need to rest.' It was an order rather than advice. 'You've suffered a trauma to the—'

'Ben.'

She was smaller than I remembered, stretching on tip-toe to reach around and plump the pillows. A faint whiff of the cinnamon gum she favoured. Up close her eyes were no less hypnotic than they'd been the last time we'd been that close, although I'd have remembered them more fondly if they'd met mine when she spoke about Ben.

'He's fine, Harry. Stable, in no danger.'

An entirely practical woman, Pamela Burns. Efficient and cynical and not given to overtly feminine ploys. At least, that's how she looked from a distance, petite and largely unremarkable and unconcerned with convincing strangers otherwise. But if you were to jog her elbow at a crowded bar – Fiddlers, say – and spill some of the three G&Ts she was carrying away onto her wrist, and she was to glare up at you with those round brown eyes flecked with a kind of green mica, the crown of her head just about level with your chin, and she was to say something harsh that you didn't hear because the music was too loud and you'd had two pints too many, and were already perning in the gyre of those eyes, round as moons and exerting roughly the same gravity – well, you get the gist.

It had ended badly between us, but then such things end badly or they don't end at all. Sligo being the size it is, we'd bumped into one another a couple of times afterwards, and a détente had been established, one that had thawed a little when Ben arrived – I'd met her the night he was born, staggering out into a shiny new world as she came on for the early shift – and later became a fully fledged truce, and we the battle-scarred veterans not quite capable yet of sharing our war stories, when she got married herself and had two kids, boys or girls I could never remember.

I hadn't seen her since I'd gone away, and now here she was, a thumb on my pulse. Her fingers felt cool and dry and somehow essential.

Slowly, very slowly, I raised my right hand to my face and touched fingertips to my left eye. It felt swollen and gauzy. Above the swelling where my eye should have been I came upon a soft wadding. An eye-patch of sorts.

'Where is he?' I said.

'Who?'

'Ben.'

'Ben's fine,' she said again. Her gaze flickered away as she tugged a sheet corner straight. 'And you need to relax and get some rest. You really shouldn't be awake yet.'

'Sure. Okay.'

She plucked a pen from her breast pocket and moved away to the bottom of the bed, unhooked the chart. The sip of water sloshed around greasily as I threw back the sheet, slid out. She glanced up in time to see me pluck the tube from my arm. A three-inch needle came away too. Spots of blood spattered the sheet, Pollock-style, but Pamela had never been a fan of abstract expressionism.

'Harry! What the *fuck* are you—'

'Where is he?'

She backed away to the door. 'You can't leave,' she said. She was firm on the principle although her voice was a bit shaky. I was still holding the tube, the needle pointing at her. I put it down on the bed.

'Where's my clothes?'

'It's not me who'll be stopping you,' she said. She put a hand behind her and twisted the handle, and I realised she wasn't checking her escape route but ensuring it was still locked. This was when she told me about the cop stationed outside. There were more downstairs, waiting for me to wake up so they could take a blood-level reading.

'For what, booze?' She nodded. 'They won't find anything,' I said. 'I haven't had a drink since God was a boy.' Then it occurred to me. 'What time is it?'

'Nearly midnight. But look, they want to talk to you about the accident too. Best if you just take it easy for now, get as strong as you can.'

'I'm grand, really. And I'm not going anywhere they won't find me. All I want is to see Ben.'

'I told you, Ben is doing—'

'Pam,' I said. 'I'm not a good person. We both know this. But I'm not dangerous to you or anyone else in the hospital, and I'm definitely not dangerous to Ben. What matters now is I was the one driving when we got rammed, when Ben was my responsibility, so I need to—'

'Rammed?'

'Rammed, yeah. The guy ran us off the road.'

'The Guards say it was a one-car accident. That you lost control.'

'They didn't see the dents in the side of the car?'

'They're saying the car's a write-off.' A doubtful note. 'It rolled over three or four times. They say it's a miracle you both got out alive.'

'What else are they saying?'

She was wavering. 'I really shouldn't be telling you anything. I've been ordered to ring downstairs as soon as you're awake, let the Guards—'

'Ordered?'

'That's right.' Her lips thinned. 'It's an order. Just like we were ordered to sign you in under Gerry Smith, and Ben as Francis Browne.'

'Listen, Pam.' I gripped the sheet as a wave of nausea rippled up my throat, the adrenaline buzz already starting to seep away. 'Someone tried to kill me and didn't care Ben was in the car. My only kid, and when it mattered most I couldn't fucking protect him.' I closed my eyes, squeezing tightly, then opened them again. The world was still fuzzy around its seams. 'When the cops ask what happened, I'll tell them I threatened you with the needle, you had no choice. And I'm begging you.'

I swallowed against some rising bile and maybe she thought I was choking back a sob. Anyway, she took a deep breath and let it out slow, shook her head, then went to the wardrobe to retrieve my jeans and T-shirt, laying them on the bed along with my socks and jocks.

She had to help me dress, filling me in on the events of the past four hours as she eased my limbs into various openings.

Dee had heard the accident happening, the crunching and glass smashing, rang 999 straight away. Christ alone knows how long we'd have been in the gully if she hadn't. I'd taken a blow to the face, from the steering wheel they guessed, which had fractured my cheekbone and left my eye so swollen it was completely closed. On the plus side, and apart from the concussion that was causing thirst, blurred vision, nausea and disorientation, I'd had a solid four hours of sleep for the first time in a week. I've walked away from stag parties in worse shape.

Ben didn't walk anywhere. The Audi had hit passenger-side first. They'd had to cut him out and he had yet to regain consciousness. His left arm was broken in two places and he had a compound fracture in his left femur. A tangerine-sized lump on his right temple was bleeding into the brain pan.

The cops were downstairs in the canteen, scarfing free coffee and complaining about the stale muffins. Pamela was supposed to tell the doctor the minute I woke up.

'Do it,' I said, trying to tie my trainers in through a blur of fingers and laces. 'I don't want to cause you any problems.'

'A dollar short and a decade late.' The hint of a sad smile. 'Wait here.'

She unlocked the door, went outside. I snuck up to the door, heard her tell the cop I was coming round, I'd be fit for interview in another ten minutes or so. No, he couldn't use his mobile phone, and she didn't care if his two-way was on the blink, the use of mobile phones was banned on this floor in case they interfered with hospital equipment. Twenty seconds later she slipped inside again.

'I'd say you've about fifteen minutes,' she said.

She stuck a Band-Aid on the needle's oozing wound and told me the ICU was three floors up. Then she gave me two Dilaudid and a ten-minute start. Which is as fair as you can ask of any woman.

21

The corridor looked no longer than the Marianas Trench. It didn't help that I'd been operated on by some fiend who'd replaced every last bone with a strand of hot cotton wool, which left me zig-zagging a course between wheelchairs and beds, stern-faced nurses and blank-eyed porters. Dizzy, weak and sick, the polished floor lurching up then falling away.

The elevator lobby was a safe haven. I propped myself between two doors and dry-swallowed one of the Dilaudids waiting for the lift to arrive. My vision seemed to be getting worse. Not only was everything shorter and narrower due to the patch on my left eye, but I was suffering a kind of blurring in the good one. Or maybe that was just the artist's impression of a fiery sunset hanging on the opposite wall, a vermillion blaze that did my thumping headache no favours.

Three minutes burned up already. The elevator door dinged, then opened. I staggered inside. The doors closed and the floor rose and I stared at the fuzzy reflection in the mirror, something that looked a lot like the Elephant Man after fifteen rounds with Jake La Motta. I found myself wondering why they put mirrors into elevators and decided it was for the claustrophobics, fully aware that I was trying to distract myself from the dread slithering up my spine at the prospect of what lay three floors above, a tangerine-sized lump bleeding into his brain pan.

By the time I left the elevator and stepped out onto the ICU floor, the Dilaudid had gone off like a depth-charge. I was queasy below and woozy upstairs, giddy as a three-legged donkey on wet cobbles. I went through to a waiting area of low chairs, low tables and people who paced, fretted or wept quietly. No worst there is none, Hopkins reckoned, although he'd never had a child comatose in ICU. You could taste the desperation on the dead air. Salty, like an offshore mist in the early dawn.

Two of the people were Dee and an angular guy in his early forties, sandy hair brushed across his forehead, wide eyes. A chin like a soft-boiled egg. He was wide in the shoulders and wore a mauve shirt under a checked sports jacket with leather patches at the elbows.

She saw me coming. Closed her eyes, allowed her chin slump forward onto her chest. Then she turned her head away and held up a hand to ward me off.

'Don't even come near me,' she said. Sounding dull, raspy. The guy unfolded from his seat and got up in stages. I had to peek under his armpit to speak to Dee.

'Whatever they told you, it's not true.' My own voice was a croak. 'We were rammed, ran off the road.'

'Jesus, Harry. Do you really think I give a fuck *how* it happened?'

She had a point. I looked up at the guy. 'Hey, d'you mind? I'm trying to talk about our son here.'

'She says she doesn't want you near her.' He sounded smooth, controlled. Or maybe it was just that he didn't rasp or croak. He pointed over my shoulder. 'Why don't you sit over there? There's a seat free.'

'Why don't *you* sit over there?'

'I'm already here,' he said.

'I don't know who the fuck you think you are,' I said, 'but—'

'Frank.'

'Right.'

I gave Frank some fish-eye. By now someone had iced the cobbles and the donkey was down to two legs. I tilted my head to peek under his armpit again and the room swam away, seemed to loop around on itself, then settled down into a whirlpool groove. Frank put out a hand, maybe to steady me, maybe to fend me off, as I began to topple in towards Dee. I swiped at it, missed, and wound up with my jaw planted on Frank's chest.

Dee whipped around, using the heels of her palms to swab her cheeks. Eyes red-limned and raw. A mascara tear-streak had curved outside her right cheekbone to head for her ear. 'Christ's sakes, Harry, I'm trying to fucking *pray* here.'

I've had worse moments, although most of those were idled away in front of a gun. 'Pray?'

It was bad, then. I struggled away from Frank, which is to say he stood me upright, just as a barrel-shaped Sikh doctor came through the double swing-doors at the end of the room. Every head turned but he barrelled straight for us, a clipboard tucked under one arm. I don't know why, he didn't refer to it once. Dee stood up, a hand to her mouth. Frank put an arm around her. He looked solid, dependable, so I lurched up against him.

'Mizz Gorman?' the Sikh said.

She nodded. He took a deep breath. 'I am very sorry,' he said, not so much rolling his Rs as bowling them at skittles, 'but I have very little to report. No significant change, yes.'

'O Christ,' Dee whimpered.

The Sikh held up a forefinger. 'This means, you understand, that he has no deterioration. But soon he will need the transfusion. He has lost a lot of blood.' A hint of reproach, as if it were Ben's fault. 'The boy has had two transfusions in four hours. At this rate . . .' He tailed off with a shrug, turning his palm upwards.

From behind her hand Dee emitted a sound that was somewhere between sob and stifled screech. Frank squeezed her shoulders. The Sikh glanced from one to the other as if waiting for applause.

'So give him the transfusion,' I said.

'It's not that simple,' Frank said over his shoulder.

The Sikh looked at me for the first time. 'Who is this?' he said.

'The father,' Frank said.

There followed a conversation I didn't fully follow, its natural flow clogged up with AB negatives, anti-Ds, antigen factors and incompatibilities, but as the room swirled away, then came rushing back, I realised they were all staring at me, waiting for an answer.

'What the fuck are we waiting for?' I said, ripping the dressing off my forearm. Drops of blood flew, spattering the tiles, the Sikh's penny loafers.

The effort, or the momentum, tugged me sideways. Frank half-turned to grab at me. The donkey, down to one leg, gave one last kick.

I don't remember making it all the way down.

22

More tubes, crisp sheets, muted beeps. A different room, another nurse, this one a pert blonde with a luscious overbite. Tohill leaned against the wall at the foot of the bed, hands jammed in his pockets, his face now looking like they'd just pulled the boot out of a canal.

'Don't mind the cop,' I told the nurse. I felt sharp enough, even though I heard myself chewing tinfoil. 'It's what they call community policing. He's just taking an interest.'

She flushed a little, averting her eyes as she fussed around, checking this, measuring that. My jaw still throbbed but the Dilaudid had bedded in. The pain was there, constant but tolerable.

I'd slept again. Long enough to allow them round up the donkey, take him away to some sanctuary in the hills. The nausea was gone and my vision had cleared, although the world was still shorter and narrower than God intended. 'How's Ben?' I croaked.

The nurse glanced at Tohill. He blinked once. 'No change,' she said. 'Stable but no change.'

'I'm compatible?'

'Already done,' Tohill said. 'They'll be giving him a transfusion once they know it's clean.'

'You won't find any booze in it,' I said. 'And even if you do, you'd have needed prior permission before it'll stand up in court.'

He nodded, grim. 'You nearly finished?' he asked the nurse.

'Nearly,' she said. When she was done, she asked if I wanted a cup of tea, some toast.

'Coffee'd be nice.' But my heart was a cotton puff, so tea it was. The nurse left. Tohill locked the door, opened the window and produced a battered pack of Marlboro Lights, sparked us up.

'Sorry about the kid,' he said.

'He's not gone yet.'

The niceties observed, he jumped in. 'Tell me again,' he said, 'how you weren't boozing.'

'We were rammed. Maybe it looks like a one-car deal to you, but we were rammed.'

'By who?'

'The fuck would I know? He came up from behind, hit me blindside.'

He had himself a drag while he thought about that. 'Convenient,' he said, 'that the only person who can verify your story is in a coma.'

'So we wait 'til he comes out of it.'

His stare was a deadpan 'If'.

'We found the stuff,' he said. 'I suppose you'll be telling me the guy who rammed you planted it.'

'What stuff?'

'The coke,' he said, patiently. 'About ten grand's worth, although we'll work it up to fifty. Plenty enough to put you back where you belong.'

He wasn't kidding. Given my record, ten grand worth of coke was enough to see me deported to the dark side of Jupiter. I took a long hit off the Marlboro while the prickles of cold sweat dried cold into my back. 'I've no idea what you're talking about,' I said.

'Probably the bang on the head,' he said. 'Temporary amnesia. When you remember, be sure to let us know. Some of the boys are keen to know where it was going, who stumped up the ten grand. Unless it was all for personal use, hey?' He winked, the grin that of a hyena with bad gas. Then he stubbed out his smoke in a kidney-shaped metal dish and took a pair of gloves from a side pocket. For one horrific moment I thought he was aiming for a cavity search, but instead he reached into his breast pocket, drew out a padded envelope. The cling-film had been unwrapped, hung loose. 'Personally,' he said, 'I'm more interested in this.'

'What's that?'

'You tell me. We found it on the back seat.'

'Back seat?'

He stared, the bleak eyes tightening. Then he tossed the envelope onto the bed.

'Try this,' he said. 'We have a one-car accident that looks like you lost control, probably as a result of your driving under the influence.' He waved away my attempt at protest. 'In the car we find a load of Class A, this in a car also containing your young son. Sordid, sure, but at least it's open-and-shut. Except then we find this.' He indicated the envelope. 'So take a quick look inside before you start talking.'

'First off, I know nothing about any Class A.'

'So your prints won't be all over the gear?'

'Matter a fuck if they are, I was unconscious when it was found, or when you say it was. Who's to say it wasn't you had me fondle it? Reasonable doubt, Tohill. Especially when I've no previous for anything drug-related.'

'You think that'll stand up?'

'You're fishing, Tohill. And you're gonna need a bigger boat.'

He shrugged that one off. 'What about this?' he said, nodding at the envelope.

'I haven't the faintest clue what's in there. You can check with the cop at the PA, I went around there to feed Finn's dog. I needed to piss, then the toilet wouldn't flush, and when I looked inside the cistern I found that under a false bottom. I presumed it was his suicide note, so I brought it with me to give to his mother.'

'A suicide note?'

'I know, yeah. You wouldn't be giving it to me now if it was a suicide note. But that's what I thought it was at the time.'

'Says you.'

'Check with Saoirse Hamilton. She'll confirm she asked me to find it.'

'And you didn't even take a sneaky peek inside?'

'At a suicide note?'

He scratched his nose, then gestured at the envelope. My prints were already on the cling-film, so I opened the envelope. Inside was a passport that had been issued six months previously. Tucked inside its inner sleeve, folded neatly in half, were ten crisp, pink five-hundred euro notes. For a second I thought they were fakes. I'd never seen a five-hundred euro note before.

The passport bore Finn's photograph, a signature that looked a lot like Finn's writing and a date of birth that was Finn's own. Oddly, the passport appeared to belong to one Philip Winston Byrne.

'Tell me this,' Tohill said. 'What kind of suicide stashes a fake passport and five grand for a quick getaway? And while you're at it, tell me some more about how you just so happened to be at the PA when he jumped.'

I stubbed my smoke and beckoned for another. The Marlboro tasted harsh and dry but I needed a little thinking time.

'I'm presuming you had a warrant to search the car,' I said. 'Otherwise anything you found'll be thrown out as inadmissible.'

'Still with the legal shit.' A lupine grin. 'Your kid had to be cut out of the wreck and you're worrying about procedure?'

'The law's the law.'

'Not when it's bent into knots by fuckers like you. And anyway, there was no search. The shit was just lying there.'

'Says you.'

'Says about ten cops and firemen, all of us with honest faces. So fuck your warrants and procedure. If you don't play ball, right now, I'll turn you out to the boys want you for the coke. And my best guess is, they'll keep you just long enough to get whoever owns the gear wondering about what you're telling them.'

'I know nothing about any—'

'Here's how it is, Rigby.' He ticked off on his fingers as he went. 'We have you cold on trafficking Class A while transporting a minor in a vehicle you're not insured to drive. And then,' he nodded at the passport, the money, 'there's the incriminating evidence in what's starting to look like a murder investigation.'

'Circumstantial, and only because you want it to look that way. So you can screw Gillick and Hamilton Holdings.'

The heat was getting to him. He slipped out of his jacket, draped it on the bottom of the bed, leaned back against the wall. 'Explain the fake passport,' he said. 'The five grand.'

'You don't know when Finn stashed them. Maybe he had plans and changed his mind.'

'According to you, he had those kind of plans about twenty minutes before he went walkabout on the window ledge.' He eased himself away from the wall, started pacing. Three strides to the window, a turn and three strides to the door. 'See it my way,' he said. 'The first thing you do is bolt, leave the scene. Then you come in and make a false statement. Next thing we know you're driving around with the guy's fake passport and five grand in cash.'

'I called it in,' I said. 'Gave the medic my number, went off to tell Finn's mother. Then I came in, voluntarily, to make a statement. All the Good Samaritan shit. And that envelope was sealed. I didn't open it because I thought it was Finn's suicide note, I was giving it to his mother.'

He quit pacing, turned to face me. Open his arms wide, as if pleading. 'That might even work,' he said, 'except for the kicker.'

'What kicker?'

'Your rep, Rigby. You've already put one guy away, your own brother.'

'Try to use that in court and you'll be laughed out of the building.'

'It's not what's said, Rigby.' The lupine grin now an incisor short of a howl. 'It's what's known.'

I nodded. He folded his arms, triumphant.

'Sorry,' I said.

'Sorry what?'

'For not playing along. I didn't realise this was a *CSI* episode.'
I glanced up into the corners. 'Where's the cameras?'

'Rigby,' his teeth grinding, 'what you don't fucking realise
is—'

'Bullshit. Okay? Bullfuckingshit.'

'You think? I say the word, you're in a cell and—'

'First off,' I said, 'you're CAB. So any and all crap about murder or homicide or any of that shit, it won't be your call. Two, if
you had enough to put me in a cell I'd be there already. Three, it's
not what's *known*, Tohill, it's what you can prove. You take a case
to the DPP on what's *known*, you'll be out on your arse so fast you
won't even bounce.'

'You want to take that chance?'

'I'm taking it. Because this is a game here, and you're trying to
push me into some corner where I have only one way out.
Because it's not me you want, it's the Hamiltons and Gillick, or
whoever they're fronting for. And I'm fucked if I'll be your boy.'

'You'll be fucked if you don't.'

'Then I'll be fucked my way.' That was the cue for a staring
game, a little glowering. 'Look,' I said, 'I don't know what Finn
told you about what he saw from the PA, but the man's dead. That
angle is dead. Close it down, start again.'

'No problem, yeah. Hey, maybe we could even put that five
grand there to the new budget.'

'That's what this is about? Budgets?'

'We're *close* is what this is about. And you need to pull your
head out of your hole, have a look around. See how you can make
this work for you.'

'Make what work?'

'Finn's number is in your phone,' he said patiently. 'He rang you, you knew where he was, you knew he'd be alone. Then he goes out the window. You're about to sign off on a false statement when Gillick arrives, walks you out. Then we find shit in your car makes it look like you're trying to cover some tracks. Maybe your own, maybe Gillick's, we don't know.'

'If you think I'm fronting for—'

'We have your phone, Rigby. You want to tell me now who you were calling today or wait until we work it out ourselves?'

'I'll wait, thanks. Because you'll need a warrant to go checking my phone records, and you'll need a rock-solid reason to arrest me, besides what's *known*, before you can get it. Meantime, I'll have my phone back, cheers. Unless you're looking to screw the investigation before it gets started.'

'How about the coke, hey? You want that back too?'

'For the last time, I know nothing about any coke.' I held out my hand, palm down. 'You want to go ahead and rap my knuckles right now, go ahead.'

From the way his fingers curled into his palm, it looked a lot like he was planning something a little more dramatic than a knuckle rap or fist-bump. Except then he sat down heavily on the end of the bed, squeezed his eyes shut, dry-washed his face. He looked drained.

'Okay,' he said. He sounded almost normal. 'Cards on the table. We think Gillick had Finn done. Maybe he did it, maybe he had you do it, and maybe you just happened to be there when it happened. Either way, it's sweet for Gillick because you're standing in the way and we can't see around you. So here's the thinking. Why not put you on the witness stand? Tell the world what we know, let it all fall out.'

'I perjure myself or you frame me for Finn.'

'You can go up there hostile if you want. But you might want to take a look at this first.' He shifted his hip, took a small tin-foiled lump from his back pocket. Placed it on the sheet.

The old black hole opened up in my gut, started sucking. 'What's that supposed to be?'

'It isn't supposed to be anything. It's hash. About two joints less than a ten-spot. Poxy slate, but still.'

'So?'

'We found it in the kid's pocket, Rigby. Which means he was holding it for you or you were punting dope on to your kid.'

'Bullshit.'

'Tell it to the tabloids.' He laughed, sounding like a Ducati trapped between gears. 'I'm thinking something along the lines of,' he held up his hands, as if framing the headline, '"Coke Trafficking Killer Peddles Dope To Schoolboy Son".' He dropped the hands, wiped the grin, gave me the dead eye. 'How d'you think that'll read on his CV in ten years' time?'

23

Tohill locked the door, mumbling something I couldn't hear to the cop parked outside. I gave it half an hour to let everyone settle down, then availed of the phone on the bedside locker, one of the very few perks that go with being unofficially jailed in a private hospital room under a false name while the Guardians of the Peace wait to see if black ops will work the oracle.

Directory Enquiries put me through to the hospital's reception desk, where I asked the receptionist to connect me with Pamela Devine. There followed a couple of minutes of clicks, brrrs and false starts, and then she picked up.

'Hello?'

'Hey. It's Harry.'

A sigh not notable for its quality of unrequited longing, then: 'Did you get to see him?'

'Not exactly. But I just wanted to say thanks.'

'My arse. What do you want?'

'It's my eye.'

'Don't worry about it. The trauma to the—'

'Not that one. My good eye. It's dazzled.'

'Dazzled?'

'By your radiance. I'm thinking martinis on the terrace at dusk.'

The old familiar dirty chuckle. 'Let's just get through to dawn first. We'll see how we go after that.'

'It's a date. Meanwhile, I need an X-ray. I'm getting shooting pains in my eye.'

'Which one?'

'My Jap's eye. Which one d'you think?'

'Then that's perfectly normal. Buzz the nurse, ask for some pain relief. No, wait – did you take the Dilaudids?'

'One of them.'

'Okay. Then you'll just have to sweat it out.'

'No kidding, Pam. It's pretty intense. And I don't want to go blind and have to sue you for negligence.'

'If you're blind, how'll you find me?'

'I'll be like Homer, seeing all. C'mon, do the right thing here. Who's one X-ray going to hurt at this time of night?'

'It'd need to be an emergency. You're seriously in pain?'

'Is there any other way?'

I heard the tappity-tap of fingernails on plastic. 'Okay, hold tight. I'll see what I can do. I'm making no promises, though.'

'You're a star. Oh, and Pam? The cop in the corridor, he'll try to keep you out.'

'Good. He looks like he could use the exercise.'

Never tell a woman what she can't do on her own turf.

*

She was wrong. The new cop they'd stationed outside was tall and trim. He was also keen on the idea of not looking a complete plum. So he did it all by the book, getting on the phone to inform his superior that I needed an X-ray and waiting until it was all confirmed in triplicate before he allowed Pam push me out into the corridor in a wheelchair, sticking so close all the way to the radiography department that I could count the hairs in his nose.

There was a patient already in situ, sitting in the row of bright yellow bucket seats, a thin bald man with big ears and tiny ragged clouds for eyebrows, dressed in a tatty brown bathrobe over maroon-blue striped pyjamas. He was barefoot and looking for company, so Pam pushed on by him, through the next set of double-doors. She parked me beside the bed and helped me up on board, got me as comfortable as anyone is likely to get on a second-hand anvil. Then she draped the protective covering over my groin, glanced across at the cop.

'You're welcome to stay if you want,' she said.

The cop eyed the covering. 'It wouldn't be, ah, dangerous or anything?'

'Not particularly,' she said over her shoulder as she scuttled for the sanctuary of the glassed-in booth in the far corner. 'But it's up to you.'

He weighed it up and came down on the side of his potential progeny, retreating through the double-doors as the radiographer came through from a door to the right of the booth. A sharp-faced blonde, hair scraped back in a bun, a dun-coloured folder under her arm. She didn't so much as glance in my direction as she clip-clipped to the booth, put some X-rays up on the light box. Nor did she meet my eyes as she swung the X-ray into place over my head, got it positioned just so. Her own were glazed, and

I wondered how long she'd been on shift.

She went back to the booth. Her voice came amplified, metallic, as she reminded me not to move. I waited for the hum, then took a quick peek at the double-doors. The cop was crowding the rectangular window, keeping tabs. A loud click-*tung* sounded from beneath the table.

'Please, Mr Rigby.' Her voice frayed with irritation. 'It is vital you don't move.'

I held up a hand. 'I need to use the toilet. Sorry.'

'Just hold still. This won't take a—'

'Okay. But I need to go now. When I get nervous . . .'

'There's really nothing to worry about, Mr Rig—'

I sat up, lifting off the covering that was protecting me from whatever it was I really didn't need to worry about. Slid down off the table, pointing towards the door beside the booth. 'Is there a bathroom through there?'

'Yes, but that's a restricted area. There are facilities available to – *Mr* Rigby.'

But by then I was already through the door, closing it behind me, sliding the snib across. Tall filing cabinets either side of the corridor, darkened cubicles, one at the end with a light showing. The sharp blonde's, I presumed. Beyond that were a set of emergency exit doors.

An alarm went off about two seconds after I kicked them out, by which time I was halfway across a deserted delivery area and aiming for an alleyway in the far corner. Picking up the pace now, from crabby shuffle to crippled jog. The alleyway was softly lit with an orange light and opened up into the harsh sodium glare of the hospital car park. Here, and for once, the universe chipped in on my side. The car park was huge and terraced and neatly landscaped, its levels dug out of a gentle slope, and I let gravity do the work as I zigzagged from one tidy clump of bush to another, lungs burning, the cotton-puff heart long since split in two and thumping in both ears.

At the bottom of the car park I put a rock through a Sierra's window, jump-started the engine at the second attempt, took off for Connaughton Road. Pulled a right at the lights, drove north towards the plum bruise of Benbulben in the false dawn.

I was in bad shape. Weak and dizzy, wheezing hard, brain fizzing like bath salts in Perrier. And driving can be tricky when you're only using one blurry eye and the other is hosting what felt like a rerun of Guernica.

Still, it could have been worse. I might have been in a coma with a tangerine-sized lump bleeding into my brain pan.

How long before the Sierra was posted stolen and the cops made the jump that it'd been me who boosted it? A couple of hours, at least, but probably more.

Plenty of time to soak the grieving Saoirse Hamilton for a quick ten grand.

24

I leaned on the buzzer until I heard a click, then a tinny, angry voice asking who I was and what the fuck I thought I was doing. A metaphysical gambit, bordering on Cartesian, but I wasn't in the mood, so I told him I was there to see Saoirse Hamilton at her request and if he didn't open the door quick smart the art gallery hallway would have a new installation comprised of a Ford Sierra wearing a busted front door and a fake elephant-trunk knocker.

Three minutes later I was standing in the great hall again. Simon struggled into a glare while he knuckled sleep from his eyes, half-dressed in a rumpled white T-shirt, grey tracksuit bottoms sans piping, pool-deck flip-flops. The bloodshot eyes could have been the result of too little sleep or too much brandy, and probably both. 'This better be good,' he muttered sourly.

'Look at me. Will you take a good fucking *look* at me? Do I look like I'd be here if I didn't have to be?'

He stifled a yawn. 'What happened?'

'Doesn't matter. I need to see your boss.'

'She's asleep right now. And she hasn't been getting much—'

'She wants to see me. I'm here.'

The quick lift of his eyebrows might have been surprise, disbelief or scorn, but whatever it signalled it meant he was out of the loop. 'Is this to do with Finn?'

'If she wants you to know, she'll tell you later. So let's go, chop-chop.'

He stared. I let my eyes go dead. He took a step back without realising it. 'Wait here. I'll ask if she'll see you.'

'Tell her if she doesn't, she won't be seeing me again.'

'That'll break her heart,' he sniped, but it came from over his shoulder as he flip-flopped away up the staircase. I waited until he'd turned left into the corridor at the top of the stairs, then ducked into the study and found the phone.

'Hello?'

'It's me, Dee.'

'Shit.'

'How is he?'

'Fine, yeah. Great. Fantastic, actually.' The bitterness was a mustard gas wafting down the line. 'I don't think I've ever seen him so peaceful for so long.'

'You're still at the hospital?'

''Course.' Then: 'Why, where are you?'

'I had to leave. I've some arrangements to make.'

'And they're more important than Ben?'

'You wouldn't let me see him anyway.'

'Not the point, Harry.'

'So what is the point?'

'The point,' she said, 'is that you put him in fucking hospital and now you've fucked off to make some fucking arrangements.'

'I didn't put him in hospital. We were—'

'Save it for the cops. You were the one driving, on a mobile phone.'

'Dee – it was you rang me.'

'You're saying it's my fault?'

I could almost taste the menace. 'I'm trying to tell you we were run off the road.'

A long silence, then, 'If I find out you're lying, Harry, I'll stand up in court and testify myself.'

'Ask Ben. When he wakes up, ask him. He'll tell you.'

A choked-back sob. 'You think he's going to be alright?'

'Of course he is. Look, I can't say too much about these arrangements I'm making, but . . .'

'But what?'

I swallowed dry. Saying it made it real. 'I'm going back inside, Dee. There's a cop on my case and he's putting me away.'

'For what?'

'Does it matter?'

She sounded distant, half-dreamy. 'No,' she said. 'I don't suppose it does.'

'I'll stay in touch. If there's any change in Ben, let me know.'

'Yeah.'

'Be strong, Dee.'

'Fuck you.'

She hung up. I depressed the connection, rang Herb. In the silence the whole house seemed to lurk at my shoulder, one ear cocked. And maybe that was just the faint echo I was hearing, the kind you get on an open line.

'Yello.'

'It's me.'

'About fucking time, too. Where are you?'

'Be cute. I'm on an unsecured line.'

'Why, where's your phone?'

I filled him in, ending with Ben's condition.

'Fucking hell. Will he be alright?'

In his cautious tone I heard the real question, the same one Dee had been asking, the one that ended with the words 'brain' and 'damage'.

'We're hopeful,' I said. 'Signs are positive.'

'Anything I can do from this end?'

'Not much, Herb. But cheers.'

'Okay, but if you think of anything . . . Listen, Harry? What about the—'

'Not now, Herb. You're on my list and I'll get to you as soon as I can. But not now.'

'Alright. But don't go lost. Don't make me send someone out to find you.'

'Herb, man – I'm your reducer. It'd be me you'd be sending out.'

'So don't make me do it. You're fucked up enough without turning schizophrenic.'

He hung up. I waited a full three minutes before hearing a funny kind of whispering click on the line, and then I hung up too.

25

I wondered if my new eye-patch would stir up some memories of Big Bob's piratical mien but Saoirse Hamilton was polite enough not to comment when she received me on the balcony of a morning room adjacent to her bedroom. Or maybe, consumed with grief, or not generally disposed to noticing the little people, it just didn't register. She wore a lilac peignoir, the rustles of sleep in her face and hair giving her the blowsy appearance of a prosperously retired madam.

The drop beyond the low pillared wall fell sheer to the crooked black teeth of an inlet a hundred feet or so below, so I retreated to the wicker armchair angled towards her own, propped my feet on the low wall. It was some view. The sun was crowning gold on the horizon, the air already balmy, and depending on how I tilted my head I could have watched a corona gild Queen Maeve's grave on Knocknerea, the Atlantic take on a patina of silvery leaf or Saoirse Hamilton's cleavage blush a rosy hue. Not being a man for nature in the raw, I focused on the coffee she was pouring.

She dropped two lumps into the bowl without asking if I was sweet enough already and handed it across. I stirred and sipped and closed my eyes. It was probably the finest coffee I'd ever tasted.

'You're not Greek,' she said.

I opened my eyes again. 'I never said I was.'

'I mean, Mr Rigby, that you come bearing no gifts.'

'Ah, right. Classical.'

She lit a menthol More, easing back into her seat and settling her bowl of coffee on her midriff, so I had to look twice to be sure it wasn't her cleavage that was steaming. 'Why so?' she said.

'When I spoke with you yesterday I thought I had what you wanted.'

'Finn's suicide note. Let's not be coy.'

'Fair enough. It was actually a passport with five grand cash inside.'

She held up her bowl in both hands, so that she could sip from it without taking her eyes off mine. She thought I was lying, was waiting for the tell, some flinch, for me to brush my nose or look away. So I blinked, grazed a forefinger across my nose and glanced out at the sunrise, just to see where it might take us.

'But if Finn was planning to . . .' She heard the words she was about to say. Her wince was practically audible, the Botox *skreek* of tectonic plates grinding. 'You told me,' she said in a firm voice, 'that Finn had plans to travel. To Cyprus.'

'What I said was, he was moving there. To live. But it's not just the passport.'

'Yes?'

'The cops want to know why it's a fake.'

'A fake?'

'It's that or he stole Philip Byrne's passport, stuck his own mugshot inside.'

She flapped some eyelash so hard that a hurricane started to brew in Brazil. 'But why would Finn need a fake passport?'

'At a wild guess, I'd say he wanted to travel incognito.' I swallowed off the last of the coffee, put the bowl down on the hardwood table. I'd resisted long enough but I hadn't had a smoke in over eight hours, so I filched a menthol More, sparked it up with her dinky gold Cartier. It didn't exactly taste like mint-roasted cowpat, but it was close.

'Mrs Hamilton,' I said, 'let's just accept at this point that when it comes to Finn and why he did what he did, I know nothing. What's bugging me is that he stashed the passport where someone was bound to find it eventually.'

'I'm afraid I don't follow.'

'That makes two of us. I'm just saying, you should mention that to the cops. They don't seem to think it's all that important.'

'Why should they?'

'Well,' I exhaled hard, 'mainly because they feature me for pushing Finn out the window. So I'd appreciate it if we could crack on with this job you have in mind, because there's a good chance that I'm under arrest at the moment, technically speaking, and I don't have a lot of time to play with.'

But I'd lost her at window, the full lips pursing into a cat's-bum pucker. 'How *dare* you,' she began, but by then I was waving the More around to distract her, a Yoda-sized lightsaber.

'I didn't push anyone anywhere,' I said, 'and I don't do poetry either. It's late, I'm knackered, and I've more to worry about than whether Finn bit the big one or wafted off into the ether on angels' downy wings. I'm here because you want me to do a job.

So just tell me what it is and how much it pays and we'll see how it goes from there.'

She bridled, quivered and damn near danced a Cuban hokey-cokey. 'You haven't the manners you were born with,' she hissed.

'True enough, but I'm guessing etiquette isn't a prerequisite for this work you need done. So what is it you want?'

She simmered a while. I dunked the More in the coffee bowl. The fizz-spit seemed to bring her back. She sat forward and placed her own bowl on the table, flicked some silk and lace into a froth while she gathered her thoughts.

'One prerequisite,' she said, sounding starch, 'would be an ability to actually deliver on your promise. Regardless of what it was you found in Finn's studio, you singularly failed to bring it to me. As you said you would.'

'Yeah, well, that had a lot to do with being rammed off the road and being hauled in by the cops. Next time I'll be what they call forewarned, keep a weather eye out for the *deus* trying on his *machina* shit.'

'Yes, the Guards. Why do you say you are technically under arrest?'

'I said I might be, but I don't know. The boys don't believe I was rammed. So they're thinking, a one-car accident, I was probably drink-driving, on drugs. Right now they're waiting for the blood tests to come back.'

'They didn't breathalyse you?'

'I was out for four hours, maybe more. And they'd have needed my permission to go poking around in my mouth.'

'Should I ask if you were under the influence?'

'Ask away. But time's a-wasting.'

She took her time lighting another menthol and didn't offer

one across. I took one anyway, snapped off the filter, beckoned for the Cartier. When she handed it over I knew she was in deep schtuck. Desperate enough, at least, to take a one-eyed desperado into her confidence.

'Finn had a laptop computer,' she said. 'It belongs to Hamilton Holdings. I'd like very much for it to be retrieved.'

'From his apartment?'

She inclined her head.

'What's the catch?' I said.

'There is no catch.'

'On a repo gig, there's always a catch.'

'Perhaps some people are more prone to being caught than others.'

'Yeah, well, I'm one of the happy few.'

'Then it's just as well there is no catch in this particular instance.'

'I take it we're talking the same fee.'

An eyebrow ripped free of its Botox moorings. 'Ten thousand euro? To retrieve a laptop?'

'Sounds a bit excessive, I know, but if we're talking break-and-enter, well, that's illegal. And the cops don't much like my face as it is.'

'You won't be breaking and entering.' She reached into the side pocket of her robe and placed a key-ring on the table. There were two keys attached. 'The apartment also belongs to Hamilton Holdings. Finn just lives there.' She choked down a tiny hedgehog, compressed her lips. 'Lived there.'

'And you can't send Simon because . . .'

'My reasons are my own.'

'The main one being, I'd imagine, that you don't want Maria to know you have Finn's laptop.'

Something Arctic seeped into the Aegean-blue eyes. 'That would be one benefit, yes.'

'So just to clarify. You're not paying me to break in and steal, you're paying me to make it look that way.'

'Correct.'

'Okay. What're the other reasons?'

'They are none of your business, Mr Rigby, and I'll thank you to keep your impertinence in check.'

I grinned. 'Impertinence, Mrs Hamilton, is a fundamental characteristic of the human condition. You should brush up on your Milton.'

Red spots appeared high over her cheekbones. Anger, I was guessing, turning the Botox to lava. 'Ten thousand euro is a substantial sum, Mr Rigby. Will you provide the service required or not?'

'Absolutely, yeah. Once I know I'm not someone's stooge.'

'But if you believe I am trying to manipulate you,' she said tartly, 'then how could I possibly convince you otherwise?'

'A few questions should do it.'

'You're really in no position to—'

'What, interrogate my betters? Sorry, but that lark went out with rack-rents and the slow boat to Van Diemen's Land.'

I couldn't tell if it was the rack-rents or Van Diemen's Land but something cut where it counts. She executed a class of reclining flounce, then went through the old routine of rearranging the silk and lace. 'What questions?' she said.

I struggled up out of the leather recliner and went and sat on the balcony wall, a strategic move designed to occupy the high ground and force her to look up at me as she answered. A bad idea. The surf swirled and swushed around the black rocks far below, spraying up on the little boathouse perched out on the point. A dizzying fall even if you hadn't given blood a couple of hours before, a one-eye perspective skewing your depth of vision.

'First off,' I said, squirming, 'Gillick reckons you knew he was up in the PA with Finn before he jumped. True?'

'Yes.'

'On your behalf?'

'Yes.'

'Why?'

She was still having trouble with my insubordinate attitude. The words came short, clipped and damn near pedicured. 'Mr Gillick was there in his capacity as solicitor for Hamilton Holdings. He was authorised to employ whatever method he felt was appropriate to convince Finn he was making a mistake.'

'Authorised by you.'

'Yes.'

'I thought you said Finn wasn't entitled to sell the PA.'

'He wasn't.'

'So what was his mistake?'

'I think we both know the answer to that, Mr Rigby.'

'Maria.'

She nodded.

'So Gillick was there,' I said, 'to tell Finn dump Maria.'

'Crudely put, but correct.'

'Appropriate method. What does that mean?'

'Exactly what it says.'

'A bribe?'

'It would certainly have been in Finn's interests not to marry that woman.'

'His financial interests.'

'Among others.'

'Such as?'

She looked away and down, to where she was rubbing the lacy hem between her fingers. 'I believe you have a son, Mr Rigby.'

'Go on.'

'No doubt you want the best for him.'

'Sure.'

'Then surely you can appreciate why I felt the same way about Finn.'

'Finn believed Maria was the best thing for him.'

She was shaking her head even before I said her name. 'She wanted to take him away, Mr Rigby. To Cyprus. The north coast of Cyprus, to be precise, a poverty-stricken hell-hole run by Russian gangsters. Where my grandchildren would eventually sink into penury while she squandered Finn's inheritance on her whims and fancies.'

'And the noble Hamilton name goes down the tubes.'

'You betray yourself, Mr Rigby. Reverse snobbery is every bit the vice of its mirror image. And is it really such a crime to hope that your grandchildren might enjoy a superior quality of life?'

'I don't suppose it is. But maybe that's why Finn was bailing out.'

A flash of something lethal in the azure eyes, a bolt from the blue so vicious it damn near toppled me off the wall. Then she glanced away, bowed her head. 'Sit down, please, Mr Rigby. Looking up at you is giving me a pain in the neck.'

I swallowed the quip, settled into the wicker armchair again.

She pointed out across the bay, all the way to Queen Maeve's grave on Knocknerea. Gilded now, shimmering. Not a cloud in the sky. It was going to be another scorcher.

'Do you know your local history, Mr Rigby? I'm asking specifically about Queen Maeve.'

'I've heard of her, yeah.'

'An iron woman. Fierce.'

'Dead, I'm told.'

She nodded. 'Dead this two thousand years and more,' she said, 'and yet here we are, still talking about her.'

She was, anyway. 'And Finn, you're saying, doesn't get it.'

'Finn, as we know, was always prone to overreacting. He had panic attacks as a boy, did you know that?'

'No, I didn't know that. Look, Mrs Hamilton—'

'This is an old country, Mr Rigby. There are passage tombs up on the hills of Carrowkeel and their stones gone mossy long before the pyramids were built. There were Greeks sailing into Sligo Bay when Berlin was still a fetid swamp in some godforsaken forest. Take a detour off our shiny new roads and you'll find yourself in a labyrinth, because no Roman ever laid so much as a foundation brick on this island. Hibernia, they called it.' A wry smile. 'Winterland.'

'Well, the roads run straight enough now.'

'Indeed. Irish tyres hissing slick on the sweat of the German taxpayer, who will tell you that he has paid for every last yard of straight road built here in the last forty years. You know,' she said, 'there have always been those who turned their back on Brussels and Frankfurt, and not everyone who professes to ourselves alone is a Sticky or a Shinner. But I could never understand that. I quite liked the idea that Herr Fritz was spreading around his

Marshall Plan largesse to buy himself some badly needed friends.' She shrugged. Her voice gone dead and cold, as if she spoke from inside a tomb. 'Perhaps I was wrong. Herr Shylock has returned demanding his pound of flesh, and it appears he is charging blood debt rates. Straight roads, certainly, and more suicides in the last year than died in traffic accidents.'

'It won't last,' I said. 'Nothing ever does.'

A hard flash of perfect teeth. 'My point entirely, Mr Rigby. I'm told that the latest from Frankfurt is that our German friends are quietly pleased that the Irish are not Greeks, that we take our medicine with a pat on the head. No strikes, no burning of the bondholders, or actual banks. Apparently they're a little contemptuous, telling one another as they pass the latest Irish budget around the Reichstag for approval that we have been conditioned by eight hundred years of oppression to perfect that very Irish sleight of hand, to tug the forelock even as we hold out the begging bowl.

'They are children, Mr Rigby, our German friends. Conditioned themselves, since Charlemagne, to believe want and need are the same instinct. Hardwired to *blitzkrieg* and overreach, to forget the long game, the hard lessons of harsh winters bogged down in foreign lands.' Tremulous now. Not the first time she'd delivered this speech. 'The Romans were no fools. Strangers come here to wither and die. Celt, Dane, Norman and English, they charged ashore waving their axes and swords and we gave up our blood and took the best they have, and when they sank into our bogs we burned them for heat and carved our stories from their smoke and words.'

I got the message. Big Bob was long gone and Finn couldn't take the heat. But Saoirse Hamilton was still foursquare at the furnace, smelting away, an Iron Queen beating ploughshares back into swords.

'I blame myself, Mr Rigby, for allowing Finn to lead something of a sheltered existence. As a result his understanding of life's requirements weren't always rooted, shall we say, in practical concerns.'

'No nose for the long game.'

'That is one way of putting it.'

'And soft enough to let Maria scam him.'

'I have always believed so, yes. And what you told me about this ridiculous notion of building a property empire in Northern Cyprus only confirmed my suspicions.'

'For what it's worth,' I said, 'Maria's no con artist.'

A faint, ghastly smile. 'A moot point now, wouldn't you say?'

'I might, yeah, if you weren't offering me ten grand to rip off Finn's laptop. What're you worried about?'

'I don't understand.'

'I'm asking,' I said, 'what it is you want from the laptop.'

'I want his computer, Mr Rigby. That is what I am paying you for and all you need to know.'

'Not good enough.' I flipped the More out into the void and stood up, watching the tiny orange ember whirl down towards the waves. 'You'll be needing someone else.'

But I made no effort to leave. We stared one another down, both knowing she had no other option.

'You haven't already realised?' she said eventually.

'Obviously not.'

'Think, Mr Rigby. Who gains from Finn's death?'

'Seeing as how he jumped, I'd have to say Finn.'

She brushed that one aside. 'You have no way of knowing this, but Finn had a comprehensive life assurance policy.'

'Which'd pay out on suicide so long as it was in place more than two years before he jumped. Except that puts you in the frame, as his next-of-kin. Finn and Maria weren't even engaged.'

'In theory,' she nodded, 'yes. But there is the not insignificant matter of Finn's will.'

'Of course. The will.'

The cobalt skewers glittered. She flung the coffee bowl aside, shattering it against the near wall. I really didn't know what Saoirse Hamilton's problem was with Finn marrying Maria. She'd have had a whale of a time at a Cypriot wedding.

I settled back on the balcony wall, folded my hands in my lap. 'So,' I said, 'the will.'

She composed herself by smearing some coffee stains into the silk. Then, low, she said, 'I have very good reason to believe that that tramp was being unfaithful to my son, Mr Rigby. And I'll be damned if I'll allow her to benefit from his naivety.'

'I don't know where you're getting this idea that Maria was—'

'If I find a single reference to an infidelity on his computer, even the vaguest hint, then I will deploy every resource I possess to have her charged with contributing to my son's death. Are you satisfied?'

'You'll need a better lawyer than Gillick to make that one stick. I mean, even if you were to plant something on the laptop . . .' I shrugged. 'Not that I'm suggesting that the thought had occurred.'

'In that case,' she said, 'I will be forced to explore other avenues.'

The threat was there. She was obviously distraught and lashing out, but even so I made a mental note to tip off Maria.

'So that's it,' I said. 'Swipe his laptop and mess the place up, make it look like a break-in.'

She inclined her head. 'Naturally, while you are at the apartment, I would like you to see if you can locate his suicide note.' Fainter now. 'If it exists.'

'Without, presumably, checking the laptop for one.'

'Correct.'

'And we're saying, ten grand the lot.'

'There is one other item.'

'The will, sure.'

She turned the Aegean blue up full blast. 'A gun, Mr Rigby. It belonged to Finn's father. Finn stole it when he left home. I would like it returned.'

For some reason I thought of Hemingway, how his mother had sent him the gun his father had used to kill himself. It seemed appropriately perverse, in that brooding museum of a home, that a weapon should be considered a sentimental token.

'What kind of gun?'

'There will be only one.' An acid bite to her tone. 'Finn wasn't in the habit of collecting firearms.'

'The reason I ask is, if it's a .22 for shooting crows or some shit, then fine, it's probably licensed. Otherwise, and presuming I find it, I'd be carrying an illegal gun. Bit of a nightmare, that, if I got run off the road again.'

'It is not licensed.'

'Then no dice.'

'I will double your fee.'

'Twenty grand?'

A nod.

'Deal.' She made no effort to shake on it. I swiped another

More, sparked it up. 'Anything else you need? Some plutonium he has stashed away? A Chinese takeaway on my way back?'

She waved me off as if swatting flies.

Saturday

26

There was a time when twenty grand was a lot of money. Used to be, you went along to a play called *Twenty Grand*, you could be pretty sure it was about something more than the stamp duty someone was paying on an upmarket kennel.

She was desperate, sure.

But still, twenty grand, cash. Just like that.

Way too easy.

I plodded down the staircase to the gloomy great hall with that nape-tickling sensation of being watched. Eyes everywhere. Hardly a blank space on any wall. Dead eyes, unseeing, no more than swirls of oil, but I felt disembodied under their pitiless gaze, a soul descending into Hades through malign vapours, not only watched but judged as well. I half-expected Simon to materialise out of the shadows with a thickly muttered threat against double-crossing the Iron Queen, but he didn't show. Maybe he was too busy manning a phone somewhere, hoping I'd make another call. Or out on the balcony squirting oil into her joints.

Outside it was already warm, a fresh new day. I patted my pockets as I crossed to the Sierra, just to be sure I hadn't missed a message from Dee, then remembered Tohill had taken my phone. I sat into the Sierra and got it sparked, giving it more rev than it needed and sorely tempted, as I reversed back to the Hamilton fleet of cars, to plough on, do some damage. A harsh crunch of gravel as I skidded to a stop, and then I punched into first and took off, wheels spitting stone. For a split second I was blinded, jamming on as the dazzle of the rising sun caught the rear-view mirror, and then I realised where the violent impulse was coming from.

Bell jars away . . .

I'd been here before, at this time, the sun coming up. There'd been a marquee pitched on the front lawn then, the once perfect lawn that by dawn had been strewn with streamers and confetti, crushed paper plates and broken glass, a prone body or two. The night of Paul and Andrea's wedding, the next morning if we're keeping score, Paul bliftered to the point where he'd almost forgotten he needed a cane. Finn being best man, he'd hosted the reception under canvas in the sheltered dell in front of The Grange, although by then those still standing, most of them the hardcore surf crew, were straggling towards the woods and the path that led down to the little cove below the house. Paul out in front in white tails, waving a bottle of Chateau de Piss '95.

Fun and games to come. Finn's gift to Paul.

What a waste. All that energy and grace, gone. Snuffed out in the time it takes to plummet nine floors.

And all the while a little boy lay still in a hospital bed, dead to the world, his own body conspiring to shut him away in order to preserve the bare minimum of life.

I got out of the Sierra and tossed away the More, crossed the gravel to the woods, falling in again with Finn's cabal as they wound down through the woods, tripping on bare roots, stumbling and staggering, the expectant air an electric current on the salty breeze. The pants of Paul's tux sandy at the cuffs as he shuffled barefoot across the rock outcrop overlooking the cove and its tiny jetty, the fingernail of sandy beach, the boathouse that had been carved from the base of the cliff. High tide, the sea snapping at rocks bared in a snarl.

Showtime.

They settled in to wait, some rolling spliffs, others spreading blankets and pouring the last of the champagne. Paul scanning the rocks above, then rearing back stiffly from the waist, pointing his cane at a spot about twenty or thirty feet below the balcony that crowned the half-pipe of ragged cliff.

'Cometh the hour,' he declared.

Heads swivelled to follow Paul's wavering cane. Most of them, more used to beaches by day than at dawn, instinctively shaded their eyes as they glanced up, so that it looked like they were engaged in a mass salute. Finn was spotted, awkwardly perched like some wing-broke hawk, hunched beneath an overhang with one knee bent up into his chest, the other leg trailing.

Behind me, horrified, a woman asked in a stage whisper if Finn was going to like actually *jump*?

'No,' Paul said without taking his eyes off Finn, 'he's going to dive.'

Andrea the only one not watching. She sat her with her back to the cliff, staring out to sea and the flickering whitecaps. In her retro-mini '60s wedding dress, sitting on the edge of the outcrop, she wasn't unlike a whitecap herself. Thinking about marrying a twenty-nine-year-old who needed a cane, maybe, who wore a neck-and-back brace in the shower, a drummer who still sat behind his kit even if his drumming was now reduced to pressing buttons on a laptop, manipulating the pre-programmed rhythms.

A low chant began. 'Finn-Finn-Finn-*Finn*.'

Hands clapping, feet pounding sand. The rhythm funnelling up the half-pipe cliff.

Maria looked across at me, rolled her eyes. 'Christ,' she drawled, 'it's not like he needs the fucking encouragement.'

But they adored him. They adored him because they wanted to be adored themselves, and had they been Finn they'd have expected no less.

Citius, Altius, Fortius: Finn Hamilton was a one-man Olympics, and for all their gnarly argot they understood, consciously or otherwise, that he was a throwback to the ancient games, the man who becomes a demigod, semi-divine, by dint of his superhuman feats, and in their chanting, their witnessing, they celebrated his courage, endurance and daring.

They knew nothing.

Had he been a lightning bolt Finn couldn't have been less interested in their praise, the champagne toasts, the backslapping. His was an instinctive philosophy, generated by a mind perversely wired to self-destruct, a brain marinated in a chemical soup long ago soured and poisoned by misfiring synapses.

They knew his history, of course. The switchback moods, the arson, the rubber rooms. Paul, when called upon, could recite from memory Finn's A&E rap sheet of broken bones and concussions, a twice-fractured skull, a detached retina. Awed tones when they spoke of the cruelly irrepressible energy that crackled in his veins as it burnt off caution and fear, driving him up the sheer cliffs, down the blackest runs.

They knew nothing.

What Paul thought he knew, and was anxious now that everyone else should know, this particular offering being in his honour, was that Finn wasn't just another overgrown kid with an ego deficit. That jumping off a cliff into the rock-fringed surge below wasn't simply the dumb bravado of an early mid-life crisis, and nor was it Finn's perverse take on tossing the bouquet. In fact it was a ritual, Paul claimed, an ancient, ageless testing.

He rather spoiled the rococo tone by pausing to take a toke. 'Behold the man,' he exhaled, squinting through the haze, 'pitting himself against the fundamental elements.' A few croaky cheers, not all of them ironic. 'Pitting himself against the void itself, the triumph of life and time snatched from the very jaws of, of . . .' He'd faltered then, frowning as he tried to recall the specifics of Finn's best man speech, when he'd lauded Paul with the very same words. His shoulder stiffened, which was as much of a shrug as Paul could muster, then he swigged from the neck of the Chateau de Piss in his other hand. 'Anyway,' he mumbled, 'it's all good,' and then inclined his head, bowing to accept the good-natured raspberries and boos, pounding his cane on the rock to start the foot-stamp drumming again.

He was wrong, of course, but then Paul was the kind who was nearly always wrong, stumbling along through life piecing together answers from second- and third-hand information and choosing the wrong option every time and never realising it until it was too late, if at all. Christ, the guy was a drummer.

Finn wasn't just another endorphin junkie. His was a compulsion that scorched the wings of any adrenaline addict unthinking enough to flutter too close to his flame. He was textbook Freud, the unsettled soul shattered by too harsh a light and ceaselessly beating back towards some shadowed peace.

One time I asked Paul why he still hung around when he couldn't surf anymore, couldn't drum. How he could stick the sight of Finn.

His shoulder stiffened. 'When you're in,' he'd said, 'you're in.'

I couldn't fault him on that.

From above, faint but clear, came Finn's cry.

Bell Jars awaaaaaaay . . .

The drumming ceased. The chanting shushed.

A nervous giggle. Surf washing on sand.

Finn rose from his crouch. For the longest moment he hung poised on the ledge, cruciform, face raised to the rising sun.

Then he pushed off, arms arrowing, and sliced into the light.

27

She was waiting for me in the woods. Sitting on the trunk of a fallen tree, smoking, facing out over the little cove below. Dressed for mourning this time, black T-shirt, black denims. At first I thought she'd been beaten up, but a closer look revealed a make up job of shaded purples and thick kohl.

'Hey,' she said.

'Hey,' I said, not stopping to discover which Carmen she was today, the vicious Miss Sternwood or the gypsy lover driven to operatic hysterics by unrequited arias.

She dropped the cigarette and ground it out, hurried to keep up. 'Wait,' she said. 'I owe you an apology.'

'Don't worry about it,' I said. I was a half-stride ahead, staying out of range of her nails, which weren't any shorter than when she'd raked me in the hall. 'You were in shock, bombed on pills, you didn't know what you were—'

'Not *that*.'

'Oh.'

'I was listening in on the phone,' she said. 'Before, when you were talking to your wife about your son.'

'She's not my wife.'

'Well, I hope he'll be okay.'

'Thanks, yeah.'

'So what does she want?'

'Ben to get well. What d'you think?'

She put on a spurt as we reached the fringe of the woods, placed a hand on my arm, tugged on it. I stopped, took a step back.

'You know who I mean,' she said.

She'd given the nails about four coats of black varnish. I prised her hand free as gently as I could. 'If it's your mother you're asking about, then that's between her and me. Client confidentiality. Sorry.'

Which wasn't strictly true, there being no ethical contract existing between a B&E man and the person who commissions them to steal. Unless it's good old-fashioned honour among thieves.

'But it's to do with Finn, right?'

'Sorry, I can't say.'

It was still gloomy beneath the trees but even so her eyes were a delicate faience-blue. She tried to bat the eyelashes but there was too much gunk plastered on. 'Can't or won't?' she said.

'Same difference, really.'

I walked on down into the grassy dell, across the gravel to the Sierra. She caught up as I opened the driver's door, put a hand on it.

'This is stolen,' she said. 'Am I right?'

'You're better off not knowing.'

A sickly smile. 'Have you any idea,' she said, 'how often I've heard that in the last two days?'

'None. Now take your hand off the—'

'You could probably do with a car the cops won't be looking for,' she said. 'Sounds like you need a phone, too.'

'Trust me, you don't want to get involved.'

'Finn's dead,' she said. 'How can I not be involved?'

'That's not what I meant.' I was acutely aware that we were having the conversation in full view of about twenty windows, from any of which a pair of eyes could be watching. 'What I'm saying is, I have a job to do. And I don't need any—'

'I can help.'

'I doubt that very much.'

'I can.'

'You don't even know what the—'

'She wants the laptop,' she said. 'And the gun.'

*

We agreed that she should do her very best to slap my face without drawing blood, this for the benefit of any watching eyes, and then storm over to her Mini Cooper and drive off, and that I would shrug and get in the Sierra and follow at a more sedate pace, and that we would rendezvous at the gates of The Grange. And so I shrugged and watched her go, a hand to my poor abused cheek, and got into the Sierra, and followed her down the driveway.

At the gates I pulled up beside her and indicated that she should wind down her window, the Sierra's being already busted and needing no winding in either direction, and told her to follow me.

Out to the main road and straight across, up the back road to Ballintrillick that winds around the rear of Benbulben. Half a mile or so up the road I branched off onto a narrow track and pulled in at the first bog cutting. I told her to get turned and face back down the mountain, borrowed her cigarette lighter. Knotted together six tissues from the box of Kleenex in the footwell of the Sierra's passenger side, unscrewed the petrol cap, got the tissues nicely soaked.

Two minutes later we were on our way again, the Sierra blazing merrily. The sun cleared the mountain as we reached the main road, spangling the landscape a luminous gold.

It was another beautiful Sligo morning, another glorious fucking day.

*

Grainne favoured Marlboro Lights. I snapped the filter and sucked on some poison that didn't taste of mint. 'Tell me about the gun,' I said.

'You first.'

'I don't know anything about it.'

'Not the gun. Finn.'

'What about him?'

'Finn's dead,' she said. She sounded solemn but then came a half-gulp and it all rushed out in a sulky wail. 'My only brother's dead and something's going on and no one will tell me *any*thing.'

'Maybe there's nothing to tell.'

'Oh come *on*,' she said. 'I'm not a fucking child.'

I couldn't contradict her there. She had her mother's genes and they were brewing up nicely, swelling to plateaus in all the appropriate places. But it was in the eyes you saw it best, the eyes that didn't film with tears despite the tremulous voice. Her mother's eyes, pellucid and skewering.

'What do you think is going on?' I said. A shrink's gambit.

'I don't *know*. It's like . . .' She paused. 'You were at the PA,' she said. 'Right? Thursday night.'

'Yeah, I was.'

'And you saw it happen.'

'Correct.'

'That's why you came out to the house, to tell my mother.'

'Sure. I thought it'd be better that way. Rather than—'

'But you actually saw him jump, right?'

'I did, yeah.'

'Did he say anything?'

About her, she meant. For all that she was trying to play the sullen ingénue, she sounded as plaintive as a woman querying the salt content of the ocean in which she was drowning.

'He said lots of things. If you're asking if he said anything about you specifically, then no. Same goes for wanting to end it all. He was in pretty good form.'

'So why did he jump?'

'I don't know.' I'd always wondered what the number umpteen felt like. Maybe I needed to get *I Don't Know* tattooed to my forehead. 'My best guess is he cracked under the pressure.'

'Pressure?'

'Well, your mother doesn't seem to be very fond of Maria.'

She hooted at that, loud and harsh. 'You mentioned Maria's name?'

'A few times, yeah.'

'Did she call her a trollop?'

'Let's just say there were variations on a theme.'

'She called her the Whore of Babylon once.'

'Nice, yeah. Biblical.'

She adjusted her visor as we rolled down into Drumcliffe, the sun streaming in. 'Problem there is,' she said, 'that was always a bonus for Finn. Anything that pissed off Saoirse was good with him.'

'If you say so.'

'I *do* say so.'

'Good for you.'

'So if it wasn't the pressure, why did he jump?'

'I haven't the foggiest clue.' I stole another Marlboro Light, got it lit. 'If it's any consolation,' I said, 'the cops don't believe he jumped. They think he was pushed.'

'Pushed?'

'Yeah, but don't get your hopes up. They think it was me pushed him.'

I was glad I'd stolen the smoke before breaking that one. A chill settled between us. 'Why would they think that?'

'Because I was there and they can't think of any reason why he'd want to jump. And before you start thinking like a cop too, I should point out that Finn'd have taken me with him if I'd been sitting in the cab when he landed on it.'

'I didn't know he . . .' She swallowed hard.

'Well, he did.' It was the first time I'd said it out loud, one of those moments when you realise you've been thinking something a long time and not really known you were thinking it. *I should be dead.*

I felt the crash coming on hard, this on top of damn all sleep and too much coffee, the concussion and the shock, and Ben,

238

Christ, Ben in a coma. I laughed out loud, heard it thin and shivery. 'It's kind of weird, y'know? Like drowning witches in a pond. If I'd been in the cab, I'd be in the clear but dead. Except I wasn't, so now I'm in the frame. Jesus,' I said, 'I never thought I'd need an alibi for someone's suicide.'

She flinched, then glared across. 'You're a horrible human being.'

'Keep your eyes on the road.'

'Why would you even say such a thing?'

'Because you're asking all these bullshit questions so you won't have to face the fact that Finn's dead and gone and didn't care enough about anyone to say goodbye before he went.'

I guess that one made us even. It wasn't exactly a slap in the face, but she recoiled, her colour draining away, and then she flushed. I edged towards the door in case she reached and raked, but when she took a hand from the steering wheel it was to cup her mouth, perhaps to catch the single precious whimper that emerged.

'Grainne,' I said. I tried to soften my tone but it came out like a frog gargling gravel. 'In the long run, it's better if you deal with it sooner rather than later. Trust me.'

Her eyes were wet, hard and bright. For some reason I thought of Fiver in *Watership Down*. Then she ruined it with a sneer. 'Oh yeah? Your only brother committed suicide?'

It wasn't just the eyes. She had her mother's way with the hired help, too.

'Not exactly,' I said. 'I killed him.'

That bought me a nifty goldfish impression. 'You . . . ?'

'Killed him. And watch the fucking road before you kill the rest of us.'

'But why would you . . . ?'

'Doesn't matter. What matters is I buried it when I should have been purging and now it's too late. So my advice to you is to take yourself off to a dark room and have a good long think about how Finn's gone. And I mean, forever. You know how you were hoping he'd be the one to link you up the aisle the day you get married? It'll never happen now.'

'Jesus,' she whispered, 'why are you saying these—'

'Because it's *his* fault it'll never happen. Stop blaming yourself, start blaming him. Otherwise you'll go daft.'

'But—'

'But nothing. Maybe, okay, he had his reasons. But whatever they were, they had nothing to do with you. So let it go, cry him into the ground, move on.'

'You're a cold fucking bastard.'

'Yeah, well, someone has to be.'

We were on the long straight into town now, passing Bertie's Pitch & Putt, which was just as well, because she jammed on and swerved onto the hard shoulder without so much as a glance in the rear-view. I reached over, knocked on the hazard lights. She sat with her shoulders hunched, knuckles white on the steering wheel, staring straight ahead without seeing much of anything at all. Not so much Fiver, now. More Bigwig. Or Woundwort, maybe.

I did a quick tally of the pros and cons of swiping another couple of Marlboros, decided against. Reached for the door handle.

'Don't get out,' she said, still staring ahead, the words softly desperate, an old monk's prayer.

'Grainne . . .'

'He didn't *do* it. He didn't jump.'

'If that's the way you need to—'

'Just listen a second,' she said quietly. 'Listen, okay?' And then the rocket fuel sparked in the back of her mind and she punched the steering wheel and suddenly she was screaming at the windscreen. 'All I want is someone to fucking listen to me for *once!*'

I got the message.

In behind the pellucid eyes and layers of kohl and Arctic cool, the grief and the rage, Grainne Hamilton was very badly scared.

28

All the Hamilton women wanted me to read their personal correspondence. Maybe it was my manly baritone and sensitive poet's eyes. Or maybe they were congenitally illiterate.

'There,' she said, handing across her iPhone.

Finn had set her up with the email address years ago, when she first went off to Kylemore Abbey Boarding School for Girls, so Grainne could bitch without worrying about Saoirse sneaking a peek. The mail I was looking at had the subject header, *To Be or Not*.

'Shakespeare,' she said.

'Sure.'

'As in, *Will* Shakespeare.'

'Ah.' I scrolled down to the body text, said, 'Listen, we probably shouldn't be parked on the side of the road. Looks odd.'

She drove like she walked, hunched forward ever so slightly around the shoulders, as if hunted, but for so long that it'd become a part of who she was.

A Gra, the email began, which was a cute touch, *Gra* being short for Grainne and the Irish for 'my love'.

Quick one, just to let you know I've had to make changes to the TF. Can't say too much now but you'll understand – just didn't want to do it without keeping you in the loop. ALL WILL BE REVEALED (LOL!). Seriously, you'll love it when it all falls out – the Dragon will roast Gillick. God, I'd love to be there for that. Take pictures. Kodak moments!

Anyway, the update is lodged with Cenk Mehmet, 7C Mustafa Çağatay Cad., Girne (number below). And do me a solid – don't mention this to Maria, not until you get the green light. Okay? I'll take that as a promise . . .
Chat soon,
Love 'n' hugs,
F

I scrolled on down, but apart from the attachment, that was it. We were up on Hughes Bridge by then, the traffic building even at that early hour, Grainne edging along in first gear, her slim fingers a-tremble where they rested on the gear-stick. I put the phone down on the pile of CDs stacked behind the seats and claimed another Marlboro as my consultancy fee.

'Well?' she said.

'Well what?'

'Why would he write that?'

'I'm guessing he wanted you to know he changed the TF. Like it says.'

She puffed out her cheeks. 'What I'm asking,' she said none too patiently, 'is why he'd *want* to change it. Unless, y'know . . .'

'Go on.'

'Unless he knew something was going to happen. Or thought it might.'

'Something like what?'

'*I* don't know.'

My stomach grumbled. 'I don't suppose there's anything I could eat?'

'Eat?'

I told her I couldn't remember the last time I'd eaten, and thought longingly about the tea and toast I'd been promised in the hospital but which hadn't arrived before I bolted for the emergency exit, making a mental note to write a letter to the *Irish Times* about the disgraceful state of the Irish health service. She gave a harsh kind of sigh but she rummaged around in the driver's door pocket and came up with half a pack of Polo Mints. A thin ring of mint around a big fat nothing. The cosmos, I presumed, up to its old tricks. I'd have been better off eating the paper and foil wrapping.

'This TF,' I said around three mints tucked into my cheek. 'That's a trust fund, right?'

She nodded.

'And you think Finn was pushed, or was pushed into jumping, because he changed this trust fund, or was trying to. And because you're the beneficiary, you're next for the old heave-ho. How am I doing so far?'

She stared straight ahead, chewing on her lower lip. Another nod.

'I wouldn't worry about it,' I said.

'You don't know Saoirse.'

'True enough. Let me put it this way. How much is the trust fund worth?'

'I've no idea.'

'Probably not north of half a million, though.'

'Half a *million*?'

'Look, I don't know what your mother tells you about her finances, but between you and me, she's struggling. Finn reckoned NAMA has everything, and the only reason she still has The Grange is that someone, probably Gillick, had the wit to sign it over to your mother personally before the hammer came down.'

'But that can't be.'

'Well, it is. Why d'you think Finn was bailing out?'

'Bailing . . .'

'He didn't tell you?' She shook her head, her eyes searching mine. 'Finn was leaving, Grainne. Moving to Cyprus. Setting up his own company, marrying Maria. He had an apartment complex development all planned as her wedding present.' I wasn't slapping her face anymore, I was stabbing her in the back. 'I'm guessing he never mentioned that.'

'No.'

'Well buckle up, because here's where it gets complicated. Finn reckoned he was selling the PA building to Gillick to pay for the Cyprus development. Your mother says that's impossible, because the PA wasn't in Finn's name, although my guess is that it's because NAMA owns it now. Anyway, she says the reason Gillick was with Finn that night, with her blessing, was to persuade him to kick Maria to touch.'

'He wouldn't do that.'

'We'll never know now, will we? Anyway,' I gestured at the iPhone, 'I'm guessing Finn was bullshitting Gillick about buying the PA building back from NAMA, at a rock-bottom price, telling him he'd need to kick some seed capital loose from the trust fund to do it. Except Finn had this development in Cyprus lined up.'

A gap opened on our left. She indicated and slipped into it, got off the bridge, drove in along Markievicz Road. 'He could have told me,' she said dully.

'He did. He sent you the email.'

'About Maria. Moving to Cyprus.'

'I'm sure he would have, once the time was right. It was supposed to be a big surprise for Maria.'

She followed the one-way system until we were on Connaughton Road, the hospital just visible over the crest of the hill. I closed my eyes and pictured Ben prone in his bed and heard a kind of gulping laugh. I looked across at her. 'Christ,' she said, 'I'd have loved to have seen her face.' Defiant now, despite the tears on her cheeks.

'It wasn't pretty.'

She made the right turn down Lake Isle Road, heading for Thomas Street. 'She *knows*?'

'Yeah.'

'But how . . . ?'

'I told her.'

'Why the fuck would you tell her?'

'She asked.'

'And you betrayed his confidence. Just like that.'

'It wasn't that simple.'

'She *paid* you, Harry. It's not exactly rocket science.'

'She hasn't paid me a penny. And if you want the truth of it, it was Finn's fault. He lied to me, told me he was selling the PA. Your mother said there was no way he could do that. Things kind of moved on from there.'

'To where, exactly?'

I took a last drag on the Marlboro, popped it out the window. Got settled in the seat. I sympathised with her, I really did, but I couldn't muster the strength to play along. It's all black and white when you're a teenager, all rights and wrongs, us and them. Takes a lot of excess energy to sustain that quality of idealism, or naivety, or stupidity, and I was just about wiped out, a long and fraught day to come.

'If your mother wants you to know,' I said, 'she'll tell you.'

A deft little snort. 'Saoirse likes it when I don't know anything.'

'I'm sure she has your best interests at heart.'

'Like she had Finn's?'

'Maybe she thought she did.'

'She had a funny way of showing it.'

You're funny when you try to be funny, dad . . .

We came off the bridge and turned left onto Kennedy Parade, out along the river.

'Tell me about the gun,' I said.

'You're so smart,' she said, 'you know everything, you tell *me* about the gun.'

We'd arrived at what they call an impasse and I was too tired to care about trying to get around it. We drove the next minute or so in silence until she pulled in at the gates of Weir's Folly, zapped the gates. They sounded a dull *thung* as they jerked open, and she nosed into the half-empty car park. I had a good look around while she found a space close to the waterfront, a view clear up the river to the lake beyond, but all the cars were empty, no shady types peering from behind upside-down newspapers. No reason there should be. If I'd been Tohill, and staking out Finn's apartment, I'd be inside with a good cup of coffee and the sports pages, waiting for fly Harry Rigby to step into my parlour.

I opened the car door and Grainne said, 'The gun was my father's. Finn took it with him when he left home, a kind of memento.' She fumbled a couple of smokes from the pack, passed one across. I snapped the filter, took the light she offered. 'I think it was supposed to be some kind of warning,' she said. 'Y'know, *Don't follow me*, some shit like that. Finn wouldn't talk about it.'

'And this is when they became estranged.'

'Estranged?'

'That's the word your mother used.'

She shook her head. 'That's just the way we are, Harry. Or were, anyway. We'd blow up, there'd be a massive row, then ten minutes later it was like it never happened.'

'So what changed?'

'Maria. Saoirse won't even allow her name be said in the house. Says she's a tramp whore slut.' She rolled her eyes.

'You like her, though.'

She shrugged. 'She can be a bit up herself sometimes, a bit high maintenance, but yeah, she's okay.' She took a hit off the Marlboro, stared off up the river. 'She was good for Finn, and that was good enough for me. I mean, you know him, right? Finn was a total flake before Maria came along. Don't get me wrong, he was a pretty cool big brother, he'd let me stay over some nights when I was home on holidays, we'd drink beers, smoke a joint.' She had a good long look at her reflection in the black polish of her thumbnail. 'But it was like every night I stayed, there'd be a different girl. One night I got in and the girl got up and left straightaway and when I asked who she was, he couldn't remember her name. He made a joke of it, but I'm pretty sure she was a prostitute. Jesus,' she said, a bitter half-smile, 'I'd love to see Saoirse's face if I told her *that*.'

'She'd probably cope,' I said, 'seeing as she reckoned Maria was screwing Finn for his money.'

Her lips thinned. 'That's just Saoirse,' she said. 'With her, it's *all* about money. No one does anything for any other reason.'

I was sitting in a car park delaying a commissioned B&E to nab a gun and a laptop, so I stared wistfully up at the high moral ground and kept my trap shut.

'I just wish she'd seen them together,' Grainne said. 'Last time I stayed over, the Easter break, we had a hoot trying to come up with Irish-Cypriot names for their kids.'

'I think that was the issue,' I said. 'Your mother was worried Maria was taking him away.'

'To Cyprus? It's four fucking *hours* away.'

Flying time, sure. Ten if you factor in the security checks. I crushed the smoke, *tempus fugit*ing onwards. 'Listen,' I said, 'I don't suppose you know what this gun looks like?'

'Small,' she said. 'Heavy.'

'He showed you it?'

She shrugged. 'He leaves it lying around.'

'Seriously?'

'Phil's messy. You'll see.'

'There's messy,' I said, noting the present tense, 'and there's leaving a gun lying around.'

She wrinkled her nose. 'It'll be right there,' she said, deadpan, 'in the bottom drawer of the filing cabinet in his office.'

'In plain sight.'

'Sometimes I have X-ray vision.'

'Did he keep the drawer locked?'

'Of course.'

'But he left the key where it could be found.'

She nodded. 'Taped behind the U-bend under the kitchen sink.'

'That's careless.'

An impish grin. 'Isn't it, though?'

I opened the door, said, 'Who's Phil?'

She flushed. 'Pardon?'

'Phil. You just said, "Phil's messy".'

'Did I?'

'You did.'

'Well, I meant Finn. Obviously.'

'Obviously. An easy mistake to make, confusing the name of your dead brother.'

I waited. She stared straight ahead, apparently entranced by the sight of Lough Gill glistering beyond the burger wrappers trapped against the chain-link fence. When she realised I wasn't going anywhere, she looked across at me, conceding.

'His real name is Philip. When he was adopted, Saoirse changed his name to Finn. She reckoned Philip sounded too English.' She shrugged. 'So I call him Phil when we're on our own.'

Still with the present tense. 'I never knew he was adopted.'

'No?' Another shrug. 'We both are. They couldn't have kids, there was some issue with conceiving. Saoirse never wanted to get into the details.'

'That's a pity.'

She bridled. 'Why?'

'I don't know. For them? Sorry. A stupid thing to say.'

It made sense of a few things, though. Maybe it meant the

passport issued under the name of Philip Winston Byrne wasn't a fake, for one. And maybe, if you're built a certain way, it's easier to feel estranged from an adopted child than from your own flesh and blood. But it still didn't explain why Finn had stashed the passport in the cistern, five grand tucked inside.

'Okay,' I said, 'you stay here. I'll go up and—'

'No *way*.' She opened the car door. I leaned across and grabbed her forearm with my right hand, pulled her back into the seat. She looked down at my hand, outraged. Which was ideal, because it meant she wasn't watching what I was doing with my left.

'Maria *needs* me,' she said. 'I've been ringing and ringing and she hasn't picked up. She must be—'

'Gone.'

'Gone? Gone where?'

'I don't know. Back to Dublin. Cyprus, maybe.'

'But why would she . . . ?'

'Why'd Finn send you an email? How come he didn't just call, or arrange to meet so he could tell you about the trust fund himself?'

'*I* don't know. Why?'

'I found a passport in his studio, Grainne. Hidden in the toilet cistern, five thousand euro inside.'

'So?'

'So it was a fake passport. Put that with the email, the trust fund being changed with a lawyer in Cyprus, and I'm guessing he was planning to duck out. Before anyone copped to the changes.'

'And Maria?'

'He'd hardly have left without her, would he? If it was me, I'd have sent her on ahead.'

'But, but . . .' In her confusion she sounded like a small out-board engine. 'If that's what he was planning, why would he . . . ?'

'I haven't a clue. If you come up with a solid theory, be sure to tell the cops.' I got out of the car, hunkered down. 'You have the apartment's phone number, right?' She nodded, still dazed and processing the new information. 'Good stuff. You keep sketch. If anyone shows up looking a bit shifty, ring twice and then hang up.'

I stood up. 'Harry,' she said. She sounded far away.

I leaned in. 'What?'

'I'll pay you,' she said. 'Whatever she's paying you to steal the laptop, I'll pay it.'

'Done deal. You have twenty grand cash handy, right?'

That got her focused again. 'Twenty *grand*?'

'Anyway, your mother wants me to try and find Finn's suicide note. There's a chance that'll be on the laptop.'

Her chin up-jutted. 'Maybe it will,' she said. 'And maybe if she was more worried about how Finn felt when he was alive she wouldn't need to read any suicide notes now.'

'I'd say what your mother needs right now is comfort. From her daughter, say.'

'Mother doesn't need people. People are just something else you buy.'

'Like you just tried to buy me?'

She'd been poised ever since I'd pulled her back into the car. Now she struck, already gouging, but by then I'd slammed the door closed, so the black-polished nails made a rattling sound on the glass. I waggled a finger at her, then dangled the car keys, pushed the button that central-locked the doors. Then, ignoring the muffled screams and thumps, I hauled my weary bones towards the apartment block. Across the river, high on the hill above the tree-line, the hospital blazed as the early sun set its glass frontage aflame.

I wondered if Dee's parents had arrived yet, and hoped they had. The vitriol bandied about when my name was mentioned might distract her from Ben's condition, even for a minute or two.

The stab in my gut answered one question, at least.

No, it wouldn't be any easier to become estranged from an adopted child.

Love, whatever the hell it might be, and wherever the hell it comes from, has nothing to do with flesh or blood.

29

Once upon a time Weir's Folly had been pretty well secured. You needed a zapper to get past the car park gates, and tap a four-digit code into the pad beside the lobby doors to access the building itself. Once inside, getting to the lifts meant passing a booth manned by a concierge who doubled as a security guard, who'd ring ahead just to be sure you were expected.

These days, with the recession in full slump and burglaries on the up, they'd cut back on administration fees by letting the security guard go. Perverse, but there it is.

I went on up to the penthouse floor, which had its own lobby, bare but for a potted bamboo standing in one corner, its leaves crisp and turning brown. Not a good look for prospective customers, given that the penthouse suite was also home to Fine Arte Investments, but then, when business gets sluggish up at the high end of the market, the potted plants are always first to feel the pinch.

The alarm didn't go off when I stepped inside, which suggested someone was home, a fact more or less confirmed by the sound of a humming shower, its splashes echoing down the narrow hall. Finn had split the penthouse into business and home, the hallway opening into a living room converted to a spacious reception area that had the feel of a gallery, with examples of Fine Arte's wares, or reproductions of same, dotting the walls. The far wall was floor-length windows, or would have been had the curtains been drawn back. In the corner was a closed door on which was a small black plaque with the legend 'Finn Hamilton, Fine Arte Investment' embossed in gold.

I crossed the reception area into another hallway, paused outside the bathroom door. The shower hummed merrily on but the showeree wasn't in any mood for singing. Beyond that hallway was a living room proper, strewn with cardboard pizza boxes, foil cartons, empty bottles. Wine, mostly. The curtains were drawn there too and the light had that gritty quality that coagulates when darkness is allowed fester.

I stepped into the kitchen expecting to find unscraped plates stacked in the sink but here everything was pretty much in order except for the nine or ten wine glasses lined up atop the dishwasher, each one of them stained purple. Maria favoured a fruity red. Even the bin under the sink was tidy. I reached past it, found the U-bend, the key taped behind. Thus armed, I crossed the living room again, the shower still humming, past the master bedroom and into Finn's study. A scuffed roll-top desk under the window, a filing cabinet behind the door. In the corner stood a recession-proof spiky palm, and diagonally opposite that a slender lava lamp mocked up to resemble a Joshua Tree. There was an overflowing bookcase beside the desk, but otherwise the walls were a collage of scenes of Cyprus: postcards, photographs, pages ripped from magazines and calendars. The single cardboard box on the polished pine floor made me wonder why I hadn't seen others, or any sign at all that Finn had been packing to go away.

The laptop was sitting amidst the usual detritus on the desk, on and open but in hibernate mode. Above it, Blu-tacked to the desk frame, was a hand-written Bukowski quote: *When you leave your typewriter you leave your machine gun and the rats come pouring through.*

Looked like Finn had walked away from his typewriter just that once too often.

The desk's bottom drawer was already unlocked. It took five seconds to confirm that the gun wasn't there and that the drawer didn't have a false bottom. All I found was a thick buff-coloured folder labelled *Cyprus*, which contained sheaves of research notes, internet and email print-outs, bank statements, letters to and from real estate agents, most of them based in Girne. A quick flick-through elicited nothing that looked like a suicide note, about which I was mightily pleased.

The laptop, when I nudged it, came to life straight away. I found Finn's iTunes, scrolled down, clicked on Melanie Safka's 'Look What They Done To My Song, Ma'. Cranked up the volume as high as it'd go. Then I went back out into the living room and liberated a cigarette from the pack on the coffee table, got it lit. I was just relaxing back into the creased old leather couch, Melanie wailing about how they'd picked her brain like a chicken bone, when the music cut out.

There was a framed poster on the kitchen door of a woman dressed in food: a pineapple for hair, a dress of assorted nuts, strawberries for earrings, that class of a thing. In the reflection of the glass I could see the darkened outline of the woman behind me, her damp hair a tangle of rats' tails, legs apart and braced. She was using both hands to point something at the back of my head.

Her voice was cold, burnished.

'Was it you?' she said.

'Don't be daft.'

The reflection blurred as she moved forward. Cocking the gun, the click loud as a shot. She touched the muzzle to the top of my spine.

'Was. It. You.'

'Maria,' I said, 'you're not thinking—'

'I'll be gone before they find you.' She ground the barrel into my neck, forcing my head forward. 'Last time. Was it you?'

'No.'

'Good.' She relaxed, allowing the muzzle fall away. I was twisting my head to look up at her when she poked it under my cheekbone. 'And if you ever try to tell me what I'm thinking again, I'll blow your fucking head off.'

'Duly noted.'

*

The first time I met Maria I told her that her eyes reminded me of Lauren Bacall's. Narrow green slits under severely cropped brows. Now, like Lauren's, they were dead. The nose was still imperious, though, straight as a tent pitched on a downhill slope, its haughty aspect softened by cheeks left rosy by the shower and a tiny apple chin. The mouth was wider than a melon slice and luscious as split peach.

I guess I was hungrier than I'd thought.

'You couldn't have rung ahead?' she said. Hungover, her voice had the metallic whine of a wasp trapped in a pipe. 'Christ, I nearly shit myself in the shower.'

I put the pair of coffees down on the glass-topped table and liberated a bottle of Courvoisier from the sideboard, slopping a generous dollop into both mugs. She bypassed the coffee and went straight for the bottle, taking a three-swallow slug before coming up for air.

I took a decent wallop from the coffee and then rolled a smoke from the detritus of Finn's makings on the table while the brandy hectored my corpuscles like a Sarn't-Major bawling drills. She made a brusque gesture. I tossed across the cigarette. She dug a lighter from the pocket of the kimono-style dressing gown that didn't contain a .38 Detective Special, lit up and exhaled without taking her eyes from mine.

'So how've you been?' I said.

'How would you be?'

'Drunk.'

'That's how I've been.'

She sat back into the high-winged armchair, tucking a bare foot under her thigh. The kimono damp where it stuck to her shoulders, dark stains on the pockets from the film of oil on her palms. For a memento, Finn kept the .38 in good working nick.

Maria didn't look too bad either.

Dried out and spruced up, Maria Malpas was hands down the most beautiful woman I'd ever seen in the flesh. Bereft, hungover and raw from the shower, hair like Medusa's in an Arctic gale, she was still top three, easy.

'How'd you hear?' I said.

'Yesterday morning, at work. I'd only just got in. Mary saw me coming and started flapping around, how brave I was. She'd heard it on the news in the car.' Her mouth went thin. 'The fucking bitch couldn't make one fucking phone call.'

Said bitch, I presumed, being Saoirse Hamilton. She sucked down another couple of inches of brandy. 'How about you?' she said.

'I rang, but I didn't want to tell you in a message.'

She nodded a vague acknowledgment. 'I mean, how did you hear about it?'

'I was there.'

'There?'

'When it happened.'

Her mouth was a bouncy castle, the words a helpless tumbling. 'And did he . . . ? Was he . . . ?'

I told her what I'd been telling everyone else, except this time I included the bit about being at the PA to deliver grass. I expected a big hoo-hah about how no one orders in that much smoke and then jumps off nine stories, but all she did was crack a grimace that was half-smile, half-snarl. 'That'd be right,' she said. 'That's Finn.'

'Was.'

'Yeah, that was Finn.' She toasted me with the bottle, had herself another swig. Eyes wet and hard as black ice. I felt a guilty twinge at not taking the brandy away, but Maria wasn't the kind who looked fondly on intervention even when she wasn't packing a gun in her pocket. And I had twenty grand to earn.

'Y'know what?' she said. 'Fuck Finn, fuck his mother, fuck the whole shitty inbred lot of 'em.'

'Skol,' I said, raising the coffee mug. 'So what're your plans?'

A sloppy shrug. 'Wait for the funeral, I suppose. Then go home. But I don't know, even the thought of packing up . . .'

She was trapped in the moment, unwilling or unable to deal with the fact that she had to move on.

'I'm guessing the salon's a non-runner,' I said.

'I won't be going back *there*.'

'I mean, the one in Cyprus. Finn's development.'

Her eyes became arrow slits. 'Fuck are you talking about?'

'Finn had plans,' I said. I told her about the apartment complex, Finn selling up, the changes to Grainne's trust fund. 'It was supposed to be a surprise. A wedding present, like.'

She stared for a moment, then shook her head, and then she laughed, but it cracked halfway through and she wound up on a coughing jag. I crossed over to the armchair and patted her between the shoulders. She cringed away. Chastened, I shuffled back to my pew on the other side of the glass table.

'Finn move to Cyprus?' she said. 'You're kidding, right?'

'That's what he told me.'

'Finn said a lot of things.' She was staring again, and I wondered if I shouldn't look at her in the reflection of the glass-topped table, lest I be turned to stone. She tapped the cigarette's filter with the ball of her thumb, so that ash toppled onto the carpet. 'He'd talked about it, yeah,' she conceded. 'But he kept *on* talking about it. A whole *year* he was talking about it. But he was never leaving, Harry. Never. She had him on a leash, and, and . . .'

She choked something back, then launched the bottle at the red-brick fireplace. It shattered, showering the rug with splinters of glass and a not inconsiderable amount of expensive brandy. I'd have paid good money to see her and Saoirse Hamilton let loose in a china shop. 'The latest thing,' she said, 'was he reckoned we should think about taking a break. Can you believe it? I'm the one waiting a year for the bastard to make up his mind, and then *he* says maybe we should take a break.'

'He say why?'

'Why do you think?' The smile was a raw wound. 'The bitch was on his case. Dump me or she writes him out.'

'He actually said that.'

'In so many words.'

'What did you say?'

'What *could* I say?' She waggled her hands, a crude caricature of a zany clown. '"Hey, pick me instead, I'm worth millions."'

'You'd have been selling yourself short.'

She closed her eyes. 'Not now, Harry,' she whispered. 'Now's not the time.'

'Maria, he'd changed the trust—'

'Ssssh.' She put a finger to her lips, the eyes still closed. 'Not now,' she said again. She let the cigarette fall away and cradled herself, rocking in a mute keening. I got up and went around the table, retrieved the cigarette, put it in the ashtray. Then I sat down beside her.

'Let me do this,' I said. 'It doesn't mean anything. But it might help.'

I put an arm around her shoulders, gave a gentle squeeze. She didn't respond, but she didn't pull away either. I increased the pressure, pulling her towards me, and suddenly the tautness in her shoulders snapped. She turned into me, burying her face in my chest, bawling as she gripped a handful of T-shirt in each white-knuckled fist. I rested my chin on the crown of her head and felt each sob shiver my ribs like a jump-start to the heart. Something hard grinding into my side.

'You put the safety back on that gun, right?' I said.

She nodded and snuffled, then half-laughed. 'I fucking *hate* you,' she told my sternum, the words coming muffled.

'I know.' It's cruel, really, but I can't help liking women who don't like me. I think it's that I respect their intelligence. 'Listen, Maria – are you listening?' The head bobbed. 'I think you're in shock. You should see a doctor, get some painkillers prescribed, a sedative. I'll take you if you want.'

She blew a sigh that set my athlete's foot tingling, then struggled upright, smearing the tears from her cheeks with the heels of her palms. She pushed me away and looked around, and it was as if she was seeing the place for the first time.

'Shit,' she said.

The phone rang, once, twice, three times, cutting off midway through the fourth ring. Maria didn't even glance in its direction. 'Guilt's a bitch,' she said. She was staring into space, at some point that lay between where we were and who she used to be.

'You've absolutely no reason to feel guilty,' I said, trying to remember the speech Dutch had given me. 'If he really wanted to go, there's no way you could have stopped—'

'Not me.' The words were dry feathers. 'Finn.'

'Y'think?'

'I know.'

'That's my theory, yeah. Finn being Finn, his mother bearing down, he couldn't stick the—'

'His father, Harry. His father.'

She reached into her pocket, took out the gun. An ugly sight. Maria had fine slim fingers, the manicure perfectly finished, a hand capable of creating the most subtle of artistic strokes. The gun, its sheen of oil notwithstanding, was dull, black, blunt and snubby. A purely functional killing machine.

'What about his father?' I said.

'No one told you?'

'Finn told me he drowned.'

'Did he tell you he was there when it happened?'

'No,' I said. The lies came easy with Maria too. 'He forgot to mention that bit.'

She poked at an oily stain on the kimono with the barrel of the .38. 'Apparently he was giving Finn the one-day-all-this speech. Just the two of them, down at the deepwater. Anyway, his father asked Finn to get out of the car, he was parked pretty tight to the edge of the dock. So Finn got out. Afterwards they said it was just one of those things, he put the car into first rather than reverse. Not used to the new gear-stick.'

I'd done it myself, except never on the edge of a deepwater quay.

'Finn says the last thing he saw was his father's face,' she said, 'he was hunched up over the steering wheel. Then he was gone. Just like that. Toppled over. Finn freaked out. But what's he supposed to do, jump in after him? Finn wasn't much more than a kid at this stage, hardly out of his teens. And by the time he got to a phone . . .' She made a meaningless gesture with the hand not holding a gun. 'Afterwards he had to make a statement to the cops, then the insurance company had to have their own investigation. It all dragged on for about two years.'

'That has to be tough.'

'I honestly don't know if he ever got over it.'

'And she blamed Finn.'

She looked up at me, taking a second or so to focus. The brandy bedding in nicely now. 'Who, Saoirse?'

'She told me they were estranged. I thought it was an odd

word for a mother to use about her son but I guess it makes sense.'

A sardonic twitch pulled at the corner of her mouth. 'Estranged?'

'That's what she said.'

'Saoirse fucking Hamilton doesn't make many mistakes, Harry. If that's the word she used, then that's exactly what she meant.' She hesitated, then slid me a sly look. 'Y'know, with Finn being there, the only witness, no one could say for sure it wasn't suicide.'

'Guys driving Beamers don't generally top themselves, Maria.'

'No one could say it was, either.'

'What're you trying to say?'

'We were down there one night last summer,' she said, 'just sitting on the dock, smoking a draw. Finn was supposed to be up in the studio but he'd left a CD playing, he had the car doors open, the radio on. One of those lovely half-moons up over Cartron . . . Anyway, out of nowhere he said he'd killed his father.'

That one hung in the gritty, festering air. She was drunk, cunning and mean with it, lashing out just like Finn's mother and sister before her. On balance I preferred Grainne's raking nails. A primitive approach, sure, but at least it had the virtue of being instinctive, honest.

'You said it yourself,' I said. 'He was young, he saw it happen. That's a lot to take on your shoulders, and at that age you think everything's your fault, wars and famines, the whole lot. And if his mother held him responsible . . .' She waited me out, smirking now. 'I'm guessing,' I said, 'that he already had the guilties about not jumping in, trying to pull his father out. Give that kind of shit enough time, enough pressure, and it's bound to – whoa, point that somewhere else.'

She was aiming the .38 at my good eye, about twelve inches from my face.

'Finn said he killed him, Harry.' She lowered the .38, laid in on her thigh. 'Put a gun against his head, pulled the trigger . . .'

'And now he's dead, yeah. Christ, Maria, he was quoting you Bohemian fucking Rhapsody.'

'I got that, thanks. Saoirse say why she wanted the gun back?'

'No, she didn't. But that's bollocks. The autopsy would've—'

'Autopsy?'

'Sure. There's always a coroner's report when—'

'There was no *body*, Harry. Officially, they reckoned Bob made it out of the car alright, through the open window, and then got swept away.'

I stared at her, trying to remember exactly what Finn had told me about his father's drowning. If he'd said anything about their not finding a body. 'Maria,' I said, 'why the fuck would Finn want to shoot his father?'

'Harry,' she mimicked my tone, 'why would Saoirse even think about wanting the gun back?'

'It was her husband's. She's entitled.'

'Sure, yeah. Except it's a bit fucked up that the first thing she thinks of when her son commits suicide is the gun that Finn says he used to kill his father.'

There was something in that, and there might even have been something in it for me if I gave a shit about Finn, Saoirse and Big Bob Hamilton. But I had a job to do. Saoirse Hamilton wanted the gun and was prepared to pay to get it. Story, end of.

'Forget about the gun,' I said. 'Forget about Finn and his

father. What you need to worry about is that Saoirse blames you for Finn jumping, and was talking crazy earlier on, making all sorts of threats. If you want my—'

The phone rang again: once, twice. It went dead, then rang again. I reached over and picked up. 'Yeah?'

'I need to use the bathroom.'

'We're on our way down. Cross your legs and sit tight.'

'But—'

'Sit fucking *tight*.' I hung up, faced Maria. 'I'm serious about Saoirse. She could cause you problems.'

A sardonic smile, albeit a little sloppy. 'Saoirse's been causing me problems since I got here, Harry.'

'Yeah, well, I'm talking about her doing you actual harm. No kidding, the woman's not well right now. And when she wants shit done, it gets done.'

'She can try.'

'You can take her. Is that it? In a bitch-fight, you'll slap her down.'

The shrug was flip, arrogant.

'It won't be her, Maria. It'll be a couple of blokes, boozed up and well paid to fuck you over. Maybe all the way.'

This time she waved an airy hand.

'Sound,' I said, getting up. 'If that's the way you want to play it . . .' I stepped around the coffee table balling my fist, leaned in and punched from the shoulder.

She squealed and shrank away, curled into the corner. 'Imagine that's your face,' I said, pointing at the cushion I'd crumpled.

'You fucking—'

'Pretend I have a knife. Or a chisel. I'm the kind of guy who doesn't like women, can only get the horn when a woman's already screaming and bleeding.'

She bellowed something harsh and came up fast, hurling the cushion and lunging hard in its wake, wielding the .38 like a small, stubby hammer. I made a grab for her wrists but only caught one. The other fist flailed at the back of my head. I backed away, still gripping her wrist, and bunched my hand again, cocked it high. She flinched and ducked away and her adrenaline rush went south. She sagged, went limp. I hauled her upright again, and we lumbered around the room like the last couple in *They Shoot Horses* until I got her propped and steady on her feet. I put a finger under her chin and tried to tilt her face upwards, but she twisted away, jerking her head back. I prised the .38 from her fingers, then let her go, stepping back in case she was playing passive as a bluff.

'Pack a bag,' I said. 'Put your passport in it. You get five minutes.'

She gave a defiant sniffle, but she turned on her heel and stalked out of the room. I waited until I heard her shuffling around in the bedroom, then had a quick look at the .38. Found the release and pushed out the cylinder. Five rounds, just waiting to go. I emptied them out, then pushed the cylinder home and slid the safety off, cocked the hammer and dry-fired. Even the dry click sounded lethal.

I went through to the kitchen and washed the oil off my hands, then wiped down the gun. Wondering why, when he had such a perfectly designed killing machine to hand, Finn had jumped. With such whimsical diversions we fill our days. I swaddled gun and shells in kitchen towel, found a stash of green cotton shopping bags under the sink. Then I followed Maria up the corridor, went into Finn's study. The folder went into the bag on top of the gun, and I was about to close down the laptop when I spotted my name in Finn's iTunes.

Skinny for Harry.

I clickety-clicked on the listing and away they went, 'Swingboat Yawning' booming out, the laptop still set to full volume. I clickety-clicked again and silence filled the room. The kind that echoes.

It didn't make any sense. I'd thought it was a mistake that night at the PA, that Finn had burned off the wrong CD and given me Rollerskate Skinny instead of his latest compilation. Except here was his iTunes telling me he'd planned it in advance. But why would he think I'd need a burned copy of *Horsedrawn Wishes* when I already had a perfectly serviceable version at home?

One last pathetic gesture, maybe. A reminder of how we'd met, and why. And typically Finn, landing somewhere between quixotic and sentimental.

I closed everything down and was about to switch off the Mac when I remembered something Tohill had said. So I brought up Google, typed in *James Callaghan hospital car bomb.*

It wasn't quite as dramatic as Tohill had claimed, possibly because I had visions of Jimmy detonating a car bomb in the underground parking lot of a hospital, planning on bringing the whole edifice down, but it was there alright, how the upstanding James Callaghan had been convicted, this back in '94, of planting a bomb under the engine of an Assistant Commissioner's Ford Sierra while the man was inside Derry's Altnagelvin hospital, visiting his wife and newly arrived baby daughter. The guy had lost both legs, apparently, but survived, this because the engine block took the brunt of the blast. Jimmy had served four years and then strolled on a Good Friday pardon.

Which was useful to know. The laptop went into the bag on top of the folder and the gun. Another wonderful swag.

I watched her pack from the doorway. The bed unmade, floor littered with the shrapnel of a laundromat bombing. She was bundling clothes into a suitcase propped open on the floor, changing her mind, unpacking half of them, packing some more. She had her back to me, bending over, the damp towel clinging to the sinuous curves where her thighs narrowed into her waist and flared again. A faint hint of perfume, all the more seductive for being elusive, undefined. I put down the bag and took two steps forward, placed a hand on her hip. She stiffened, then straightened up. 'Don't,' she said.

'I won't,' I said, drawing aside the tendrils of straggling hair and kissing the fine, silvery hairs at the nape of her neck. She shook her head and her hair brushed my face like some subterranean apple-scented fronds and then she was turning into me muttering something crude and for a while, a very short while, we were tensed flesh and thrumming blood and there was no love in it, no love at all.

30

Afterwards she rolled away from me and got off the bed and went into the bathroom. When she came back she wouldn't look at me, just knelt on the ground and resumed packing the suitcase.

'If you forget anything,' I lied, 'I'll come back for it later.'

'Fuck you.' She gathered two handfuls of pants and bras, dumped them into the suitcase, then half-zipped it closed. When she straightened up to face me, flushed but somehow drained, her expression was a lot like a rusty tuba might sound. 'Do you think he knew?' she said.

'Knew what?'

'About you.'

I got up and went to the doorway, retrieved the bag. 'I wouldn't think so, no. But even if he did, it wouldn't have been the me part that bothered him.'

'You're saying, it'd be the me part.'

'Let it go, Maria. Finn wasn't the type to die of a broken heart.'

'Something made him jump.'

'It generally takes more than just one thing.'

'Maybe so,' she said. She hoisted the suitcase, shouldered past me in the doorway. 'But maybe we were the one thing that pushed him over the edge.'

*

There was much weeping and falling upon necks when the sisterhood reunited, the Mini Cooper's interior dripping humid with professions of undying solidarity. Most of them, as it happened, Grainne's.

'Okay,' I said, getting in. 'Miles to go before I sleep and so forth.'

Grainne extricated herself from the grapple-hold, knuckling tears up her nose. 'Where to now?' she said.

'There's a gun in there,' I toed the green cotton bag, 'and I don't want to be around it any longer than I have to.'

'You're still doing it?'

'I am.'

She twisted around to look back at Maria. 'Did he tell you about Finn's email?'

'Now isn't the time, Grainne,' Maria said. She sounded like a bank's answering machine. Metallic, disembodied, heedless.

'But if we give Saoirse the laptop, she'll know *everything*.'

'She's already guessed he was up to something hinky,' I said. 'The laptop'll just confirm the details.'

'I know *that*. But if we can keep it away from her long enough to—'

'Who's this "we"?' I said. I glanced back at Maria. 'Do you want to tell her, or will I?'

271

'Tell me what?'

There was a very long moment when it could have gone either way, but then Maria blinked and looked away to Grainne. 'Harry says Saoirse is making threats,' she said.

'Threats?'

'So he says.'

'What kind of threats?'

'Your mother,' I said, 'isn't in a good place right now. She blames Maria for Finn's suicide and she's looking for proof. So I'm suggesting we get the laptop to her straight away, let her burn out searching for some reason to blame Maria. While she's busy, we get Maria somewhere safe until we can put her on a flight out of here.'

'And in the meantime,' Grainne sneered, 'you get paid for bringing her the laptop.'

'There's that.'

'Where's this somewhere safe?' Maria said.

'Friend of mine. He'll put you up for now.' I nudged Grainne's elbow. 'Let's go. Drive.'

'But—'

'I'll put you out and make you walk.'

'It's best this way,' Maria said from the rear. Dull, resigned.

Grainne's jaw tightened, but she started the car. 'What about the cops?' she said.

'The cops want me for a hold-all of coke. I'm guessing they'll keep the road-blocks to a minimum.'

Grainne nosed out of the car park, turned right along Kennedy Parade.

'This coke the cops want you for,' Maria said. 'Is that what Finn ordered?'

'Different score.'

'But the cops know you were there when he jumped.'

'Yep.'

'But they don't think you pushed him.'

'Some of them do.'

'Are they right?'

'Nope.'

The way Grainne had her ear cocked, she might well have been trying to tune in to a satellite orbiting Io.

'You're sure,' Maria said.

'I'm positive,' I said. 'I was there. If I was the one pushed him I'd have remembered by now. Especially when everyone keeps asking the same fucking question.'

'Why,' Grainne said, her voice strained, 'would Harry want to push Finn?'

'No reason,' Maria said. 'I'm just asking. No one's telling me anything, so I'm asking.'

'Fine by me,' I said. 'Only next time, before you open your mouth? Remember you're drunk.'

'Bite me.'

'Fucking ingrate.'

'Asshole.'

We kept it up all the way to Herb's. My strategy was to distract Grainne from asking dangerous questions about why I might want Finn out of the picture. Maria's ambition appeared to be to maximise her insults using the minimum of vowels.

Inside, I pointed Grainne at the downstairs bathroom and Maria towards the kitchen, the kettle and as much black coffee as her kidneys would bear. Some buttery toast for yours truly wouldn't go amiss either.

Herb watched it all, appalled. Then he took me out to the kitchen.

'The fuck're you doing, Harry?'

'She needs somewhere to stay for a few hours. Once we get a flight sorted, I'll drop her down to Knock, put her on the plane.'

'Now? Are you fucking mental?'

'Getting that way.' I dug out the makings I'd liberated from the coffee table at Finn's, started rolling a smoke. 'You wanted to see me,' I said. 'I'm here.'

'What I wanted,' Herb grated, 'was for you to turn up with Toto's coke, late being a hell of a lot better than never when it comes to Toto fucking McConnell. What I got was Finn's tart pissed to the gills and some underage minge looks like Marilyn Manson with a hangover. And you,' he gestured at the eye-patch, 'looking like Jolly fucking Roger.'

'Actually, the Jolly Roger was—'

'I'll fucking Jolly Roger *you*. Where's the coke?'

'The cops have it.'

'The fucking *cops*? How the fuck?'

'Well, I'm guessing here, but I'd say it happened when I was spark out after been run off the road, the car being swarmed by cops and firemen.'

'Run off the road?'

'Rammed, yeah.'

'But who the fuck'd—'

'Dunno. This guy in Galway, Moore. How well do you know him?'

'I don't, he's Toto's guy.' He thought about that. 'What're you saying, the guy's ripping off Toto?'

'Could be. Only this way it looks like the rip-off's coming at your end.'

He squinted at me. 'What's that supposed to mean?'

'It means our boy in Galway handed over the coke, that's all he knows. And all Toto knows is there's no product. So that puts you and me in the middle, the cops holding the coke and needing names to join the dots.'

He took a half-step back, as if only now realising I was dangerously insane. 'Tell me,' he said, 'you're not thinking of giving up Toto McConnell.'

I closed my eyes, the sun streaming warm into the kitchen, and for a split-second allowed myself to see it all laid out in a perfect daisy-chain. How I'd give up Herb for the coke, and he'd give up the McConnells, and we'd all live happily ever after in a pink palace in the clouds. A tidy little fantasy, sure, even as the iron weight in my gut reminded me I was only indulging it so I wouldn't have to dwell on Ben lying still as a statue amid the crisp white sheets, a tangerine-size lump bleeding into his brain.

I tuned back in to Herb's rant. ' . . . how it looks on *me*, Toto's thinking you're playing both ends, laying side bets with the fucking cops.'

I let my eyes go dead. 'Say that again?'

This time, when he took a full step back, he was under no illusions as to how dangerously insane I was feeling. He took a deep breath, let it out slow. 'I'm just talking through the options here,' he said.

'Keep talking. Maybe you'll end up in a bed beside Ben.'

'What's that, a threat? Jesus, Harry. You lose ten grand in product and you're the one threatening *me*?'

'Wise up, Herb. I'm not the one put Ben in that bed. And

you're wasting your time talking to me. I was you,' I said, 'I'd get on the blower to Toto, feel him out. Because if it wasn't Toto's boys ran me off the road, then it's someone else fucking around on his patch. And radio silence from your end might get him to thinking it's you.'

His expression lacked the sickly green pallor of Munch's *Scream* but it wasn't a bad stab. 'Something else you should know,' I said.

·'This better be good fucking news, Harry.'

'A cop told me Finn was onside.'

'He was touting?'

'Not about the grass. But he was cosy, yeah.'

He said nothing to that. He didn't have to. Herb'd said all along that Finn was a flake, and the whole sorry mess had kicked off with a call from Finn ordering up three bags of grass Herb'd questioned from the start. And I'd vouched for Finn.

We stared awhile, neither us composing any odes about limpid pools. 'There's good news,' I said then.

'Yeah?'

I told him about Saoirse Hamilton and the laptop, skipping the bit about the gun in case he melted down right there. The twenty grand cash, ten of which was Toto's for the impounded coke, ten going to the cost of replacing the torched cab.

'Toto really wanted that coke for tonight,' he said.

'Yeah, well.'

'Shit,' he said. 'Fuckity-fucking *shit*.'

There wasn't much I could add to that. 'Listen, about Maria. A couple of hours is all she needs, somewhere to kip down.'

'Anyone looking for her?'

'I wouldn't think so. Anyway, they'll never look for her here.

While I'm gone,' I said, 'you could be booking her out of Knock on the first flight to London.'

'I'm a travel agent now?'

'The quicker it's done, the sooner she's gone. And it'll look better with Toto, he comes looking for his coke, if we have his ten large ready to go.'

He accepted the logic. 'When'll you be back?'

'Soon as I get the money and work out some way of seeing Ben.'

He nodded. 'What's the latest there?'

'Last I heard he was holding on. Dee isn't keen on hearing from me right now.' Something wobbled up through my chest, a bubble that broke at the back of my throat. Herb stepped in, put a hand on my shoulder.

'Want me to ring her?' he said.

'That'd be good, yeah.'

We went back into the house, through to the kitchen. There was no black coffee, no buttery toast. Grainne was at the table hunched over the laptop, smoking and sullen. I made the introductions, asked where Maria was. She jerked a thumb in the direction of the living room.

Maria was panned out on the couch, snoring gently.

'Mi casa, su casa,' Herb observed as he scrolled down through the contacts list on his mobile. He found Dee's number, pressed call.

He didn't get to say a lot. There was much by way of sympathetic grunting, and then he asked Dee if there was anything he could do.

'If I see you,' he said after he hung up, 'I'm to kick your balls into your throat and then suck them out and spit them

277

into a blender. Then bring her the blender.'

'Is he okay?'

'Better, she says. He squeezed her finger about an hour ago, although the doc says that could be just a reflex reaction, nothing to do with anything.'

'Shit.'

'Think positive,' he urged. 'If he was really bad, they'd have transferred him to Dublin by now. What're you looking for?'

I was hunkered down beside the couch, rummaging through Maria's suitcase. Came up with her passport. I flipped it open on the off-chance but it looked genuine, no five grand stashed inside. 'You'll need that to book her flight,' I said. 'Her purse must be around here somewhere, her credit card.'

'How long will you be?'

'Couple of hours, tops.'

'So I should book her flight for . . .'

'This evening. Late as you can. Give me a chance to get back here, drive her down.'

'We could always stick her in a taxi,' he said, and for the briefest of moments something glittered in his bleak eyes, a faint hint of humour.

Sometimes that's enough. For the first time in I couldn't remember how long I felt like everything might just work out okay.

I fetched Grainne from the kitchen, hit the road. It wasn't until we were pulling out of Herb's drive that it hit me. That maybe Ben hadn't been transferred because he was too fragile to be moved at all.

31

We drove in along the Strandhill Road and I thought I was smart directing Grainne down Orchard Road and through Rathedmond, cutting out the town's traffic and coming out near the quays and Hughes' Bridge. Except there were road works just beyond the Eircom building, temporary traffic lights. She sat stiffly, back straight and hands at ten-to-two on the steering wheel.

'What Maria said about you pushing Finn,' she said.

'What about it?'

'Why would she ask that?'

'She was drunk.'

'I know, but—'

'This is the last fucking time I'm saying this,' I said. 'I didn't push Finn anywhere. Okay? I liked the guy. Now I'm not so sure I like him anymore, every time I turn around I'm tripping over another lie he told me. But I didn't push him. Maria, she was drunk, she has plenty to worry about with your mother coming on all Cromwell at the gates of Drogheda. So she's looking to push her crap onto someone else, and that someone is me. Right now I'm just counting my blessings that she didn't try to rake my fucking eyes out.'

She flushed. 'All I'm trying to do is—'

'I know exactly what you're trying to do. What I'm saying is, find some other sap to practise on.'

'Practise what?'

'Being your mother.'

She whipped around to face me. 'You dirty fucking—'

'Guilty as charged. The lights are gone green, by the way.'

Face set in a bitter pout, she edged forward a couple of car lengths, knocked the car out of gear again. The temporary lights had an erratic sequence, which led to the first few cars jumping the red, snarling things up further. In the middle of it all a motor-cycle cop in leather strides and fluorescent yellow jacket was waving his arms around like an arsonist on the apron at Heathrow.

'Maybe,' she said through clenched teeth, 'I should tell him who you are.'

'The cops aren't morons, Grainne. If they seriously thought I'd pushed Finn off the PA I'd be banged up in a cell right now.'

'What about the gun?'

'What about it?'

'If they find you with a gun,' a triumphant note, 'you're screwed.'

'Find *me* with a gun? Whose car are we in?'

She frowned. 'The gun's on your side,' she said, sounding nowhere as peppy.

'I don't *have* a side, Grainne, it's not my car. And anyway, the gun's your mother's. Anyone wants to know, I'll say she asked me to fetch a bag of stuff from Finn's apartment. How was I supposed to know what was in it?'

She edged the car forward, knocking it out of gear three lengths back from the junction. Close enough to see the whites of the cop's eyes.

'You'd expect them to believe you didn't look in the bag,' she said.

'There's a marvellous legal invention called reasonable doubt, you might want to look it up. Besides, if the cops find the gun, they'll impound the laptop too. What'll happen your little scheme then?'

'What scheme?'

'There's more than one?'

She'd got more than her blue eyes from her mother. The imperious tone could have cut glass. 'I'm afraid I haven't the faintest idea of what you're—'

'No? Then you're not trying to follow up on Finn's changing the terms of the trust fund, see if you can't play with that, maybe even tweak it some more so you buy yourself leverage with your mother. A little independence, so you can move out, get away from all the bullshit back home. Am I warm?' If her flushing cheeks were any guide, I was two degrees off self-combusting. 'Here's the deal, Grainne. If I get nabbed, you get nabbed, everything gets fucked. Your call. Now, *go*.'

The light was already red as she accelerated through the junction, waving airily at the irate cop. I twisted in the seat to see if he was noting her registration, but he only stood with his hands on his hips as a mustard Peugeot and a metallic-green Phaeton filtered in behind us.

We trundled towards the bypass and another set of lights, more traffic backed up. She cut left towards the quays, the atmosphere in the car a kind of cold simmering. Right onto the docks, more traffic lights, less traffic. I dug out the makings and rolled a smoke.

'What happens when you're caught?' she said. She was staring straight ahead.

'I don't know.'

'So why don't you run?'

'Where to?'

'*I* don't know.' The lights turned green. 'Anywhere,' she said as we turned on to Hughes' Bridge.

'There'd be cops there too.'

'Sure, but—'

'If I run, I keep running. I don't get to come back.'

A grimace. 'I think I'd cope.'

'You don't have a kid.'

'You won't see much of him in prison.'

'I wouldn't imagine, after the last couple of days, that I'll be seeing a lot of him anyway. Jesus, this fucking *traffic*.'

We were stuck in the middle lane on the bridge, aiming for the Bundoran Road, the main artery north out of town. The left lane, which filtered off at Cartron and headed for Rosses Point, was tipping along nicely. It was the long way round, but I was too tense for sitting still. Better to be moving. 'Head for the Point,' I said.

Maybe she thought I was having second thoughts about delivering the swag, because for once she didn't protest. She indicated, eased into the left lane, put the Cooper into third. We sailed up over Cartron Hill and down again, out along the breakwater parallel to the Bundoran Road, the Atlantic lapping at the low stone wall.

'Does Saoirse know about the drugs?' she said.

'No idea.'

'I mean, that Finn was buying some that night.'

'She didn't hear it from me, if that's what you're asking.'

'At least you managed to keep that much from her.'

'The reason Saoirse knows so much,' I said, 'is because your sainted brother was a lying fuck. If he'd been straight with me, she'd know nothing. Alright?' I turned in the seat to face her. 'And before you start in with your but-fucking-buts, you should probably know that Finn wasn't planning to smoke three bags of premium weed all on his lonesome. And I'm not talking about him handing it out for free at some surf-'n'-bake, either.'

It took her a moment or two to digest that. 'Finn,' she said. 'Dealing drugs.'

She said the word 'dealing' like she'd handle a moist turd.

'That's right,' I said, 'Finn was *dealing*, and I'd be shocked if you weren't one of his best customers. You want me to tell Saoirse all that?'

'But why would Finn need to sell drugs?'

'I don't know. Maybe people kept sponging off his own stash, he thought he'd try to break even.'

She laughed at that. 'One thing Finn was never worried about,' she said, 'was money.'

'Yeah, well, maybe that was it.'

'What was what?'

'Weed isn't as lethal as money, Grainne. Nowhere as addictive. An entirely more pleasant drug to *deal* in. You get into peddling dope it's like playing the markets in reverse, illegal but not immoral.'

'Bullshit.'

'Look, I could give a fuck about why Finn was dealing dope. Right now all that matters is the leverage it gives me.'

She considered that. 'You'll tell the cops,' she said.

'If it comes to it.'

'What good will that do when he's already dead?'

'I said, *if* it comes to it. Saoirse plays ball, sets me up with a good legal team that buys me the minimum time served, then it doesn't have to wash out.'

'Fuck, you're cold.'

'I wasn't born this way. Oh, and one more thing.' I took a drag off the cigarette and turned my face away to exhale into the rear of the car, came back to her. Then glanced into the rear again, where I'd caught a glimpse of metallic-green through the back window. 'Fuck,' I said, settling back into the seat again. '*Shit.*'

'What's wrong?'

We were coming up on Ballincar, the Radisson visible to our right. 'Cut across at Cregg House,' I said.

'Why?'

'Just fucking *do* it.'

Thirty seconds later, she did it. Just as we passed the gates of Cregg House, the metallic-green Phaeton swung around in our wake, the unmistakably boxy nose of the classic Volkswagen, and followed us up the leafy lane. I gave it a couple of seconds, on the off-chance the driver was headed for Cregg, but once it passed the gates I knew.

'Where's your phone?' I said.

'What?'

'Your phone. I need to make a call, and fast.'

She fumbled the phone from her pocket, and I rang directory

enquiries, asked to be put through to the cop shop.

'Sligo Garda Station.'

'Detective Tohill, please. Criminal Assets, liaising with this station.'

'And who shall I say is calling?'

It took a Homeric effort not to say Leonard Cohen. 'Harry Rigby.'

'Hold the line.'

We were out in the country by now, the road narrowing to a twisting lane between drystone walls and ditches of thorny hedge. Grainne tooling along in third gear, shifting down to second for some of the sharper bends. 'Aim for the mountain,' I told her, pointing at Benbulben. 'You won't go far wrong.'

Tohill came on the line.

'Smart fucking bastard. Where are you?'

'Forget that. I'm on my way in.'

A moment's hiss. I wondered if the call was being recorded. 'You're coming in?'

'Call off the dogs and give me an hour. I'll be there.'

'What dogs?'

'The dogs in the Phaeton.'

'What fucking Phaeton? Rigby, I'm only saying this—'

I killed the call. 'Fuck.'

'What is it?' Grainne said.

'That car behind us, I thought it was the cops. Jesus, watch the *road.*'

She clipped a pothole, swerved onto the verge, got us back on track. 'So who is it?'

'Dunno.' I dipped into the green cotton bag, came up with the .38 and the paper-wrapped shells. 'But they're not out here for the good of their health. Ever seen *Rebel Without a Cause*?'

'Harry . . .'

'Before your time. Jimmy Dean. Gets in a chicky-run and dives out of the car before it goes over a cliff.'

'You're diving out of the *car*?'

'You just watch me go.' I slotted home the fifth shell, clicked the cylinder closed. Checked the safety was on. Glanced over at her. She had one eye on the road, one on the green cotton bag.

'Grainne,' I said, 'listen to me now. That fucking laptop's more trouble than it's worth. I'm serious. Best thing you can do is take it home, hand it over. You'll be better off in the long run.'

'You mean, *you'll* be better off. Twenty thousand euro's worth.'

Which was true, in theory at least. And she knew she had me. Diving out of a moving car is one thing. Doing it with a laptop in tow, and expecting us both to survive intact, was another thing entirely.

'Make me an offer,' I said.

'What?'

'Cut me in. Twenty grand from the trust fund. I'll help you track down this guy in Cyprus, we'll screw Saoirse.'

We were on a straight section, the Phaeton a couple of hundred yards behind, coming up on a bend that cut a sharp left beyond a small copse. I tucked the .38 into my belt at the small of my back.

'I should probably remind you,' I said, 'that yesterday I got rammed off the road, my kid ended up in a coma. So this would be a good time to—'

'Deal, yeah, it's a deal. Okay?'

'Deadly. Whatever you do, don't stop. Head back to Herb's, she'll never find you there. Right, this next bend'll do it. Ready?'

She nodded again. We hit the bend past the copse and she jammed on, tyres skidding. I threw open the door and tumbled out, turning my shoulder so the impact caught me high on my back and bounced me sprawling into the long grass on the verge. A blackthorn branch ripped into my right arm, tore a gash as I pulled away reaching for the gun.

By the time the Phaeton rolled around the bend, I was up on one knee, shoulder burning from the road burn, both hands braced on the butt of the .38.

The Phaeton jerked, then slowed, eased to a halt.

A one-man job. I stood up, twitched the gun.

Slowly, very slowly, he got out and stepped away from the car and stood in the middle of the road. Arms cocked like a gunfighter itching to draw.

It wasn't intentional. When you're built like an upside-down cello, your arms just tend to hang that way.

'You looking for me, Jimmy?' I said.

The eyes were bright, his features impassive. It wasn't the first time he'd been at the business end of a gun barrel.

'Just passing on a message,' he said.

'You couldn't have rung?'

'I rang. The cops answered.'

'What's the message?'

'Is that even loaded?'

'What's the message, Jimmy?'

'Gillick wants a chat.'

'What about?'

He up-jutted his chin in the direction of the long-gone Mini Cooper. 'Her, mainly.'

'Who, Grainne? What about her?'

'She has the laptop, right?'

'Why's Gillick wanting to talk about Grainne?'

'At a guess,' he said, 'I'd say it's because she can make him money.' He shrugged. 'But that's just a guess.'

32

I asked Jimmy if he'd mind wearing his peaked cap while he drove me back to Herb's, and he asked me if I wanted to lose my other eye, and after that we motored along in a companionable silence until Jimmy got us off the country roads and headed back to town.

'So where'd you pick us up?' I said.

'Finn's place.'

'You were there?'

He jabbed a thumb at his eye. 'A patch,' he said, 'can fuck with what you can see. You think you're scoping everything but, y'know . . .'

He was being generous. 'How'd you know I'd be at Finn's?'

'Gillick reckoned you'd turn up there sooner or later.'

'He knew about the laptop.'

'Sounds like it.'

'So why didn't you brace me there?'

He tapped ash out the window. 'Because I rang Gillick when you came out, told him the score.'

'That Maria was with me.' He inclined his head. 'And he told you not to jump in, just see how it played.'

'Something like that, yeah.'

'Just so we're clear,' I said. 'I was at Finn's picking up the laptop for Saoirse Hamilton. Gillick knows this, right?'

'He knows.'

'Does he know she's paying twenty grand for it?'

He nodded. 'Okay,' I said. 'Get him on the blower.'

'What for?'

'I want to be sure, if he wants the laptop, he has twenty grand cash lying around.'

'Don't worry about that.'

'I'm a worrier, Jimmy. Get him on the phone.'

'Don't sweat it. He's Saoirse Hamilton's bagman. You think she has twenty gees stashed under the mattress?'

'Wouldn't surprise me in the least.'

A flash of white teeth. 'I wouldn't mind a tumble in that mattress,' he said, 'just to find out.'

We came over the hill at Cartron and down onto Hughes Bridge. The traffic a trickle, but steady. Across the bridge and up the bypass, cutting right at the train station and out along Strandhill Road. Jimmy cleared his throat. 'By the way,' he said, 'that's hard lines about your kid. How's he doing?'

'Alright, yeah. Stable.'

'Is he a fighter?'

'He'll be grand, Jimmy. He takes after his mother.'

A sympathetic grimace. 'I'll light him a candle,' he said, 'first chance I get.'

'Appreciate the thought.'

The traffic was slower on Strandhill Road for some reason,

the cars dawdling along like a fat kid early for school, but I was still trying to picture Jimmy hulking over a bank of flickering candles in the back of a church when he pulled in at Herb's gate. I took his phone, rang Herb, told him I was outside. The gates swung open and in we went.

Herb cracked open the front door, had a quick scan left and right, ushered us in and through to the living room. Maria, still bedraggled, still luminous, was slumped in an armchair facing the TV. Grainne was perched in the corner of the couch, her eyes vacant orbs, as far from Maria as it was possible to get without actually hanging herself out the window. The green cotton bag tucked between her and a cushion. The mood was tense, possibly because Herb was holding a gun, and maybe because they'd been wondering, having dived out of the Mini Cooper, if I'd ever resurface. And maybe it was because the TV was tuned to a *Coronation Street* repeat, mousey Sally having yet another affair. It really is the quiet ones you have to watch.

As for Herb's gun, I presumed that was because he was half-expecting a frontal assault from the McConnells. It looked square and blocky, like a cut-down SIG.

'Where'd you get that?' I said.

'Toto,' he shrugged. 'Where else?'

'Toto gave you a rod?'

'He *sold* me a rod, back when we hooked up.'

Jimmy was more intrigued than put out. 'Toto McConnell?' he said.

'That's right,' Herb said. 'You know him?'

'You could say that, yeah.' He sounded cautiously impressed, as if Herb had announced he kept a tiger in his kitchen, was thinking about letting it out for its afternoon romp. He made a point of glancing at his watch. 'Listen,' he said, 'I'd love to stay and shoot the shit, but, y'know . . .'

'Yeah,' I said. 'Maria? Hey, Maria?'

It took her a few moments to tear her gaze away from the TV. She'd been crying, and had reapplied the mascara with what must have been a shaky hand, leaving her looking a lot like a sultry Sioux racoon. Whether the look was intended as camouflage or war paint was hard to say. 'You want to take Grainne through to the kitchen?' I said.

Her eyes seemed to swim a backstroke as she focused on me. 'What?' she said.

'We've had a wee, ah, chillum,' Herb said. 'Just to take things down a notch.'

'Ah.' That would explain Grainne's dislocated stare. She was out to lunch, in Rio. 'Alright, let's take it next door.'

We trooped through to the kitchen, Herb gesturing for Jimmy to go first, me bringing up the rear. Jimmy perched a butt-cheek on the kitchen table, said, 'So where's this laptop?'

I jerked a thumb over my shoulder. 'Grainne has it, it's in that green bag on the couch. But let's be cool, alright? We try to take it away from her, she's liable to start—'

Herb's phone went off, a tinny 'Ride of the Valkyries' pealing through the kitchen. He held up hand, apologising, as he slipped it from his pocket, answering as he went out into the hallway, closing the door.

Jimmy tapped his watch. 'Time's money, Rigby.'

'Fucking everything's money lately, Jimmy. I just want to be sure—'

'And that's twice now,' he nodded at the closed door, 'I've had rods pulled on me in the last hour.'

'He didn't *pull* any fucking rod, for fuck's sake. He had it out when you came in.'

'I'm just saying, I get nervous around guns when it's other people have them.'

'You want mine?' I hauled the .38 out of my belt, held it up. 'Will that make you feel any—'

The door opened. Herb stood there, SIG in one hand, phone in the other. He seemed to have lost weight in the few seconds he'd been gone, most of it around the shoulders and chest. His eyes bright and dead as they found mine.

'Fuck, Harry . . .' he croaked.

And I knew.

33

It hit like cold lightning. I buckled at the knees and staggered back, reaching for the countertop. For a split second I thought I was having a heart-attack, couldn't breathe past the pain, the tectonic plates grinding in my chest.

From a very great distance I heard Herb say, 'Harry, I'm so fucking sorry, man, Jesus,' but faintly, very faintly, from the heart of some roaring storm. The world gone black, shot through with blood.

Then came a single thought, a question, piercing:

Would Ben have died had Gonz killed me?

The storm dropped away. The clarity was surreal. Herb, frozen in place, a helpless expression etched on his face. His lips were moving but I couldn't hear a word.

My lips felt numb, throat locked shut. But from somewhere I heard, 'Herb? It's Ben?'

He nodded.

'He's dead?'

Herb closed his eyes. 'That was Dee. She said,' he swallowed hard, 'that you might want to know.'

The tectonic plates began to grind again, some deep Antarctic fault line I'd never even suspected was there. Beneath, a poisonous lava bubbling up a vicious brew. A cold and savage rage.

It was just Jimmy's bad luck he was there.

Bad luck that he felt moved to say, 'Hard lines, Rigby. Sorry for your troubles.'

Bad luck he'd offered to light a candle for Ben.

'How'd you know, Jimmy?'

'What?'

'About Ben being in hospital. How'd you know?'

He came up off the table with his hands out, palms facing me. Watching my eyes, the .38. 'Wait a minute, Rigby. You're not thinking—'

'I *wasn't* thinking, Jimmy. Too fucking worried about laptops and twenty fucking grands to think straight. I'm thinking now, though. So how'd you know?'

'Back the fuck off,' he said, and it was only then I realised I was moving. Something flickered in my peripheral vision, Herb raising the SIG, and it was Jimmy's bad luck, again, that he let himself be distracted. By the time he came back to me I'd reversed the .38, was smashing its butt into the bridge of his nose. A squelchy crunch. He went down hard, as only big men can, bringing a chair with him, tangling himself up. I stomped his face, once, twice, blood spraying up my shins. Bone cracking. He tried to scream but it came out a choked gurgle, and I reared back and booted him up under the chin. His head flopped back, leaving his throat open, so I got myself a good grip on the table for leverage and stomped down on his Adam's apple.

If Herb hadn't pawed at my shoulder, dragged me off-balance, I'd have killed him where he lay. My heel connected too high, glanced off his chin and punched into his cheekbone. His face seemed to billow, then flatten out slow.

Herb was screaming something in my ear. It took a couple of seconds to work it out, and then I realised he was saying, 'Not here, Harry, not fucking *here*.'

I stepped out across Jimmy, turned and hunkered down. Reversed the .38 again, clicked the safety off. His breathing coming now in ragged bubbles.

'Jimmy,' I said, 'you have three fucking seconds before I blow your fucking head off. How did you know?'

*

His face looked a lot like a melting balloon. Nose busted, a cheekbone crushed, the mouth a raw hole, both eyes swollen shut. So I guess he was literally swearing blind, in words that came slow and gloopy, when he mumbled he knew nothing about running the Audi off the road. That he'd heard about Ben from Gillick.

How Gillick knew he couldn't say, even after I cocked the .38 and ground the muzzle into his forehead.

'He's not worth it, Harry,' Herb said, and he was right, but not in the way he thought.

Herb was trying to feed me the old line. How blowing a hole in Jimmy wouldn't bring Ben back. That revenge might be sweet, but knee-jerk retribution wasn't worth twenty years in a cell.

Sound advice, at least where Jimmy was concerned.

Gillick, though. Depending on how he'd heard about Ben, Gillick would be a different matter entirely.

I de-cocked the .38, put it away. Herb went to get a roll of masking tape. We got Jimmy nicely trussed, ankles and wrists, then Herb pulled the Phaeton around to the kitchen door. Jimmy wasn't exactly a dead weight but he was a big man, no easy job to cram into the boot. He lay there half-blind and snuffling.

'What if he chokes?' Herb said. 'On his own blood, like.'

'That's on me.'

'Yeah, but—'

'I'll need some clean clothes.' My jeans were spattered to the knee, shoes and socks stained red. 'D'you mind?'

''Course not. Work away.'

'And do me a favour. Find Gillick's place, Google-map it for me.'

'Will do. But Harry, listen to me.' A hand on my shoulder, a faint squeeze. 'You need to go see Ben.'

For a moment I found myself puzzling over how best to stand, where my hands should go. 'I will, yeah.'

'I mean, now.'

'Not yet, Herb. Couple of things to do first.'

'Harry . . .'

I shrugged off his hand and told him that there would come a time to mourn, for sure. When I'd sit myself down and acknowledge Ben was gone, and cry first for what he had been to me, the one and only good thing I'd ever known in my life, and then for Ben, for what he might have grown up to be, all the things he'd never get to do, the sights he'd never see, the music he'd never hear. For the sheer *waste* of it.

I told Herb that the world was already pointless without Ben in it. That in time his absence would metastasize into grief, a cancer hollowing me out from within, with no reason to go on other

297

than my dying would mean Ben would have one less person to remember him.

I reminded him about the TV documentary we'd seen last week, the one about the Bronze Age, two guys making a sword, molten metal being poured into a mould, the fiery, viscous bronze that quickly dulled and hardened into a lethal weapon.

I told him all that with Jimmy lying there in the boot of the Phaeton, moaning, although how it sounded was, 'I can't see Ben like this, Herb. Not like this.'

That much he understood, so I left out the bit about pulling up at the hospital in a chariot, Hector's body broken and bloody in my wake.

'Don't do it,' he said.

'It's doing me, Herb. It's doing me.'

34

The scream came while I was upstairs changing into a pair of Herb's jeans.

I took the stairs four at a time, beat Herb through the living room door by a short head.

The sisterhood was no more, or else the initiation rituals were a lot more arcane than I'd imagined.

Grainne crouched low, coming crab-like at Maria, a scissors clutched in her right hand. Maria backing into a corner, the laptop she was using as a shield already scored a couple of times.

I hurdled the coffee table, clamped a forearm around Grainne's throat, grabbing her forearm with the other hand. Forcing the hand holding the scissors down and around, behind her back.

'Drop it,' I hissed.

A schoolboy error. She was a bag of drowning cats, spitting and twisting, her left hand clawing for my eyes. The point of the scissors pierced my right thigh just above the knee. A dart of pain, the shock enough to send me stumbling backwards, hauling Grainne with me as we tumbled over the coffee table and bounced off the couch. The rebound threw us sprawling onto the carpet, Grainne still gripping the scissors. I balled a fist and punched down on the back of her wrist. Her fingers splayed, the scissors fell free. I tossed them out of reach and fell back against the couch again. Her nails dug into my forearm, so I tightened the choke-hold. 'Do that again,' I panted, 'and I'll snap your neck.'

For a second or two she seemed to be considering it, weighing up the pros and cons. Then she relented, went limp. I relaxed my grip and gave her another couple of seconds, then pushed her off, slipped out from underneath. I was half-expecting her to rear up again, start lashing out, but she only turned away and stretched out beside the couch and bawled into the carpet.

By then Herb was easing Maria into an armchair. I got to my feet. 'What the fuck was *that* all about?'

Maria shook her head, bewildered. 'I just wanted to check the flight times,' she said. Stunned, the laptop still braced in both hands, protecting her midriff. 'All of a sudden, she was screaming, coming at me with, with . . .' She broke off, shuddered.

'Next time use your phone,' I said. I nodded down at Grainne. 'She's a bit protective of the laptop.'

I sat down on the couch, pulled up the jeans to the knee. The scissors had punctured the skin but the cut wasn't so deep I'd bleed out any time soon. I rolled down the jeans again, leaned across to pat Grainne on the shoulder. 'Hey, are you okay?'

Muffled sobs.

'Listen,' I said, 'the laptop's yours. No one's taking it away. Alright?'

Right on cue Herb placed the Mac on the coffee table. 'Here,' I said. 'See? It's all yours.'

She told the carpet something.

'Grainne,' I said, 'I can't hear a word you're saying. And I don't have time to be sitting—'

She turned her head, looked up at me. 'You said we had a deal.'

'Yeah, well, all bets are off. The laptop's yours. I don't want it.'

She wriggled into a sitting position. 'But it's no good . . . I mean, I thought we were doing it together.'

'That was never happening. You were paying me to give it to you instead of your mother. Now I don't need the money.'

'But . . .'

'Forget it.' I looked across at Maria. 'You okay?'

She nodded.

'Change in plan,' I told her. 'Herb's going to drive you to the airport.'

'Like fuck,' Herb said. 'And anyway,' he gestured at Grainne, 'we can't leave her here on her own.'

'Not my problem. Not right now.'

Herb swore. Maria snorted, like she'd heard it all before. Grainne tugged at my jeans.

'What?' I said, looking down at her, but she didn't have to say anything. She was staring up at me, her expression half-hopeful, shyly expectant and desperate not to be refused. She might as well have stabbed me in the heart with the scissors.

I'd seen that expression not twenty-four hours ago, Ben glancing up at me from under his fringe, his wan smile anticipating my latest failure, the latest round in the raising and dashing of hopes. The unsaid promises, the wordless craving of a fatherless child for something he didn't fully understand except in its absence.

'I don't have anyone else,' she whispered.

I looked across at Herb. He shrugged. Maria had her head tilted to one side, eyes watchful, a sneer on the brew.

'There's no way I'm driving the two of them anywhere,' Herb said. 'Are you kidding? Fucking world war three it'd be.'

'Okay,' I said. 'Okay.'

*

Herb said he'd take care of the clean-up, burn my trousers and socks, the shoes. He didn't say anything more about my going to see Ben. I was guessing that meant he'd only brought it up as a way of buying time, hoping the rage would burn itself out. Which was why he wanted me to be the one to take Maria to Knock, put her on a flight. The idea being that an hour there and an hour back would help me cool off. Herb with no idea the rage was ice cold.

Saoirse Hamilton rattling around my head, her voice scabrous as she asked me if I honestly believed one day might make any difference to how she felt about her dead son.

We turned out of the driveway onto the Strandhill Road, headed for town. It felt like my brain was swimming in black ink. Ben a stab in the heart every time I drew breath and suffering a weird kind of horizontal vertigo, the world accelerating away. The sense of loss like a black and poisoned kind of light. It was everywhere, infusing every last thing with a corrosive despair, eating away even as it fed on itself. The heart turned iron, so that all I felt was the gaping, tugging vortex he'd left behind and a hatred of everything alive, of the world itself for being the world without Ben in it.

' . . . fucking disappointed when she opens that baby up.'

'What?'

'I said, Grainne'll be . . .' She paused, looked across. 'Have you been listening to *any*thing I've said?'

'No.'

We'd reached the railway station, were stalled in traffic on Lord Edward Street, the lights red. I had no memory of getting there.

Maria sipped from a bottle of water, tapped the cap home again with the heel of her palm. 'I'm talking about the laptop.'

'Forget it. We're not going back.'

'Who said anything about going back?'

'I'm getting you out. That's all you need to know.'

'I'm owed, Harry.' The brandy still working its old black magic. A bolshy tilt to her chin. 'Finn made promises.'

'Finn said a lot of things.'

'Maybe he did, but it's not just about me.' She placed her hands, very deliberately, on her midriff. 'Is it?'

'You don't even know it's his,' I said.

She conceded that by pursing her lips and nodding slowly. 'Maybe not,' she said, 'but see it my way. It's either Finn's or it's some flake who killed his brother, already has a kid of his own. Sorry,' she needled, '*had* a kid of his own.'

The lights turned green. I eased off the clutch and trundled around onto the bypass, knocked the car out of gear again as we rolled up behind a Ford Focus.

'Someone's going to die for Ben,' I said. 'It doesn't have to be you.'

'Oh yeah? You'd kill your own kid, maybe? Just when you've lost another? Oh, wait – he wasn't actually yours, was he?' She patted her tummy. 'At least this time,' she said, 'you know there's a chance it's yours.'

'Maria, I know you're drunk but I swear to God, one more fucking word about Ben and I'll drive you straight to Saoirse Hamilton myself.'

'And tell her what?' she said. 'That Finn jumped because you got me pregnant?'

I had a sudden urge to vomit. A flash of Gonzo flopped prone in a chair, a hole punched in his chest, the gun in my hand and the thick whiff of cordite. The sickening thrill of it.

'Don't tempt me,' I said.

'You never wondered?' she said.

'About what?'

'Well,' she said. 'Why you.'

'Not really. You're a gold-digging bitch who got bored, needed to kick-start Finn. And I was, y'know, there.'

She seemed pleasantly surprised, if a little disappointed I'd stolen her thunder. 'And here you are again,' she said.

The lights turned green. This time we managed to make it through two sets before getting caught behind a red again. 'What're you saying?' I said.

'I'm saying, the Hamiltons will do okay. Me and you, we're walking away with nothing. But if we were to—'

'Forget it. You're going to Knock and you're getting on that plane.'

'Right. And then go home and tell them I'm pregnant and we all live happily ever after.'

'Not my problem.'

'No?'

'Not right now.'

'Except you don't know the baby isn't yours.'

'You want me and you to play happy families?'

'I'm saying, Harry, that you already lost one kid today. You want to make it a twofer?'

She was good, no doubt about it. The lights went green again. We cleared the roundabout opposite Summerhill, heading south now, the road clear.

'I'm serious,' she said. 'I'll abort. No way I'm going home to Ozanköy carrying some kid I don't even know who the father is.'

I pulled over onto the hard shoulder, parked up, got the hazard lights flashing. She watched me roll a smoke, spark it up.

'Forget the laptop,' I said.

She smirked. 'You're the one keeps banging on about the laptop. You seriously think Finn'd be dumb enough to keep anything useful on it? Saoirse could've sent some scumbag in any time she wanted, break into his apartment, the studio.'

'So why's everyone want the Mac?'

'Saoirse wouldn't be exactly up to speed on the latest in computing. So long as she thought everyone else wanted the Mac . . .'

'The woman's looking for a suicide note. Wants to know why her son—'

'Come on, Harry. You still believe that crap?'

It didn't matter a fiddler's fuck what I believed anymore. 'So if there's nothing on the laptop . . .' I prompted.

'There's a flash drive.'

'Right.'

'Finn buried it all.'

'I hope he marked it with an X.'

'In cyberspace,' she said.

'Christ.'

She was talking about Grainne's trust fund. How Gillick had worked with Big Bob Hamilton on a rewrite of his will, this not long before Big Bob went for a header off the dock. Essentially, the changes put Finn in control of the trust fund once he came of age.

The flash drive had all the codes, the passwords, the details of the electronic transfers Finn had been making over the last couple of years as he bled the fund dry.

'How much are we talking?' I said.

'Well, the downturn has changed everything. It's not worth anything like—'

'How much?'

'One-point-eight million,' she said.

'Jesus.'

I wondered how Ben might have turned out, bright kid that he was, had there been a trust fund waiting for him when he came of age. A tidy little nest egg to put him through college, maybe set him up in business designing his own computer games.

The pain of him throbbing now, as if I'd become entirely an abscess, skin stretched taut across a pus-filled void.

'What's wrong?' she said.

'I'm just wondering,' I said, 'what happens if you get your hands on this one-point-eight.'

'We do a split,' she said.

'Wrong answer. But what I'm asking is, what's to stop you taking the money, aborting the baby and taking off for Monte Carlo to find another sap like Finn?'

'Because I need it for something else.'

'And what's that?'

'To break Saoirse.'

'Say again?'

'I'll be needing most of it,' she said, 'to break Saoirse.'

Which was interesting. 'How'll you do that?'

'The first thing,' she ticked it off on her finger, 'is a paternity test proving the baby is Finn's.'

'Which might be expensive,' I said. 'Especially if it's not.'

'Meanwhile,' she went on, 'I need to hire a PR company, get a campaign organised to let all the investors know where they really stand with Hamilton Holdings. Get enough of them on board to call an EGM, bring in some outside accountants to take a look at the books. At the same time we're asking some questions of NAMA, making sure the right journos have the inside line on how HaHo is setting up to buy back the choicest bits of its portfolio at rip-off prices, screwing the taxpayer.' She'd thought it through. Not all the way, maybe, but at least she was facing in the right direction. 'The newspapers love all that family feud shit, don't they?'

'Their readers do, anyway.' I took a last drag off the smoke, dropped it out the window. 'You're serious about this?'

She got herself half-turned in the passenger seat so she was facing me. 'You can think what you want about me and Finn,' she said, 'all that gold-digging crap, but I never gave a fuck about his money. It was Saoirse who was all about the money. And now Hamilton Holdings is fucked, about all that's left is Grainne's trust fund. Which was why Saoirse was pressuring Finn, giving him all this family-first bullshit. Time to circle the wagons, start again. Why do you think he started making transfers out of the fund in the first place?'

'Knowing Finn, I'd say it was because he reckoned one-point-eight million would buy him a nice slice of the easy life in Cyprus.'

'Because you're like all the rest. One time,' she cracked a grimace, 'Saoirse told him the money was his crutch. Saoirse, of all fucking people. Telling him he needed to stand up straight, learn to walk on his own.'

'Maybe she knew him better than you think.'

She nodded at that, slowly. 'She knew him well enough to know what buttons to press,' she said. 'And I don't care what any inquest says, it was Saoirse who walked him out that window and pushed.'

And then he came down on my cab and blew my life to shit, taking Ben with him as collateral damage.

It had a nice symmetry, alright. Grab Saoirse Hamilton's blood money and make her choke on it.

'This flash drive,' I said. 'It could be anywhere.'

'Sure,' she said. A nasty little grin. 'Except you knew Finn, his perverse sense of humour. If Saoirse was giving him grief about money being his crutch, where would he be likely to hide the flash?'

35

The PA yard still stank of burnt petrol, warm tar. The crime scene tape hanging limp.

'Didn't take them long to move on, did it?' Maria said.

Budgets and resources being what they are these days, I was more surprised they hadn't taken the crime scene tape with them when they left. The chalk outline, too.

We gave the scorch mark a wide berth, the jam stain on the tarmac that was still purple at its centre but mostly sun-browned and flaking. It was worth trying the door, on the off-chance the cops had wandered away without locking up, but no joy. So I left Maria out front and went around the side, scaled the rusted fire escape again. Came in through the studio as the phone Herb had given me beeped, a text message to say Maria's flight was booked, 7.30 PM to Gatwick out of Knock. Which gave us about three hours. I went on down the metal stairs to the ground floor, padding across the silent gallery. Let Maria in, directed her to the window.

'You keep sketch,' I said. 'If anything moves, do that scream thing again.'

Then I crossed to the rear of the gallery, went through to the storage area behind. Opened the metal door and got a half-second warning, the clickering of nails on concrete, realising too late I hadn't announced my presence. A furry Panzer exploded out of the dark. Jaws open, teeth gleaming in the gloom. I ducked away, rearing back, so the crown of his head hit me full-force in the chest. Heard the jaws snap and then I was down, bowled over. He skittered on the concrete as his paws scrabbled for grip, and then he bunched and sprang again.

Sprawled on my back, winded and weak, it was all I could do to meet his lunge halfway, bounce an elbow off his snout, grab a handful of rough fur beneath his throat. Gobs of spittle spattering my face as he slavered and snarled, forepaws on my chest, the rear scraping in my groin like he was rucking out a scrum. I tried kneeing him off but he had all the weight and momentum, his relentless twisting and snapping wearing me down.

There came a shrill whistle with a neat little trill. His head shot up as if jerked by a chain, ears pricking. A plaintive whine.

'*Bear*,' Maria urged. 'C'mere, Bear!'

One last gouge in my groin and he was gone, launching himself at Maria like some grotesque teddy bear, all snuffles and short barks, skittish now. I sat up, shaking so hard I could barely tug my shirt free, wipe the drool from my face.

Starving, I guessed, and maddened for the want of water cooped up in that heat. Had the cops fed him before they'd left? Doubtful.

I went into the storage room and opened a couple of well-gnawed cans of dog food, scooped them into a bowl. Brought that outside and put it down on the ground, slid it across the concrete in his general direction. He'd wolfed it all down when I got back from the bathroom with a bowl of water, Maria hunkered along-side tugging his ears, so I opened another couple of cans of food while he inhaled the water, lapping at it so fast he splashed more than he drank.

'He's just a big dopey kid really,' Maria crooned, tears in her eyes as she tickled Bear under the throat. 'Aren't you, Bear?'

A big dopey kid, sure. When you weren't eyeball to eyeball, his jaws crunching, eyes rolling back white in their sockets. All the better, my dear, to inspect the instinct that had taken his lupine ancestors all the way from the tundra to the ground floor of an art gallery a couple of million years later.

A big dopey stone-cold killer.

Except it wasn't really Bear she was talking to. It was the other big dopey kid, the one with the Brian Jones fringe and shit-don't-matter grin, the one who'd walked away forever when he'd taken a stroll off nine stories out into the big empty. I was tempted to suggest she'd be better off talking to the jam stain out in the yard, but I let it slide, went through to the storage room again. The place stank of stale piss and shit, although at least Bear'd had the good grace, or sense of self-preservation, to leave all his deposits in one corner. The pile of crutches lay loosely stacked behind his kennel. I picked one up, shook it. Then another. The rattle of their hitting the concrete alerted Maria to the reason we were there, and she slipped in beside me, picked up a crutch.

She swallowed hard, although whether that was from the rancid stench or some repressed emotion was anyone's guess. 'We were supposed to be bringing these home to Cyprus,' she said.

'I heard, yeah.' Finn, the part-time philanthropist. 'Noble as all fuck, he was.'

She shook the crutch, tossed it aside. Bear wandered in, licking his chops. 'No need to get pissy,' she said.

'I just said he was noble as all fuck. What more do you want?'

She shook another crutch, threw it down. Bear had a nuzzle at it, wandered off. 'Some people used to get sniffy about it, alright,' she said. A tart edge now to her tone. 'Mainly because it made them feel bad about not helping out.'

'Not me.'

She gave a light shrug. 'I guess some people are more inclined to help.'

'Spare me the *noblesse* fucking *oblige*, alright? The guy had more time and money than was healthy, he was working off his guilt and impressing the pants off you in the process. Nice work if you can get it.'

'Jealous much?'

'Keep talking,' I waved a crutch at her, 'and you'll be needing one of—'

A dull clunk. Her eyes widened.

The crutches were telescopic, the kind with holes punched in the lower half so they were adjustable to the user's height. I pushed the metal knobs in, twisted the bottom half of the crutch free. A silver-grey flash-drive dropped out onto the concrete.

Neither of us reached for it. Instead we stared at the rolled-up canvas protruding from the top half of the crutch.

'What's *that*?' Maria said.

I slid the canvas free, unfurled it. A landscape scene, some upland moor of rock and heather, a vast sky, a storm brewing.

There were sixty-plus crutches in the pile. We went through

them all. Twenty minutes later we were staring at nine canvases in total, all landscapes. Each one signed, none of them by Finn.

The one that caught my eye was a fiery sunset, a vermillion blaze I could've sworn I'd seen in the very recent past, hanging opposite a bank of elevators in a hospital lobby. Not that my testimony would've been worth shit. Any half-decent lawyer would've torn me to shreds, this on the basis that I'd been pie-eyed on pills at the time, and perhaps understandably distracted as I staggered upstairs to visit my son, comatose in intensive care.

'I don't get it,' she said.

'Maybe the crippled orphans were supposed to pin them on their walls,' I said, 'brighten up the place a little.'

36

Maria pocketed the flash drive, got the leash on Bear. More of a chain, really, with a plaited-leather grip. The canvases went back into the crutches. Originals, I was guessing, their fake twins hanging on walls all over the country. I wondered if they were all Finn's work, or if he hadn't brought some of the Spiritus Mundi crew in on the scam.

Either way, they'd come in useful the next time I saw Tohill. Nine originals in oil had to be worth at least the equivalent of ten grand in coke in a trade, especially when the oils could well be that thread Tohill was looking to pull.

We stepped out into the blazing sunshine, blinking against the glare. Bear tensed, growled low in his throat.

He was leaning back against the Phaeton, shades on, face upturned to the sun. Basking, both hands in the pockets of the waist-length leather jacket.

Toto fucking McConnell.

'So I'm on my way over to Herbie's to see what the story is

about a certain delivery I'm expecting,' he said, 'because for some reason Herb isn't answering his phone, when I get a call from one of the boys, says he's seen Jimmy's motor only it's not Jimmy driving, it's this guy he thinks he knows from the taxi rank, Harry Rigby, only he's wearing an eye-patch so he can't be sure. Now this is interesting, because Harry Rigby should know something about this certain delivery I'm waiting on, so I ring Jimmy to see what the score is, why Rigby has his car. Except Jimmy isn't answering his phone either. So I tell the guy to stay with the Phaeton, keep me posted. Next thing I hear, Rigby's down at the docks, the PA building, where the guy he vouched for a couple of nights back took a dive onto one of my cabs. So here I am, wondering what's what.'

There was no one in the battered Golf he'd parked to one side, but that meant nothing. He could've had a couple of guys staked out anywhere, maybe waiting outside the yard.

'I vouched for Finn that he'd pay for his weed,' I said, stacking the crutches against the Phaeton's boot, 'not that he wasn't suicidal.'

'Sure,' Toto said, 'only Herb says you got the paying bit wrong too. What's with the crutches?'

'They're for a charity Finn used to run with Maria here,' I said, nodding back to where she stood rigid with the effort of restraining Bear. 'They were planning to get married.'

'Sorry to hear it,' he said, dipping his head at Maria, a brief bow. 'Condolences on your loss.'

'Who's this?' she said.

'Just some business I need to take care of. You get in the car.'

Toto slipped his left hand out of his pocket, held it up. 'Stall the ball. No one's going anywhere yet.' The gesture, his tone, got

Bear growling again. 'Keep a good grip of that hound,' he told Maria, 'or I might get nervous.' He came back to me. 'So what's the story? Jimmy being family, you can start with him.' He saw something in my eyes, stood away from the car. Tightened his grip on whatever it was he had buried in his right pocket. 'Rigby,' he said, 'I got enough problems right now. And the last thing I need is my sister chirping in my ear, wondering where Saint fucking James is, if he hasn't done another runner, send out a search party. Where's he at?'

Jimmy, as it happened, was lying prone and semi-conscious about two feet from where he stood. Sweat sliding down the back of my thighs at the prospect of Toto's sister trying to ring him, Jimmy's phone sounding from the boot.

'It's complicated,' I said.

'So give me bullet points.'

'That, uh, delivery,' I said, 'it's gone.'

'Gone?'

'I got run off the road coming back from Galway, ended up in hospital.' I shrugged. 'The cops have it.'

'They found it in the car?'

'That's right.'

'What'd you tell them?'

'Said I knew nothing about it, they must have planted it there.'

'And they just let you waltz out free.'

'No, I bolted from the hospital when they brought me down for an X-ray.'

'So they'll be looking for you right now.'

'It's not exactly a manhunt, and no one got around to reading me my rights, but yeah. If they find me, they'll pull me in.'

'Fuck.'

'Toto,' I said, 'it's on me. I know that. And I'm making it good.'

'Oh yeah?'

'I got this gig going on, someone's asked me to retrieve their personal belongings. Paying me ten grand to do it.' No point in telling him about the twenty straight away, he'd want the lot off the bat. 'Soon as I deliver, the ten grand goes to you, leaves us clean on the, y'know, delivery.'

'First off,' he said, 'that delivery was needed for tonight, I was specific on that. And I was guaranteed. So there's penalties.'

'I know all that.'

'Yeah? So how're you going to pay that off, you're up the fucking Swannee on ten grand worth of product? And where the fuck,' he said, 'is Jimmy?'

'Jimmy's guy, Gillick, the solicitor, he's brokering this gig I have going on. His client being too posh to dirty her hands with cash. So Gillick told Jimmy, seeing as I didn't have any transport, to lend me his Phaeton to get the deal done.'

'So why isn't he answering his phone?'

'I don't know. Gillick lives up the back of Lough Gill, out in the sticks. Maybe there's no coverage, all the mountains.'

The shades made it impossible to read his eyes. 'When do you kick this ten grand free?'

'I'm on my way there now.' I picked up a crutch, hefted it. 'Soon as I get these loaded up.'

'So you wouldn't mind if I tagged along behind, just for the spin.'

'It's a free country.'

'Okay,' he said. 'But listen, Rigby, if I get the feeling you're—'

There came a tinny, muffled sound from the Phaeton's boot. A mobile phone ringtone. Wings, 'Live and Let Die.'

Toto's head turned instinctively, just a fraction, but that was enough. It helped, too, that whatever he had buried in his pocket snagged as he stepped back already drawing. I was only going to get one chance so I swung from the knees, aiming for the bleachers. The crutch smashed into the side of his head, sent the shades flying. He staggered and reeled back, then went down on one knee, toppled over onto his side. I stepped in, Bear snapping and snarling behind me, stepped on his wrist and reached in, eased the gun from his pocket. A Beretta, if the legend stamped on its barrel was any guide, 9mm. The safety off.

I thumbed the safety on, pointed the Beretta at his face. 'Up,' I told him.

The crack on the head had been hard enough to put a bend in the crutch. Dazed, blood seeping from a ragged gash over his ear, he dragged himself to his feet, stood there swaying. I popped the Phaeton's boot, gestured at it. 'Get in.'

It boasts a roomy trunk, the Phaeton, but Jimmy was a big man. It was going to be a tight fit. Toto, eyes glazed, didn't move.

'Get in,' I said, 'or I'll lock you into the PA with the hound.'

'Rigby,' he said. Sounding drunk, or delirious. 'You don't know what you're doing.'

'I'll figure it out.' I stepped in behind him, put a hand on his shoulder, pushed him on. A pity I hadn't brought the masking tape from Herb's. 'Now get in.'

It took him a couple of attempts, but he finally clambered inside. 'Turn over on your front,' I told him. Once he was in position I patted him down. Came up with two phones and a four-inch blade he had taped to his right calf. Jimmy's phone was more of a struggle, it being jammed in his pocket, but eventually I came up with it. He had seven missed calls.

I slammed the boot closed, went weak at the knees. No going back now.

Like the man said, when you're in, you're in.

The Beretta went into my belt alongside the .38 Special. Getting crowded back there now, a Gatling gun short of starting a revolution.

I tossed the crutches into the back seat, slammed the door. Bear snuffing at the Phaeton's boot, intrigued by the scent of blood. I glanced over at Maria to chivvy her on and realised she was staring at me, standing stock still, her expression caught somewhere between horror and disgust.

Nothing new there, then.

'You can get in,' I said, 'or you can try riding Bear all the way to Knock. Your call.'

37

Maria shushed Bear a couple of times when he whined at being forced to lie doggo in the well behind the front seats, but otherwise she didn't speak again until we'd cleared the town and were heading out along the lake shore, the road meandering through a tunnel of trees. We passed Dooney Rock.

In shock, I supposed. I couldn't blame her. First I'm cracking Toto over the head and waving his gun around. And then, we open the boot, there's Jimmy drenched in blood.

I'd never paid much attention in school, but now I was wishing I'd paid none at all. So I wouldn't know that every action has an equal and opposite reaction.

I could dump the car, sure, and run, take Saoirse Hamilton's twenty grand and never look back. No Ben to keep me here now.

Except that'd leave Herb to face Toto. Dee, too.

No. We were playing for keeps now, going all the way.

I reached Herb's print-out from the dashboard, Gillick's place Google-mapped, gave it to Maria. Told her we had a pit stop to make before we headed for Knock. I was expecting her to protest but all she said was, 'He was smuggling those paintings out, wasn't he?'

Grit under her nails as she sifted Finn's clay feet.

'Well,' I said, 'they do say it'll be an export-led recovery that'll dig us out of recession.'

'You think he stole them?' she said.

'I'd say he was given them.'

'You mean, like, donations to charity.'

'Something like that, yeah. Keep an eye on the map.'

We came up on Slish Wood, Maria following the red line with a forefinger. 'Looks like the second left after this,' she said.

I turned off the main road, up a narrow rutted lane and into a forest of pines. A steep incline. I dropped down into second, then first. Maria balled the map, tossed it on the floor.

'Don't get carried away,' I said. 'We might need that yet.'

'We're going to Gillick's, right?'

'Yeah.'

She'd been before, with Finn, a couple of times. Barbecues and long boozy summer evenings on the decking overlooking the lake. 'What are we doing here?' she said.

'Jimmy reckons Gillick was the one told him Ben was in hospital. I want to know how he knew.'

'What will that achieve?'

'Depends on how Gillick knew.'

The Phaeton bounced down and out of a pothole and set the crutches a-rattle on the back seat. A dull bellow followed. Toto, feeling his chops. I reached over and punched the stereo on, was more than a little surprised to hear the delicate, unadorned tinkling of a piano. Schubert, I thought. I'd have had Jimmy down as a guitar man, Metallica, maybe some Led Zep if he was going old school.

We crested the summit, a razor-backed ridge in the pines. There the lane branched, the right tine curving away and down through the trees to run parallel with the ridge.

'Straight ahead,' she said.

We were high above a lake shaped like a crooked finger, maybe half a mile long and a couple of hundred yards wide, nestled in a steep-sided valley velvet with pine.

I pulled over, put the handbrake on. Found Jimmy's phone and brought up his list of contacts, scrolled down, jabbed the one called 'Fat Man'.

It rang twice, and then Gillick came on. 'Where are you?'

'It's Rigby.'

'Oh?'

'Jimmy's driving, asked me to ring ahead. Says we're coming in.'

'And not before time.'

'He says we have the laptop, wants to be sure it's all clear.'

'Clear?'

'He doesn't want to fetch up with the Mac if there's anyone else there.'

'Why would anyone else be here?'

I covered the phone with my hand, repeated the question, then said, 'He says there's no harm in being careful.'

'Indeed. Be so good as to put Jimmy on, Mr Rigby.'

'Okay, hold on. Jimmy? Gillick wants to talk to you.'

I hung up.

'This won't bring him back,' she said.

I wasn't sure if she meant Finn or Ben.

322

'Not the point,' I said.

'But you are going in there to kill him.'

I thought about quoting her some Shakespeare, the bit about how we first kill all the lawyers, but the time for cheap cracks was long gone.

'I want to know who ran us off the road,' I said, 'who made that call. If it was Gillick, then yeah, I'm going to kill him. You want to step out, do it now. But here's the thing,' I said. 'You believe Saoirse's the one who killed Finn, walked him out onto that ledge, gave him the nudge, okay. But she couldn't have worked him, had the kind of leverage she'd need, if Gillick wasn't backing her every step of the way. He's the legal eagle pulling all the strings. And that night at the PA, according to Saoirse, he was there to tell Finn to kick you into touch.'

Her throat tightened. She chucked Bear under the chin. 'Drive on,' she said.

I knocked the car out of gear but kept my foot on the brake as we bumped and jolted down what was starting to look a lot like the dry bed of a waterfall. The pines began to thin out. Soon we emerged into a clearing that sloped down to the edge of a cliff. The lane veered sharply to the right into a sheltered parking area of loosely packed rough stone, where I reversed and turned, pointing the Phaeton back the way we'd come. The only thing to spoil the view was a low wood-frame bungalow squatting near the edge of the cliff.

'Maybe I should come in,' she said. A dry rasp in her throat. 'Hear what Gillick has to say for himself.'

'See no evil,' I said, 'do no time.'

'I'll take my chances.'

'Except you're taking chances for two now,' I said. 'So you

don't have the right to make that kind of call anymore.'

'I need to know. About Finn, what he was really planning.'

'I appreciate that, sure. But—'

'Swear on Ben,' she said. Husky now. 'Swear you'll ask him.'

'I'll ask, yeah.'

'*Swear* it.'

I swore. Then I gave her the Beretta, on the off-chance Toto managed to kick his way out of the boot.

'I'm not asking you to shoot him,' I said. 'If he gets out, fire off a shot and make for the trees. He won't come after you knowing you're tooled up. Okay?'

It wasn't okay, not by any reasonably civilised standards, but she nodded.

I got out, crossed the parking area and strolled around to the front of the bungalow. Except it wasn't a bungalow. The house had been built into the hill, its frontage split-level, the upper half all glass. Decking ran the full length of the house and was probably exhausted by the time it disappeared around the far corner.

The sun was warm on my back as I climbed the wooden steps, the smell of fresh pine sharp and clean. Birds chirped and whittered. Below on the lake, two small islands shimmered in the haze. Then I stepped up onto the porch and saw Gillick, a napkin tucked between his third and fourth chins. He wore a pale blue short-sleeved shirt open at the neck, knee-length shorts, a dainty pair of deck shoes. Given the amount of flabby flesh on view, it was akin to arriving at Jeremiah Johnson's cabin to find Jabba the Hutt claiming squatter's rights.

'Ah,' he purred, 'the elusive Mr Rigby. Would you be so kind as to join me?'

He beckoned me on and turned without waiting to see if I'd do his bidding. I followed him inside and down a glassed-in walk-way that ran parallel with the decking outside, the wall on our right defaced at regular intervals by examples of what can go wrong when a man is given too much paint and not enough sex. At the end of the corridor he turned into an office-cum-conser-vatory with a large walnut-wood desk near the wood-panelled back wall, a two-piece leather suite angled to face the desk, two filing cabinets standing sentinel either side of the desk. On the desk sat a Mac Pro, a printer and a tidy version of the usual office clutter, loose pens and a block of Post-Its, a yellow legal pad defaced with doodles. A crystal-cut ashtray, on which was perched a cigar the cops would be requisitioning if the truncheon factory ever burned down. The shelves behind the desk were lined with legal tomes bound in green leather and nary a cracked spine to be seen.

'That night at the PA,' I said, just to be conversational. 'What was this favour you wanted to do Finn?'

He held up a hand without looking around, the forefinger extended, beckoning me on again. I expected him to turn into the office but instead he kept going, plodding ahead into the conser-vatory. There a small dining table sat before the floor-to-ceiling window offering an expansive view of the lake below, the ridge beyond tinged ruddy as the sun dipped for home. He went around the table and eased his bulk down into the chair. 'Please,' he said, 'sit down. Make yourself comfortable.'

The .38 was digging into my spine standing up, so I passed. He'd already eaten, the dirty plate pushed to one side to make room for a couple of smaller plates of grapes and crackers and what looked like a spectacularly whiffy brie. A large cafetière sat filled to the brim with hot nectar, but he reached for the bottle of red, topped up his glass. That he slid across the table towards me, then sloshed some more wine into the coffee cup.

'No sense in standing on ceremony,' he said. 'Will you join me?'

'I'm not hungry,' I said. The howls of protest from my belly were the screams of the damned. 'Just tell me about Finn and this favour.'

'At least have some coffee. It's freshly brewed.' He was slathering brie onto a cracker. 'Colombian, the real McCoy. Have you ever had the pleasure? In Colombia they say it's a better hit than cocaine. Not,' he gave a cute smile, 'that I'd know.'

'If you're waiting for Jimmy, he won't be coming.'

He'd taken a bite of cracker and brie, so his 'No?' came muffled. He swallowed. 'Why so?'

'He's indisposed.'

'Really.'

'Ring him,' I said.

His eyes were thoughtful, reassessing, as he stared. Then he dabbed at the corners of his mouth with the napkin, picked up his phone. Pressed a button. After a moment or two, the faint strains of 'Live and Let Die' wafted up from under the table. I reached into my pocket, took out Jimmy's phone and hit the answer button. 'This is Jimmy,' I said. 'I'm fucked four ways to next Tuesday. Leave a message and I'll get back to you. On Tuesday.'

I hung up and put the phone away. Gillick, nodding, laid his own phone on the table, picked up the other half of the cracker-and-brie, then had second thoughts and put it down again. 'It would appear,' he said, 'that events have taken an unexpected turn.'

'Jimmy said you wanted a chat with Grainne. She couldn't make it. I'm here instead.'

'Indeed you are. Larger than life and twice as resourceful.'

'Just pang-wangling along, happy as a sandboy.'

He smiled at that, a tired and cynical smile that fumbled for purchase on his greasy lips. 'Shall we proceed to business, then?'

'Let's do that.'

'Very well.' He drained the wine and then reached for the cafetière, poured a cup of coffee. This time he made no offers. He got up and carried the coffee through to the office, put it down on the desk and went straight to the framed nightmare on the wall behind, this one an impressionistic take on spaghetti meatballs or a grenade in the guts. I was ready to go, standing sideways on, hand hovering near my hip in case he came up with some hardware, but when he turned he was holding nothing more sinister than a brown envelope.

He tossed it onto my side of the desk, then lowered his bulk into the leather swivel chair. 'I am authorised by Mrs Hamilton to pay the agreed fee for retrieving Finn's computer,' he said. 'You'll find twenty thousand euro in that.'

I picked up the envelope, had a peek inside. Disappointed at how slim a bundle was twenty grand cash. I slid it out, balled the envelope, dropped it on the floor.

'We'll consider this a deposit,' I said, holding up the twenty grand. 'Ring Saoirse, tell her the fee's changed. I'll be wanting one-point-eight million.'

'Pardon me?'

'I'll also be wanting to know what it is on the Mac she's so desperate to find.'

'But Mr Rigby.' He seemed genuinely outraged. 'That deal was made in good faith.'

'Is that a fact?'

'Well, yes, it is.'

'So what kind of faith was it that had Jimmy scoping out Finn's apartment when I was picking up the laptop?'

His lips flattened. 'That was simply a case of Mrs Hamilton protecting her investment.'

'You're saying, she didn't trust me not to bunk off with the Mac. Dig into it, maybe, find out why she really wants it back. Put the squeeze on.'

He'd had enough of being lectured by the undeserving poor. He leaned back in his chair, crossed one flabby calf over the other, joined his hands on his paunch. 'It is not my place, Mr Rigby, to question Mrs Hamilton's motives. And now that she has commissioned you to provide a service, neither is it yours.'

'You want me to remember my place.'

'I want you to focus on what you are doing here.'

'What I'm mainly doing here,' I said, 'is getting ready to put a bullet in your fat fucking face.'

'Excuse me?'

'You heard.'

He had, but he'd heard it all before. The kind of defendants Gillick specialised in, that line was probably something of a negotiating tactic, an opening gambit to keep him on his toes. 'I'm afraid I don't understand,' he said.

'I'd imagine the idea was for me to do the dirty bit, the break-and-enter, truck the laptop and young Grainne out here. Then Jimmy'd step in, swipe the Mac, turn me out. Where am I going to go, the cops?'

'That's a rather lurid leap to make, Mr Rigby.'

'Meanwhile, you're having a cosy chat with Grainne about the trust fund, the one-point-eight mil. Trying to persuade her that now is not the time to go making drastic decisions, that she's a little fucked up, not thinking straight. Best to leave these things to the grown-ups, for now anyway. Am I anywhere close?'

'I am the executor of Finn's will, Mr Rigby. I would be derelict in my duty were I not to do my utmost to convince Grainne that certain decisions would not be in her best interests.'

'The girl knows what she wants.'

'She's distraught, Mr Rigby. Bereaved. She and Finn were very close, you know.'

'So she says. Close enough that he told her about the changes he made to the trust fund.'

The porcine little eyes glittered, as if he'd caught sight of a trove of truffles. 'Is that a fact?'

'I saw it myself.'

'Did you, indeed?' He sat forward and reached for the coffee and had himself a sip, the pinky finger shooting the moon. 'And what else did you see?'

'Not much.'

A wry smile. 'Please, Mr Rigby. According to Jimmy you were in Finn's apartment for approximately forty minutes. I can only assume that you found this information on the laptop.'

'Assume again.'

'Where else might you have seen it?'

'That's between me and Grainne.'

Another sip of Colombia's finest. 'I do hope,' he said, 'that you're not taking advantage of that girl's misfortune. It's perfectly understandable that she's angry right now, and disappointed, and seeking, in that unfortunate way people have, to strike out and cause others to feel a pain akin to her own. Mrs Hamilton wants only the best for Grainne, but that's not always how—'

'What Mrs Hamilton wants is the Mac.'

'Well, yes, she does want her property returned. But in terms of the bigger picture, her instincts are to—'

'And the gun.'

'Gun?'

I reached around and untucked the .38, laid it on the table. A couple of chins wobbled as he slumped in the chair. From the expression in his eyes he was watching the trove of truffles being carted away. Then he heaved himself more or less vertical and reached for the gun.

I snaffled it back. More nodding, more chins a-wobble. A weariness to him now. 'I can only assume,' he said, 'that this is why the price has jumped so exorbitantly.'

'You'd want to rethink that whole assuming lark,' I said. 'It's getting you nowhere fast. This,' I pointed the gun at his face, 'is here to kill you. Simple as that.'

This time I got through. Maybe it was staring down that little black hole, and maybe it was the way I said it, but he realised there was no negotiating involved, no tactics.

'Mr Rigby,' he said, 'I must tell you that I'm not in any position to pay over any more money than has already been—'

'Forget the fucking money, Gillick. This isn't about money.'

Now he was truly at a loss. Eyes wide, mouth agape. I could almost hear the cogs whirring in the back of his head.

If it wasn't about money, what could it possibly be?

It was fascinating to watch on a purely anthropological level. Gillick looked a lot like a squid that had found itself high and dry on a mountain peak with a sudden but somewhat vague understanding of Heisenberg's Uncertainty Principle.

To confuse him further, I lobbed the bundle of notes at his face. Notes fluttered in the air, and his instinct was to reach and grab.

By then I was halfway across the desk, landing ankle-deep in a wobbly mess of chins. We hit the floor in a tangle of leather, chrome and flailing limbs. Being about a hundred pounds lighter and feeding off a murderous rage, I was first to my knees. Yanked the chair out of the way and cracked him flush on the mouth with the butt of the .38, followed up with a left cross to his right jaw that cracked the knuckle of my little finger. I heard myself yelp. Gillick flopped back, his eyes rolling up in their sockets.

By the time he came back I'd ripped the sash-cords off the blinds and got his hands bound behind his back. No mean feat when the knuckle of your little finger has swollen to the size of a decent conker.

I clenched my left fist, felt the pain shoot up into my elbow and ricochet off into the icy core.

'How'd you know about Ben?' I said.

He blinked, groggy, the eyes round and owlish. 'Wha . . . ?'

'Jimmy said he heard from you that my boy was in hospital. How'd you know?'

The flattened prim beak leaked blood and a couple of teeth as he half-spat, said, 'I don't—'

'Slow down. You're not thinking.'

I got up and righted the chair. Put the gun on the desk and retrieved the crystal-cut ashtray, the cigar, from where they'd landed near the filing cabinet. Then I sat down on the chair. When the cigar was glowing I leaned in and exhaled in his face.

'Cuban,' I said. 'Am I right?'

'Rigby, I know nothing about your kid.'

'You knew enough to know he was in hospital.'

'It was on the *news*, for Chrissakes. The accident.'

'The accident, maybe. Our names were strictly under wraps.' I took a good pull on the cigar, got the tip glowing again. Held it close to his lower lip. His eyes flared and he twisted his head away, so I singed his earlobe instead. He squealed.

'That's so you know I'm serious. Every time you move, you get burnt. Okay?'

He nodded.

'Jimmy told me,' I said, 'that he heard it from you. So that means you called it, or whoever called it told you. Which?'

He shook his head and half-shrugged, helpless. I scooched in close, placed the tip of the cigar half an inch from his chin. His head tilted back so that he was looking into my eyes.

'Are you religious?' I said.

'No.'

'Me neither. Lapsed Catholic. Still, the old learning dies hard.' I tapped my eye-patch. 'An eye for an eye and all that.'

'But I don't *know*—'

'Gillick,' I said gently, 'there's no cavalry coming. Jimmy's fucked. So focus, man. It's you and me, and I just lost my son. Which pretty much means I've got nothing left to live for. I don't know, maybe that'll pass, they say it does. But right now I don't give a flying fuck what I do or who I do it to. Are we clear?'

We were, albeit a little too clear. Somewhere in there I'd lost him, taken away his last hope.

Do that, all you leave a man is his dignity.

The way his hands were tied it was physically impossible for him to square his shoulders. But it was there in his eyes. A sudden hardness behind the damp gleaming, as if he'd scraped through to bedrock.

'Fuck you,' he whispered. Then he spat a bloody gob.

He was nowhere as practised as Tohill. The gob flopped to one side, dribbled away down his cheek. I puffed on the cigar again. His jaw muscles tightened. There was pain in the post but his mind was a-swirl, drunk on dignity. Sweat glistening on his forehead.

'Last chance,' I said. 'From here on in, there's no rules.'

'Fuck. You.'

'Your call.'

I flexed my fist, felt the pain burn. Then I sat back and placed the cigar on the crystal-cut ashtray. Bent in again, thumbs cocked.

He started to frown before he realised what I was about. He shrieked, but by then I was already digging in.

I had no idea a man's eye socket could be so deep. My thumb was buried to the second knuckle when I scraped back and out. His scream set the fillings in my teeth a-shiver as I puffed again on the cigar. The eyeball lay on his cheek like a wobbly marble, still attached by stringy muscle. Tears seeped out of the socket and down his cheek, under the eye. I touched the tip of the cigar against the wetness. It hissed.

'Jesus Christ *no*,' he rasped.

The coming together of a glowing ember and the vitreous substance encasing an eyeball is an unedifying sight, but I'd been expecting that. What I hadn't factored in was the smell. It was that of a half-boiled egg jammed against a hot pan.

Twice I raised gritty blisters singeing the eyeball.

The second time he knew there'd be a third, a fourth.

'Grainne,' he gulped. 'It was Grainne Hamilton.'

'Bullfuckingshit.'

'She heard you . . .' He gasped. 'Heard you on the phone. When you rang the hospital from . . . from the Grange.'

That made a kind of sense. 'And she told you?'

A nod.

'No way Grainne Hamilton ran anyone off the road,' I said. 'So who did it?'

He didn't know. Or so he said. I had myself another pull on the cigar and he broke. Everyone does in the end. He started babbling, begging. His theory being that so long as he was talking, I wouldn't be singeing.

It took a couple of slaps around the head to get him focused, and then I pointed the .38 at his good eye, slipped the safety off, cocked the hammer.

'Listen good,' I said. 'If it wasn't you, you don't need to die. But I know you have a best guess.'

He did, and when it all tumbled out it sounded like I was mostly to blame for Ben's dying, this because I'd told Saoirse Hamilton on the phone that I'd come see her after I got back from Galway, and that I already had what she was looking for.

There's only one Galway-Sligo road. I'd been driving Finn's Audi. The rest had been easy.

'She thought I had Finn's suicide note,' I said. He closed his good eye and nodded. The raw socket mocked me, its eyelid flopping. 'What was she so worried about?' I said. 'What'd she think it'd say?'

'The safe,' he moaned. 'The safe.'

I got up and crossed to the painting of exploding meatballs, pushed it aside. Inside the safe were a number of slim manila envelopes of varying sizes, all blank. A small case in black velvet, inside of which was a matching necklace-and-earring set in jade. 'What am I looking for?' I said.

He directed me to the top right-hand corner of the rear wall, told me to feel around. 'There's a catch,' he mumbled.

'Isn't there always?'

I slid my finger up the right side of the safe, felt a small bump. I jiggled it back and forth, up and down, then pressed hard. There came a soft click. The back wall of the safe sprung, leaving a half-inch gap. Behind was a single buff manila envelope. Inside was a blank CD in clear plastic and two pale blue Basildon Bond envelopes, one blank, the other with an address handwritten in Finn's flowing cursive script.

Back at the desk I slipped the CD into Gillick's laptop. When the folder popped up, I clicked it open. It contained a single document, a spreadsheet. The first page was titled 'Irish'.

O'Leary, George: 17/3/2010 – €12k
Smyth, Val: 24/5/2010 – €14k
McCaul, Manus: 09/6/2010 – €21k
Walsh, Padraig: 11/8/2010 – €8k
Callaghan, Cormac: 21/9/2010 – €11k
O'Toole, Hugh: 14/11/2010 – €17k
Byrne, Brian: 05/2/2011 – €13k
Kelly, Paul Christopher: 12/3/2011 – €9k
Flynn, Bryan: 23/3/2011 – €19k
Morris, Colin: 04/5/2011 – €12k
Carruthers, John: 27/6/2011 – €5k
O'Rourke, Laurence: 19/8/2011 – €27k

And so it ran, for almost six pages, the lists divided into various nationalities. The total topped out close to seven hundred grand.

'Who are they,' I said, 'shareholders?'

'Artists,' he whispered.

The Fine Arte portfolio, I presumed, but as always I was just that bit behind the curve. The list did detail some of the Fine Arte portfolio, but only those artists who'd been copied, strictly one per artist, the originals sold on to private collectors, the fakes left hanging in courthouses and libraries and county council offices to gather hefty tax deductions for their philanthropic owners along with a thin film of dust.

It had been Gillick, not Finn, who'd tipped off Tohill about the scam, buying himself some credit when CAB started to squeeze.

It wasn't fool-proof, of course. It helped that Finn had focused entirely on impressionistic takes on landscapes, but even so it depended heavily on the art world's assessors and experts being largely incapable of differentiating between a modern masterpiece and a blurry fart.

Finn had needed Gillick for the legal side, cutting him in for a percentage. They'd left Saoirse Hamilton out of the loop. The first she'd heard of it was when the Italian art dealer with a keen eye for a blurry fart had sued for breach of contract, and the defendant pointed the finger at Fine Arte for originating the fake.

She wasn't, to put it mildly, best pleased. It wasn't so much the Italian suing, this on a blood-from-a-stone basis. No, Saoirse Hamilton was far more concerned about the public ridicule that would inevitably follow.

Being wiped out financially was one thing, and just about

bearable so long as everyone else in the Golf Club was leveraged up the ass all the way to the tonsils and beholden to NAMA for a modest stipend to keep themselves in freshly pressed silk kimonos. But the idea that the Hamiltons were grifters, and were to be dragged through the courts as petty thieves who had preyed on the gullibility, greed and unsophisticated eye of their peers, was a social embarrassment that would deliver the coup de grace to her reputation. And all for what was, by Hamilton standards at least, chump change.

The kicker, and the reason Gillick wanted a squint at the laptop before handing it over to Saoirse, was that Gillick had taken it upon himself to invite some valued clients of his to the party. Specifically, the rootin' tootin' McConnell boys, who were always keen to avail of the opportunity to give a dirty wedge a nice spring-clean.

It made sense, of course, that a man of impeccable Republican credentials and sewer-level morals like Gillick would represent Ted McConnell, ex-INLA killer and bank blagger of note.

'Now Saoirse's pissing herself Finn made a confession in his suicide note,' I said.

He was a pitiful sight, had there been anyone in the room capable of pity. Like an abused child baring his gritted teeth, desperately clinging to the belief that if only he could smile hard enough it would all go away. He raised a trembling hand and pointed at the pale blue envelope, the blank one. 'The proof,' he whispered.

The document inside was a birth certificate. The date seemed right – October 28, 1994 – and the stamp looked official. But it was a fake.

'I don't know what this is supposed to be proof of,' I said, 'but whoever put it together got the name wrong.'

From somewhere he found a second wind, even if the words came halt and hoarse. 'The name is correct.'

'She was adopted, Gillick. They both were, Big Bob Hamilton was shooting blanks. So the birth cert wouldn't read Grainne Hamilton, it'd be Grainne something else. And the way Saoirse likes changing her kids' names to Irish, maybe not even Grainne.'

'Genuine,' he said, although it took him about four seconds to push it all the way out.

'Bullshit.'

'Finn,' he said, then swallowed thickly. His good eye closed. I looked around for some water but there was nothing to hand.

'What about Finn?'

Nothing. I tapped him on the chin with the .38. 'Gillick?' I said. 'I'm giving you five fucking seconds to—'

'Robert couldn't live with that.' He meant the birth cert.

'But why would he want to kill himself over—'

Except Gillick wasn't saying Big Bob topped himself. He was saying Bob couldn't live with knowing what his wife had done, was moving back to London and planning to divorce her.

Saoirse had panicked, even though Gillick had reassured her that Bob had confirmed the truth would stay hidden.

'What truth?'

'That truth.' Again he meant the birth cert.

'What fucking *truth*?'

For a moment he found himself, the old Gillick, supercilious and smug, although the effect when he smiled was rather ruined by the fact that his teeth were pink. 'No wonder,' he whispered, 'you failed as a private detective.'

That did it. I reached behind myself, scrabbling on the desk for the cigar, and came up instead holding the ornate paper-knife.

'We could've done this the easy way,' I said. I plonked myself down on the broad saddle of his chest, a knee either side. He gasped a fine spray of blood. 'But this way we'll have ourselves some fun.'

I gripped him under the throat to hold his head steady. His good eye bulged. He tried to say something but it came out a strangled squawk.

'Day late,' I said, 'dollar short.' Then dug in.

When I'd finished carving the 'T' into his forehead, and eased off on his throat, it all fell out like some third-rate Jacobean farce, Gillick squealing like a one-man chorus about murder and incest, blood and gore. How Saoirse Hamilton had seduced her teenage son, maybe even convincing herself it was somehow okay given that he was adopted, not flesh and blood. Then falling pregnant, Grainne arriving, Big Bob not knowing shit from shinola, but suspecting shinola. Blazing rows, threats of violence, the inevitable mooting of divorce. Saoirse taunting Bob about being half the man Finn was.

All this Gillick knew from Finn, who'd gone to Gillick as some perverse kind of priest. A scared and very confused young man, no more than a boy, with nowhere else to go and confusing the idea of client confidentiality with the sacred oath of the confessional.

Telling Gillick, putting the gun on his desk, that he'd shot his father down at the docks, tumbled him into the water, then reversed the Beamer into the quays.

'With that gun,' Gillick gasped.

'So I've heard. Paranoid bullshit.'

Not so, apparently. And Gillick being Gillick, he'd sniffed

leverage, juice. Started grooming Finn as some kind of dauphin, this with one eye on the Hamilton Holdings fortune Finn would some day inherit. Never guessing for a second that he might be the one being groomed, manipulated into a false position of power, as they schemed their way towards isolating and under-mining Saoirse Hamilton's position.

It made a lot of sense. At least, it went a long way towards explaining Finn's bipolar mood-swings, the arson, the constant need to reinvent himself, to lose himself in his art or in diving off cliffs. And why, just when he believed that he was getting out from under it all, squirreling away enough nuts to get him a new start in Cyprus, he might take a stroll off the ninth floor when he discovered that Maria was pregnant, only not with his kid. Going down in style and up in flames, taking everyone with him, yours truly included.

What didn't make sense was the big finale. The sick punch line, so ludicrous I actually laughed out loud.

I got the dull point of the paper knife under Gillick's chin, pushing up so that his head strained back, leaving his throat exposed.

'This is true?' I said.

'On my fucking *life*,' he rasped at the ceiling.

He had nothing left. No reason to lie. Besides, if what he said was true, it would take only a short journey to prove it beyond doubt.

'Okay, that's us. We're done.'

I slipped sideways off his chest as his entire body sagged with relief. The good eye closed again, although it snapped open when I wrenched off his shoe, tugged his sock free.

'What're you—' he began but then I dropped an elbow into his groin. He *oooofed* and gagged, his mouth dropping open. I jammed the sock in his mouth, saddled up on his chest again. Picked up the paper-knife.

A muffled croak came from behind the sock as he strained his head away. I seized him by the throat, held his head steady, my knuckle throbbing all the way up into my shoulder. Then I dug in again.

It took some time. He gurgled and squawked and squealed behind the sock all the while, a Philip Glass overture, Agony in C Minor. Blood seeping down to pool in the empty socket and blind his good eye. But the naked eyeball, singed as it was, saw all.

I found a bathroom down the hall, washed off the blood as best I could. Then I went to retrieve my latest swag. The birth cert, the pale blue envelope addressed in Finn's hand, the twenty large in loose notes. Gillick had toppled over onto his side, lying snuffling like a beached elephant seal, badly gored and dying slow. Low moans coming muffled from behind the sock.

I still was picking up hundred-euro notes, leaving behind the ones spattered with blood, when he developed the power of ventriloquism. Amazing stuff. Projecting his voice behind me, and not so much as a wobble from the sock, when he said, 'Put the tool down, Rigby.'

38

He stood in the double doorway with a hand on Maria's shoulder, the Beretta nuzzling her ribs. Blood drying on the side of his neck.

Maria looked to be on the point of vomiting, a faint bulge to her eyes.

'Arthur,' Toto said without taking his eyes off mine. 'Arthur?'

Gillick gave a sock-muffled groan, turned his head towards the sound like some light-dazzled mole dug out of a burrow.

'First you lose my coke,' Toto said, 'and then you batter my brother-in-law. Now you're hammering my solicitor.' A bleak smile. 'I was the paranoid type, I might start thinking you've some kind of vendetta going on.'

He was generous enough not to mention my assault on his dignity with a crutch. Or maybe he was trying to pretend it had never happened.

'Nothing personal,' I said.

He made a clicking sound, regretful. 'Put the gun down on the ground,' he said, 'slide it over here.'

I shook my head.

He raised his right hand, tapped the Beretta against Maria's stomach. She closed her eyes. 'Don't think I won't do it,' he said.

'Seriously?' I said. 'You're going to blow her away, you don't even know who she is, for *this* piece of shit?' This last being directed in Gillick's direction. 'Think about it,' I said, lifting the .38, pointing it at his face. 'Because it'll be the last fucking thing you'll ever do.'

Toto took it all under consideration. 'So where are we now?' he said.

'I was just leaving,' I said. 'Taking her with me.'

His grin was a cold slash. 'Just like that.'

'Something like it, anyway.'

'You know that's not going to happen.'

'That'll be Ted's call.'

'Ted?'

'There's something he should probably know. About Gillick here, what he just told me.'

'Tell me.'

'I'll tell Ted.'

He thought about that, his eyes on mine, not the gun. 'You want us all to arrive at Ted's,' he said, 'a three-ring fucking circus.'

'Ring him.'

That put him in a bind. To ring Ted he'd have to let Maria go or put the Beretta away.

'Okay,' he said. He released Maria, put a hand in the small of her back, urging her towards the nearest seat. So she was still in his theoretical field of fire. 'Sorry, love,' he said. 'No harm meant.'

Still looking at me, waiting for the quid pro quo. I gave it a beat, lowered the .38.

'So go ahead and ring Ted,' Toto said, nodding at the phone on the floor beside the desk.

Which would have been hilarious, me hunkering down to dial some number Toto was calling out, getting a kick in the side of the head for my troubles.

'Gillick's phone,' I said, 'is on the table.'

He thought it through, then backed away to the table. Still facing me. Scrabbled through the detritus of Gillick's meal.

Once he found the phone, though, it was relatively straight-forward. Coming forward again, stabbing a couple of buttons. Gillick with Ted McConnell, former INLA killer turned post-Peace Process Robin Hood, on speed-dial. The boys back at Blackhall would surely have been proud.

Toto's eyes never left mine.

The call connected. 'Ted?' he said. 'It's me.'

He was sharp, was Toto. It took him about thirty seconds to sketch it all out, this including a number of his own yeahs and uh-huhs. Then he pressed the speaker button, held out the phone. 'You're up,' he said.

'Ted?' I said.

'This Rigby?' A faint metallic hum charged with feedback.

'Yeah.'

'Go.'

'Your boy Gillick just mentioned that my kid's in hospital.'

'Yeah?'

'My kid was in a coma.'

'Yeah?'

'Now he's dead.'

'So?'

'So the only person who knew my kid was in hospital, in a coma, was a guy called Tohill.'

'And?'

'This Tohill being Detective Sergeant Tohill.'

Silence. Then, 'Oh yeah?'

'You mightn't have heard of him yet. He's been seconded here from CAB.'

'CAB?'

'The Criminal Assets—'

'I fucking know what CAB is, Rigby.'

'Right.'

A metallic click, a faint echo of feedback, and the phone went dead. Toto and I made eyes at one another some more to a soundtrack of a sandpaper symphony of Gillick choking something back behind the sock.

Maria sitting rigid on the chair, hands clasped between her knees.

The phone rang again.

Toto took the call. 'Ted?'

More yeahs and uh-huhs, the cold grey eyes drifting away down to Gillick. A final, definitive nod. He tossed me the phone.

'What do you know about Gillick and this Tohill?' Without the tinny effect of the speaker-phone, Ted McConnell had a surprisingly mellow baritone.

'Someone told Gillick about my kid. Tohill's the only one who knew.'

'They're in bed?'

'I'm telling you what I know.'

'Yeah.' Silence. Then, 'I'm thinking I should probably have a chat with Gillick.'

'He's all yours.'

'Then I'll be wanting to talk to you.'

'That's doable, yeah. Just not right now.'

'You don't tell me when—'

'Ted,' I said, 'I've given you Gillick.' Toto wincing at my interrupting Ted. 'And let's be crystal fucking clear on this. I'm walking out of here now. Anyone gets in my way, I'm putting him down. End of story.'

A long silence this time. 'Can't say I like your attitude, Rigby,' he said finally. 'Can't say I like what was done to Jimmy, either. Gillick's one thing. Jimmy's family.'

'Fuck you and what you think about my attitude,' I said. 'Jimmy, okay, I can say there's ten grand in it for him.'

'Ten?'

'I've twenty grand cash here right now. Ten's owed to Toto. The other ten's Jimmy's. Final offer.'

'Put Toto back on.'

I tossed the phone across. Toto went through another round of yeahs and uh-huhs. Then he hung up, untucked his shirt, gave the phone a good wiping down. Dropped it.

'Alright,' he said. 'The deal is this. Jimmy gets his ten grand, I get mine, we take Gillick for a spin. You and me, we were never here.'

'Only one can say we were,' I said, 'is Gillick.'

'And her,' Toto said.

'She's leaving the country,' I said, 'in a couple of hours.'

He nodded. 'Okay. Give me a hand getting Gillick to the car.'

'Fuck off.'

'Fair enough.' He went and hunkered down beside Gillick, slapped his cheek. 'Let's go, fat-chops,' he said. 'Time's money.'

I told Maria to go ahead, wait for me outside. She stalked out, her face pale, although whether that was because she was holding down a puke or repressing her fury I couldn't tell.

I left the blood-spattered notes where they lay, put the wad in my hand on the desk.

Toto had Gillick propped against the wall by then, Gillick emitting some gravelly groans. Toto's hands smeared with blood.

'Ted'll try to square it with Jimmy,' Toto said. 'But I'm making no promises. Jimmy's his own man. Might be no harm to go missing for a while once he's back in business.'

'Run once,' I said, 'and you never stop.'

Toto rubbed his bloody hands together, cracked a bleak grin. 'And wouldn't that be just fucking grand?' he said.

'You and me,' I said. 'Where are we now?'

He sat back on his haunches, considering. 'Let's get the business sorted first Rigby. Then we'll talk personal.'

'You'll want to confirm this with him,' I nodded at Gillick, 'but he just told me Jimmy was working a little freelance Thursday night, down at the PA.'

'Oh yeah?'

'Yeah. Keeping himself busy while I was upstairs talking with Finn and Gillick.'

'Busy how?'

'Finn came down on top of the cab when he jumped,' I said, 'blew it to shit. The cab sitting directly under the window because Jimmy directed me into that exact spot.'

'So?'

'So cabs, or any kind of motors, don't tend to blow up just

because someone lands on top of them. Unless it's a movie you're watching.'

'What're you saying, Rigby?'

'Our boy Gillick,' I toed his foot, 'reckons Jimmy's a dab hand at improvising petrol bombs from the good old days. A wee magnet to clamp it to the petrol tank, a mercury-tilt switch, Finn hits hard enough to rattle the lot . . .' I shrugged. 'I'm telling you what Gillick said. Maybe you'll get more out of him.'

'But why the fuck would they want to blow the cab?'

The sixty-four thousand dollar question. Actually, the one-point-eight million question.

'Point I'm making,' I said, 'it's Gillick and Jimmy on the hook for what I owe.' I nodded at the desk. 'And Jimmy's ten grand is just sitting there.'

He pursed his lower lip. 'It's tidy,' he said. 'This providing Gillick backs it up.'

'Tell him if he doesn't,' I said, 'I'll be coming for his other eye.'

'Okay,' he said. Nodding to himself, slow. He touched the tips of his fingers to the gash above his ear, had a look at the blood. 'So now, you and me, all we're left with is personal.'

39

The evening was closing in, the sky a rotten peach. I told Maria to get her stuff from the Phaeton and went and had a look at Gillick's Saab in the garage. Unlocked, no keys. A minute later I was easing in beside the Phaeton.

I put her bags on the back seat, debating whether to leave Bear where he was. Maria wouldn't hear of it. So he got transferred to the Saab too.

I drove up the steep track and into the pines, flicking on the lights against the thickening gloom. The Saab so quiet, even in first gear, that I heard an owl whoo-hoo over the engine's hum. Up across the razor-back ridge, down into the valley again.

'How'd he get out?' I said.

A hardy joker, Toto McConnell. Had squirmed across Jimmy and kicked in the back panel, come scrambling through from the boot, Bear trapped in the well behind the front seats. Maria'd bailed out and made for the trees, squeezing the Beretta's trigger. Its safety on.

The rest I knew.

The dash lights gave her pallor a ghastly blue sheen. Hands trembling, the adrenaline rush sending her into delayed shock, how close a gun had been to her belly and what was in it.

'Stop the car,' she said.

'We don't have time to—'

She gagged, put a hand to her mouth. There was no hard shoulder, nowhere to go.

'Harry!'

I jammed on, skidding. She was pushing out the door even before we'd stopped, and vomited quietly onto the verge.

It was a one-puke deal. She sat back into the seat, eyes closed. Pale as raw vellum now, a diamanté gleam to the sweat prickling her forehead.

With her eyes still closed she found her bag, fumbled inside. Came up with a bottle of water, some tissues.

'You alright?'

She took a swig, gargled, spat onto the verge.

'Just get me to the airport,' she whispered.

It was that horrible time to drive, dusk sifting into night, when the lights of the oncoming cars are harsh, dazzling. My skull a damp sandbag, grit drifting in at the back of my eyes. Trees flooding by on both sides. Tremors in my hands that had nothing to do with the swollen knuckle, the adrenaline effort of carving 'TOUT' into a man's forehead.

I was fritzing, the synapses shorting out even as they fired and flared, trying to process what Gillick had said.

It made no sense.

It made perfect sense.

Exhausted now, long past the brink.

Maria didn't speak until we hit the roundabout at Carraroe and I turned off, heading back towards Sligo.

'Where're we going?' she said.

'One last pit stop.' I heard myself sound hollow, as if on the other end of a long-distance call. 'Then we're good.'

'I'm going to miss that flight, Harry.'

'If you do I'll drive you to Dublin.' I looked across at her. 'Maybe get on the plane with you.'

'The fuck you will.'

'And what if it's mine?'

'All the more fucking reason,' she said, placing her hands on her stomach, 'to keep it a million miles away from you.'

Maybe she had a point.

I shifted in the seat, pulled the pair of pale blue envelopes from my back pocket. The one with a cheque for seventy-five grand inside, and addressed in Finn's handwriting to Andrea Toner, 18 O'Neill Crescent, Carton – I tucked that under my thigh. Handed Maria the other.

'You might want to see that,' I said.

She was only mildly curious opening the envelope, and had to peer at it closely in the bluey light. Then she realised it was a birth certificate.

'Gillick had this?' she said.

'That's right. He reckons Finn is Grainne's father.'

'So?'

'You knew this?'

'Sure. Finn told me. That night he told me about killing his father. He told me everything, Harry.'

I doubted that. The best liars tell only mostly the truth.

'Kind of sweet of him really,' she said. An acid bite to her tone.

'I mean, I was taking him in sickness and in health, right? The least he could do was tell me how sick he could actually be.'

She didn't know the half of it.

'And you told Grainne you knew,' I said. 'Which is why she went for you with the scissors.'

'She wanted everyone to pretend Finn was some kind of saint.' She shrugged. 'About fucking time she grew up, learned a few things about how the world really works.'

'Right. Because every girl needs to find out, at some point, how her brother is her father too. Doing her a favour really, weren't you?'

'Don't shoot the messenger.'

'And now you're going to steal her trust fund, use it to destroy the Hamilton name. Maybe drop some incest into the mix to spice things up.'

'That's the general idea, yeah.' She held up the envelope. 'Mind if I keep this?'

'It's all yours.'

40

O'Neill Crescent lay on the outer fringe of the Cartron estate, a left-hooking curve of semi-ds that petered out just before the pocked tarmac crumbled into a shallow ditch, its muddy stream choked with brown weeds and rusting bike wheels, used condoms and shopping trolleys that looked brand new. In the bare field sloping down to the water two emaciated ponies snuffed for grazing among the blackened circles of dead bonfires and the dark hulks of burnt-out cars.

When I U-turned the Saab at the end of the street, reversing into the high weeds, a rabbit-sized rat went scuttling across the road to disappear up the driveway of number 26.

Maria shuddered. 'This better not take long,' she said.

'It won't.'

Leave a Saab sitting out on O'Neill Crescent and you're asking for rats a lot bigger than rabbits to come swarming.

For now, there wasn't a single human face to be seen.

The driveway of number 19 hosted a battered caravan up on breeze-blocks, and even at that it was in better nick than the house. Three of its facing windows were either fractured or boarded up and the front door had been patched at least twice with plywood.

Number 18 was still holding on, or trying to. The window boxes on the first-floor sills were empty, but at least their chipped and flaking paintwork gave the place a splash of yellow and blue. The tiny lawn out front was ragged but recently cut. The front door all of a piece.

There was no bell, so I rat-tat-tatted on the reinforced glass. When I turned around I could see why the planners had once thought O'Neill Crescent worth building. Away to the north, Benbulben was a delicate swash of amber-tinged plums and lavenders as the sun sank for the horizon. To the west the bay gleamed silvery-green, still as mercury where it funnelled up towards the docks.

I rat-a-tat-tatted again, giving it serious knuckles. That won me a shadow lurking back in the hall and a muffled, querulous tone. 'Who is it?'

'You don't know me.'

'What do you want?'

'It's Andrea, right? I've a delivery for you.'

'Fuck off.'

'I'm not a bailiff.'

'Fuck off away from that door *now*.'

No threat to back it up. Even through the door the deadened tone sounded strained, defeated.

I hunkered down, prodded in the letterbox. 'It's from Gillick,' I tried.

'I don't know any Gillick.'

'He knows you.'

A pause. 'What're you delivering?' she said.

I slipped the envelope out of my pocket, pushed it halfway through the letterbox. 'This.'

'So drop it in.'

'Sorry. I need to hand it over in person.'

'Fucking bailiff. Fuck off.'

'Go back inside,' I said, 'and look out the window. If I look like a bailiff, then fair enough, I'm gone. But I should warn you, there's a cheque for seventy-five grand in here.'

The shadow didn't go away in search of a window. Hard to tell with shadows, but I got the impression its shoulders slumped. Then it seemed to swell, come closer, and I heard the rattle of a chain. She opened the door a crack. One glimpse was enough to convince her that, whatever my business was, it was a long way from being official.

She unhooked the chain, stood back. I pushed the door in and stepped into a tiny hallway. She backed away into the sitting room. I closed the door and followed. The curtains were pulled tight, leaving the room dark except for the glare of the muted TV. It felt like stepping into a cave, the TV a coldly flickering fire. An emptiness in that room IKEA would give up Stockholm to be able to mimic, the kind of minimalism only functioning poverty can carry off with any degree of authenticity. She shuffled around the low table and sat on a couch that had much in common with a Swiss Protestant's pew. The low table was bare but for an overflowing ashtray, a pack of smokes and a tumbler with about half an inch of wine.

The place stank like a grow-house, that sickening smell of stale dope that seeps into the walls. She didn't look stoned, though. Eyes like new coins, bright and shiny and hard.

'It's Harry,' she said, not looking at me as she fumbled a

cigarette from the box. She didn't offer me one. She knew why I'd come. 'Isn't it?' The tremble in her voice made it all the way down to her fingers. She had to snap the plastic lighter three or four times before she got the cigarette lit. 'Harry Rigby. Right?'

'That's right.'

Her face was pinched, pale but blotched with crude pinks and angry reds, and I didn't have the kind of time it'd take to work out which was make-up and which tough living. Late twenties and hard with it, time as a kiln forging a mask of her face.

The last time I'd seen her she'd been sitting on a rock staring out to sea, her back hunched against the sight of Finn perched high on the cliff, the retro-mini '60s wedding dress rucked up and wrinkled in the small of her back.

I put the envelope on the table, pushed it across. She glanced at it once, biting her lower lip, then looked at me, the eyes still hard and shiny and bright. I looked past her, to where a cane stood propped in the corner.

'Paul around?' I said.

'Not right now.'

'Will he be back later?'

'You'd need to ask Paul.'

'Where'll I find him?'

'Your guess,' she exhaled, her voice flat now, 'is as good as mine.'

From outside came the fat parp-parp of the Saab's horn. I crossed to the window, twitched back the curtain. Maria spotted the movement and held up her arm, tapping at her wrist. I gave her the thumbs up. 'It's Maria,' I said. Andrea nodded, then wrinkled her nose. I pulled the curtain all the way back. 'Finn's fiancée,' I said.

'I know who she is.'

'Come here,' I said.

'What?'

'Come over to the window. I want to show you something.'

'I think you'd better go.'

'I'm going. Just let me show you this one thing. That way I
don't take the cheque with me when I leave.'

She picked the envelope off the table and folded it in two,
rammed it into the front pocket of her jeans. Stubbed the cigarette and got up, came around the couch. I pushed back the other
curtain.

A pretty view, so long as you looked long and far. Benbulben
dissolving into dusk, the bay suffused with the faintest of pinks.
On the far shore, down at the deepwater, the PA building stood
out stark as a warning finger against the coppery sky. It took a
moment or two, but it was there her eyes were drawn.

'Did you watch?' I said.

She twitched. 'What?'

'Were you watching,' I said, 'when he jumped?'

'Who, Finn?'

'Paul. Did he give you a time, when it was likely to happen?'

'I don't know what you're—'

'Come on, Andrea. Seventy-five grand? Sounds a lot like a life
insurance policy on a cardboard box like this. Unofficial, maybe,
but it's in the ball-park. Am I right?'

She stood rigid now, the eyes shiny and bright, no longer hard.

'Just nod,' I said. 'The cheque's going nowhere. It's yours.
Christ fucking knows you've earned it.'

She turned away from the window, muttering something I
didn't catch, and went to perch on the edge of the couch again.
Hunched forward, with the effort of maintaining a defiant stare

deranging her features, she wasn't unlike a gargoyle. She reached for the smokes but her hands were shaking so hard that I had to take away the cigarette and lighter, spark it up. She took a quick hard drag, spat out the smoke.

'You can fuck away off now,' she said.

I perched on the other end of the couch, shifting my position as the .38 dug into my coccyx. 'Andrea,' I said, 'I can appreciate—'

'Oh can you? Really? What is it you can fucking appreciate?'

'That you've lost—'

'Me?' she sneered. 'I've lost fuck-all.'

'Lucky you. I lost my kid today.'

It didn't penetrate straight away. Then her brows wrinkled and she sat back. 'What're you talking about?'

'My boy. He died today.' I gave her the short version, how we were run off the road, the coma. How it'd all started Thursday night at the PA, when someone jumped and came down on the cab and blew my life into a million pieces. That I needed to know the how and why, for closure.

Which was true, in a way.

'Christ,' she whispered.

'All I'm asking,' I said, 'is if Paul said anything before he went.'

Another parp-parp from outside. Andrea jerked, and a half-inch of ash toppled onto the carpet. She looked down at it, glanced up at me. Then, slowly, very deliberately, she rubbed the ash into the carpet with a pointed toe.

She was still putting it together for herself, so it came out in pieces, like shards of pottery unearthed at some dig, broken and brittle but sharp enough to slice deep.

Paul diving off a cliff and getting it wrong, just a fraction out when he jumped.

Coming down hard on the unforgiving rock.

'At the start he thought it was a slipped disc, it was bad down here.' She half-twisted to indicate her lower back, the left side. 'Except it kept getting worse. After a while he couldn't even drum, wasn't able to walk sometimes. He'd have to sleep down here.'

'What'd the doctor say?'

She shrugged. 'He thought it'd sort itself out. In the beginning, like. And the dope, the grass, it seemed to help. When it kept on getting worse he thought maybe it was some kind of early arthritis, he could treat it himself. Later on, whenever it got bad enough for him to want to go to the hospital, he was in too much pain to move. In the end I told him I was leaving, packing up, if he didn't just go and get it seen to.'

'And?'

'Spinal stenosis, they called it. He'd cracked his spine in the jump, and there were complications, an infection in the spinal canal that wouldn't stop spreading. Degenerative, the doctor said.' She said the word carefully, giving all the syllables it deserved. 'He said it'd take a major operation, but it'd be risky, Paul could be left, y'know.'

'Paralysed.'

'Yeah. And Paul goes, what's the fucking point, pay a fortune for some operation that leaves him paralysed anyway. That was even if we could get it in time.' She gestured around at the bare living room. 'I was the only one working, and health insurance . . .' She shrugged. 'So there was a waiting list, all these criteria we had to meet.' She choked back a giggle. 'Paul says, "Here's me fucked on the flat of my back and the bastards want me to jump through fucking hoops."'

'And all Finn wanted him to do was fall off a building.'

Another shrug, this one fatalistic. 'He felt guilty all the time,' she said. 'I mean, I know people thought Paul was a flake but no one really knew him. Didn't know what he was like up here,' she tapped her forehead. 'One night he started on about for better or worse, said it was a load of shit, there was no way he was dragging me down with him. This was when we were talking about how we'd need to re-do the house, make it wheelchair-friendly, maybe put in one of those stair-lifts. Just talking, really. I mean, we could hardly afford his painkillers, let alone any fucking stair-lifts. And every day there was something new he couldn't do.' Reliving it now, her voice raw with smoke and maybe a hint of desperation. 'I mean, it was bad enough when I was having to wash him in the shower. But wiping his arse?' A bleak light in her eyes. 'I'm not . . .' she began, and then she looked up at me. 'It was worse for him than me,' she said. 'He'd actually cry, get into this rage . . .' A quick hard drag on the cigarette. 'Then one day, it was actually one of his better days, he was just lying here on the couch, he said Finn had a gun. If he could only get his hands on it. Before it got so bad he wouldn't be able to, to . . .'

'He asked Finn for the gun?'

'I don't know. He must've said something, though. Finn'd call around during the day when I was out at work, I'd come home and the place'd be stinking with grass, the two of them toking away, having a fucking laugh.'

I tried to picture him there, half-stoned on the couch, paranoid, Finn calling around with his baggies of grass and rolling spliff after spliff, pouring his poison into Paul's ear.

'Did he tell you it was Finn's idea?' I said.

She shook her head, her fringe falling forward to hide her

face. A tear dropped from the end of her nose. 'He left a note.' She sniffed. 'I came home from work and he was gone, just the note on the table saying he'd had enough, he was taking care of it. Nothing packed, all his stuff still here. I tried ringing him but he never picked up.'

She looked up at me, the eyes raw. Defiant again. 'What could I do, ring the cops? Tell them my husband was out there somewhere planning to kill himself?' She cradled herself, rocked back and forth. 'And then, the next morning, I heard about that fucker Finn, how he was supposed to have jumped off the PA building. The bastard. The dirty fucking *bas*tard.'

Another parp-parp from outside, and another. I stood up. 'Andrea,' I said, 'I have to go.'

I don't know what she'd thought, that maybe we were going to hang out all night swapping hard luck stories, weeping and wailing about lost loves and how unfair was life, how cruel and cold.

'Yeah,' she sneered. She snuffled again, wiped her nose with the back of her wrist. 'Now you've got your fucking closure.'

'Not nearly,' I said. 'Not even close. And at least you got a cheque.'

In a way I was pleasantly surprised that Finn had at least honoured the debt. This providing, of course, it didn't bounce when Andrea took it to the bank, Finn writing a cheque to buy himself time.

I stepped out the front door and pulled it behind me as gently as I could. Strolled out to O'Neill Crescent with its burnt-out cars and rusting bike wheels, the starved ponies still snuffing and caravans propped high and dry on their cement blocks.

I flashed back on that night in the Cellars and the boys' Rollerskate Skinny tribute band, Paul hammering the drums in a lather of sweat. In the corner of my eye a lemon arcing towards the stage and Finn with his eyes closed, chin tilted, singing, 'I love this compromise, you've finally got me, swallowing miracles, the whole way down . . .'

By now the black finger of the PA was invisible against the night sky.

Somewhere inside I felt a pang for Paul. A glimmer of why he might've wanted just one last dive. The air rushing by, the rush of what it means to be totally free, even for a couple of seconds. Those gloriously precious final few.

Like the man himself said, when you're in, you're in.

41

'Forget Knock,' Maria said when I got back in the car. Thumbing her Blackberry, the Expedia website up on her browser. 'We'll never make it.'

'Fine by me. Dublin it is.'

Might be for the best. A three-hour drive would give me plenty of time to decide if I should tell her Finn was alive and well and very probably grooming another suicide, this in case his latest scam didn't work out.

My best guess was that Finn'd been playing everyone off. Stringing Maria along with the promise of a new life in Cyprus, offering Gillick some ground-floor action on the new development in the sun. Giving Saoirse just a glimmer of hope that he'd see the light, give up Maria and come back to the fold, revitalise Hamilton Holdings and become her warrior and king, her future legend.

All of it predicated on ripping off young Grainne's legacy, the one-point-eight million held in trust by a man who was both brother and father. Her life strip-mined even before it began.

And maybe Finn might have pulled it all off, too. Squared all those circles. Until a certain Harry Rigby got involved, started slipping between his sheets.

'Belfast's a better bet,' Maria said. 'There's a flight tomorrow morning to Larnaca, connects through Birmingham.'

'Sound,' I said.

Anything that postponed the moment when I'd finally have to look down at Ben, waxy and lifeless on a morgue slab, was good with me.

We turned out of Carton and up the hill, down onto Hughes Bridge. Hardly any traffic. The bypass clear under the orange glow of the lights. A faint snoring from behind, Bear panned out with his nose on his paws. The crutches a-rattle on the rear seat.

Empty, now. Drained. No rage, no pain. Running on fumes and guilt.

We cut across past the hospital, out by the college. Got onto the Enniskillen road. I knocked the Saab into cruise mode, got comfortable.

It didn't last.

It never does.

The phone rang.

'Herb?'

'Where are you?'

'Heading for Belfast. What's up?'

'She's gone.'

'Who, Grainne?'

'Who fucking else?'

'Christ. How'd she—'

'I was helping her with the laptop, some shit she wanted to

find. Then she picks up the SIG, says, nice gun.'

'And?'

'And she locks me in the fucking utility room.'

'You're shitting me.'

'Don't get fucking smart with me, Harry, bringing fucking lunatics around here, shitting all over—'

'She say where she was going?'

'What d'you think, we had a nice fucking chat through the utility room door?'

'When was this?'

'An hour ago, maybe more.'

'And she said nothing at all. About where she was going, like.'

'I told you, she said nothing.'

'She bring the laptop?'

'Yeah.'

'What shit was she trying to find?'

'We found it. Her birth cert, scanned in.'

'Fuck.'

'Fuck is right, Harry. It's not like we don't have enough—'

'We're sorted with Toto, Herb. That's done.'

'Done?'

'Mostly, yeah.'

'How come?'

'Long story. I'll tell you later. Listen, you're sure Grainne said nothing about where she was going?'

'She wouldn't talk to me. Wouldn't listen. Just kept singing.'

'Singing?'

'Girl's off the charts, Harry. If you see her coming, you'd better—'

'Herb? What was she singing?'

'Something about speed to her side, nobody every told her something something something . . . I don't know, she isn't exactly fucking Adele, y'know?'

I hung up.

Our old friends Rollerskate Skinny. *Speed to my side, nobody ever told me that this sort of thing could come alive . . .*

'Let me guess,' Maria said. 'The little witch promised him a blowjob.'

I didn't want to hope. But it was worth a try.

'Give me your phone,' I said.

'What's wrong with that one?'

'It doesn't have Grainne's number in it.'

She rummaged in her bag until she found the phone, scrolled down through her contacts, pressed Grainne's number. I plucked it from her hand, clamped it to my ear.

She answered on the sixth or seventh ring. Amused, cold. 'I am led to believe,' she said, 'that you are pregnant with an ex-convict's bastard. I do thank you for confirming my long-held suspicions.'

'Mrs Hamilton,' I said, 'it's Harry Rigby.'

'Oh?'

'I'd like to speak with Grainne, if I may.'

An iron-sounding chuckle. 'Grainne is nowhere to be found, Mr Rigby. We've tried ringing her, of course, but for some reason she left her phone here this morning when she drove away with you. Naturally, it would be remiss of me not to mention that to the Guards when I file a missing persons report.'

'You do that. On the off-chance that she does turn up, though, tell her I have the paintings Finn stole. My guy in CAB tells me that the finder's fee, the reward, should be enough to tide her over for a few months, keep her going until she's old enough to access the trust fund herself.'

'Is that a fact?'

'It is. I've got the gun, too.'

Silence then, and the faint hiss of static.

'Perhaps you should come here, Mr Rigby. When Grainne does turn up, you can tell her about her unexpected good fortune in person.'

'I can do that, sure. Should I bring the gun?'

'If it's not too much trouble.'

'No trouble at all, Mrs Hamilton. I'll see you soon.'

42

I got turned in a laneway, drove back to town. Pulled up at the taxi-rank opposite the Town Hall, double-parked.

'You're really going after her,' Maria said.

A flash of some eyes behind a fringe, the hopeful up-and-under look, pleading.

'Yeah,' I said.

'She's insane,' she said. 'You know that.'

'Troubled, some'd say. And with good reason.' A horn parped from behind. I acknowledged it with a wave as he pulled around me, then knocked on the hazard flashers. 'You told Grainne you were pregnant, didn't you?'

'So what?'

'Did you tell her Finn was the father?'

'Why wouldn't I?'

'Mainly because you couldn't know for sure. Unless you've already had a test done.'

'Don't go getting any ideas, Harry.'

'Ideas aren't really my thing.'

'Good. Keep it that way. Now let's—'

'I need to know.'

She sat there with her hands on the steering-wheel, thumbs tapping the soft leather grip. 'Archú,' she said, so softly I barely heard her.

'What?'

'You don't recognise your own name?'

'Who told you that?'

'Finn.' She looked up at me then, and there was hate in her eyes, and hurt, and something that might even have been tender. 'He said it was the night you pulled him back from the edge. Telling him about your brother. How you killed him over a kid who wasn't even your own.'

Odd. The way I remembered it, Finn had been the one who'd dragged me back from the edge. Telling me about the arsons, the pressures that opened up the fissures deep inside, left him bipolar, suicidal and clinging by his fingertips to that sheer black cliff.

We'd ended up laughing at one another. The way you do when a spark of hope flares. That god-given moment when you realise there's someone even more fucked-up than you. That there might even be a way back.

Of course, we traced it all back to our mothers. Saoirse for changing Finn's name from Philip, starting him early down that road of hiding who he really was, the brain-bending strain of pretending to be someone else, always.

'Is it true?' she said.

'Nope.'

'No?'

'You know what Finn was like,' I said. 'He wanted everyone else to be someone else too.'

She nodded. 'Pity,' she said. 'Archú, the Hound of Slaughter. Has a nice ring, just trips off the tongue.'

'I like Harry better.'

'I'll bet you do.'

I got out of the Saab and went around to the first cab in line. When I told him he was up for a run to Belfast, he nearly shit. Hopped out, scuttled around the back of the Saab, started transferring Maria's bags.

I sat back into the Saab. Maria with the sun-shield down, touching up her eyes in the mirror.

'You haven't had any tests done,' I said, 'have you?'

She found that funny in a sour kind of way. 'What're you saying, Harry?' She cocked an eyebrow. 'You actually give a shit?'

'If it's mine, yeah.'

'And what if I said it was?'

'Then I'll come find you.'

She closed her handbag with a sharp click. 'The baby's mine, Harry. Right now that's all I know for sure.'

'That's enough to get started.'

A wry smile. 'You've never met my father.'

'Fuck him.'

'Maybe I will,' she said. 'It seems to be all the rage.'

She got out, went around the Saab to where the cabbie was holding the door open. I watched the taxi pull away from the kerb, roll down to the intersection, pause and cut right. She didn't look back.

43

In the end it was all pretty civilised, if a little cold and excessively formal. But that's the way of it with executions.

I turned in at the gates of the Grange and drove on a couple of hundred yards until I hit a narrow stretch, the forest encroaching on both sides. Eased the Saab to a halt and then reversed back in a half-circle, blocking the road. I checked the .38, gave the cylinder a spin, tucked it back into my belt.

'Okay, Bear. Let's go.'

He loped along beside me as we advanced towards the clearing, ears pricked, a querulous whine in the back of his throat. Familiar territory, even if the smells and sounds were strange. He sniffed greedily at the night air, head turning and twisting, and I wondered how long it had been since he'd found himself outside, in his ancient environment of sycamore and oak. The trees densely bunched, a black-on-dark chiaroscuro charcoal etching. From somewhere came an owl's whoo-whoo and Bear's head jerked up, whipped around. A low growl.

'Sssshhh, boy.'

Not that it'd have mattered if he'd tap-danced up to the house wailing be-bop on a kazoo. I had no plan other than kill or be killed.

Duty and the protocols demanded the former.

As for the latter, well, that had its fringe benefits too.

I paused on the fringe of the forest, clicked my tongue at Bear. He pawed at the ground as I dug out the phone, dialled Grainne's number.

'Mr Rigby?'

'I'm outside.'

'Please, Mr Rigby. Do join us.'

Eighty yards away the faux-Georgian monument to survival stood stark and silent, the upper storey's windows ablaze with light. The front door dark and gaping open, as if the house was about to scream.

Us.

Maybe she meant Grainne, and maybe she meant Simon. But I didn't think so.

He was there.

I could almost taste him.

There came a piercing whistle that cut off with a little trill. Bear stiffened, nostrils flaring as he sifted the night. Then he tossed that massive head, reared back and howled. Lunged forward across the immaculate lawn, howling still, cleared the ornamental pond in one leap.

I stepped out of the trees, followed on. Just strolled across the lawn, angling wide of the pond and the fountain, cutting back again towards the broad steps leading up to the front door.

An easy target, sure. But there were no marksmen in the

Grange that night, no snipers. I figured they'd let me get close, talk up the paintings, try something to distract me and then put me down.

Sweat dripping from my fingertips, pooling in the arches of my feet.

Another balmy night.

I went up the steps one at a time, easing the .38 from my belt. The cross-hatched grip feeling clammy. Half-expecting someone to step out of the hallway's gloom, maybe a herd of suicidal giraffes stampeded in my direction.

Getting through the door, I reckoned, would be the toughest part. I'd be back-lit going through, a black shape against the moonlit lawn behind, unmissable for anyone lurking behind the potted bamboo.

So I hauled out the Jimmy Dean roll for one last tired tumble, ducking through the door low, rolling to one side, coming up fast with the .38 extended.

Nothing. Only the door at the end of the corridor slightly ajar, offering a thin slice of yellow light.

I trudged along through the deep carpet, both hands braced on the butt of the .38, a weather eye on the balcony above. A murmur of conversation growing louder from the end of the hall.

Don't go in there, Rigby.

There's lunatics in there with guns, Rigby.

Desperate folk, Rigby, and at least two of them want you dead.

And all the while I was moving towards the door, realising, or finally admitting, that I hadn't trekked all the way out to the Grange to kill or be killed.

I'd come to be wiped out. For all to be void.

And yet when I pushed in the door I found myself stepping

back, half-expecting the SIG to start blazing away.

The only sounds the crackle of burning logs, a snuffling from Bear.

I stepped inside.

'When you said you would bring the gun, Mr Rigby,' said Saoirse Hamilton from the couch, 'I didn't realise you planned on arriving like John Wayne.' Her tone mock-severe, as if chiding a spectacularly stupid child. 'Should I raise my hands?'

Grainne crouched in the other corner of the couch, feet drawn up beneath her, arms wrapped around her shins. Chin resting on her knees and staring blankly into space. Eyes dull, blank.

On the far side of the coffee table, angléd away from the fire, Finn sprawled in an armchair, one leg hooked over its arm. The lazy grin starting.

'Harry,' he said. 'You're a hard man to put down, y'know it?'

Tickling Bear's ear, scratching at the fur on the back of his head. Bear squirming pleasurably, driving his head into Finn's lap.

Of the SIG there was nary a sign.

I crossed Grainne off the list, figured Saoirse Hamilton would be too slow if she tried to draw, put the .38 on Finn.

There were questions I wanted to ask, things I'd have loved to know. If Finn had been committed for arson, or if he'd put himself away, grooming some crazy paranoid to take the fall for him when the time was right. If he'd gone to Cyprus specifically to find some woman who'd offer a back-door escape when the hammer came down.

If he'd known Ben was in the Audi when he'd side-swiped us off the road.

But I was bone-tired by then, and anyway, none of it mattered.

'To business, Mr Rigby,' said Saoirse, sitting forward on the couch. 'Have you a fee in mind for the paintings and the gun? Or should we open the negotiations now?'

'If you so much as blink again,' I told her, the .38 still on Finn, 'I'll blow your fucking head off.'

She paled. 'Mr Rigby, I must—'

'I'm here,' I said, 'to kill him. No fee charged. What anyone does with the gun and the paintings after that is up to them.'

'But Mr Rigby—'

'Only fair,' I told Finn. 'You've had two goes at me now, at the PA and running me off the road. One question, though. Did you know Ben was in the car before you rammed us? Or did you just not give a fuck?'

'It doesn't have to be like this, Harry.'

'But it *is* like this. Ben's dead. There's no other way it can be.'

'As I understand it,' Saoirse said, 'you were the one who stole Finn's car and took your son along for a joyride. Not,' she said, 'that he was actually your son. But the point pertains.'

I twitched the gun so that it was pointing at her face. What she said was true, on all counts. Didn't mean I wanted to hear it.

'Say that again,' I said. 'Please. Just say those exact same—'

'Sic 'im, Bear!'

With a snarl Bear sprang out of his sitting position across the coffee table, the massive head turning, jaws wide.

It was no contest. A .38 Special, pointed in the right place, will take down a charging rhino.

Bear's massive, unmissable head was about two feet from the muzzle of the .38 when it blew apart. The impact arresting his momentum, so that his headless body reared back in mid-air, came crashing down on the low table.

There was a moment's stunned silence, the air ringing. Then Grainne gulped and began to sob. I stepped across the table, Bear's body, the pool of blood seeping black into the carpet. Cocked the .38 and aimed at Finn's face.

'Harry . . .'

His face the colour of buttermilk. No shit-don't-matter grin now, just those wide blue eyes filled with the horror of extinction.

'Jesus, Harry, I didn't know the kid was in the fucking *car*.'

'Doesn't matter.'

'Mr Rigby.' Saoirse, sounding hoarse now, realising there was no fee to be paid, no more buying to be done. 'Surely we can discuss this like—'

'No.' Except I was feeling it now, the sick burn, the anticipation of the jolt in my wrist, seeing Finn's eyes widen in agony, then dull, go lifeless.

My gorge rising at the prospect.

'An eye for an eye, Finn. It's how it is.'

She came up off the couch with a strangled bellow, dragging the SIG free from where she'd tucked it between the cushion and the couch's arm. The Iron Queen, raging as the pillars collapsed and the chunks of masonry went tumbling all about.

I put one in her upper chest, knocked her sprawling back the way she'd come, then swung backhanded, the .38's butt catching Finn high on the side of the head as he drove out of the armchair. Not a brutal blow, but enough to deflect him wide, so that he head-butted my hip and sent me staggering backwards. His arms around my thighs now, trying to heave me over the coffee table. I got a good grip on the .38 and drove it down into the nape of his neck, the top of his spine, and after that he didn't do an awful lot of anything much.

It was only then I realised the ringing in my ears wasn't a ringing at all, but Grainne, eyes closed, arms still wrapped around her shins, screaming into her knees.

'Shut that fucking noise *now*,' I told her. She didn't even hear me. I hunkered down beside Finn, put the muzzle of the .38 to the back of his head, told him how it was going to be. Took a handful of shirt-collar and dragged him to his feet, pushed him towards the French windows. 'Some kind of dispute over money, I'd say,' I told him. 'She wouldn't cut you in, you blew a hole in her, couldn't live with yourself. You know the drill, right?'

I pulled the doors open, shoved him outside. He stumbled up against the low wall, almost tipped over. I reached and dragged him back, got him steady.

'Step up,' I said.

'Harry . . .'

'Step fucking up or I blow a hole in Grainne too.'

Still stunned, blinking heavily, it took him three attempts to stand up on the low wall. Below, maybe forty metres straight down, the surf rolled in to break on the jagged jaws of the rocks.

He straightened, wobbled a little. Then he found himself and tensed into a crouch. A crippled kind of grace.

One last dive. One final delicious falling away from the world and all in it.

'Harry,' he whispered.

'Yeah?'

'All I ever wanted,' he whispered but that was as far as he got. The vocal cords tend to give up the ghost pretty quick when a bullet punches through the side of a man's skull.

He turned end over end twice before bouncing off an outcrop and pinwheeling into the surf.

'Bell jars away, motherfucker.'

44

I shuffled back in from the balcony hollowed out and ready to drop. Preparing a little speech for Grainne, how she'd be needing her passport and a big wide smile for Maria whenever she tracked her down in Cyprus, this presuming she was interested, given her piss-poor experience to date, in trying the whole family malarkey again.

Too blitzed to realise the screaming had stopped.

She was gone.

Yeah, and I needed to be gone too. One last thing to do.

So I dragged myself down the long hallway, past the gallery of staring eyes. Out the front door and down the steps.

The Rav4 was gone, but there was still enough cars out front, and plenty enough petrol to be siphoned off. A jerry can in the boot of the Land Cruiser.

I made three trips, splashed the petrol through the hallway, the drawing room, the living room. Smashed some bottles of brandy.

Stinking of petrol and cordite and blood.

Back out to the steps, where I rolled a cigarette and got it sparked, tossed the Zippo in through the open door. Then I went down the steps and across the manicured lawn and took a pew on the rim of the fountain, watched the flames take hold. Panes cracking, glass splintering.

The smoke in one hand, tasting foul. The .38 in the other, and it probably wouldn't taste any better.

Something blew deep in the bowels of the house, a generator maybe, and a million sparks went rocketing off towards the stars, heading back home, and as they glowed and dissipated and faded away I conceded that it didn't really matter either way if I ate the gun or sat on that fountain rim for the millions of years it would take the sun to go cold and wink out, because life was nothing but a pointless bloody farce, just this impossibly brief flaring between being nothing and dead matter, everyone who ever lived just a constellation of atoms stuck together for long enough to realise it's just that bit too aware for its own good, and how it didn't really matter, not when you lean back and have a good long look up into that endless night, that Ben had only lived twelve years instead of surviving to shamble into a hole in the ground, deranged and broken, leaking sticky stuff from every orifice that counted.

But even if it all meant nothing I still wasn't entitled to put myself away. Didn't have the right. I could point the finger at Finn or Saoirse Hamilton or Gillick or anyone else I chose, it didn't change the fact that it was my fault Ben was dead. And the very least I owed him was to live with that, to suffer that torment.

The Grange was burning so hard now my skin felt singed. The roar of the flames so loud that it took me a second or two to realise the phone was ringing.

Herb.

'Yeah?'

'Harry? Where are you?'

'You don't want to know.'

'Listen, Harry.' Maybe my hearing was still off from my eardrums being blasted by the .38, or maybe it was the popping and crackling from the house. But he sounded different, something choking his throat. 'Dee rang, there's been a development with Ben.'

A surge of irrational hope. 'Yeah?'

'Yeah. She said, uh, fair warning, she's filing charges against you, reckless endangerment, some shit like that.'

'Aye, right.'

'Harry, maybe you should, y'know, take off.'

'Yeah, maybe.'

'If you need anything, let me know. I can bring it anywhere.'

'Appreciate that, Herb. I'll be in touch.'

I hung up and heard her coming, the angry whine of an engine in reverse, then the crunch of gravel as she emerged from the trees. A gear-change, and the Rav4 came roaring around the fountain, braking hard, the tyres spitting stones.

The .38 like an anchor in my hand.

I thought she might come on raging about how someone had parked a Saab across the road, boxed her in. Instead she simply opened the door and stepped out onto the gravel.

She was her mother's daughter, alright.

The ice-blue eyes, the iron will. The SIG pointing at my chest, both hands braced on the butt.

'Just put it down,' she said softly. 'Just let it go.'

The .38 hit the grass with a muffled clunk.

She'd played me from the start. Letting me think she was a crazy, scared kid. Because we've all seen the same movies, haven't we? Read the same books.

Grainne Hamilton was seventeen going on seventy and about as crazy scared as a marble slab.

Not once did she glance at the blazing house.

'I can't get the Saab started,' she said. 'So let's go. You drive.'

I got in. She crammed herself back against the passenger door, the SIG pointed at my ribs.

We drove into the forest. She hadn't killed anyone yet and I didn't know if she had what it took to go that far. So I asked, just to gauge where she was, when she'd realised Finn and Saoirse were ripping off her trust fund to start all over again in Cyprus.

'Just drive,' she said.

'Was Maria in on it?'

'Maria, Jesus.' She shook her head. 'All she had to do was play the game, sit tight, marry Finn when the time was right.'

'Which'd net him a Cypriot passport.'

'Except she couldn't help herself. Started screwing around with you. Thinking she'd teach Finn a lesson.'

'And then she gets pregnant.'

She shrugged. 'He couldn't be told. Couldn't go without taking you out too.'

'He was here all along,' I said, 'wasn't he?'

She nodded. 'In the boatshed, yeah. I thought, yesterday morning, you'd worked it out. When you went for a stroll down to the cove.'

'Which is why you started on about the will, Finn making changes to the trust fund. Just to see how much I knew.'

'Pull in here,' she said. The Saab looming large in the headlights. I eased the Rav4 to a halt, careful not to make any jerky movements. 'Okay,' she said, 'get it out of the way.'

I got out and went around to the Saab, sat into the driver's seat. She came and stood by the driver's off-side, the SIG still braced. I reached under the dash, found the wires. A couple of sparks, then a low hum. I gave the accelerator a nudge, let the engine roar.

'Now get it off the road,' she said.

I put the Saab in reverse, went bumping down into the under-growth.

She waited on the verge of the road as I climbed back up the incline. When I was close enough so she couldn't miss, she said, 'Far enough. Down.'

Not so much as quiver in those delicate hands. I went down on one knee, then the other.

'Grainne,' I said, 'think it through. Right now you're walking away clean. You want to give them a reason to hunt you down?'

She took it onboard, a faint glitter in the ice-blue eyes. Hunkered down so that we were on the same eye-level, the SIG in one hand now, resting on her knee.

'And you'll do what?' she said. 'I mean, when the cops ask you what happened here, what'll you say?'

'I won't even be here. I'll be gone.'

'Chasing Maria?'

'There's a good chance the kid is mine.'

'And you wouldn't be even slightly interested in the money.'

Seventeen years old and neither woman nor girl nor fully human, but flesh drawn tight over the machinery of greed.

A survivor, this one. She'd do okay.

'I'll do you a deal,' I said. 'I find you Maria and you get the money. She has Finn's flash-drive, the codes.'

She nodded slowly, pursed her lips. 'Y'know,' she said, 'I'd probably be just as quick tracking her down myself.' Then squeezed the trigger.

Not a knee-capping, exactly. She wasn't all that precise. But she was so close she couldn't miss and the round punched through my thigh.

No pain at first, just the shock of the impact sending me into convulsions as I keeled over into the dead leaves. I was vaguely aware of her standing up and dropping the gun, swearing as she cradled her wrist. Then a spurt of flame and pain bolted through my thigh, set my bones on fire. Screaming made it worse, every nerve scraped raw. And no one to hear anyway, not after the drone of the engine finally faded away.

I lay still in the leaves with my eyes closed and teeth clenched, trying not to breathe. After a while the pain dulled and I began to get cold. I heard a whoo-whoo, the sound faint, its tone curious. Then the shakes started, just a shiver at first, but soon I was shuddering all over. Numb below the waist and faintly damp, the artery pulsing slow now, draining out.

This motionless ease, measure me by . . .

It could have been minutes or hours. No way to know.

Just as it all started to fade away, the world bleeding dark from the edges in, I had one last glimpse of a shadowy Ben, those hopeful eyes peering up from under his fringe, but when I reached to brush the hair from his eyes I found he had no eyes, no features at all save a raw hole of a mouth twisted into a leer and it was Gonzo, yes, Gonz waiting for me and saying put it down, just let it go, you can't go on, you'll go on, and the leaves faintly rustling, whispering, yes, I will, yes, yes

Acknowledgments

My deepest thanks, as always, to the good people at Liberties Press: my editor, Daniel Bolger; PR gurus Caroline Lambe and Alice Dawson; and publisher Sean O'Keefe.

I owe a great debt to Ed O'Loughlin, for taking the time to read this story and bring to it an eye as sharp as his opinion is blunt.

As always, John McFetridge and Adrian McKinty have provided sterling support from opposite ends of the planet. The borderless Peter Rozovsky, too, went far beyond conventional kindness.

Much of what is good in this book belongs to them; all of its failings are mine.

Thanks too to my agent, Allan Guthrie of Jenny Brown Associates, an endless source of advice and support.

I will always be grateful to my parents, Harry and Kathleen Burke, for making books part of the furniture as I was growing up.

As for the Three Regular Readers of my blog, Crime Always Pays, this book would not have been written without their invisible presence at my shoulder, urging me on.

Unfortunately, I can never get back the time I stole away from my wonderful wife and daughter, Aileen and Lily, in order to write this book. Hopefully the inevitable fame and riches to follow will be some compensation.

Oh, and Lily? Perhaps next time I'll write a book that isn't broken, with pictures to go along with its words . . .